Special thanks to Kate Cary

ALLEGIANCES

RIVERCLAN

LEADER **HAILSTAR**—thick-pelted gray tom

DEPUTY **SHELLHEART**—dappled gray tom

MEDICINE CAT **BRAMBLEBERRY**—pretty white she-cat with black-spotted fur, blue eyes, and a strikingly pink nose

WARRIORS (toms, and she-cats without kits)

RIPPLECLAW—black-and-silver tabby tom

TIMBERFUR—brown tom

MUDFUR—long-haired light brown tom

OWLFUR—brown-and-white tom

OTTERSPLASH—white-and-pale-ginger she-cat

CEDARPELT—brown tabby tom, stout and short-tailed

LILYSTEM—gray she-cat

BRIGHTSKY—nimble white-and-ginger she-cat

PIKETOOTH—skinny brown tabby tom with a narrow face and protruding canine teeth

LAKESHINE—pretty, long-haired, gray-and-white she-cat

SHIMMERPELT—night-black she-cat with glossy pelt

APPRENTICES (more than six moons old, in training to become warriors)

SOFTPAW—small, lithe, white she-cat with tabby patches

WHITEPAW—pure white tom with tabby-striped tail and brown paws

QUEENS   (she-cats expecting or nursing kits)

ECHOMIST—long-haired gray she-cat, fur tipped with white to give her a soft, cloudy appearance (mother to Volekit, Beetlekit, and Petalkit)

RAINFLOWER—pale gray she-cat (mother to Stormkit and Oakkit)

FALLOWTAIL—light brown she-cat with blue eyes and soft fur (mother to Graykit and Willowkit)

ELDERS   (former warriors and queens, now retired)

TROUTCLAW—gray tabby tom

TANGLEWHISKER—long-haired tabby tom with a thick, knotted pelt

BIRDSONG—tabby-and-white she-cat with ginger patches around her muzzle, flecked with gray

THUNDERCLAN

LEADER   **PINESTAR**—red-brown tom with green eyes

DEPUTY   **SUNFALL**—bright ginger tom with yellow eyes

MEDICINE CAT   **GOOSEFEATHER**—speckled gray tom with pale blue eyes

    APPRENTICE, FEATHERWHISKER

WARRIORS   **STONEPELT**—gray tom

STORMTAIL—blue-gray tom with blue eyes

ADDERFANG—mottled brown tabby tom with yellow eyes

TAWNYSPOTS—light gray tabby tom with amber eyes

SPARROWPELT—big, dark brown tabby tom with yellow eyes

SMALLEAR—gray tom with very small ears and amber eyes
APPRENTICE, WHITEPAW

THRUSHPELT—sandy-gray tom with white flash on his chest and green eyes

ROBINWING—small, energetic brown she-cat with ginger patch on her chest and amber eyes

FUZZYPELT—black tom with fur that stands on end and yellow eyes

WINDFLIGHT—gray tabby tom with pale green eyes
APPRENTICE, DAPPLEPAW

SPECKLETAIL—pale tabby she-cat with amber eyes

QUEENS

SWIFTBREEZE—tabby-and-white she-cat with yellow eyes (mother of Leopardkit: black she-cat with green eyes, and Patchkit: black-and-white tom with amber eyes)

MOONFLOWER—silver-gray she-cat with pale yellow eyes (mother of Bluekit: gray she-cat with blue eyes, and Snowkit: white she-cat with blue eyes)

POPPYDAWN—long-haired, dark red she-cat with a bushy tail and amber eyes

ELDERS

WEEDWHISKER—pale orange tom with yellow eyes

MUMBLEFOOT—brown tom, slightly clumsy, with amber eyes

LARKSONG—tortoiseshell she-cat with pale green eyes

SHADOWCLAN

LEADER

CEDARSTAR—very dark gray tom with a white belly

DEPUTY

STONETOOTH—gray tabby tom with long teeth

MEDICINE CAT

SAGEWHISKER—white she-cat with long whiskers

WARRIORS

RAGGEDPELT—large dark brown tabby tom

FOXHEART—bright ginger tom

CROWTAIL—black tabby she-cat
APPRENTICE, CLOUDPAW

BRACKENFOOT—pale ginger tom with dark ginger legs

ARCHEYE—gray tabby tom with black stripes and thick stripe over eye

HOLLYFLOWER—dark-gray-and-white she-cat

QUEENS

FEATHERSTORM—brown tabby she-cat

POOLCLOUD—gray-and-white she-cat

ELDERS

LITTLEBIRD—small ginger tabby she-cat

LIZARDFANG—light brown tabby tom with one hooked tooth

WINDCLAN

LEADER HEATHERSTAR—pinkish-gray she-cat with blue eyes

DEPUTY REEDFEATHER—light brown tabby tom

MEDICINE CAT HAWKHEART—dark brown tom with yellow eyes

WARRIORS DAWNSTRIPE—pale gold tabby with creamy stripes
APPRENTICE, TALLPAW

REDCLAW—dark ginger tom
APPRENTICE, SHREWPAW

ELDERS WHITEBERRY—small pure-white tom

CARRIONPLACE

SHADOWCLAN
CAMP

THUNDERPATH

THUNDERCLAN
CAMP

GREAT
SYCAMORE

SANDY
HOLLOW

SNAKEROCKS

TALLPINES

TREECUT PLACE

TWOLEGPLACE

THUNDERCLAN

RIVERCLAN

SHADOWCLAN

WINDCLAN

STARCLAN

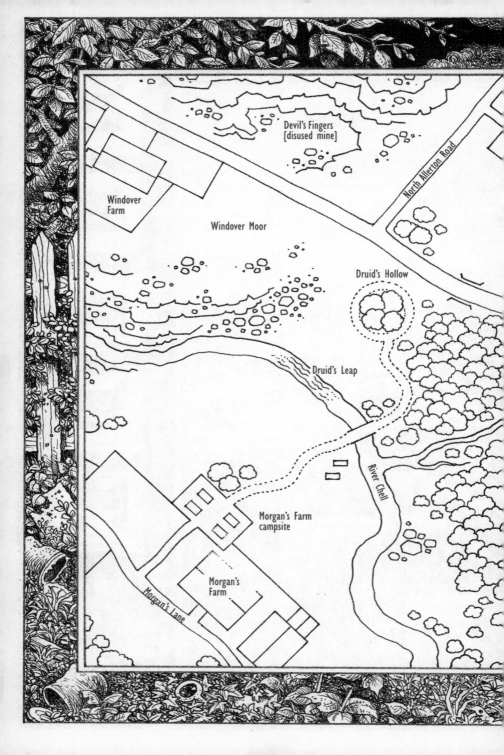

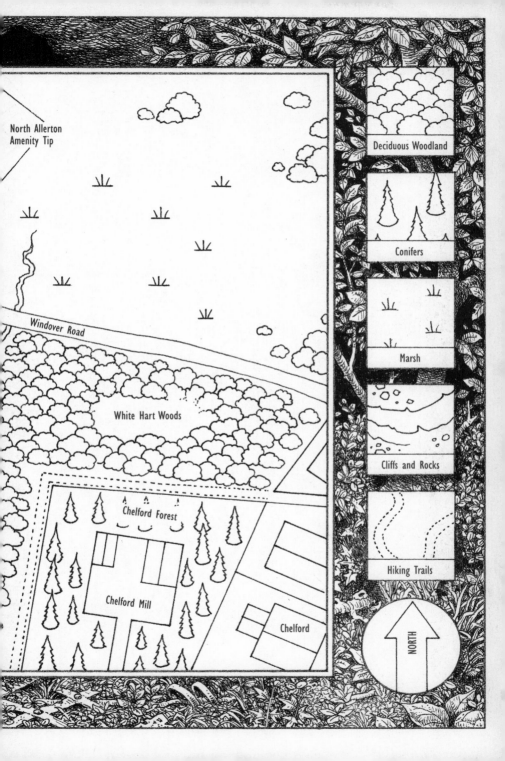

North Allerton
Amenity Tip

Windover Road

White Hart Woods

Chelford Forest

Chelford Mill

Chelford

Deciduous Woodland

Conifers

Marsh

Cliffs and Rocks

Hiking Trails

NORTH

PROLOGUE

❧

Wind rattled the branches of the willow trees and tore the reeds from their beds.

"Hailstar!"

Thick storm clouds swirled across the night-dark sky. Rain battered the tightly woven dens where the RiverClan warriors had been sleeping.

"Hailstar!"

The RiverClan leader flattened his ears as he heard his mate's terrified cry. He dug his claws into the mud, steadying himself against the water that swirled around his legs. The river had broken its banks and was streaming into camp. He twisted his head around, searching the shadows.

"Hailstar!" Echomist shrieked again. Her cry was muffled by the kit who swung from her jaws. Another clung to her back. She was staring at a nest of twigs that was spinning away from her on the floodwater. A small kit was struggling to cling to it as the woven twigs collapsed like loose leaves.

Hailstar dived for the nest and grabbed the kit just before he disappeared beneath the water. He thrust his son at Timberfur, who was chasing another nest. "Take Volekit to the elders' den!" The brown tom took the dripping scrap of fur and bounded toward the high end of the camp where the elders' den was still untouched by the rising water.

"Follow him!" Hailstar ordered Echomist. She nodded, her eyes huge with fear, her long gray fur flattened to her body by the rain.

Hailstar scanned the camp. Gleaming pelts darted in the darkness like panicked fish. A lithe ginger-and-white she-cat was clinging on to the remains of the warriors' den, trying to claw together its fast-fraying walls. A stout tabby tom tried to block the foaming channel where nests swirled out into the river.

The sky lit up with a white flare as lightning blazed. Thunder crashed and the wind hardened. A new wave of water surged through the camp.

"Shellheart!" Hailstar called to his deputy. "What's your opinion?"

A dappled gray tom, peering upriver from a beech stump among the reeds, called back, "The water's rising fast, Hailstar! The elders' den isn't going to be safe for much longer."

Hailstar lashed his tail. "We'll have to abandon camp!"

"No!" The ginger-and-white she-cat let go of her den and faced the RiverClan leader.

"We *must*, Brightsky!" Hailstar urged.

"We can't leave everything our ancestors built for us!"

"We can rebuild it!" Hailstar snapped.

"It won't be the same!" Brightsky plunged through the floods and clamped her paws around a floating nest.

Shellheart bounded down from the stump and splashed toward his Clanmate. "Together we can rebuild anything," he insisted. "Except cats who have drowned trying to save bits of twig."

Brightsky reluctantly let go of the nest and watched it spin away into the reeds, then raced for the high end of camp.

Black, bubbling water surged around the edge of the elders' den, making the woven willow stems sway with the flood. Hailstar bounded up the slope and shook the den with his paws. "Get out!"

Echomist slid through the entrance. Three kits, like half-drowned mice, followed her. She stared at her mate. "Where should we go?"

"Head for high ground." Hailstar flicked his tail uphill, where the riverbank climbed toward a swath of trees and bushes.

A tangle-furred elder slid out of the den. "I've never seen a storm like this."

A tabby-and-white she-cat followed. "Where are we going?" she rasped.

The tom stroked her spine with his tail. "Further inland, Birdsong, where it's safe."

Birdsong's eyes widened. "Away from the river?"

"Just for now," Hailstar promised. "Come on, everyone."

"Wait!" Shellheart stopped halfway up the slope and stared over his shoulder. "Where's Rainflower?"

"Here!" A pale gray queen picked her way carefully through the swirling water toward him. Her belly was swollen with unborn kits.

"Are you all right?" Shellheart asked, sniffing her.

"I will be when I get my paws dry." She was out of breath, and rain ran off her fur in steady rivulets.

A small white she-cat wove around the queen, her eyes flashing. "She's been having pains."

Shellheart narrowed his eyes. "Are the kits coming, Brambleberry?"

"I don't know yet," the medicine cat meowed.

Rainflower gazed at the RiverClan deputy. "Go and help Hailstar. I'll be fine."

Shellheart blinked at her, then turned away. "Rippleclaw?"

"Here!" A black-and-silver tabby tom was holding open a gap in the reeds beside the elders' den while his Clanmates streamed through, heading for higher ground.

"Make sure every cat heads straight into the trees."

Rippleclaw nodded to the deputy and nudged a graying elder who was refusing to go through the gap.

"I can't go without Duskwater!" The elder dug his claws into the wet earth. "She went to make dirt before the camp flooded. She hasn't come back yet."

"We'll find her," Rippleclaw called over the wind. He glanced at his leader, who was rooted on the slope, eyes wide as he stared at his devastated camp. "Can you see her, Hailstar?"

Hailstar shook his head. "I'll make sure the dens are empty!" He plunged back toward the nursery, stuck his head through the entrance, and sniffed for warm bodies.

It was deserted. He checked the place where the apprentices' den had been next, and then what was left of the warriors' dens. It smelled only of sodden reeds. He glanced around the camp, fighting to keep his balance as water tugged and pushed him. Then half running, half swimming, he crossed the clearing and followed his Clan.

"Are we all here?" he asked as he caught up with his Clanmates on drier ground.

Rippleclaw scowled. "There's still no sign of Duskwater."

Brightsky stepped forward. "I'll go back and find her."

Hailstar nodded. "The rest of you keep moving up to the trees," he ordered.

As Brightsky dived down the bank, Rainflower let out a low moan.

Shellheart stiffened. "Rainflower?"

The queen was crouching, her face twisted in pain.

Brambleberry ducked down beside her, then lifted her head. "The kits are coming," she announced.

"Right now?" Shellheart demanded.

"They won't wait for the storm to end," Brambleberry retorted. "We must get her somewhere safe."

"Into the middle of the trees," Shellheart suggested. "The water never reaches that far."

"That'll take too long." Brambleberry glanced up at the wide, low branch of an ancient oak that hung overhead. "Do you think you can get her up there?"

Shellheart blinked. "I will if I have to." He grabbed Rainflower's scruff and, half guiding, half dragging, propelled her toward the thick trunk. "Up you go."

Rainflower glanced upward and groaned. She opened her mouth as if she was about to protest, then her flanks convulsed and she shrank into the spasm, looking small and wretched with her fur slicked down.

"Come on!" Brambleberry meowed briskly. "We don't have long."

Rainflower dug her claws into the bark, and Shellheart shoved from behind. Panting, the queen hauled herself up until she reached a hollow in the trunk where the low branch jutted out.

Brambleberry skittered up the trunk, lithe as a squirrel, slipping past Shellheart. She glanced at the hollow where branch met trunk and nodded. "Here will do." Then she blinked at Shellheart. "Can you get herbs from my den?"

Shellheart nodded. "I'll try."

"Be careful!" Rainflower gasped, but Shellheart had already leaped from the branch onto the slippery ground below and was racing back toward the flooded camp.

Brambleberry cleared wet leaves out of the low dip between branch and trunk. "Good. There's plenty of room for you to lie down here." She nosed Rainflower into the hollow and crouched beside her on the dripping bark.

"Will he be all right?" Rainflower whispered. She stared into the darkness where Shellheart had disappeared.

"He can take care of himself," Brambleberry told her. Her fur was spiked, wet to the skin. She'd been RiverClan's medicine cat for fewer than three moons since her mentor, Milkfur, had joined StarClan. This was the first time she'd dealt with an emergency on her own.

Rainflower shuddered as a fresh wave of pain passed through her belly. Brambleberry took a deep breath, blocking out the howling of the wind and the growl of thunder. She laid her forepaws gently on Rainflower's flank as another contraction gripped the queen.

Brambleberry scanned the reed bed far below. No sign of Shellheart. "Here." She nipped off a twig with her teeth and laid it beside Rainflower's cheek. "Bite down on that when the pains come."

"Is that all you have?" Rainflower hissed.

"It's all you need," Brambleberry told her. "Queens have been kitting since the ancient Clans. It's the most natural thing in the world."

Rainflower groaned and bit down on the stick, her body shuddering.

Claws ripped bark as Shellheart scrambled onto the branch. "Sorry," he panted. His fur was drenched. "I had to swim to your den. I managed to get inside, but your herbs have all been washed away."

Brambleberry closed her eyes as she thought of how many moons it had taken to build up that supply. Before she could reply, Rainflower hissed and the stick crunched between her teeth.

The first kit was coming.

Brambleberry leaned down in time to see a kit slither out on to the rough bark. She gave it a lick, and then passed the tiny, wriggling bundle to its father. "Don't let it fall," she warned.

"Is everything okay?" Brightsky was calling from the bottom of the tree. Water lapped her paws. The flood had reached the tree.

"One kit and one more to come," Brambleberry reported.

Shellheart looked down, keeping one forepaw over the squirming kit. "Did you find Duskwater?"

"No sign of her," Brightsky replied heavily.

Shellheart lashed his tail. "Join the others. We're fine. Come back for us when the waters have gone down."

The stick Rainflower had been biting on crumbled into splinters as the second kit slid out. Brambleberry caught it in her teeth and placed it at Rainflower's belly.

Rainflower reached for it at once, licking it roughly till it mewled. "It's a tom."

"So's this one." Shellheart gently placed the tiny kit beside its littermate. His voice cracked. "They're perfect," he whispered.

Rainflower purred as Shellheart rubbed his cheek against hers. "I name this one Oakkit for the oak that protected us from the flood," she rumbled, "and this one Stormkit for the storm that drove us here."

"Kits born into a storm like this one are destined to be great warriors," Shellheart murmured. He gazed at his queen with pride. "It's just a shame they can't both be leaders of RiverClan."

CHAPTER 1

❧

Stormkit edged farther along the slippery branch. Volekit's dare rang in his ears. *Bet you fall off before you get to the end!*

He unsheathed his claws and dug them into the frozen bark. From here, he could see a long way downstream, as far as the bend in the river. He could just glimpse the first of the stepping-stones beyond. And on the far shore, Sunningrocks! Its sheer side shadowed the water and its wide, smooth stone summit sparkled with frost. Stormkit fluffed out his fur. He'd seen farther than any other kit in the Clan! They'd never even seen past the reed bed.

"Be careful!" Oakkit called from the camp clearing.

"Shut up, Oakkit! I'm a warrior!" Stormkit looked down, past the fat, mouse-brown bulrush heads, into the dense forest of reeds that jutted out of the icy river. Minnows flitted between the stems, their scales flashing.

Could he reach down with a paw, break the thin ice, and scoop them out? He pressed his pale brown belly to the bark, wrapped his hind legs around the narrow branch, and swung his forepaws down toward the tiny fish. Tingling with frustration, he felt his claws brush the tips of the bulrushes.

I was born in a storm! I'm going to be Clan leader one day! Stormkit stretched harder, trembling with the effort.

"What are you doing?" Oakkit yelped.

"Let him be!" Stormkit heard Rainflower silencing Oakkit, a purr rumbling in her throat. "Your brother has the courage of a warrior already."

Stormkit clung tighter to the branch. *I'll be fine. I'm stronger than StarClan.*

"Look out!" Oakkit squeaked.

A rush of wind tugged Stormkit's fur. A flurry of black-and-white feathers battered his ears.

Magpie!

Talons scraped his spine.

Frog dirt and fish guts! Stormkit's claws were wrenched out of the bark. He plummeted into the reeds and crashed through the thin ice. The freezing water shocked the breath from him. Minnows darted away as he thrashed in the water.

Where's the shore? River water flooded his mouth. It tasted of stone and weeds. Spluttering, he struggled to swim, but the stiff reeds blocked his flailing paws. *StarClan, help me!* Panic shot through him as he fought to keep his muzzle above water.

Suddenly the stems beside him swished apart and Tanglewhisker plunged through.

"I'm okay!" Stormkit spluttered. Water rushed into his mouth again and he sank, coughing, beneath the ice.

Teeth gripped his scruff.

"Kits!"

Stormkit heard Tanglewhisker's muffled growl as the elder hauled him up.

Shivering with cold, Stormkit bunched his paws against his belly, wincing with embarrassment as Tanglewhisker pushed his way through the reeds and deposited Stormkit on the bank next to his mother.

"Nice dive, Stormkit!" Volekit teased.

"Like a kingfisher," Beetlekit added. "Maybe Hailstar should change your name to Birdbrain."

Stormkit growled at the two kits as they crowded around him. One moon older, they loomed over him like crows.

Echomist paced anxiously behind them, her soft gray fur fluffed with worry. "Don't tease, you two."

Petalkit pushed past her brothers. "I wasn't teasing!" The pretty tortoiseshell she-cat stuck her nose in the air. "I think he was brave to try!"

Purring, Rainflower licked Stormkit's ears. "Next time, grip the branch harder."

Stormkit shook her off. "Don't worry. I will."

As Tanglewhisker shook water from his long tabby pelt, Birdsong hurried down the slope from the elders' den. "You'll catch cold!" she scolded.

Tanglewhisker blinked at his tabby-and-white mate. "Did you want me to let him drown?"

"One of the warriors would have rescued him," Birdsong retorted.

Tanglewhisker shrugged. "They're busy."

Rainflower purred. "I think Stormkit would have found his own way out. He's a strong little cat, aren't you?"

Stormkit felt his fur glow with the warmth of his mother's praise. He blinked water out of his eyes and looked around the clearing. This was the home of RiverClan, the greatest Clan of all. He hadn't seen it before the flood, so the smooth brown mud that covered the ground and the heaps of battered wet reeds that cluttered every corner were more familiar to him than the densely woven walls and open spaces that were emerging. Timberfur and Cedarpelt were carrying bundles of freshly picked dry reeds across the clearing to Softpaw and Whitepaw, who were weaving them into the tattered apprentices' den. Farther along the river's edge, Shellheart and Ottersplash were gathering more stems. Fallowtail was helping Brambleberry clear the last of the muddy debris from the medicine den. Owlfur and Lakeshine were dragging deadwood and bark that had been washed through the reeds and into the clearing.

A whole moon had passed since the stormy night when Stormkit and Oakkit had been born, but the camp still showed signs of being swept away. Fortunately the elders' den had held firm and only needed a little reweaving here and there. And the nursery, a ball of tightly overlapping willow branches and reeds, had been found downstream, wedged between the stepping-stones. It had been easy enough to drag it back to camp and lodge it among the thick sedge bushes. A few patches had repaired it, though it was still damp inside from the soaking. Rainflower tucked fresh moss into their nest every evening, but Stormkit still woke each morning with a cold, wet pelt.

The rest of the camp was harder to fix. It had taken half a moon's digging and levering to roll the fallen tree to the edge of the clearing where the old warriors' dens had stood. Once the broken branches and shattered bark had been cleared away, new dens could be woven against its thick trunk. Until then, RiverClan's warriors slept in whatever shelter they could find, making nests in the thick sedge walls around the camp or in the nooks and crevices of the fallen tree. No cat could remember what it was like to be warm. Newleaf might be showing in early buds and birdsong, but leaf-bare frosts still gripped the banks of the river every night.

Hailstar had been sleeping in the open, despite the cold. He insisted that his den be the last one rebuilt. "When my Clan is safe and warm, then I will sleep soundly, but not before," he had vowed.

Oakkit wound around Stormkit, soaking water from his brother's pale tabby pelt into his own bracken-colored fur. "I told you to be careful."

"I wouldn't have fallen if that magpie hadn't dived at me," Stormkit growled through chattering teeth. The cold water seemed to have reached his bones.

"You wouldn't have fallen off if you'd stayed in the clearing." A deep mew sounded from behind them.

Stormkit spun around.

Hailstar was staring down at him, his thick gray pelt ruffled against the cold. Amusement lit the RiverClan leader's yellow eyes. "Shellheart!" He called to his deputy, not taking his eyes from Stormkit.

Shellheart slid out from the rushes, his wet pelt slicked against his strong frame. He glanced at Stormkit. "Is everything okay?"

"Your kit will be a brave warrior," Hailstar meowed. "*If he doesn't drown himself before he starts his training.*"

Shellheart's tail flicked as Hailstar went on. "We'd better send a patrol to catch that magpie. It's beginning to think it owns RiverClan territory."

Shellheart dipped his head. "Should we drive it off or catch it?"

Hailstar wrinkled his nose. "We'd better catch it," he growled unenthusiastically. Few cats in RiverClan liked adding birds to the fresh-kill pile. "We must eat whatever we can find." The flood had killed so many fish—battered them on the rocks or left them stranded on land—that river prey was scarce.

"I'll organize a patrol," Shellheart meowed.

"Wait till Rippleclaw's patrol returns," Hailstar ordered. With so much rebuilding still to do in camp, Hailstar rarely sent out more than one patrol at a time.

"I hope they've caught something edible this time," Tanglewhisker muttered.

"I'm sure they will have," Birdsong meowed. "It's been a moon since the flood. The fish must be coming back by now."

Echomist turned away from her kits. "If only we'd buried some of the fish washed up by the flood, and preserved them like ThunderClan does with their prey in leaf-bare."

Hailstar shook his head. "Fish don't keep like forest prey. Our warriors will need the strength of StarClan to repair the damage done by the flood as well as keep the fresh-kill pile well stocked."

Stormkit stuck out his tail. "Let us help with the rebuilding, then."

Volekit hurried forward, his gray fur spiking with excitement. "Oh, yes, please!"

"We'll be really useful!" Petalkit fluffed out her tortoiseshell pelt.

Echomist swept her tail around her kits, pulling them away. "Don't be frog-brained. You'll get under everyone's paws."

Stormkit plucked at the ground. "No, we won't!"

Hailstar's whiskers twitched. "I'm not going to turn down a genuine offer of help, Echomist. As long as they stay in the camp, I don't see a problem. We'll have a kit patrol!"

Stormkit puffed out his chest as he stood shoulder to shoulder with Oakkit, Beetlekit, Volekit, and Petalkit. "Great! What should we do?"

Hailstar thought for a moment. "If you take the reeds that Ottersplash is gathering to Softpaw and Whitepaw, then Timberfur and Cedarpelt will be free to join Shellheart's hunting patrol."

"Come on!" Stormkit raced for the shore where Ottersplash was tossing reeds.

"Careful!" Cedarpelt was pawing together a freshly harvested pile as Stormkit skidded to a halt next to him.

"Don't knock them into the river!"

"I won't!" Stormkit sank his teeth into a stem and began dragging it across the clearing to the apprentices' half-built den.

"Well, well." Whitepaw paused from weaving stems on the roof of the apprentices' den and looked down. "We have new volunteers."

"Is that a whole reed?" Softpaw peered from inside the framework of woven willow stems, her tabby-patched tail quivering. "We'll be finished before we know it with help like this."

"I can carry more," Stormkit boasted, puffed up with pride. He dropped the stem and turned away, nearly crashing into Beetlekit.

"Watch out!" mewed the black kit, tripping over the reed he was dragging.

"Sorry!" Stormkit dashed back toward the reed bed, past Volekit, who had three reeds clamped between his jaws. "I'm bringing four next time," he called over his shoulder.

He pricked his ears as he heard paws splash on the marshy earth beyond the entrance tunnel. A cat was racing toward the camp. Stormkit halted, blinking, as the sedge wall of the camp rustled and Rippleclaw pounded into the clearing.

"Any prey?" Birdsong called.

Rippleclaw shook his head, his silver flanks heaving. "Sunningrocks!" he gasped. "ThunderClan has taken Sunningrocks!"

CHAPTER 2

"ThunderClan!" Stormkit *raced for the fallen* tree, scrambled onto the trunk, and scooted back along the icy branch that stretched over the river. "Those snake-hearts!" He could see the scrawny pelts of ThunderClan warriors swarming like rats over the huge gray rocks that had always been RiverClan's despite ThunderClan's grasping claims.

"How dare they?"

Stormkit heard his father's growl and turned to see Shellheart leap up the trunk of the ancient willow and hurry along one of the low boughs that reached out over the water. The RiverClan deputy peered through the trailing branches. "I don't believe it! Pinestar's stretched out in the sunshine like it's his territory!"

Stormkit saw a massive fox-red tom sprawling on the rocks, his soft belly fur glittering where it had brushed the frosty stone.

Rippleclaw paced the clearing, his black-and-silver fur spiked up. "They must think we've lost our teeth and claws!"

The sedge swished as Mudfur and Brightsky raced into camp. Piketooth followed, his tabby fur bristling, a fat carp skewered between his long front teeth. He dropped the fish and stared at Hailstar. "Who's going to lead the battle patrol?"

Stormkit lashed his tail. Why couldn't he be an apprentice already? Then he could join his Clanmates in driving the mangy ThunderClan cats off RiverClan territory.

"What's going on?" Troutclaw padded stiffly out of the elders' den. His gray tabby pelt was ruffled from sleep.

"There are ThunderClan warriors on Sunningrocks!" Stormkit called from his perch.

Hailstar swung his gaze around. "Get down from there, Stormkit," he growled. "This isn't a time for games."

"I'm not playing!" Stormkit objected. But he backed along the branch and jumped down from the trunk.

Shellheart scrambled down from the willow and faced Hailstar. "Are we going to let those squirrel-chasers stay there?"

Rippleclaw growled. "They must know we can see them."

"Which means they'll be ready for us if we attack." Troutclaw padded down the slope. "How could we win a battle that they're more prepared for than we are?" He shook his matted head. "Haven't we lost enough?"

Stormkit wondered if the old tom was thinking of Duskwater. He'd heard Rainflower telling Echomist that the she-cat's body had never been found after the flood. "We'll win this time!" he mewed.

"Hush, Stormkit!" Shellheart snapped his head around.

Timberfur crossed the clearing, his eyes dark. "We might lose."

Cedarpelt joined Troutclaw and swept his tail sympathetically across the old cat's shoulder. "Sunningrocks has always been hard to defend."

Stormkit stiffened. "That's no reason to let ThunderClan have it!" He stepped back as Shellheart brushed in front of him, muffling his mew.

"You're too young for this debate," the RiverClan deputy warned.

Rainflower scooped Stormkit aside with her tail. "Hush, little one. You have a warrior's heart as brave as any cat's. You'll get your turn."

You bet I will! Stormkit shut his mouth and curled his claws. *One day I'll be leader and then I'll decide when we go into battle.*

"Ow!"

He felt a tail beneath his paws and turned to find Oakkit glaring at him.

"That's my tail you're digging your claws into!"

"Sorry!" Stormkit guiltily hopped off his brother's tail. "We have to punish those squirrel-chasers for stealing our territory, right?"

Oakkit didn't answer. He was watching Brambleberry. The white medicine cat had slid out from her den among the sedges.

"Do you think we should fight, Brambleberry?" Hailstar asked.

Brambleberry shook her head. "Not now. I have no way to treat battle wounds. The flood took my herbs and my store will stay empty till newleaf brings fresh crops. I can only use the most basic remedies."

"And we're half-starved," Troutclaw added.

Stormkit blinked. He hadn't been hungry. Rainflower always had enough milk for him and Oakkit. He studied his Clanmates and noticed for the first time how thin they were looking. Nearly as scrawny as ThunderClan cats.

Hailstar sighed. "I don't want to start a battle we are likely to lose. And I don't want warriors with injuries that can't be healed."

Rippleclaw lashed his tail. "Then we're just going to let them take as much territory as they want?"

"They only want Sunningrocks," Echomist pointed out. "They'd never try to cross the river."

Piketooth growled, "There's prey at Sunningrocks. Forest prey that could make up for the lack of fish." He kicked the carp lying at his paws. "It took all morning to catch this."

Echomist dipped her head. "But it's almost newleaf. It won't be long before we have more prey than we need. And right now I'd rather go hungry than lose another Clanmate." She glanced at Troutclaw.

Piketooth dug his claws into the earth. "Are we going to give up Sunningrocks without a murmur?"

"No." Hailstar crossed the clearing and leaped onto the low branch of the willow. He glanced toward Sunningrocks. "Rippleclaw, Shellheart." His tail swept the bark. "Take Ottersplash and Brightsky to Sunningrocks. Don't fight. Tell Pinestar and his Clanmates that they may have Sunningrocks today. But warn them: Those rocks are

RiverClan's and we will defend them soon."

"Don't worry. Those snake-hearts will get the message!" Shellheart's claws sprayed soft earth as he charged for the entrance tunnel with Rippleclaw, Brightsky, and Ottersplash pounding after.

"Quick!" As his Clanmates bunched into anxious, murmuring groups, Stormkit hissed in his brother's ear and dashed back to the fallen tree. He scampered along the trunk, checking over his shoulder.

Oakkit was following. "Where are we going?"

"To watch."

"Watch what?"

"We're going to watch Shellheart tell Pinestar off!" Stormkit scampered along the branch. "Dig your claws in," he warned his brother. "It's slippery."

When the branch grew thin enough to dip under his weight, Stormkit halted and ducked down to let Oakkit watch over his shoulder. Only four ThunderClan warriors remained on Sunningrocks. Pinestar was still lying on the smooth, flat rock, showing his belly to the leaf-bare sun. A bright ginger tom sat beside him, eyes closed, tail wrapped over his paws.

"That must be Sunfall, the deputy," Oakkit whispered. "Volekit said he was ginger."

Two lithe warriors paced back and forth beside the leader and deputy: a blue-gray tom and a mottled tabby. Their eyes were wide and their ears pricked. Suddenly the tabby halted and stared at the river.

Stormkit followed his gaze. Shellheart was swimming toward Sunningrocks. Water splashed as Rippleclaw, Brightsky, and Ottersplash plunged in after him. On Sunningrocks, the gray tom's pelt had bristled along his spine. He darted to the edge of the rocks and showed his teeth, his gaze fixed on the RiverClan patrol.

Pinestar jumped to his paws, quickly followed by Sunfall. The four ThunderClan warriors lined up on the crest of the rock as Shellheart launched himself, dripping, from the water. In two bounds, the RiverClan deputy scaled the smooth cliff face. Sunfall arched his back and hissed as Shellheart approached. Pinestar narrowed his eyes.

Stormkit felt Oakkit tense behind him. "Will they fight?" Oakkit breathed.

"Wait." Stormkit's paws trembled with excitement as Rippleclaw leaped up onto Sunningrocks with Brightsky and Ottersplash following.

Stormkit pricked his ears, straining to hear.

"You're on RiverClan territory," Shellheart growled.

Sunfall took a step forward. "Make us leave, then."

Shellheart flicked his tail. "This is not *yet* a battle worth fighting," he meowed. He looked back toward the RiverClan camp, clearly visible through the leafless trees. "But we'll be watching. You should watch out, too, because this is our land and we *will* defend it."

The gray tom's lip curled. "But not today?"

Rippleclaw darted forward, flattening his ears. "If it comes to a battle," he hissed in the gray tom's face, "it'll be me who shreds you first."

"Rippleclaw!" Shellheart called the warrior back and met Pinestar's narrowed gaze. "You can have Sunningrocks for now. Help yourself to any fresh-kill you find here. RiverClan doesn't need mice. But we'll take it back when we want it back."

Stormkit could feel his brother's heart pounding. "Mangy mouse-eaters," he muttered. "Enjoy Sunningrocks while you can."

Shellheart jumped down to the riverbank and waited while Rippleclaw, Ottersplash, and Brightsky dived past him into the water. He glanced back up at the rock face once more before following his Clanmates.

"Watch out!" Oakkit's yelp made Stormkit jump. "The magpie's coming back!"

Stormkit looked up and saw a flash of black-and-white feathers outlined against the gray sky. "Hold on to me!" he ordered.

As Oakkit sank his claws into his pelt, Stormkit reared up on his hind legs. He lashed out at the magpie with his forepaws just as it swooped level with the branch. Held firm by Oakkit, Stormkit slashed again and again until he felt his claws slice through feather and reach flesh.

Squawking, the magpie wheeled away, and Stormkit dropped to four paws.

Oakkit let go and blinked at him. "Nice move!"

"Thanks for hanging on to me." Stormkit looked at the bloody feathers caught in his claws. "I don't think that magpie will be back for a while." He blinked triumphantly at his brother. "We're going to be the best warriors RiverClan's ever seen."

CHAPTER 3

Stormkit stretched in his nest, feeling the muscles slide underneath his glossy fur. He could almost reach from one wall to the other in this corner of the nursery. Early-morning sunshine filtered through the roof, making the reed walls glow. In the three moons since ThunderClan had stolen Sunningrocks, the sun had grown hotter and higher in the sky. New growth speared up through the old reed bed and the sedge bushes smelled sweet and lush.

"Wake up!" Stormkit whispered in Oakkit's ear.

Rainflower stirred sleepily and wrapped her tail over Stormkit's belly. "Go back to sleep, little warrior," she purred. "It's still early."

Stormkit shook off her warm, soft tail and sat up. He poked Oakkit with a paw.

"What is it?" Oakkit grumbled, his eyes tightly shut.

"Let's go explore."

"Remember to stay in camp," Rainflower murmured sleepily.

"Of course," Stormkit promised. He poked Oakkit again.

Oakkit hid his nose under a paw. "Don't you ever sleep?"

"We've been asleep all night. The dawn patrol left ages ago."

In Echomist's nest, Beetlekit struggled to his paws, his black pelt rumpled. "Is it time to eat?"

Volekit opened his eyes. "Yeah, I'm hungry."

Petalkit was already sitting up and washing. "The hunting patrol will bring something back for us." She leaned forward to lick Beetlekit's head, smoothing the fur tufted between his ears. Echomist rolled over and began to snore gently.

Stormkit hopped out of his nest and stretched. "*We're* going to catch our own prey."

Oakkit sat up. "Are we?"

Rainflower lifted her head. "I hope you're not going to get your brother in trouble again, Stormkit."

"Why are you blaming me?" Yesterday they'd made it as far as the stepping-stones before being spotted and escorted back to camp by a very cross Mudfur. "It's not my fault Oakkit followed the patrol."

"He wasn't following the patrol," Rainflower reminded him. "He was following *you*."

"He was?"

As Stormkit blinked at her innocently, she flicked his ear with her tail-tip. "I suppose I'm lucky to have such a brave, handsome kit." She rested her chin on her paws.

"I'm brave, too." Oakkit leaped out of the nest and headed for the entrance.

"Wait for me!" Stormkit caught up and slid past him out of the nursery.

The clearing was already warm and bright, though the sun was barely higher than the ancient willow. Hailstar and Shellheart sat beside the fallen tree, their heads dipped in quiet conversation. Troutclaw, Birdsong, and Tanglewhisker were sunning themselves on the smooth earth outside the elders' den. Timberfur and Ottersplash were poking among the reeds at the edge of the river, their ears pricked, tails twitching, clearly hoping to find a minnow among the watery stems.

Brambleberry was laying out limp leaves in the sun, her snowy paws tinged with green sap.

"What are those for?" Stormkit crossed the clearing and sniffed the leaves. He screwed up his face. They smelled sour.

"They're coltsfoot leaves," Brambleberry told him. "Good for coughs."

Stormkit nudged a leaf with his front paw. "How?"

"You have to chew them to get the juice out." Brambleberry smoothed another leaf out on the warm earth. "Then you swallow the juice and spit out the leaf."

Oakkit skidded to a halt beside them. "Where'd they come from?"

"I picked them beside the falls," Brambleberry meowed.

"Can we come with you to pick more?" Stormkit asked hopefully.

Brambleberry's whiskers twitched. "Perhaps in two moons' time, when you're 'paws."

"I'm sure Hailstar will let us go now if he knows we're with you," Stormkit pleaded.

Brambleberry glanced at the RiverClan leader. "Why don't you go and ask him?"

Stormkit scowled. "Maybe later." He'd asked Hailstar if they could leave the camp before: once if they could help Shellheart hunt, twice if they could shadow Rippleclaw's patrol, but the answer had always been the same: "Wait until you're apprentices."

Stormkit stared enviously at the apprentices' den, tasting the air. There was no warm scent of sleep drifting from it. Softpaw and Whitepaw must have left with the dawn patrol. "Lucky furballs," he muttered.

Oakkit shrugged. "I thought we were going hunting."

"We are."

"Where?" Oakkit scanned the camp. "In the sedges?"

Stormkit fluffed out his fur. "I want to catch more than butterflies!"

"We could try hunting for minnows with Ottersplash and Timberfur," Oakkit suggested.

Stormkit rolled his eyes. "Minnows?"

"What's wrong with minnows?"

"Do you *want* to stay in camp?"

"We have to."

"Oh, come on." Stormkit butted his brother with his head. "Let's sneak out and hunt like real warriors."

"What if we get caught again?" Oakkit lowered his voice. "Hailstar said he'd make us wait an extra moon to get our apprentice names if we got into any more trouble."

"He didn't mean it!" Stormkit scoffed. "RiverClan needs

warriors. Hailstar's not a frog-brain. The sooner we're out patrolling and fighting, the better it'll be for the Clan." He flicked his tail. "When I'm leader I'll let kits go out of camp whenever they want."

Stormstar. What a great name!

"Hey!" Oakkit jabbed him with a paw. "Rainflower says I was born first so *I* get to be leader."

"You? Leader?" Stormkit ruffled his brother's ears. "You wanted to hunt *minnows!*" he scoffed, then added kindly, "I'll make you deputy when *I'm* leader."

"Thanks a lot."

"Come on! Let's go and hunt."

Before Oakkit could answer, mewling filled the clearing. Volekit and Beetlekit were tumbling noisily out of the nursery.

"Wait for me!" Petalkit scrambled after them, pawing at their tails as they scooted across the clearing and skittered to a halt by the reed bed.

Beetlekit thrust his nose into the stalks beside Ottersplash, making the reeds tremble. "Have you seen any fish?"

"Don't scare them off!" Ottersplash grumbled, not taking his eyes from the patch of water beneath his nose.

Stormkit nudged Oakkit. "Come on, before Beetlekit starts asking *us* questions."

"Which way?" Oakkit asked. "We can't just walk through the entrance tunnel."

"Dirtplace. Then we can squeeze through the sedges out on to the marsh."

Stormkit headed toward dirtplace. He ducked through

the fronds, Oakkit on his tail. Through the gap lay a sandy clearing, clumped in places and stinking. Oakkit poked his paw through a clump of sedge. "Through here?"

"Let me see." Stormkit pushed past and nosed his way through the stems. They were sharp and grazed his nose but he pushed on, eyes half-closed, until he broke out into sunshine. A wide marshy plain stretched ahead of him, grassy and lush, filled with patches of reed and sedge and white billowing flowers.

"It's huge!" Oakkit slid out behind Stormkit and stared at the green wetland. It stretched far along the riverbank and sloped up toward a smooth meadow where horses grazed.

"Let's head for the river," Oakkit suggested.

Stormkit tilted his head on one side. "Don't you want to cross the marsh?"

"I thought we were going to find prey," Oakkit reminded him. "What lives in the marsh?"

"Frogs?" Stormkit guessed.

"If you want to spend your morning hopping after a frog, then go ahead, Storm*star.*" Oakkit padded away. "I'm heading for the river."

"Okay!" Stormkit's paws sank into watery moss, cool and springy beneath his pads. He bounced along behind Oakkit, following the sedge wall.

"Wait!" Oakkit halted.

Stormkit stumbled into him. "What?"

"We're near the camp entrance," Oakkit whispered.

Stormkit recognized the well-trod grass track that led out

from the sedges and weaved between the thick bushes and grasses that swathed the riverbank.

"Follow me." Stormkit slid ahead, and pushed his way into the rich greenery at the side of the path. Nosing his way through the soft leaves, he kept to the bushes. Where water puddled the path, he crossed deliberately through it, hoping the mud would disguise their scent. Then, glancing over his shoulder to make sure Oakkit was following, he plunged into the long grass on the other side of the path. The ground fell away from beneath his paws and he tumbled down the bank.

He landed with a thump on a muddy flat at the river's edge. Water lapped his pelt as he scrambled to his paws. He moved just in time. With a yelp, Oakkit tumbled after him.

Jumping up, ruffled, Oakkit shook out his fur. "Nice route," he muttered.

"It's not my fault I don't know the whole territory yet," Stormkit defended himself. "Hailstar won't let us explore, remember?" He gazed downriver, watching the water flow away in a lazy brown flood that moved with such ease it was hard to imagine the same river had once destroyed the camp.

"Look, the stepping-stones!" Stormkit spotted smooth boulders breaking the surface farther downstream. "We can get to Sunningrocks!"

Oakkit blinked. "Why would we go to Sunningrocks? It belongs to ThunderClan."

"No, it doesn't!" Stormkit answered hotly. "They're invaders." He glanced at the far bank. A stretch of sandy shore lay in the shade of Sunningrocks. Stormkit stiffened.

A cat was moving along the water's edge, tugging at weeds that clung to the rocks and streams in the current. "Look!" he hissed to Oakkit.

"It must be a ThunderClan warrior!" Oakkit gasped.

"A warrior? No way!" Stormkit sniffed. "Look at him. He looks older than Sunningrocks." The ThunderClan cat was unkempt, his thick gray coat clumped with burrs and twigs. His ears were ragged and his whiskers frazzled like chewed grass.

"What's he doing?" Oakkit whispered.

The tom was nosing intently through the weeds along the shore, sniffing each one, tasting the air, and then hesitating a moment before tugging out a leaf or two with his shaggy paws.

Stormkit bristled. "He's stealing our herbs!"

"They're not exactly ours. Hailstar gave Sunningrocks to ThunderClan."

"No, he didn't. He just didn't fight them. Besides"— Stormkit glanced up at the huge gray boulders that loomed over the river—"that old cat is on the shore, not the rocks, and that's definitely ours."

"Should we go and tell Shellheart?" mewed Oakkit.

Stormkit stared at his bother. "Are you frog-brained?"

"He's on our land."

"If we tell Shellheart, he'll know we were outside camp."

Oakkit frowned. "So what should we do?"

"Let's chase him off!"

"Chase him off?" Oakkit's eyes widened. "He's bigger than both of us put together."

"But look at the state of him!" Stormkit pointed out. "He can't even wash himself. He's obviously not a real warrior. He might not even be ThunderClan. He might be a loner."

"I think we should tell Shellheart." Oakkit dug his claws into the mud.

But Stormkit was already padding along the shore. "Let's deal with this ourselves."

Oakkit scurried after him. "We can't take on a full-grown tom."

"Why not? There are two of us."

"But we—"

"Shhh!" Stormkit crouched and began stalking along the riverbank. "Or the mange-ball will hear us."

The ragged tom was still sniffing his way from plant to plant.

Stormkit paused and pressed his belly to the mud, feeling water soak his fur. The stepping-stones began about a tail-length from the bank. A narrow stretch of water stood between him and the first rock. The river wasn't flowing particularly fast, but it looked deep and cold around the base of the stone. Stormkit tensed, then leaped, clearing the channel and landing with a soft skid on the first stepping-stone. It felt smooth beneath his paws, worn by countless moons of lapping water.

Oakkit joined him with a muffled *oof*. There was only just enough room for both of them. "I still think we—"

Stormkit flicked his tail over Oakkit's mouth. "Shhh!"

The river gurgled between the stepping-stones, making

tiny whirlpools at the edges of the rock. Stormkit took a breath and launched himself toward the next stone. He landed with his paws splayed out, feeling dizzy; the river streamed around the rock so smoothly it seemed for a moment as though the rock were moving. Stormkit steadied his gaze, fixing it on the ragged tom who was still skulking in the shade of Sunningrocks, then jumped on to the next rock, and the next, keeping low and praying that the swirling river would camouflage their approach. He felt Oakkit's pelt brush his as his littermate kept pace. One more stone and they'd be on the shore.

Oakkit breathed in his ear. "He's going to see us for sure!"

"Not if we land over there." Stormkit nodded toward a clump of mallow clinging at the river's edge. "We'll hide behind that."

He sprang, pushing off hard, and swished through the mallow clump. Wet sand spattered around his paws as Oakkit landed clumsily beside him. Stormkit froze and glanced at the tom. Had he spotted them?

The tom was tugging at weeds, his pelt smooth, his gaze intent on his leaves. Then he looked up. His cold blue gaze bored into Stormkit's.

"Did you think I wouldn't notice you?" A growl edged his mew.

Oakkit's fur bushed up. "Let's get out of here!"

"Not yet." Stormkit showed his teeth. "You're on RiverClan territory!" he hissed at the tom. "Get off our land."

Oakkit unsheathed his claws. "Go and steal someone else's herbs!"

The tom's gaze narrowed. "How dare you?" His ears flattened.

Stormkit felt sick.

"He's going to kill us!" Oakkit croaked.

"Run!" Stormkit turned and scrambled through the mallow. He skidded to a halt on the first stone, then leaped again.

Oakkit landed beside him. "Help!" he wailed as his hind paws slipped off the stone. Stormkit grabbed his brother's scruff before Oakkit could slide into the swirling river.

"Thanks!" Oakkit regained his balance and jumped for the next stone. The tom yowled behind them. Stormkit hurtled after his brother.

"You don't get away from Goosefeather that easily!" the old cat snarled. Stormkit felt hot breath on his heels and jagged claws spiked his tail. Unbalanced, he leaped for the final stone. His paws hit water as he plunged into the river.

StarClan help me!

Pain shot though his face as he collided with the base of the rock. Cold water engulfed him and the world turned black. Churning his paws, Stormkit flailed for the surface but he had no idea which way up was. Gravel grazed his belly, then his spine, as the river tumbled him downstream like a leaf.

Water stung his eyes as he opened them, searching for sunlight. Shadowy shapes raced past him. He struggled against the current, trying to swim, but another submerged rock slammed against his side, knocking the last of his breath from him. His chest heaved as he fought not to suck in water. Then he saw a shape moving steadily toward him. A she-cat. Orange and white, he could just make her out in the gloom.

Had StarClan come to claim him? Terror clawed Stormkit's belly and he fought harder, praying for air, for the surface, for something to grab on to that would stop him being washed into StarClan's hunting grounds. He couldn't die yet!

The orange-and-white cat swam closer.

Go away! I don't want to come with you! The words screamed in Stormkit's mind.

"Don't worry, little one." He heard the cat's words as though she were whispering in his ear, even though she was still a tail-length away. "It's not your time yet. You have a great destiny ahead of you." Her amber eyes shone in the green water and then she was gone.

Teeth gripped Stormkit's scruff. With a jerk, he was above the rushing water, dangling from the jaws of Mudfur. The brown warrior turned against the current and swam for shore. Stormkit gulped air, coughing and trembling, suddenly aware of an agonizing pain in his cheek.

Mudfur scrambled from the river and bounded up the bank.

"Is he okay?" Oakkit yowled.

Stormkit could hear his brother but he couldn't open his eyes because his whole face felt as if it were on fire. He felt liquid bubbling at his lips and tasted blood. He started to shake. *What's wrong with me?*

Mudfur didn't speak or put him down, just headed along the path toward camp with Stormkit swinging limply beneath his chin.

"What's wrong with him?"

The sound of fear in Oakkit's voice frightened Stormkit more. Each jolt as Mudfur's paws hit the ground shot through his face like lightning. Stormkit tried to open his eyes. Grass, sedge, and willow herb streamed past in a blur. He could hear his own breathing. He was terribly cold and his paws felt numb.

It's not your time yet. It's not your time yet. He clung to the orange-and-white cat's words, repeating them as though praying to StarClan. He smelled the warm scent of Brambleberry as Mudfur ducked through the sedge tunnel into camp.

"Where did you find him?" Rainflower's shrill mew cut through the anxious murmur that greeted them. "Oakkit? Oakkit!"

"I'm here."

"What happened?"

"Stormkit fell and hit a stepping-stone."

Brambleberry's mew sounded calm among the others. "Take him to my den, Mudfur."

Past the haze of pelts and worried eyes. Past the deep olive sedge and into the green calm of Brambleberry's den. It was a wide space, almost a clearing, thickly walled by sedge with a nest hollowed out at one side where Brambleberry slept. Stormkit smelled his mother close by, her scent edged with fear.

Rainflower moved around him, pushing past Brambleberry, nudging Mudfur as the brown tom laid Stormkit gently down. "What has he done to himself?"

"Let me see." Brambleberry nosed the queen away.

Stormkit tried to focus on the white medicine cat, but the black spots that dotted her fur swam before his eyes.

"His face! His handsome face!" Rainflower's wail sent a new wave of terror through him.

Mudfur's pelt brushed Stormkit's flank as he huddled facedown on the smooth earth floor. "Come on, Rainflower. You need to check on Oakkit. He's pretty shaken up."

As the warrior steered Rainflower from the den, Brambleberry leaned closer to Stormkit. "Don't worry, little one. I'll take care of you."

Stormkit lay numb and trembling as Brambleberry disappeared for a moment. When she returned she was carrying something that had a strong, sour tang.

"I'm going to squeeze juice into the side of your mouth," she told him. "It'll taste bad and it'll hurt to swallow, but you must take it." Her mew was firm. "It'll help you feel better."

Stormkit tried to speak but his mouth felt thick and strange, and another jolt of pain made him cry out.

"This has willow bark, thyme, and poppy extract in it," Brambleberry went on, her voice low and soft.

Stormkit felt wetness at the side of his mouth and then a

stream of liquid trickled in. He forced himself to swallow in spite of the agony.

"Good kit." Brambleberry stroked his flank with her tail. "Have a long sleep and when you wake up you'll feel a lot better than you do now." As she talked, the medicine cat pulled moss around him until he felt warm and cozy. Her words drifted into a low murmur until the green clearing and the sharp scents of herbs faded into darkness.

CHAPTER 4

Stormkit blinked at his mother. "Are you leaving already?"

"I've got to," Rainflower meowed, glancing up at the sky.

Why won't she look at me?

"There's a lot of hunting to do now the fish are back," she went on.

Oakkit rested his paws on the edge of Stormkit's nest. "I'll stay," he promised.

Stormkit tried to catch Rainflower's eye. "I wanted to tell you about the moth I caught last night."

Confined to the medicine den for a moon, he'd had little chance to hunt. It'd been pure luck the moth had flitted into Brambleberry's den; he'd snatched it out of the air with a single paw.

Oakkit shuffled closer. "You can tell *me* about the moth."

"It was huge." Stormkit leaned toward his mother, but Rainflower was already halfway to the entrance.

"I promised Rippleclaw I'd join his patrol," she called.

"Rainflower!" Brambleberry backed out of the small hollow in the sedge wall where she stored her herbs. Strange green scents clung to her fur, and there were fragments of leaf on her muzzle where she'd been sorting through her supplies.

Rainflower halted. "Yes?"

"Stormkit can go back to the nursery today," Brambleberry told her.

"Really?" Oakkit tumbled into Stormkit's nest and started pummeling him playfully with his hind paws. "That's great! Come on, lazybones!"

"So he's better?" Rainflower's eyes darkened. She glanced at Stormkit. "You can't do any more for him?"

Oakkit froze, mid-pummel.

"He's got all his ears and whiskers." Stormkit heard sharpness in the medicine cat's mew. "He can play and practice hunting like any other kit. What more do you want?"

Rainflower turned away and ducked through the entrance. "Fine. Send him back to the nursery then," she called as the tip of her tail disappeared.

Stormkit tilted his head on one side. "Is Rainflower okay?"

"She's just tired from all the hunting," Oakkit mewed.

Brambleberry flexed her claws. "Tired," she echoed drily.

Oakkit flicked Stormkit's ear with his tail. "Come on!" He leaped out of the soft moss nest. "You've been lying around too long. We need to get you fit. We'll be apprentices in less than two moons."

"I'm afraid not." Brambleberry crossed the den.

Stormkit's heart lurched. "What do you mean?"

Her blue gaze was clear. "You'll have to wait a while

to become a 'paw, little one."

Stormkit leaped out of his nest. "Why?" His paws trembled beneath him.

"You broke your jaw," Brambleberry reminded him.

"But it's healed," Stormkit told her. He opened and closed his mouth to show her. It still felt stiff and lopsided, and it ached if he lay on it during the night, but he knew the bones had mended because the pain wasn't so sharp it made him feel sick.

"You hardly ate for a half-moon, and even now you find it hard." Brambleberry's gaze flicked along Stormkit's flank. "You need to fill out a bit before you start your apprentice training."

"It'll be okay," Oakkit mewed. "I bet you catch up to me even if you start your training late." He nudged Stormkit with his shoulder.

Stormkit almost fell over. When did Oakkit grow so much? He was strong and weighty, more like a 'paw than a kit. Stormkit felt tiny beside him, with hollow flanks and thin legs. He sat down. Was this going to stop him from becoming a warrior? What about Clan leader? Could he still be Clan leader if he was apprenticed late?

Brambleberry touched his head with her muzzle. "Oakkit's right," she murmured. "You'll grow in no time. Just eat well and get some exercise. StarClan is watching over you. There's no reason why you won't be as big as Shellheart by next newleaf."

StarClan's watching over me. Stormkit dug his claws into the soft ground. "I'm going to get big and strong and be the best apprentice ever."

Oakkit flicked his tail toward the tunnel. "Come on! Everyone wants to see you." He bounded away and Stormkit followed, suddenly excited to be out in the camp again.

"Thanks, Brambleberry," he called over his shoulder.

"I'll check on you tomorrow," Brambleberry promised. "Make sure you eat well and rest whenever you get tired."

Stormkit burst out into the clearing, dazzled by the sunshine and surprised by the heat. The river chattered beyond the reed bed and wind swished the rushes. New warrior dens had been woven around the fallen tree. The apprentices' den had grown a warm coating of moss, and the nursery, tucked away in the sedge wall, looked as cozy as ever. Hailstar's den had been rebuilt, its willow stems bright and freshly woven among the roots of the ancient willow. Beetlekit, Volekit, and Petalkit were chasing a ball of moss in the clearing. Mudfur was lying in the shade with Cedarpelt. Shellheart was sharing fresh-kill with Hailstar, Tanglewhisker, and Birdsong at the top of the slope while Softpaw hauled stale moss from their den.

"Are you almost finished, Softpaw?" Fallowtail, her mentor, was calling from the camp entrance. "I want to teach you a new battle move."

"Won't be long," Softpaw answered.

Stormkit breathed deep and smelled the mouthwatering tang of newly caught fish. "Are you hungry?" he asked Oakkit.

"I ate when the dawn patrol got back, but there's fresh-kill left if you want some." He flicked his tail toward the pile of fat trout lying beside the reed bed. "Let me get you one." Oakkit raced away.

"Stormkit!" Mudfur's rumbling mew sounded across the clearing. The warrior clambered to his paws and padded across the clearing. "It's good to see you up and about."

Volekit caught the moss ball Petalkit had just tossed and turned to stare at them. "Stormkit!" He left the ball and came charging across the clearing, Beetlekit and Petalkit on his tail. They dived around Mudfur, nearly tripping over the brown tom's feet, before skidding to a halt in front of Stormkit.

Volekit gasped. "H-how are you?"

Petalkit pushed past her brother. "We kept begging to visit you but Rainflower wouldn't let us." Her eyes glittered. "Would she, Mudfur?" She looked up anxiously at the brown warrior.

Why does she sound weird?

Mudfur sat down behind the kits. "She was worried you were too sick."

Stormkit frowned. He'd begged Rainflower for visitors. Had he really been too sick to see anyone? He'd been in pain, but after half a moon he'd been as bored and frustrated as a turtle up a tree.

Beetlekit was staring at him. "You look funny."

"Hush, Beetlekit." Echomist came trotting across the clearing. "He looks very well considering what he's been through." She licked Stormkit between the ears. "I'm so pleased you're out of the medicine den," she purred. "The nursery's been quiet without you." She glanced at Volekit. "Well, *almost* quiet."

Volekit swallowed. "We've—er—made a training corner

in the nursery." He looked away. "You'll love it. We've got bulrushes and moss to help us practice."

"He can see it later." Echomist silenced her kit. "Right now he needs sunshine and food." She glanced at Stormkit. "And plenty of it."

Even Echomist sounded strange.

Stormkit frowned. "Oakkit's getting me some fresh-kill," he told her.

"Stormkit!" Birdsong's mew sounded from the top of the bank.

"Is that Stormkit out of the medicine den?" Tanglewhisker appeared beside Birdsong, whose tail curled over her back.

Stormkit looked past them to see his father but Shellheart was already on his paws and bounding down the slope. "Stormkit!" He nudged Stormkit's cheek with his muzzle as though he hadn't seen his kit in moons.

Stormkit wriggled away. "You just saw me yesterday!"

"It's just good to see you out of the medicine den at last! You have lots to catch up on. I've been giving Oakkit some training to get him ready for his apprenticeship. You need to get to the same level as fast as you can."

Stormkit purred. He glanced across the clearing wondering if Oakkit had found him a fish yet. His belly was growling.

He stiffened.

Rippleclaw was staring at him from underneath the ancient willow. The silver-and-black warrior looked away as Stormkit caught his gaze.

The whole Clan was acting odd.

Confused, Stormkit turned back to the friendly faces crowding around him. Everyone was making a fuss, saying how pleased they were to see him, how much they'd missed him, but there was something peculiar about the way they were looking at him. Because they *weren't* actually looking at him. Stormkit realized with a jolt that, despite the purrs and kind words, none of them was looking directly at his face. A cold chill ran through him.

He shouldered his way past Echomist and Mudfur and headed for the reed bed.

"Stormkit?" Oakkit dropped the fish he was carrying as Stormkit dashed past him.

Stormkit stopped at the shore, by a patch of clear water, and stared down.

"Stormkit!"

He hardly heard Oakkit's mew. He was staring at the strange cat reflected in the water. That wasn't his face! This cat's jaw was twisted from just below his ear, hardly visible beneath one cheek, sunken horribly beneath the top lip. His nose was stretched sideways and up, and his tongue poked out at one side, lolling between his teeth like a fat pink worm.

"What happened to me?" he whispered.

Oakkit pressed close to him. "You're lucky to be alive, that's what," he mewed fiercely. He stroked Stormkit's spine with his tail. "Brambleberry thought you'd die of shock and then infection. She fought really hard to keep you alive. And Shellheart sat with you night after night."

"What about Rainflower?" Was this why his mother had

hardly visited him? Because he was so horrible to look at?

"Rainflower was upset," Oakkit told him.

Stormkit felt a flood of guilt. "I'm sorry," he whispered.

"What for?"

"That I hurt Rainflower so much."

"Don't say that. It wasn't your fault." Oakkit's voice sounded as if it was stuck in his throat. "Come on." He sat up and nudged Stormkit away from the water's edge with his nose. "We're supposed to be fattening you up!"

Stormkit let his brother guide him toward the fish he'd dropped. He felt weak.

"Eat," Oakkit ordered, stopping beside the fish.

Stormkit crouched down and took a mouthful. He could hardly taste it. All he could think about was how strange it felt when his tongue kept trying to slide out of the side of his mouth. How oddly he had to move his jaws to chew. In the medicine den, it had seemed normal. *It's just part of your recovery,* Brambleberry had told him as he clumsily munched the fish she'd brought him. But he was better now. Back among his Clanmates. Why was eating still so difficult? He must look weird, trying to keep the food from dribbling from the twisted side of his mouth. He glanced up, wondering who was watching.

"I can't do it," he whispered.

"Yes, you can." Oakkit picked up the fish and carried it to a shadowy spot behind a jutting branch of the fallen tree. "Come over here." He beckoned to Stormkit with his tail. "It's quiet. You can eat in peace." Oakkit pushed the fish toward Stormkit and padded back to the clearing.

Stormkit's belly rumbled as if to remind him that he was still hungry. Hidden behind the fallen tree he took another bite of fish. He glanced up to see if anyone was watching. But Oakkit had found him the most private spot in the camp. No one could see him here. Relieved and grateful, Stormkit gulped down the fresh-kill. Pain raked along his jaw, but he kept chewing. At last, his belly full, he sat up. A small pile of half-chewed fish sat by his paws where it had dribbled from his mouth. Stormkit quickly dug a hole in the soft earth and buried it. He jumped, hot with embarrassment, as Oakkit appeared around the end of the branch.

"Are you done?"

Stormkit nodded.

"Come and see the training corner we made in the nursery."

Stormkit padded after his brother and squeezed into the nursery. "Wow!" He stared in delight at the far end of the den. The nests had been pushed back and moss laid on the floor.

Oakkit bounded past him and landed on the moss. "This is so we can fall without hurting ourselves."

"What are those?" Stormkit glanced up at the fat brown bulrush heads sticking out high up the nursery wall.

"Watch!" Oakkit crouched, his head tipped back as he focused on the bulrushes. Then he leaped. Mid-leap he reached out both forepaws and grasped a thick brown rush, then fell back, landing deftly on his hind legs before wrestling it to the ground.

"That's great!" Stormkit felt a surge of excitement. "Can I try?"

"Of course," Oakkit mewed. "That's what it's for. Me and Volekit climb up and thread in fresh bulrushes every morning. It's to practice hunting skills. By the time we start training we'll be able to hit a mouse from three tail-lengths away."

The den rustled as Volekit, Beetlekit, and Petalkit fought to squeeze in.

"Hey! I was first!" Beetlekit complained as Petalkit climbed over him and scampered across the nests to the training corner.

"Have you tried it yet, Stormkit?" Volekit demanded. He crouched down, wiggled his hindquarters, then flung himself at the wall and snatched a bulrush head.

Stormkit pressed his belly to the floor and looked up. A fat bulrush was dangling teasingly over his head. He narrowed his eyes and leaped. Stretching out his paws, he reached for the long fuzzy head. His paws clapped together, grabbing thin air, and he fell back on to the moss panting. "Frog dung!"

"You nearly had it," Petalkit mewed encouragingly.

Stormkit lashed his tail. "*Nearly's* not good enough."

The nest behind him rustled. Echomist squeezed into the nursery, her soft gaze on Stormkit. "It's good to have you back."

Petalkit purred. "He's trying the training corner," she mewed. "He can jump pretty high already."

Volekit stared thoughtfully at the wall. "We're going to have to add more bulrushes."

The den trembled. "You're not going to clog up that corner with more mess, are you?" Rainflower pushed her way in and sat down. She licked her paw and ran it over her pale gray face.

"Can't you play outside like normal kits?"

"Okay." Oakkit nudged Stormkit toward the entrance. "Come on," he called to the others. "Let's play moss-ball."

Beetlekit bounded across the den. "I'm catcher!" he mewed.

"You were catcher last time!" Petalkit scrambled after him.

As his denmates crowded past him, Stormkit stumbled over a pile of woven reeds at the edge of the den. "What's this?" It looked like a nest. Had a new queen moved to the nursery?

Rainflower paused mid-lick. "That's your nest," she meowed.

"*My* nest?" Wouldn't he be sleeping in her nest with Oakkit, like before?

"You'll need your own space," Rainflower told him. "Your jaw must be sore. You'll probably fidget in your sleep. I don't want Oakkit disturbed just because you're injured."

Stormkit blinked at his mother. "It doesn't hurt now," he mewed. "I won't fidget, I promise."

"Still, it's better if you have your own space." Rainflower returned to her washing.

Volekit nudged Stormkit's shoulder. "Come on. Let's go and play."

Stormkit stared at his mother. Was she angry because he'd worried her by being so ill?

Shellheart poked his head through the entrance. "How are you settling in?"

"I've got my own nest," Stormkit mumbled.

Shellheart narrowed his eyes. "Have you got your own nest, too, Oakkit?"

Oakkit stared at his paws.

"Rainflower." Shellheart's mew was more like a growl. "I'd like to speak with you outside."

The fur along Rainflower's spine bristled as she hopped out of the den.

"Come on, kits," Echomist mewed cheerily. "How about another go at the training wall?"

"But we're going outside to play." Beetlekit's mew was drowned by Shellheart's angry snarl beyond the nursery wall.

"His own nest?"

"He has to grow up eventually," Rainflower answered.

"But *Oakkit* can stay in your nest?" Shellheart hissed.

"Stormkit must be used to his own nest after so long in the medicine den."

Shellheart snorted. "At least you're still calling him Stormkit."

"And I'll keep calling him that till Hailstar changes his name formally."

"So you're still determined to rename him Crookedkit?"

Stormkit froze. *Crooked*kit?

"It will suit him."

"Don't you think it's a bit cruel?"

"If he'd stayed in camp he'd never have had the accident."

She does blame me!

Rainflower carried on. "Then he wouldn't be the ugly mess he is now." The icy coldness in his mother's voice made Stormkit feel sick. "He'd still be my handsome young warrior."

He began to tremble. Soft fur brushed beside him. Echomist

pressed close as Shellheart growled at his mate.

"How do you think Stormkit must feel?"

"He'll get used to it," Rainflower retorted.

"To what?" Rage sharpened Shellheart's mew. "His new name? Being scarred for life? Being rejected by his mother?"

"The accident wasn't my fault! I shouldn't have to deal with it," Rainflower spat.

Stormkit's chest tightened. A sob welled in his throat.

"She's grieving," Echomist murmured in his ear. "She doesn't realize what she's saying."

Shellheart's voice was little more than a whisper. "I never knew you could be so heartless, Rainflower," he growled. "If you insist on Hailstar going ahead with the renaming ceremony then we are no longer mates. I will never share a den or a piece of fresh-kill with you again."

"Very well."

Stormkit couldn't listen to any more. He jumped to his paws and rushed out of the den. "Please don't argue! I don't mind sleeping by myself or having a new name!" he wailed. But Rainflower was already crossing the clearing to Hailstar's den and didn't seem to hear him. Stormkit stared pleadingly at Shellheart. "Don't argue because of me."

"It's not because of you." Shellheart wrapped his tail around Stormkit. "It's because of her." He stared after Rainflower, anger flaring in his eyes.

Brambleberry was trotting toward them. "How's the nursery?" Her cheerful mew faltered as she caught Shellheart's gaze. She turned to see Rainflower disappear into Hailstar's den. "She's really going to do it?"

Shellheart nodded. Brambleberry closed her eyes for a moment, then blinked them open and stared at Stormkit. "The seasons change, Stormkit, but RiverClan never stops being RiverClan. Shellheart will always be brave and loyal, whether there is sun or snow on his pelt. And you will always have the heart of a warrior, no matter what your name is." She touched him gently on the head with her muzzle.

The trailing moss at the entrance to Hailstar's den quivered and Hailstar padded out. Rainflower slid out after him. "Let all cats old enough to swim gather to hear my words," the RiverClan leader meowed solemnly.

Brambleberry flicked her tail. "Perhaps I should change my name." She began to walk toward Hailstar. "I could be called Swallowherb." She purred at her own joke. "See?" She looked over her shoulder at Stormkit. "Because that's what I do? I make cats swallow herbs."

Stormkit padded numbly after her. He tried to purr but his throat was dry.

Brambleberry halted and looked down at him. "StarClan is watching over you," she told him. Her blue eyes met his. "This is part of a destiny only they understand, but you must believe that they are guiding all of us, and that they care about you just as much as any cat in RiverClan."

Stormkit blinked as the medicine cat turned and trotted away. He wanted to believe her, but why would StarClan let something so unfair happen to him?

Troutclaw, Birdsong, and Tanglewhisker headed down

the slope as Echomist herded Volekit, Petalkit, and Beetlekit from the nursery.

"How can he change someone's name before they're an apprentice?" Volekit was protesting.

"Shhh!" Echomist hurried him on with a nudge of her nose.

Hailstar waited with Rainflower beside him while the Clan gathered at the edge of the clearing.

"What's going on?" Shimmerpelt whispered.

Fallowtail shrugged. "No idea. It's too soon for the kits to have their apprentice names."

Softpaw lifted her chin. "Maybe we're going to get our warrior names," she hissed to Whitepaw. Whitepaw glanced questioningly at his mentor, but Timberfur was whispering something to Ottersplash, his eyes dark.

Stormkit's heart quickened. He tried to catch Rainflower's eye but she stared straight ahead.

"Stormkit, come here." Hailstar's mew was soft.

Stormkit padded, trembling, into the clearing. He looked blindly around. The familiar faces seemed strange, menacing, all of a sudden. Was this a bad dream?

"I have gathered the Clan to witness the giving of your new name. I'm sorry you have suffered so much. The whole Clan knows how brave you've been." His mew was gentle with sympathy. "Your new name may describe your face, young kit, but it doesn't describe your heart. I know you are as true and loyal as any warrior. Bear your name bravely as a kit and nobly when you become a warrior."

Stormkit nodded.

"From this day forward, you shall be known as Crookedkit."

Stormkit tried not to hear the murmur of shock that swept around the Clan. He stared past Hailstar, confusion clouding his thoughts.

But I was born in a storm. I'm Stormkit.

How could he ever be Stormstar now?

Suddenly he glimpsed an orange-and-white pelt in the shadow of the sedges. The cat from the river! Her pelt shimmered as though caught in a heat haze. He tasted the air and found only the familiar scents of his Clanmates. She must be a StarClan cat. *StarClan is watching over you.* Brambleberry's words rang in his head. Had the orange-and-white cat been sent to remind him of their promise? *Don't worry, little one.* He heard her words again. *It's not your time yet. You have a great destiny ahead of you.*

"Crookedkit." He murmured his new name. "I am Crookedkit." He glanced around his Clanmates. No one met his gaze. Only the shimmering orange-and-white cat. Her amber eyes shone, unblinking, at him. *She believes in me.* With a rush of hope, Crookedkit lifted his chin.

"I am Crookedkit," he repeated.

CHAPTER 5

❧

"*Can I sleep in Crookedkit's nest* tonight?" Oakkit mewed to Rainflower. His eyes glistened in the moonlight that filtered through the walls. "It's my last night in the nursery."

"No." Rainflower climbed into her nest and circled, ready for sleep. "How many times have I told you? He's used to sleeping alone. You'll stop him from getting a good night's rest, and he needs as much sleep as he can get if he's ever going to grow."

Crookedkit flinched. A long moon of sleeping in his own nest had deepened his pain, not eased it. Volepaw, Petalpaw, and Beetlepaw had received their apprentice names and moved to the apprentices' den, and Echomist had returned to the warriors' dens. Crookedkit curled into his nest and tucked his nose under his paw. If only he hadn't broken his jaw, Rainflower would still love him. Instead she acted like his ugliness was contagious. He'd tried to please her, to make up for his accident. He'd fetched her prey from the fresh-kill pile until she asked him to stop. He'd offered to clean out the stale moss from her nest, but she'd shaken her head.

"Clean out your own nest," she'd told him. "Softpaw can do ours."

Crookedkit shoved his nose tighter under his paw. His belly rumbled; his jaw ached. He'd only managed to eat a fish tail earlier before pain had stopped him from chewing. If he couldn't eat, how would he even grow big enough to get his apprentice name?

"Crookedkit!"

Volepaw was calling. Crookedkit blinked open his eyes. Hot greenleaf sun shone through the reed walls. Rainflower's nest was empty. Had he missed Oakkit's naming ceremony?

"The dawn patrol brought fresh-kill!"

Crookedkit struggled groggily out of his nest, his legs trembling as he stumbled out of the nursery.

Volepaw was bouncing around Shellheart. "Look what he caught!"

Shellheart held a fat trout in his jaws. He dropped it at Crookedkit's paws. Crookedkit jumped back; the fish was almost as big as he was. Shellheart purred. "One day you'll be catching fish like that." He tore a lump from the shimmering fresh-kill. "Eat this." He tossed it beside Crookedkit. "I'll give the rest to the elders. Tanglewhisker won't believe his eyes."

Crookedkit watched his father carry the fish away, then looked down at the piece at his paws.

Volepaw was watching him.

Crookedkit ignored the trout, even though its fresh river smell was making his mouth water. He sucked back the spit that was threatening to spill over his twisted jaw. "Has Hailstar given Oakkit his apprentice name yet?" he asked.

"Not yet." Volepaw glanced toward Hailstar's den. A pale gray tail twitched between the trailing moss covering the entrance. "Rainflower wanted to talk to Hailstar before the ceremony."

Perhaps she's asking Hailstar to make me an apprentice, too! Hope flared in Crookedkit's belly.

"She told Echomist that there's only one warrior good enough to train Oakkit," Volepaw went on. "And she's going to make sure Hailstar chooses him."

"Oh." Disappointment dragged at his pelt. "Which warrior is it?"

Volepaw shrugged. "Who knows?" He glanced at the piece of trout. "Are you going to eat that?"

Crookedkit hesitated. He was hungry but there was no way he was going to eat in front of Volepaw. He still drooled like an elder. "You have it." He kicked it toward Volepaw.

"Thanks." Volepaw crouched and started eating. Crookedkit's belly growled.

"Let all cats old enough to swim gather in the clearing!" Hailstar was padding from his den, his wide shoulders sleek and freshly groomed.

Cedarpelt slid out from the sedges. A dead frog dangled from his jaws. Fallowtail jumped down from the ancient willow. She turned and called up to Softpaw. "We'll practice diving later."

Softpaw slithered clumsily down the trunk. "I don't know why we have to learn to climb. It's not natural."

Tanglewhisker poked his head out of the elders' den. "A

ceremony already? The sun's barely up!" he grumbled, but he padded down the slope with Birdsong and Troutclaw ambling after him.

Piketooth hauled himself out of the reed bed, clasping a bundle of stems between his jaws. River water streamed from his tabby pelt as he laid the reeds on the ground. Shimmerpelt followed him on to dry land, another bundle dripping between her teeth. She dropped the reeds and shook out her glossy black fur. Lakeshine, who was dozing nearby, leaped to her paws as water sprayed her.

"Sorry." Shimmerpelt flicked her tail. "I didn't see you."

Lakeshine's mottled gray pelt made her look like dappled shadow beside the shore. "It's okay." The she-cat licked her wet fur. "It'll cool me down."

Brambleberry emerged from the medicine den and sat beside Softpaw. The apprentice was lapping at her chest where mossy willow bark had turned her snowy white fur into another patch of tabby.

Whitepaw came hurtling from the dirtplace tunnel. "Did I miss anything?" He circled his mentor.

Timberfur sat down. "Not yet."

Crookedkit wondered where to sit. Shellheart was beside Hailstar. Rainflower stood apart from her Clanmates, Oakkit at her side. Oakkit's eyes sparkled. Crookedkit wanted to race across the clearing and wish him luck. But he knew Rainflower would send him away with a snarl.

Brambleberry flicked her tail toward Crookedkit. "Sit with me." She stroked Crookedkit's spine with her tail as he reached her. "It's nice and cool here."

As he settled beneath the willow beside her, Echomist joined him. "I bet you're proud of your brother."

Crookedkit purred. Soon Oakkit would be the strongest and bravest apprentice in the Clan. "He's going to be a great warrior, like Shellheart."

Echomist's scent touched his nose and nursery memories rushed back. When a bad dream woke him, she'd let him creep into her nest and bundled him among her own kits. She always gently pushed him out before dawn so he could go back to his own nest before Rainflower woke up. "It's best not to cause trouble," she'd whisper, licking his ears.

"I think Oakkit's trying to get your attention." Brambleberry nudged Crookedkit from his thoughts. Oakkit was staring at him, mouthing something. Crookedkit tried to guess what he was saying. It looked like "Crookedpaw." *He's wishing I was getting my apprentice name, too.* Warmth flooded him. *It won't be long,* he silently promised.

Hailstar dipped his head. "Oakkit, come here."

As Oakkit padded forward, Hailstar called another name. "Shellheart!"

Crookedkit blinked. Hailstar was making Shellheart Oakkit's mentor! Fathers never mentored their own kits. He stared at Rainflower. Her eyes glowed. She had planned this. Crookedkit felt suddenly cold.

Hailstar's gaze swept the Clan. "Shellheart and Oakkit share courage, strength, and loyalty." He dipped his head to his deputy. "Strengthen those talents in your apprentice,

Shellheart, and make Oakpaw a warrior who will lead RiverClan to greatness."

"Oakpaw!" Rainflower was the first to raise her voice in praise of RiverClan's newest apprentice.

"Oakpaw!" Volepaw and Petalpaw joined in. Timberfur and Brightsky lashed their tails enthusiastically as they called out Oakpaw's new name.

Crookedkit scanned the reeds, looking for a glimpse of orange-and-white pelt. The StarClan cat had come before. Would she come now to remind him of his destiny? Or was Oakpaw going to get that, too?

"Join in!" Crookedkit felt Brambleberry's breath in his ear and realized he hadn't called his brother's new name.

"Oakpaw! Oakpaw!" he yowled to the wide blue sky. *Oh, StarClan, let him be a great warrior!* As the plea flashed in his thoughts, Oakpaw padded toward him.

"Thank you." Oakpaw bent his head and rubbed his jaw along Crookedkit's. "I hope we get to train together soon. You're my littermate and I'll always be there for you."

Crookedkit purred, his jealousy melting. He loved Oakpaw too much to want anything less than the best for him. He just wished Rainflower loved them equally.

Oakpaw's eyes shone as he turned back to Hailstar. "I promise I will train hard to become the best warrior I can be."

Rainflower crossed the clearing. "Well done, my dear," she purred to Oakpaw.

Shellheart pushed in front of her and touched Oakpaw's head with the tip of his muzzle. "I'll expect you to train harder than any other apprentice," he warned. "I don't want anyone saying I'm going easy on you because you're my kit."

"Neither do I!" Oakpaw puffed out his chest.

Shellheart glanced at Crookedkit. "There's no reason I can't show you some of the moves I teach Oakpaw," he promised. Excitement fizzed in Crookedkit's paws.

"Don't be silly." Rainflower sniffed. "He's too small."

Crookedkit stared at her, his twisted jaw gaping. He shut it quickly and swallowed. Was she right? He was eating as much as he could, and he had nearly outgrown his nest in the nursery.

Pelts brushed past his nose as Petalpaw and Volepaw crowded around his brother. "Well done, Oakpaw!"

Crookedkit backed away.

"Yeah." Beetlepaw nosed past his littermates, his shoulders stiff. "Well done. Now I understand why I didn't get Shellheart as a mentor."

"Oh, Beetlepaw." Petalpaw nudged her brother's cheek with her muzzle. "Aren't you over that yet? Just because you're Hailstar's kit doesn't mean you get the deputy as your mentor. You know Hailstar matches us with who he thinks will train us best."

Beetlepaw snorted. "Then why'd he give me Ottersplash?"

"Shhh!" Volepaw hissed.

Beetlepaw stared blankly at his denmates' frozen faces. "What?"

Ottersplash had crossed the clearing and was standing right behind her apprentice, her white-and-ginger coat shining in the sunlight. "Maybe he thought you needed to learn a bit of respect?" she suggested.

Beetlepaw spun around, his pelt ruffled. "Sorry!"

Ottersplash looked steadily at him. "I think you'd better spend the afternoon cleaning out the elders' den instead of learning battle moves."

Beetlepaw's face fell, but he didn't argue. "Okay." He padded away, dragging his paws.

Petalpaw hurried after him. "I'll help!"

"Perhaps you should help, too," Shellheart meowed to Oakpaw.

"My first apprentice duty! Great!"

Crookedkit watched him charge away, envy pricking. His mother's sharp mew made him jump.

"Aren't you going to thank me?" Rainflower was glaring at Shellheart.

Shellheart narrowed his eyes. "What for?"

"Who do you think arranged for you to be Oakpaw's mentor?"

"You?" Shellheart blinked.

"Hailstar understood it made sense for the strongest warrior to train the strongest apprentice."

Echomist's anxious mew sounded in Crookedkit's ear. "Why don't you go and see if Oakpaw needs help?" She nudged him toward the slope. "Go on."

He padded away reluctantly, glancing back at Shellheart and Rainflower as they faced each other, hackles high. If he'd never had his accident, they'd still be happy.

"Oakpaw?" Crookedkit stuck his head through the neatly woven entrance of the elders' den.

Petalpaw looked up from Tanglewhisker's nest. "Oakpaw went to gather moss."

"I'll go and help him," Crookedkit offered.

"He's *outside* the camp," Petalpaw told him.

"Oh. Then can I help you?"

A bundle of stinking moss hit him on the nose.

"You'll just get in the way." Beetlepaw was clawing through Troutclaw's nest, his nose wrinkled against the stench.

"Why don't you go and play?" Petalpaw mewed kindly. "We can manage here."

Tanglewhisker was patting his nest back into shape. "He's got to learn sometime," the elder croaked.

"Well, he can come back and learn by himself." Beetlepaw tossed another ball of moss toward the entrance. "This is bad enough without having a kit underpaw."

Crookedkit bristled. "I'm only a moon younger than you!" he snapped.

"And four moons smaller," Beetlepaw answered back.

Growling, Crookedkit ducked out of the den and stomped down the slope. Perhaps Piketooth and Shimmerpelt needed help. He'd gathered reeds two moons ago. There no reason he couldn't do it now. He hadn't *shrunk*.

"Can I help?" he called from the edge of the reed bed. The water lapped at his claws, cool and refreshing.

Piketooth backed out of a thick swath of reeds. "Don't fall in!" he warned.

"You could teach me how to swim, then I could help better," Crookedkit pointed out.

Piketooth shook his head. "You're a bit small for that."

"So are minnows!" Crookedkit felt like jumping into the clear patch of water and teaching himself how to swim.

Shimmerpelt waded out of the river and dropped a mouthful of reeds on the shore. "I know you're bored," she meowed sympathetically. "There aren't any more kits to play with." She glanced around the camp. "Maybe you could practice stalking by yourself?"

Crookedkit felt his tail droop. Didn't anyone want him around?

Brambleberry was watching him from outside the medicine den. "Do you want to help me sort herbs?" she called.

"I'm going to be a *warrior,* not a medicine cat!" Crookedkit snapped. He turned and padded across the clearing. Oakpaw was trotting into camp, a wad of moss between his jaws.

Shellheart hailed him. "Oakpaw, when you've delivered that, I'll take you on a tour of the territory."

Crookedkit pricked his ears. "Can I come?" he called hopefully.

Shellheart sighed. "One day." He watched as Oakpaw raced up the slope, dropped the moss, and dashed back down. "Ready?"

Oakpaw nodded. Crookedkit sat down and watched them disappear through the entrance tunnel.

Rainflower was lying in the shade of the sedge wall, sharing fresh-kill with Lakeshine. She lifted her head and stared at

Crookedkit. "I'm moving back to the warriors' dens tonight." She turned her fresh-kill with her paw. "Lakeshine's letting me share her nest until I build my own."

You can't! Crookedkit's heart began to race. That meant he'd be alone in the nursery. His Clanmates would all be sharing tongues and snoring together while he lay on his own, like an outcast. Maybe Rainflower would stay if he did something to impress her. Maybe he could get her to love him again. He raced for the fallen tree and scrambled up the trunk. Claws stretched, he skittered along the jutting branch he'd climbed moons ago.

"Look, Rainflower!" He reached the end and stretched up, legs trembling, heart pounding, tall enough that the whole Clan could see him—the bravest kit in the Clan. "Look at me!"

Rainflower twitched her tail. "Get down before you fall!" she called wearily, and turned back to her meal. "And stop showing off. You'll be an apprentice when you're ready, not before."

Somewhere in the woods, a warbler shrieked. Crookedkit sat up in his nest. The Clan was asleep. Even through the walls of the nursery, he could hear snores and snuffles and the rustling of nests as his Clanmates stretched and rolled over. Crookedkit felt wide awake. His heart ached in his chest too fiercely to sleep. He trailed around the empty den, breathing in the scents of Rainflower and Echomist.

Perhaps the orange-and-white StarClan warrior would come now. He scanned the shadowy edges of the nursery, straining to see through the half-light. Was this loneliness part of the destiny she'd promised? *StarClan is watching over you.* He remembered Brambleberry's words. *This is part of a destiny only they understand, but you must believe that they are guiding all of us, and that they care about you just as much as any cat in RiverClan.*

If StarClan wouldn't come to him, then he'd go to them. He'd visit the Moonstone where Brambleberry shared tongues with their ancestors. When he was in the medicine den, she'd described her journeys there. He just had to head upstream and get through WindClan territory without being spotted. After that Highstones would be easy to find. It was bigger than Sunningrocks. *It makes Sunningrocks look like a pebble.* That's what Brambleberry had told him. Butterflies fluttered in his belly but he ignored them. He *had* to know whether this was part of his destiny. Padding to the nursery entrance, he peered out. The clearing was deserted, silvered by moonlight. Crookedkit slid out of the reed den and padded quietly across the clearing to the entrance tunnel.

The sedge whispered around him as he headed out of camp.

CHAPTER 6

Gentle rain began to fall as Crookedkit followed the grassy path away from the camp. The river glittered beside him. *I cross the river and head upstream to the moors. Then I*—He frowned, trying to remember the rest of Brambleberry's words. His paws pricked nervously. First, cross the river. He couldn't swim yet, which left him just one option.

The stepping-stones.

He felt sick as he remembered his fall: smashing his face against the rock, the pain, the swirling current. Then he remembered the orange-and-white cat's amber gaze burning through the green water. He had to make it to the Moonstone and talk to her. He had to find out if everything that had happened since the accident—Hailstar changing his name, being left in the nursery on his own—was part of his great destiny. How *could* it be? Nothing had been great. Everything had been terrible. But, if it *was* part of his destiny, he would bear it. He could bear anything to be truly great.

Pushing through the bushes, he slithered down the bank onto the muddy shore. The river was shallow and sluggish, lightly dappled by raindrops. It looked harmless now, lapping at the stones, but Crookedkit knew its power. It had washed away his Clan's home. It had nearly killed him.

Ahead, the stepping-stones shone, wet with rain. An owl shrieked in the trees beyond Sunningrocks. Crookedkit sniffed the air, searching for fresh ThunderClan scent, but smelled only his Clanmates. Timberfur had passed this way recently, leading the dusk patrol home. Fallowtail must have been with him; the tang of her paw steps was still fresh on the grass.

Crookedkit paused. Very fresh. Was she still here? Ducking, he scanned the shore and hoped his pale brown tabby pelt wouldn't show in the dark; but he could not hide his scent, especially now that it was tinged with fear. Ears stretched, he listened, but heard nothing beyond the river's murmuring and the soft patter of rain on leaves. Crookedkit took a deep breath and made a dash for the stepping-stones. Tensing, he leaped and landed, sure-pawed, on the first stone. The river flowed dizzyingly around him as he jumped to the next. He was *definitely* bigger than the last time he'd tried to cross the river. His paws gripped the stones more firmly, and they didn't seem so far apart. He focused his gaze on the far shore and crossed the rest of the stones without hesitating, landing on the other side with a sigh of relief.

Sunningrocks rose into the dark, drizzly sky. Clouds hid the moon and Crookedkit had to squint to see his paws on the sandy shore beneath him. His hackles lifted as he smelled ThunderClan scent drifting down from the new borderline. Was Hailstar ever going to fight for this land?

Flexing his claws, Crookedkit headed upstream. He

followed the shore, slinking into the bushes as he passed the RiverClan camp on the other side of the river. The path began to climb steadily. He was deep in ThunderClan territory now. Scent marked every bush, and he closed his mouth so the foul stench didn't touch his tongue. His ears twitched. Beyond the soft gurgling of the river, he heard water thundering. He must be nearing the falls where Brambleberry collected coltsfoot. Crookedkit sniffed, tasting the zest of it in the air and the stone tang of splashing water beyond.

The path grew steeper, climbing beside the river, the shore now a rising cliff that grew higher and higher with every paw step. Crookedkit peered over the edge. Far below him, the river rushed past, swirling in the moonlight through a deep rocky channel. The thundering water grew louder, echoing from the rock and, as Crookedkit rounded a corner, he saw the falls for the first time. Higher than any tree, throwing droplets up toward the moon, the river plunged straight down where the land fell away, hurtling into the deep gorge.

Crookedkit stiffened, suddenly aware of how narrow the path had grown. Sheer rock rose on one side and plummeted down on the other. He flinched away from the precipice, grazing his pelt on the cliff face, and flattened his ears against the roar of water as he pressed on. The graveled path scratched his paws and wind whipped rain across his muzzle. It smelled peaty and rich with the scent of pollen.

As he reached the top of the falls, the roar of water faded. The path flattened and the river flowed smoothly once more, brimming to the shore. Crookedkit gazed across the swath of land that stretched out beside him. It rose toward the moors and beyond that he could see distant cliffs. *Highstones?* He'd heard warriors and elders talk about the jagged rocky peaks, and he knew that was where the Moonstone lay.

A new scent hit his nose. ThunderClan markers had been replaced by a different stench. A new smell. This must be WindClan territory. *Then I cross WindClan's moor.* Brambleberry's words rushed back to him. His heart quickened as he turned his paws away from the river and headed upslope into the moorland. The soft bushes gave way to prickly heather and gorse. Crookedkit weaved among their stems, thankful for the cover. Ears pricked and mouth open, alert for WindClan patrols, he padded on.

A familiar scent stopped him in his tracks.

RiverClan?

He sniffed again, unable to put a cat's name to the scent through the strong smell of heather. But it was definitely RiverClan. Had Hailstar sent a patrol to find him? That seemed unlikely. He'd been alone in the nursery. Who would even know he was missing yet? He frowned and kept going.

At the top of the slope, a small pile of rocks jutted from the heather. Crookedkit scrambled onto the lowest rock and looked at the stones above him. If he could get higher he might be able to see Highstones. He glanced up at the sky, wishing the clouds would clear. He wanted to see Silverpelt and know that StarClan was near. Rain spattered his nose. Screwing up his eyes, he reached up the rock, feeling for cracks to curl his claws into. Finding one, he hauled himself up and scrabbled onto the next boulder. He was above the heather now. It stretched out ahead of him, and in the distant darkness he could just make out the jagged shape of Highstones.

A warm wind tugged his wet pelt. He tasted the air. The RiverClan scent hit his tongue again, clearer now. He could recognize it now.

Fallowtail!

A mew sounded on the breeze. Crookedkit scrabbled up onto the summit of the outcrop and crouched at the top.

"Did you hear something?"

A deep mew sounded below. Clinging to the wet stone with outstretched claws, Crookedkit crept forward and peered over the edge. Two pelts gleamed in the heather below. Crookedkit gasped. Grit showered from beneath his claws.

Fallowtail's light brown pelt glowed in the half-light. A tabby tom stood with her. Crookedkit shot backward and pressed his belly against the rock.

"Is someone up there?" Fallowtail's mew sounded frightened.

"I'll look," the tom growled.

Crookedkit froze. The stench wafting up alongside Fallowtail's fear-scent smelled like the markers he'd passed at the border. *WindClan!* As claws scraped rock, Crookedkit slithered tail-first over the edge of the boulder. He landed clumsily on the ledge below and pressed himself into the shadow, thankful he was small enough to hide in the shallow crevice where the boulders met. Drawing his tail close, he waited, trembling.

"I can't see anything," a voice called above him.

"Let me look."

Crookedkit heard another pelt brush stone.

"I can smell RiverClan!" Fallowtail gasped.

"But no one's here," the tom soothed. "There's nowhere for a warrior to hide."

"I smell RiverClan!" Fallowtail's breathing quickened. "Some cat *must* have followed me. Let's go."

Crookedkit pressed himself harder into the crack as Fallowtail and the other cat slid down past him. Paws damp with fear, he stared from his hiding place as the warriors slipped into the heather and bounded away across the moor. When his breathing had slowed, he crept out of the crevice and slithered down the rock. He padded around the outcrop, skirting the trail of mixed WindClan and RiverClan scent, and pressed on toward Highstones.

His mind whirled as he followed a track through the gorse, ears pricked and pelt bristling. What was Fallowtail doing here? Had Hailstar sent her on a secret mission? But why was she with a WindClan tom? Was he helping her? Why would any warrior betray his Clan like that?

The rain eased and the clouds drifted away until the moon was a claw-scratch of silver against a crow-black sky. Crookedkit crested a short, steep rise that stood like an island in the vast sea of heather. Highstones towered in the distance, more sharply etched against the sky but no closer than they had been before. Crookedkit gazed in dismay at the wide space between the moorland and the Moonstone. It was broken by hedges and stretches of meadow and dark shapes he guessed must be Twoleg nests.

How would he ever travel that far? His belly growled. If only he knew how to hunt! It couldn't be that hard. Echomist was always complaining about kittypets hunting on the edges of their territory. If a kittypet could do it, then so could he. And imagine Rainflower's face when he told her he'd traveled to the Moonstone and back! He tasted the air, hoping to scent prey, but smelled nothing more than heather and WindClan stink. Sighing, he padded down the rise. At least the edge of the moor was close. He could see where it tipped down toward the meadows beyond. He'd be out of WindClan territory by moonhigh.

Bushes rustled behind him. Crookedkit whipped around and glimpsed a pair of eyes flashing in the heather.

StarClan, help me!

Heart lurching, he ran. His claws sprayed peat as he hurtled through a swath of gorse. The sharp twigs snagged his pelt but he hardly felt the pain. Paws thrummed the ground behind him. Crookedkit didn't dare look back as he skidded over the crest at the edge of the moor and raced down the slope toward the meadowland.

The paw steps were gaining on him, thumping closer. Crookedkit charged through a wall of WindClan stench. *The border!* The markers were so strong it *had* to be the edge of WindClan territory. Their warriors wouldn't chase him here, surely? But the paws kept coming.

Crookedkit pelted to the bottom of the hill. His chest

screamed; blood roared in his ears. Ahead, a smooth river of stone sliced through the land where it flattened out. A hedge loomed beyond. Perhaps he could find somewhere to hide there. *If I make it.* The paw steps were a frog-length behind now. He could hear snorting and feel the earth tremble. Eyes wide, he glanced back and saw a rabbit charging after him.

A rabbit!

Astounded, he stumbled to a halt. The rabbit charged past him, its eyes gleaming with panic. Crookedkit glanced back up the slope. His breath stopped. Four WindClan warriors lined the crest of the hill, their eyes shining in the moonlight. Were they watching the rabbit? Or him?

A growl made him turn. Two giant eyes lit the stone path. A *monster* was storming straight toward him! He'd heard nursery stories about monsters. It was even more terrifying than Echomist—eyes wide, pelt bristling—had described. Huge, sharp-edged creatures with hard shiny pelts and yellow beams shooting from their eyes. Their round black paws smelled of burning stone, and the air shuddered with noise even before they appeared. But monsters were stupid, clinging to the Thunderpath as if they were afraid of venturing on to soft grass or into trees. A cat could outwit them by holding his or her nerve and getting out of the way.

Crookedkit backed away from the Thunderpath as the monster screamed by. Wind howled as it passed and its stench bathed his pelt. Fur on end, heart bursting, Crookedkit clung to the earth.

And then it was gone.

Thank StarClan, it didn't see me!

Crookedkit opened his eyes. The rabbit lay in front of him, flat, on the hard black stone. Blood pooled around from its mouth and Crookedkit shivered. The monster had killed it without even slowing down to take a bite or snap its neck. He looked back up the slope. The warriors had gone.

His breath shallow, Crookedkit padded shakily across the Thunderpath. He paused beside the rabbit, wondering whether to drag it to the grass at the edge. It was, after all, fresh-kill now. But its dead, open eyes made him shudder and he hurried past it and dodged into the safety of the hedge on the far side. Trembling, he crouched down and let his terror slowly ebb away.

Highstones was ahead of him, still distant beyond rolling fields. Crookedkit straightened up and followed the hedgerow. Keeping to the edges of the open meadows, where he couldn't be seen by any passing foxes or badgers, he pushed on, his belly growling and jaw aching. The moon climbed over Highstones and slid down behind them. Crookedkit paused. The stars were disappearing as the edges of the sky began to turn pale. He wasn't going to make it to Highstones before dawn. He wasn't even close.

Ahead, a stone wall marked the edge of another meadow. Crookedkit squeezed through a hole where the stones had collapsed. A huge nest rose ahead of him, four-sided with strips of black wood covering the walls and a curved roof. Its entrance was blocked by a smooth slab of paler wood, but a tiny hole next to it showed darkness inside, warm and sweet-smelling. It might be a safe place to rest. Crookedkit tasted the air and inhaled the scent of dry grass. More tired than he'd ever been in his life, he padded up to the small opening. He could just make out piles of dried stalks stacked high in the giant space inside the nest. There was no sign of life, no warrior scent. Paws heavy as stones, Crookedkit slithered inside and found a dark corner. Too weary to figure out where he was, he curled into a ball, tucked his nose under his paw, and gave in to sleep.

CHAPTER 7

"Crookedkit!"

Crookedkit opened his eyes. The straw he'd curled up in had vanished. Instead, he was standing on damp earth. Trees crowded around him, their trunks wet with moss, roots snaking into slimy soil. Mist swirled and darkness pressed down through their branches, hiding the sky. Crookedkit unsheathed his claws as sour scents bathed his tongue.

"Crookedkit!" the voice called again. Amber eyes gleamed from the shadows. "How could you leave your Clan?"

"I—I wanted to visit the Moonstone." Crookedkit blinked, his eyes adjusting to the gloom. The amber eyes flashed and an orange-and-white she-cat padded out of the trees. *The StarClan cat! She's come back!* "What is this place?" he meowed.

The cat weaved around him, her pelt warm in the chilled air. "You're dreaming, little one."

"Dreaming?" Crookedkit's pelt ruffled. Why would he dream of a place like this?

"Why go all the way to the Moonstone to speak with StarClan?" The orange-and-white cat stopped in front of him. "You can ask me anything, right here in your dreams."

"I was right! You are a StarClan cat!" Crookedkit gasped.

The cat dipped her head. "My name is Mapleshade. What is it you want to know, little one?"

"My destiny," Crookedkit burst out.

"Everything that happens to you is part of your destiny."

"But the accident? And not becoming an apprentice?" The words rushed out. "Was all that supposed to happen?"

Mapleshade weaved around him, her soft pelt brushing his. "Oh, you poor thing," she sighed. "Your path is not an easy one. But StarClan would never have given such a hard path to a cat who wasn't strong and brave and loyal."

"Really?" Crookedkit shuffled his paws. "Then I am special."

Mapleshade rested her muzzle on his head. "Of course you're special."

Suddenly he remembered Rainflower's scent. She used to speak to him like this. He pulled away. "How?" he demanded. "How am I special?"

Mapleshade shook her head. "I can't tell you that yet."

"Why not?"

"First you must return to your Clan." Mapleshade's eyes darkened. "A true warrior is loyal."

"I was only traveling to the Moonstone."

"There's no need to go there now."

"I guess not." Crookedkit glanced at his paws. He'd been looking forward to telling his Clanmates he'd visited the Moonstone. "What will I tell everyone?"

"That you're sorry and you'll never leave again." Mapleshade flicked her tail beneath his chin. "They must know you're loyal."

Crookedkit straightened. "I am!"

"Then you'll go back?"

Crookedkit nodded. "Which way do I go?" He glanced around the forest. "I . . . I think I'm lost."

A purr rumbled in Mapleshade's throat. "Close your eyes, little one." She brushed her fluffy white tail over his muzzle. "And when you wake, you'll know where to go."

Crookedkit closed his eyes and let darkness claim him.

Crookedkit rolled over and stretched. The air was stifling. He sneezed and rubbed a paw across his itchy muzzle, then opened his eyes and saw loose dry grasses. They were stacked high above him and smelled woody. Sun streamed in, dancing with dust. He was back in the nest he'd found the night before.

Sitting up, Crookedkit yawned. *Then you'll go back?* Mapleshade's words echoed in his ears. Suddenly he remembered Rainflower's weary mew, telling him to get down from the tree, and his Clanmates sending him off to play on his own. Crookedkit sighed. *What if I don't want to go back?* Suddenly his belly growled. *I'm starving!*

Crookedkit pricked his ears. Was that a squeak? He dropped into a crouch and crept across the dusty floor. Mouth open, he let the scents of the nest bathe his tongue. A musky odor filled his nose. *Mouse?* Maybe. He'd never smelled mouse but he'd heard elders' descriptions. Padding quietly, he slunk toward the wall at the back of the nest. The dusty stalks twitched in the corner. Crookedkit held his breath. His paws pricked as he bunched the muscles in his hind legs. Fixing his gaze on a soft lump beneath the straw, he prepared to leap.

"Oomph!"

A great weight dropped on his back. Fear pulsed through him as he smelled tom. But it wasn't any *Clan* scent he'd ever smelled. Claws dug into his spine. Stiffening with terror, Crookedkit struggled to escape. But the tom was heavy and had a firm grip.

Crookedkit flailed unsheathed claws at the air. "Get off!"

The attacker growled, tightening his grip. "Do you surrender?"

Crookedkit growled. "Never!" Memories of play fights with Oakpaw flashed in his mind. He pictured Oakpaw's favorite move and let himself go limp.

The tom's grip slackened. "You do surrender?"

Crookedkit shot backward, unhooking his pelt from the tom's claws and wriggling out from behind as fast as a fish. As the tom turned, Crookedkit reared up, claws outstretched. "I'll shred you!" He stared into the face of a fat ginger tom, nearly as big as Hailstar.

The tom's whiskers twitched. "Go on then." He sat back on his haunches and raised his forepaws to reveal a fat white belly.

Crookedkit narrowed his eyes. Was this cat mocking him? *I'll show him!* He lunged at the tom's exposed belly, paws churning. Thick, soft fur filled his nose and caught in clumps beneath his claws until he felt heavy paws push him gently away.

"Give it up, kit."

Crookedkit paused and shook the fluff from his eyes, then blinked at the tom.

"You're wasting your time," the tom purred. "By the time you've finished shredding me, we'll both have missed breakfast."

"Breakfast?" Crookedkit tilted his head. *What's breakfast?* His belly rumbled again.

"Sounds like you need some." The tom narrowed his eyes. "And it looks like you need some, too."

Crookedkit growled. Why did everyone have to point out how skinny he was? He dropped into an attack crouch.

"Whoa!" The tom held up a paw. "Let's not go through that again. You've got sharp claws." He began to pad toward the back of the nest. "What's your name?" he called over his shoulder.

"Crookedkit."

"I'm Fleck." The tom halted and sat down. "What brings you to my barn, Crookedkit?" He stared into the pile of dusty stalks that Crookedkit had been watching. It was still quivering.

"I was on my way to the Moonstone." Crookedkit padded after the tom, trying to figure out if this cat was an enemy. He wasn't a Clan cat, that was for sure. "What are you looking at?"

Fleck dropped into a crouch, his tail flicking. "I see breakfast."

Crookedkit bristled. "Stop! That's my prey!"

Before he could finish Fleck dived across the floor and landed with his paws outstretched on the small lump that Crookedkit had been eyeing. Deftly, he hooked a mouse out of the stalks and killed it with a nip to the back of the neck. He glanced at Crookedkit. "Here." He tossed the mouse and it landed with a thud at Crookedkit's paws.

Even though it wasn't fish, the warm smell of it made Crookedkit's mouth water.

"You look like you need it more than me," Fleck mewed.

Crookedkit stared at the mouse. He was starving. But could he let another cat catch food for him?

"Eat it." Fleck rummaged deeper into the straw. "There'll be another one in the straw."

Straw? Barn? This cat knew some funny words.

Crookedkit sniffed his warm prey, wondering where to begin. "I've never eaten mouse before," he admitted.

Fleck padded over. "Are you a kittypet?"

Crookedkit stiffened. "I'm a *warrior!*"

"Ah." Fleck nodded. "That explains the jaw. Got hurt in a fight? I've heard warrior cats are always fighting."

Crookedkit stared at the ginger tom. "No, we're not! I hurt it falling in the river."

"Tough river." Fleck reached farther under the straw. "I had kin with a smashed jaw." He sneezed. "He fell out of the barn loft."

"The barn loft?" Crookedkit echoed.

Fleck jerked his muzzle upward. "This place is the barn, and up there is the loft. Long way to fall."

"Where is he now?"

"Who? Domino?" Fleck stopped rummaging.

Domino? Farm cats had strange names. "The cat who broke his jaw."

"He's dead now."

"Dead?" Crookedkit's eyes widened. "Because he broke his jaw?"

Fleck sat up. "No," he mewed quickly. "He died of old age. Last leaf-bare. He looked a bit odd, like you. He learned to eat using one side of his mouth. Hunted that way, too. He was one of the best mousers on the farm."

Crookedkit quickly scanned the barn. "Are there many mousers here?"

"Just me now," Fleck told him. "And Mitzi, my littermate. But she's moved to the cornfield for her kitting."

"Is that where the nursery is?"

"Nursery?" Fleck stared at him quizzically, then shook his head. "It's quieter there. No farm monsters." He nodded toward the mouse at Crookedkit's paws. "Are you going to eat that?"

Crookedkit felt hot. "Are you going to hunt some more?" He didn't want to be watched.

"Oh, yes. You're not the only cat that needs feeding around here." Fleck turned back to the heap of straw at the edge of the barn.

Crookedkit crouched down and bit into the mouse. It tasted musky and meaty. He screwed up his nose. At least it was food. A small chunk of meat dripped from the side of his mouth where his twisted jaw gaped.

"Tip your head," Fleck called.

Crookedkit looked up sharply. Was the tom watching him? But Fleck had his tail toward Crookedkit, and his gaze was fixed firmly on the straw. Feeling awkward, Crookedkit tipped his head, cocking it sideways so the mouse meat fell to the straight side of his mouth. Chewing in quick, short nips, he crunched through the mouse, catching stray bits with sharp jerks so that he dropped only a few morsels.

"Got one!" Fleck dropped a second mouse beside Crookedkit. "Do you want another?"

Crookedkit shook his head, swallowing. A few scraps of his mouse littered the floor where he'd dropped them, but his belly was full already. He'd managed to swallow more in one meal than he'd eaten since his accident. And his twisted jaw hardly ached. He purred. "Thanks, Fleck."

"What for?" Fleck started tucking into his mouse.

"The fresh-kill," Crookedkit mewed. "And for telling me how to eat it."

Fleck gazed at Crookedkit, chewing. "I watched Domino eat. I can show you how he hunted, too, if you want. He had a special way of doing the kill-bite. Looked a bit odd but it worked."

"Thanks, but I've got to go home." Crookedkit began to wash his face. "My Clan will wonder where I've gone."

"Don't they think you're at the Mewstone?"

"*Moonstone*." Crookedkit licked a paw and wiped it along his jaw.

"Whatever." Fleck took another bite of mouse and went on, mouth full. "I'm going to catch something for Mitzi when I've finished this. She's stuck in her nest with four kits. And I promised to watch them while she went for water."

Crookedkit paused from washing. "You sound like a Clan cat."

"I don't know about that. But there's no one else to hunt for her." Fleck swallowed. "And you can't let kin starve."

"Can I help?" Crookedkit suddenly wanted to find a way to thank this cat for his kindness. "I could look after the kits with you."

Fleck purred. "They're a pawful," he warned.

Crookedkit remembered his denmates with a pang. "I can handle kits."

"Okay." Fleck swallowed the last of his mouse and sat up. "Let's hunt first."

Crookedkit followed the ginger tom behind a pile of straw that was rolled and stacked high as a mountain. Fleck didn't hesitate as he slid into the gap between the packed straw and the stone wall of the barn. Crookedkit padded after him, tasting the air. The tang of barn prey was familiar now and he smelled something warm as Fleck led him into a space shielded from the rest of the barn.

"They always hide here." Fleck's mew dropped to a whisper. Something was moving through the shadow at the bottom of the stone wall. "Can you see it?" he breathed.

A small brown creature was scuttling along the wall, pressing its body to the stone. It was heading for a crack.

Crookedkit crouched, tail swishing. With his heart pounding like a woodpecker battering a tree trunk, he shot forward, paws outstretched. Belly brushing the ground, he skidded toward the mouse.

Crash! He hurtled into the stone wall as the mouse dashed for the crack and disappeared into the shadow. *Frog dung!* He sat up and glanced sheepishly at Fleck.

Fleck shrugged. "Mice are dumb but not *that* dumb."

"I attacked as fast as I could," Crookedkit mewed apologetically.

"Speed isn't everything," Fleck warned. "The mouse had seen, heard, and smelled you before you jumped."

"How?"

"Your tail was swishing over the straw," Fleck told him. "And you were panting like a badger with your breath stinking of mouse meat."

Crookedkit scowled. "I have to breathe."

"Let me show you." Fleck beckoned him back with a flick of his muzzle and Crookedkit hurried and crouched behind the ginger tom.

"Breathe through your nose," Fleck ordered as they waited.

Crookedkit closed his mouth. His tail longed to twitch, but he held it still, copying Fleck. When a tiny nose twitched in the crack between the stones, Crookedkit stiffened.

Fleck seemed as relaxed as a basking trout beside him. "Wait," the farm cat murmured.

Crookedkit swallowed the excitement rising in his belly as Fleck padded forward, shoulders loose, belly swinging. How was he going to catch a mouse moving that slowly? Crookedkit unsheathed his claws, preparing to make the attack, but, before he could lunge, Fleck darted forward. The fat farm cat covered a tail-length fast as a kingfisher, scooping the mouse from its hiding place with a nimble paw. He tossed it to Crookedkit.

It's alive! Crookedkit stared at the stunned creature trembling on the straw-strewn stone.

"Kill it before it comes to its senses!" Fleck hissed.

Crookedkit froze.

"Bite its spine with the strong side of your jaw."

Crookedkit ducked, tipping his head sideways and clamping his back teeth around the mouse's spine. He felt it go limp and tasted blood on his tongue. He sat up. "It's a strange-tasting mouse."

"It's a vole." Fleck padded over. "Mitzi will be happy. Vole's her favorite."

Crookedkit purred. He'd killed his first prey. *Wait till I tell Oakpaw!* His heart dropped. Oakpaw was so far away. *I should go back.* With his belly full and the sun still climbing, he could be home by dark.

Fleck picked up the vole. "Come on, let's take this to Mitzi." He bounded away, climbing out through the hole Crookedkit had used last night.

"But —" Crookedkit scrambled after him.

"Keep your eyes open in the yard," Fleck ordered as he jumped down on to the hard earth outside. "There are farm monsters everywhere. You'll hear them but it's not always easy to know where they're coming from."

Crookedkit pricked his ears. "I don't hear anything."

"We're early." Fleck darted through a gap in the stone wall that circled the flat open space outside the barn. Crookedkit hurried after him, alert for any sudden monster noise. On the track beyond the wall, Fleck slowed to a trot. Green meadows lay on either side and blue sky stretched overhead. The track, speckled with pebbles and lined with ruts, wound downhill toward a golden field. Crookedkit gazed at it, eyes wide. It shone like the sun and rippled like water.

"That's Mitzi's cornfield." Fleck's mew was muffled by the vole in his jaws. "She's made a nest in that dip." He flicked his tail toward the middle of the field. They followed the track down and, as it wound around the edge of the cornfield, Fleck veered on to a tiny path that was almost invisible. Pushing through long grass, the farm cat leaped a ditch and ducked through a hedge.

Crookedkit stopped. He watched Fleck disappearing into the corn beyond the hedge, his orange tail merging into the golden stalks.

"Are you coming?" Fleck called.

I should go home. Crookedkit opened his mouth to explain. *But I promised I'd help Fleck.* He nosed through the long grass and peered into the ditch. It was wide and deep and water trickled along the bottom. Curiosity pricked his paws. *I wonder what farm kits are like? I'll just say hi.* Taking a deep breath, he sprang and at the same time grabbed for a clump of grass on the other side. His hindquarters swung down, his tail sweeping through the water. Scrabbling, he hauled himself up and squeezed under the hedge. "Wait for me!"

He plunged into the forest of corn, weaving among the stems. The stiff stalks reminded him of the reed bed. Their heavy heads rattled above him as the wind tugged at them. Crookedkit followed Fleck's scent through the corn, noticing where the stalks were bent from cats using the tiny path regularly. He caught up to him where the field began to slope down toward the dip.

"Take this." Fleck dropped the vole at Crookedkit's paws. "Mitzi's a bit protective of her kits. She'll welcome a new face quicker if it's carrying food." Mewls sounded through the corn as he spoke.

"Come on." Fleck pushed on.

Crookedkit picked up the vole and trotted after him until they emerged in a small clearing, enclosed by a wall of rustling yellow stalks. A black cat blinked up at them from a scoop in the earth. Four tiny kits fidgeted at her belly. Mitzi wriggled and sat up, heaving them away. Her nose twitched and her gaze settled on the vole in Crookedkit's jaws.

"Who are you?" Her eyes narrowed.

Crookedkit tossed the vole down to her. "Crookedkit of RiverClan."

Mitzi bristled. "What's a Clan cat doing here?" she hissed at Fleck. "There haven't been warriors around here for as long as I can remember." She glanced warily around. "Where's his kin?"

"He came alone."

Mitzi frowned. "Alone? Ain't he a bit young to be so far

from home? I thought warriors lived up on the moors."

"My Clan lives by the river," Crookedkit told her. "Past the moors."

Mitzi wrapped her tail over her kits. "And you've come all this way by yourself?"

Fleck sniffed. "He's heading for the Foodstone."

"*Moon*stone!" Crookedkit corrected.

A black she-kit scrabbled to the edge of the hollow. "Is that where the moon lives?" She stared at Crookedkit with wide green eyes like her mother's.

"Now, now," Mitzi chided. "It's rude to start asking questions before you've been introduced."

"Sorry," squeaked the kit. "I'm Soot."

"Hello, Soot." For the first time since the accident, Crookedkit felt big.

"Does the moon live there?" Soot pressed.

"No," he purred. "It's where we visit our ancestors."

Mitzi heaved herself out of the hollow and shook out her pelt. "Can you keep them busy while I eat?" she asked Fleck.

"I can!" Crookedkit offered.

Mitzi glanced at her littermate. "He's okay," Fleck reassured her.

Mitzi shifted her paws. "Hardly more than a kit himself." She nodded to Crookedkit, then crouched and hungrily began eating the vole.

Crookedkit jumped down into the hollow. The tiny kits scattered, squeaking, out of his way, then trotted back and sniffed him gingerly.

The gray tom-kit stared at him. "Where's your mother?"

"She's back at camp," Crookedkit told him. "What's your name?"

"I'm Mist," the gray kit mewed.

"And I'm Piper." A silver-tabby-and-white she-kit scrambled over her brother.

"Is there a Foodstone as well as a Moonstone?" The last kit, a black-and-white tom, nosed between his littermates. "Can we go there?"

"Don't be daft, Magpie." Mitzi looked up from her vole. "You're far too young." Magpie suddenly started coughing, ears flat, body shuddering. Mitzi stiffened. "That cough isn't getting better," she told Fleck.

Crookedkit pricked his ears. "Brambleberry would give her coltsfoot." When Mitzi stared blankly, he added, "Brambleberry's our medicine cat."

"Coltsfoot for coughing?" Mitzi frowned. "I haven't heard of that."

Crookedkit glanced at Magpie, who was still coughing. "Brambleberry says you chew the leaves and swallow the juice, and then spit out the leaf bits."

"It's worth a try." Fleck's tail twitched. "There's some by the farm track." He headed into the corn. "I'll fetch a few leaves."

Mitzi leaned into the hollow and plucked up Magpie by his scruff. She nestled her spluttering kit between her forepaws. "Are you okay, dear?" Magpie caught his breath and nodded. Mitzi licked his head gently, then straightened. "There's no spit left in me," she sighed.

"Fleck said you'd be thirsty." Crookedkit hopped up beside her. "Do you want me to look after the kits while you get a drink?"

Mitzi glanced at the corn where Fleck had disappeared. "Fleck said he'd watch them."

"I can teach them to play moss-ball," Crookedkit offered. He suddenly realized how tired and ruffled Mitzi looked.

She licked her dry lips. "I suppose Fleck will be back soon."

"I'll keep them in the hollow till he does." He picked up Magpie by his scruff and lowered him gently back into the nest.

Soot was pawing at the side of the hollow. "Let him teach us moss-ball," she begged.

Piper scrambled up beside her littermate. "We'll be good!" she promised.

Mitzi's whiskers twitched. "Okay, but stay out of the corn."

"We promise!" Mist purred at his mother.

"I won't be long." Mitzi headed through the corn where Fleck had disappeared.

Magpie blinked. "What's moss-ball?" His mew was croaky but he'd stopped coughing.

"What's *moss*?" Piper asked.

Crookedkit glanced at the churned soil and thick corn stems. No moss here. "How about corn-ball?" He reached up with his forepaws and hauled down a cornstalk till he could grab the head. "Here!" He nipped it off and tossed it down into the hollow.

Soot leaped on it and flicked it up into the air. Piper batted it away with an outstretched paw. The corn head sailed past Crookedkit's muzzle. Retrieving it from among the stems, he flung it back into the nest. Why go home today? He purred, watching the kits play. He was far more useful here than he could ever be back at camp.

CHAPTER 8

The forest loomed, dark and eerie, around Crookedkit. He shivered as the damp air seeped into his pelt.

"You've been away from your Clan for a moon!" Mapleshade glared at him, a whisker away from his muzzle, and lashed her tail.

Crookedkit met her stare. "Do you really think they've *missed* me?" Fog weaved around his paws. "Don't you think they were glad to get rid of such a useless warrior?"

"You're *not* useless!"

"*I* know that!" Crookedkit hunted on the farm every day and helped look after Mitzi's kits. Fleck didn't care that he didn't have his apprentice name yet. He had taught Crookedkit how to stalk and catch mice, how to let the kits play fight without hurting themselves, how to watch out for monsters that didn't keep to Thunderpaths but stormed over grass and mud faster than a cat could run. Crookedkit knew for sure that he wasn't useless. "But I don't know if my Clanmates would agree."

Mapleshade's eyes blazed. "Then prove yourself to them!"

"Why should I?" Crookedkit hissed. "*They* stopped believing in me!"

"Every warrior must prove himself," Mapleshade argued. "You must go home! Your destiny lies with your Clan."

Crookedkit heard pleading in her mew. "I'll go back when I'm big enough and strong enough to become an apprentice."

"You're big enough already!" Mapleshade pressed. "You've eaten so many mice you've probably forgotten what fish tastes like."

Crookedkit licked his lips, remembering the taste of the river with a pang. Then he dug his claws into the brown earth. He liked living on the farm. He liked being needed. He liked how Magpie and Mist looked up to him. And what if Mapleshade was wrong? His great destiny might lie here. "What if my Clanmates never see past my twisted jaw?" he whispered. "What if Hailstar never makes me an apprentice?"

"If you stay away much longer, he won't," Mapleshade growled. "You'll be called a loner."

Crookedkit flattened his ears. "I'm a RiverClan cat."

"Then go home and prove it." Her amber gaze held his while the forest faded around them. Then Mapleshade blinked and Crookedkit woke up.

He scrambled to his paws, relishing the warm morning sunshine streaming into the barn. "I smell mice." He nudged Fleck.

"Just you wait." Fleck stirred beside him. "It's harvesttime soon." He yawned. "Then you'll really see the mice run."

Crookedkit licked his lips. "I found a new mouse nest yesterday."

Fleck sat up. "Where?"

Crookedkit bounded out of his straw nest and trotted across the stone floor. "I'll show you." He wanted to stop Mapleshade's words from ringing in his ears. He wasn't a loner. He was a RiverClan cat. And once he was big enough for his Clanmates to take him seriously, he'd go home and prove it.

"Slow down!" Fleck lapped at his rumpled fur.

"Come on!" Crookedkit paused, swishing his tail. "I want to show you before the monsters wake up."

Puffing, Fleck hurried after him, then stopped suddenly and twisted to nibble at an itch on his spine. "I haven't had a chance to pick my fleas out yet."

"You can do that later." Crookedkit jumped through the opening, screwing up his eyes against the dazzling light. The sun blazed above the distant hills. The farm monsters lay still in their dens. Crookedkit scooted across the open space and followed the wall.

"Hurry up!" he called as Fleck appeared around the corner. Grass clung to the bottom of the wall. Crookedkit followed the clumps till he reached a green tuft, thick with nettles. His mouth began to water as he parted the stems with his forepaws. Behind, a tiny hole was just visible under a jutting-out stone. "In there," he whispered to Fleck.

Fleck peered over his shoulder. "It's a waiting hole. You'll have to let the mouse come out first."

"We can dig underneath."

Fleck shook his head. "I've tried. The stones go down a tail-length. You won't dig your way past them."

Crookedkit let the nettles swish back into place. "I'll wait, then."

Fleck's whiskers quivered. "You? Wait?"

"What?" Crookedkit cocked his head. "I can wait."

Fleck shook his head. "You may have grown this past moon, but you're still as impatient as a kit."

Crookedkit sniffed. "I'll show you!" He crouched beside the nettles and curled his tail beside him.

Fleck's eyes glowed. "While you're busy waiting," he meowed, "I'll go and see what I can catch behind the wood store."

Crookedkit shifted his paws as Fleck padded away and disappeared around the corner. *I can wait!* Crookedkit flicked his tail. He stared at the nettles, ears pricked, whiskers stiff, ready to detect any movement. Nothing stirred.

I can wait a moon if I have to.

He curled and uncurled his claws. Then he opened his mouth and tasted for mouse scent. Nothing.

They'll be out before long.

An itch made his tail quiver. Crookedkit stared at the nettles. The itch grew stronger till it was unbearable. He twisted and nibbled at it, relived when it stopped.

Perhaps the hole's empty, he thought. *It's dumb to waste my time waiting for nothing when I could be doing some proper hunting.* He stared at the corner where Fleck had disappeared. The wood store was probably alive with mice. Fleck would need help. Crookedkit glanced at the nettles. *I'll come back later,* he told himself, *when the mice are awake.* Chin high, he trotted back along the wall, around the corner, and across the open space.

"That didn't take you long," Fleck commented as Crookedkit reached the wood store. "Did you catch many?" The ginger tom was crouching at the bottom of a stack of chopped wood, staring at a gap between logs.

"They'd all gone," Crookedkit told him.

Fleck didn't move his gaze. "You can help me then." He shuffled closer to the gap. "I can hear them, I just can't see them."

Crookedkit peered into the darkness, then glanced up at the top of the woodpile. "I've got an idea." He leaped up, clearing two tail-lengths in one bound, and clung on to the logs. They shifted beneath his weight and he heard a squeak below. Scrabbling higher, he clawed his way to the top, then looked down.

Fleck had caught a mouse and laid it behind him. "Can you shift them again?" he called. "It looks like you're scaring them out."

Crookedkit jumped across the long stretch of logs. He landed as heavily as he could and heard the wood creak beneath him. Another mouse shot out from the bottom and Fleck caught it with a swift paw. Crookedkit pricked his ears. Tiny paws scrabbled behind the logs. He focused on the sound. Then, in one swift movement, he pressed his belly to the wood and reached down behind the pile. His outstretched claws felt warm as he hooked a mouse from the shadows and killed it expertly with a quick nip from his back teeth.

"Got one!" he called down to Fleck. "Should we take it to

Mitzi? I bet she's hungry."

"She will be." Fleck lined up his catch. "And the kits'll be restless." They were growing fast and exploring farther from the nest every day.

"I'll take them on an expedition to the ditch if Mitzi says it's okay." Crookedkit picked up his catch and jumped down from the woodpile.

Fleck was watching him. "Don't you miss your own kin?" he asked softly.

"Of course." Crookedkit dropped his mouse and met Fleck's gaze. "But they don't need me like Mitzi and the kits do."

"I can take care of—"

Crookedkit grabbed his mouse and ran out of the wood store before Fleck had finished. Fleck caught up as Crookedkit was squeezing through the gap in the wall. Crookedkit glanced at him anxiously. Was the farm cat going to tell him he wasn't needed here anymore?

Fleck's catch swung by their tails from his mouth. He gazed at the distant meadows. "Fine day," was all he said. The tails muffled his mew.

Crookedkit felt weak with relief. *I am needed.*

Sunshine glared on the farm track as they headed toward the cornfield. The crest of the hill cut into blue, cloudless sky. The hedgerows spilled over the verges, blousy with fading lushness, while the corn looked dull, its golden sheen dusty. Crookedkit's ears twitched. A strange noise stirred the hot air. He dropped his mouse and stared down the track. "What's that noise?"

Rumbling sounded in the distance.

Fleck halted, nose twitching. "Smells like a farm monster is working already."

"But all the monsters are in their dens."

Fleck dropped his mice. "Harvest!" Panic edged his mew. Pelt spiking, he raced away.

Crookedkit stared in surprise at Fleck's abandoned fresh-kill. "What's harvest?" he called. His pads pricked nervously as he smelled fear-scent in Fleck's wake.

"They're cutting the corn!" Fleck yowled back.

Horror gripped Crookedkit. He shot after his friend, grit cracking beneath his paws.

Fleck stopped abruptly at the edge of the field. Crookedkit skidded to a halt beside the bristling tom and stared, eyes wide, at the cornfield. A huge scarlet monster was trawling through the corn, sucking up the golden stems and spewing lumps from its hindquarters. Shorn stumps lay in swaths behind it.

"Mitzi!" Fleck's mew was filled with terror.

"The kits!" Crookedkit charged forward, pelting down the path and clearing the ditch in one leap. He shot through the hedge with Fleck on his tail and charged into the corn. The monster rumbled toward them, heading straight for Mitzi's nest. Crookedkit heard mewling as he neared the hollow. He burst into the small clearing. Mitzi stood, eyes wild, Piper dangling from her jaws. Crookedkit looked in the nest.

Magpie sat in the middle, wailing. "The monster's coming!"

Fleck exploded from the corn. "Where are the others?"

Mitzi tucked Piper between her forepaws. "I've taken Mist to the ditch," she told them. "Soot ran into the corn." Her green eyes glittered with terror.

"I'll find her." Crookedkit glanced at the rumbling monster. He could see its bloodred head advancing over the corn.

"I'll take Magpie." Fleck leaned into the nest and plucked out the mewling kit.

"Which way did Soot go?" Crookedkit demanded.

"I didn't see!" Mitzi gasped.

Magpie stabbed his paw toward the corn. "That way!"

Crookedpaw dived among the stems, nose twitching. He sneezed as dust filled his nostrils. The stench of the monster swirled around him, its rumble now a roar as it pounded down the field.

"Soot!" he yowled. He pricked his ears, then flattened them as the roaring of the monster blasted his fur. Opening his mouth, he tasted the air. A faint fragrance of Soot lingered. He hesitated a moment, then plunged deeper into the corn. With a rush of hope he spotted a tiny track through the stems. He followed, heart pounding. It was leading straight toward the monster.

Soot's scent was stronger now, laced with fear. Crookedkit weaved onward, following the bent corn stems. The monster was howling so loudly, Crookedkit could only feel the blood roaring in his ears. He glanced up, gasping, as he saw the great red body barely a tree-length from him. Gigantic claws swirled at its chest, tearing up the corn and scooping it into its gaping mouth.

"Help!" Soot's squeal shrilled against the roar. The kit's black fur was just visible through the golden corn. She was three tail-lengths away, the monster bearing down on her with a roar.

Breathing fast, pelt bushed up, Crookedkit leaped into the air. Landing beside Soot, he grabbed her scruff and pelted onward through the corn. The stalks whipped his face. He tasted his own blood as it welled on his muzzle. Pain jarred his jaw as he clasped hard on to Soot. He fought panic as he heard the monster's claws whirring at his ear. He leaped again, Soot pressing against his chest as he flung himself clear of the monster's path. Tumbling to a halt, he felt its wind tug his fur and the ground shook beneath them as it passed.

He lay trembling a moment before he let go of Soot. She crouched quivering beside him. As the monster rumbled away, paw steps crunched the bitten stalks.

"Are you okay?" Fleck ducked down beside them. The farm cat's eyes were wide.

"Yeah," Crookedkit panted. "Let's get her to the ditch before the monster comes back."

Fleck picked up Soot and waited for Crookedkit to stagger to his paws. "Did it hurt you?"

Crookedkit licked the blood from his nose. "Didn't touch us," he breathed.

Soot wriggled in Fleck's jaws. "Crookedkit saved me!" she squeaked.

Crookedkit frowned at her. "Next time, stay with your mother." He followed Fleck back across the path the monster had cut and through the corn to the edge of the field. Squeezing underneath the hedge, he padded trembling out the other side and saw Mitzi huddling her kits close to her. A purr shook her as she saw Soot in Fleck's jaws.

The farm cat placed the kit at her mother's paws. "Crookedkit reached her just in time."

Mitzi stared at him, eyes glowing. "You saved my kit," she whispered.

Crookedkit was shaking too hard to reply.

"You really are a warrior." Mitzi leaned forward and licked the blood from his muzzle.

"You could've been killed," Fleck grunted.

Crookedkit glanced over his shoulder at the monster still prowling across the cornfield. What if something like that threatened his Clan? "I need to go home," he murmured.

"But you're safe now," Fleck reassured him. "The monster won't come on this side of the hedge."

"I'm not running away." Crookedkit swallowed. "I've finished running away." He knew he had to go back and become a warrior. This life wasn't his destiny. It *couldn't* be. He was glad he'd saved Soot. But that was just the beginning. He was destined to be great—not a great farm cat but a great *warrior*. Maybe the greatest warrior ever. He didn't care if his Clan thought he was too small or too ugly. He would make them see that his heart was still as brave as any of them. And as loyal. He dipped his head.

"I'll never forget you," he promised. He was finding it difficult to swallow, especially with Soot, Mist, Magpie, and

Piper gazing at him with enormous eyes. "I wish I could stay forever, but I don't belong here." He could see Fleck and Mitzi struggling to understand. "I'm a Clan cat," he whispered. "I *have* to go home."

CHAPTER 9

As the path sloped beneath his paws, Crookedkit heard the roar of the waterfall. He had walked all night, crossing the Thunderpath and slipping through WindClan territory undetected. The sky was growing light beyond the trees. The camp would be stirring soon. He hurried down the path beside the gorge. It seemed narrower than last time he'd passed this way. He had grown. He was also more sure-pawed and he didn't peer nervously over the edge, but kept his gaze fixed ahead where he could just make out the river snaking into RiverClan territory below.

He wondered if Mist, Soot, Magpie, and Piper were awake yet. Perhaps Fleck had offered to watch them while Mitzi went hunting. Were the kits asking about him, wanting to know where he had gone and when he would be back? Crookedkit's heart twisted. He missed them already. But he was going *home*.

As the path flattened out along the bank and the bushes grew lush, he smelled the familiar scents of RiverClan and strained to see the reed bed bordering the camp. But mist shrouded the river, betraying the coming of leaf-fall. It wove around him as he skirted the shore below Sunningrocks. By the ThunderClan stench lingering there, Crookedkit guessed with a prickle of irritation that Hailstar still had not reclaimed RiverClan's land.

The stepping-stones were hardly visible in the mist, each stone only appearing when he'd reached the one before. He landed on the pebbly shore and scrambled up the short, steep bank. The grassy path was soft on his tired paws.

"Crookedkit?" A voice hailed from the mist and the dark shape of Mudfur emerged on the path ahead. Rippleclaw and Echomist flanked him, the silver of their pelts as familiar as their scent.

"You're alive!" Echomist's joyful mew rang in the dawn air.

Mudfur swished his tail. "I'm going to get Shellheart."

Before Crookedkit could speak, Mudfur had darted back toward camp and Echomist had run to him and was licking him fiercely between the ears. "Where were you? We've been worried sick. We thought a fox had taken you."

Her warm, familiar scent enfolded him. Crookedkit stared at his paws, hot with shame. *She thought I was dead.* "I'm sorry."

Rippleclaw stiffened, his gaze narrow. "Then you *did* run away. Cedarpelt was right."

Crookedkit nodded. "But I came back."

"Why?" Rippleclaw curled his lip. "Couldn't you make it as a loner?"

Crookedkit flinched. "I never stopped being a RiverClan cat."

Rippleclaw tasted the air. "You don't smell like a River-Clan cat."

Echomist hissed at the black-and-silver warrior. "You

should be pleased he's safe!"

"RiverClan doesn't need warriors who run—"

Rippleclaw was cut short by the pounding of paws and Shellheart slowed to a halt beside him. The RiverClan deputy stared at Crookedkit. "You've grown." His eyes shone.

Oakpaw pelted past his father and brushed around Crookedkit, purring loudly. "You look great! Where have you been?"

"I went to find the Moonstone," Crookedkit began to explain.

"Did you get lost?" Oakpaw mewed.

"Come on," Shellheart interrupted. "Hailstar will want to see you." He pressed against Crookedkit as he escorted him back to camp, a low purr rumbling through his pelt.

Crookedkit felt butterflies in his belly when he saw the wall of reeds that surrounded the camp. "Is Rainflower okay?" he whispered to Shellheart.

"She's fine," he reassured. "Everyone's fine." He ducked through the sedge tunnel. Crookedkit followed, Oakpaw on his tail and Echomist purring behind.

Hailstar was already in the clearing. Mudfur paced beside him, his eyes bright. Troutclaw, Tanglewhisker, and Birdsong were trotting down the slope from the elders' den. Brightsky and Lakeshine paced the edge of the clearing, exchanging whispers. Crookedkit pricked his ears as Fallowtail hurried from her den and joined them.

"Can you believe he's back?" he heard the brown warrior murmur.

Piketooth and Shimmerpelt sat together, tails neatly wrapped over their forepaws. Timberfur was shaking out his wet pelt beside the reed beds while Ottersplash slid, yawning, from her den.

"Softwing! Wake up!" The white-and-ginger she-cat stared in amazement at Crookedkit. "Whitefang! Come and see!"

Crookedkit watched them pad sleepily from their dens. The two apprentices must have been given their warrior names while he was away. He glanced at the apprentices' den. Who else had been made a warrior? He couldn't help feeling a prick of relief as Volepaw, Beetlepaw, and Petalpaw scrambled out.

"Crookedkit's back!" Petalpaw raced to greet him, Volepaw on her tail.

"You're bigger!" Volepaw purred.

Beetlepaw narrowed his eyes. "He's *fatter.*" He sniffed. "Like a kittypet."

"I'm no kittypet!" Crookedkit growled.

"Who's been feeding you then?" Beetlenose challenged.

Crookedkit lifted his chin. "I've been hunting for myself."

"Really?" Hailstar padded toward him, broad shoulders specked with dew from the morning mist. "Not bad for a kit not yet out of the nursery." His voice betrayed surprise.

Crookedkit warily searched the RiverClan leader's gaze, relieved to see warmth brimming in his amber eyes.

"You've had everyone very worried," Hailstar growled. "But it's good to have you home."

Rippleclaw padded into camp. "Are you going to take him

back that easily?" he muttered.

Tanglewhisker snorted. "Of course he is! Crookedkit's one of us."

Birdsong leaned against her mate. "That's right. We are warriors, not rogues," she rasped. "We don't turn on our own Clanmates!"

Cedarpelt slid from the dirtplace tunnel. "Is he *still* our Clanmate?" His brown-striped tail snaked behind him and he narrowed his gaze.

Shellheart's hackles lifted. "Of course he is!"

"Where has he been?" Beetlepaw called.

"He smells like heather." Lakeshine sniffed. "Perhaps he was seeing what life was like in another Clan."

Crookedkit glanced at Fallowtail. Had she reported that she'd scented a RiverClan cat on WindClan territory? She was staring at her paws.

"I'd never join another Clan." Crookedkit puffed out his chest. "I'm RiverClan."

Hailstar padded around him, his gaze sweeping the Clan. "He was born in RiverClan and that's where he belongs."

Cedarpelt exchanged a look with Rippleclaw. "How can we trust him not to leave anytime life gets tough?" he challenged Hailstar.

"Yeah!" Beetlepaw scowled. "While he's been away getting fat, some of us have been busy training."

"I'll start my training whenever you like!" Crookedkit looked hopefully up at Hailstar.

Before the RiverClan leader could answer, Brambleberry

hurried from the medicine den. She stopped beside Crookedkit and sniffed along his flank. "Are you okay?" she asked anxiously. "You *look* okay."

"I'm fine," Crookedkit told her.

A purr rumbled in her throat. "Thank StarClan you're home safely."

Hailstar narrowed his eyes. "Where have you been?"

"I went looking for the Moonstone," Crookedkit told him.

"The Moonstone!" Shellheart gasped. "That's so far away!"

Paw steps scuffed the clearing behind them. "He was always too adventurous for his own good." Rainflower's mew made Crookedkit shiver. He turned and faced his mother, trying to read her expression. Her tail-tip was flicking. Was she pleased to see him or sorry he'd come back? Her eyes reflected his gaze, giving nothing away.

Crookedkit turned back to Hailstar. "I went to ask StarClan if it was my destiny to be a kit forever."

Hailstar narrowed his amber eyes. "And what did StarClan say?"

"I never reached the Moonstone," Crookedkit confessed. "But I found my answer." He raised his chin. "My destiny is to be a RiverClan warrior no matter how long I have to wait."

Brambleberry frowned. "How did you find your answer if you didn't reach the Moonstone?" she asked. "Did StarClan *visit* you?"

Crookedkit hesitated. Should he tell Hailstar about Mapleshade? But he had disobeyed her when she told him to return to RiverClan. He shook his head. "I helped a loner save her kits and I realized I should be helping my Clan." He turned back to Hailstar. "I'm sorry I ran away. It was dumb and I won't ever run away again. I want to be the best warrior in RiverClan."

Hailstar's eyes flashed. "Better than Shellheart?"

Crookedkit glanced at his father. Shellheart's gaze didn't waver. "One day."

The RiverClan leader dipped his head. "Good. RiverClan will always need strong warriors."

"Welcome back, Crookedkit!" Petalpaw rushed to congratulate him. Echomist, Birdsong, and Tanglewhisker weaved around him, purring. Crookedkit breathed in their warmth.

"Can I welcome back my kit?" Rainflower was waiting behind Birdsong. The elder scuttled out of the way. "Welcome home." The pale gray she-cat touched her muzzle lightly to Crookedkit's head. "I'm glad you're safe."

Crookedkit swallowed. "Th-thank you." His gaze reached for hers but she'd turned and was padding toward the sedge entrance tunnel.

"Can I join your patrol?" she called to Rippleclaw.

"Of course." Rippleclaw signaled to Echomist and Mudfur with his tail. "We should be checking the borders by now." He flashed an accusing look at Crookedkit.

"I can't believe you went all the way to the Moonstone by yourself," Petalpaw purred.

"Not all the way," Crookedkit corrected.

"I bet you didn't even make it to WindClan territory," Beetlepaw scoffed.

Volepaw plucked at the ground. "How far did you get?"

Rippleclaw paused at the entrance. "Petalpaw, Volepaw, come with us. Mudfur wanted to assess your hunting today. We might as well do it now."

Ottersplash crossed the clearing and nosed Beetlepaw. "Come on," she meowed. "We're practicing hunting in the beech copse. The earlier we get there the more prey there'll be."

"Can Oakpaw come, too?" Beetlepaw's eyes flashed. "I always learn more when there's someone to compete with."

"You can compete with your littermates," Ottersplash told him.

"They're *easy* to beat."

"That's not true!" Volepaw snapped.

Crookedkit watched his former denmates follow their mentors out of camp, then turned to Oakpaw. "Do you have to train, too?" He glanced at Shellheart.

"With leaf-fall coming, we can't waste time," Shellheart meowed gently. "You can tell us about your adventures tonight."

Crookedkit nodded. He'd caused the Clan enough disruption for one day. "Okay," he mewed. "I'll see you later."

"Why don't you clean out the elders' nests?" Shellheart suggested as he padded away with Oakpaw.

Tanglewhisker rubbed a grizzled paw over his ragged ear. "They could do with new moss. The old stuff is full of fleas."

Crookedkit stifled a sigh. He'd learned so much and traveled farther than any apprentice, but he had to stay in camp and clean out nests. Suddenly becoming a warrior seemed a long way off.

Crookedkit woke into a dream. Mist shrouded the earth and trees rose around him with smooth gray trunks that disappeared into darkness above. Mapleshade slid out from behind a trunk, mist swirling around her paws. "So they took you back."

"Of course." Crookedkit swished his tail. "I'm a RiverClan cat."

"I was worried you'd forgotten."

Crookedkit narrowed his eyes. "I came back," he growled. "You don't have to go on about it."

Mapleshade sat down. "You've got guts," she muttered. "I'll give you that."

"What do you want with me?" Crookedkit wondered why she was back in his dreams. He'd come home. What more did she need?

"I want to help you fulfill your destiny." Mapleshade padded closer. Her tail slid across Crookedkit's flank.

Crookedkit fidgeted with impatience. "What *is* my destiny?"

"If you obey me and train hard, one day you will lead your Clan."

"I'll be *leader*?" Crookedkit couldn't believe his ears. "But I'm not even an apprentice yet!"

Mapleshade sat down. "Were you hoping that Hailstar

would be so impressed by your adventure he'd make you an apprentice right away?"

Crookedkit flinched. She was close to the truth. "I can hunt," he insisted, straightening up. "And I'm big enough."

"Hailstar can't reward disobedience," Mapleshade pointed out. "He'll make you an apprentice soon."

"It's dumb not to train me," Crookedkit complained. "I could be much more use to my Clan if I was trained."

Mapleshade's green eyes flashed in the half-light. "I could train you," she offered. "But you'd have to keep it a secret."

Crookedkit leaned forward. "Could you?"

"It's been a while since I've had an apprentice."

"If you make me your apprentice I'll work hard, I'll do anything you tell me." Crookedkit paced around Mapleshade. "I'll meet you every night and you can show me how to hunt and fight like a RiverClan warrior!" If he was going to be leader, he'd need to know every move. "Please make me your apprentice—like a proper 'paw!"

Mapleshade's tail swung slowly from side to side. "The first thing you're going to have to learn is patience," she murmured.

Crookedkit sat down and curled his tail over his paws. "I know." He remembered Fleck's teasing. "I promise I'll try. But I've had to wait so long!"

"The best prey is the prey longest waited for." Mapleshade gazed at him thoughtfully.

Please make me your apprentice! Crookedkit swallowed back the plea.

"Will you make me one promise?" Mapleshade's muzzle

was a whisker from his.

Crookedkit nodded vigorously. "Anything!"

"I can do more than make you leader. I can give you everything you've ever dreamed of," she went on. "Power over your Clanmates. Power over *all* the Clans."

Crookedkit's eyes widened. "I promise!"

"Wait." Mapleshade tipped her head. "You don't know what you're promising yet."

Crookedkit blinked.

"You must promise me," Mapleshade lowered her voice, "that you will be loyal to your Clan above all other things. What you want for yourself is nothing compared to the needs of your Clan. Nothing, remember?" Her green gaze bore into his. "Do you make that promise?"

Crookedkit's heart quickened. "Yes!" He unsheathed his claws. "Yes, I do!"

CHAPTER 10

❧

"No! No!" Mapleshade snapped. "Keep both hind paws on the ground or your enemy will unbalance you with nothing more than a hiss!" She nosed Crookedkit's hindquarters until his paws were firmly planted. "Try it again."

Concentrating hard, Crookedkit reared up and slashed again at the stick that Mapleshade had stuck into the slimy soil. With both hind paws steady, he found his blow was fiercer and stronger and the stick tumbled with the third hit.

"Much better." Mapleshade pushed the fallen stick with a paw. "Now, try the move on me."

Crookedkit blinked at her. "What if I hurt you?"

Mapleshade snorted. "You can try." She faced him, her thick pelt like a mane around her neck.

Crookedkit imagined that he was facing a LionClan warrior. *Only the bravest survive!* As his thoughts whirled with excitement, he reared up and struck at Mapleshade. But she'd disappeared. He stared, confused, then felt fur beneath his belly and a weight pushing him up. With a yowl of surprise, he was tossed into the air. He flicked his tail, paws flailing, and tried to turn. But the ground rushed at him and he landed heavily on his side. Winded, he struggled to his paws.

Mapleshade was sitting a tail-length away. "A warrior doesn't daydream," she growled.

"How did you know?"

"You lost your focus a moment before you reared," she told him. "I could see it in your eyes. Your thoughts were on a battle in your head. You must fight the battle you're in, not the one you could be in."

Crookedkit blinked. "Can I try again?"

Pain gripped his shoulders. He could still feel Mapleshade's claws as he opened his eyes. Dawn light filtered through the nursery roof. Fallowtail was snoring. After a moon sleeping alone in the nursery, Crookedkit had at first resented Fallowtail's arrival. The warrior was a queen now, heavy with kits. But after a night listening to her gentle snore, watching her wide belly rise and fall while her warmth filled the den, he felt happy to share again.

He longed to ask her what she'd been doing on the moorland, three moons ago. But if it was a secret mission for Hailstar he didn't dare. That was warrior business and he was painfully aware he was still just a kit. He woke every morning hoping Hailstar would make him an apprentice that day. But he knew he had to prove his loyalty to his Clan. At least his Clanmates weren't treating him like a useless fledgling anymore. He cleaned the elders' nests, helped patch the warriors' dens to get them ready for leaf-bare, and Piketooth had taught him to swim and how to catch minnows among the reeds. It needed far more skill than he'd thought; he had to have paws as fast as lightning to grasp them as they flickered in and out of the stems. He ate with his Clanmates—not as neatly as some cats, but neater than before he left and he didn't really care much anymore. Just as long as he kept growing.

"Hailstar has got to make you a 'paw soon," Brambleberry had commented while checking his jaw. "You'll be too big to fit in the nursery at this rate."

Her prediction was close to the truth after Fallowtail kitted Willowkit and Graykit. Crookedkit added reeds to her nest, making it big enough to accommodate the two fidgeting balls of gray fluff, and cleared away the training wall to make room for a bigger nest for himself. He wondered when the kits' father would visit, but no tom made an appearance in the nursery and Fallowtail never mentioned a mate.

Snow came early, when Graykit and Willowkit were only two moons old.

"Can we go and play in it?" Willowkit begged.

Fallowtail looked imploringly at Crookedkit, who was tossing stale moss out of his nest. "Would you take them outside, please?" she begged. "I want to get this nest clean and they won't stay out of the way."

"We're just trying to collect the old moss for you!" Graykit objected.

"Collecting?" Fallowtail sniffed. "Is that why you've been jumping around the den like frogs every time I tug a piece out?"

Crookedkit purred, remembering Mist, Soot, Magpie,

and Piper. "I'll take them." He squeezed through the nursery entrance, sinking into the belly-high snow outside. Thick gray clouds promised more. "We can't stay out long," he told Willowkit and Graykit as they scrambled out after him. "You'll turn to ice."

Willowkit wallowed through the snow toward him. "Can we ride on your back?" she squeaked.

Crookedkit crouched down. "Climb on." He waited, wincing as the two kits climbed his pelt with burrsharp claws. "Hang on!" Straightening, he plodded through the snow.

"Why are you still a kit when you're so big?" Willowkit asked.

"Shh!" Graykit hissed. "Fallowtail said we weren't allowed to ask that!"

Crookedkit's fur ruffled. Willowkit dug in her claws. "Watch out!" she squeaked. "I nearly fell off."

"Well, don't ask stupid questions," Crookedkit snapped.

"It's not stupid," she mewed. "Oakpaw's been an apprentice for moons. What's wrong with you?"

"I had an accident and broke my jaw." Crookedkit pushed through the snowy clearing. Beetlepaw and Ottersplash were digging tracks through the snow.

"You're better now," Willowkit pointed out.

"He ran away and Hailstar's punishing him," Graykit whispered to her littermate.

Crookedkit pretended not to hear. "Where do you want me to go?" he called over his shoulder.

"To the reed bed," Graykit mewed. "Petalpaw told us the

water gets hard in leaf-bare and you can walk on it."

"Only if a warrior has tested it first," Crookedkit warned. "It can break under your weight." He bounded over the snow where it had piled beside the apprentices' den and headed to the frost-stricken reeds.

Rippleclaw and Brightsky were clearing a space to drop the mice they'd caught. With the river so cold, the hunting patrols were scouring the willow wood for land prey.

"There." Crookedkit tipped the kits off at the edge of the river. A thin frosting of ice coated the water.

Willowkit peered over the bank. "Can we go on it?"

"It's too thin."

"Then let's play warriors!" Willowkit bounded away, so light she barely broke the surface of the frost-hardened drift. Graykit chased after her, scooping a pawful of snow and hurling it at her sister.

Crookedkit purred. He wanted to join in, but Rippleclaw was close by. It was bad enough being called a kit without acting like one. A shadow flitted over the clearing. Crookedkit looked up. A heron was circling. Its great wings flapped, white against the gray sky. Its beak was long and sharp like a newleaf reed spear. His heart lurched when he saw its beady eye fix on the camp. The kits were still small enough to be easy picking for a big, greedy bird.

"You're WindClan," Graykit called to Willowkit. "And I'm RiverClan. Try and invade my camp." Graykit was in the center of the clearing. She'd piled walls of snow around her and was ducking behind them.

Squeaking a battle cry, Willowkit rushed one and struggled over the top. "Invasion!" she mewed, throwing herself on top of Graykit.

The heron drew into a tighter circle over the clearing.

Crookedkit stiffened. "Graykit." He tried to keep his voice calm. He didn't want to panic them and send them running in opposite directions. He had to keep them together. "Willowkit, come here."

"Get away, you WindClan fleabag!" Willowkit had Graykit in a shoulder-lock and was pummeling her with churning hind legs.

"You won't take the camp!" Graykit squealed, struggling to free herself.

"Willowkit!" Crookedkit pushed his way toward them through the snow. "Graykit! Let's get back to the nursery."

"Why?" Willowkit let go of her sister and blinked at him.

"We're not cold!" Graykit complained.

Suddenly the heron stalled mid-air and dived. Its piercing cry split the air as it aimed for the kits.

StarClan, help us!

Crookedkit leaped.

"Heron!" His warning cry rang around the camp as he dived on top of Willowkit, pushing her deep into the snow. Reaching out a paw, he grabbed Graykit and dragged her underneath him.

The air whistled above him as the heron screeched down.

He held on to the kits and tensed the muscles along his back.

What about my destiny?

Closing his eyes, he prepared for sharp talons to rip his pelt. *Mapleshade! You told me I'd be leader!*

He pictured the beak spearing his flesh. He was going to die for sure.

Suddenly Ottersplash's shriek wailed over him. "You mangy river rat!"

The heron's cry turned to a screech of fury and pain. Crookedkit looked up. Ottersplash was clinging to its back, hauling it down to the ground. Beetlepaw leaped and landed on the heron's neck.

Rippleclaw reared at the edge of Crookedkit's vision, claws unsheathed, ready to attack.

The great bird struggled, flapping against the snow as Ottersplash released it.

Rippleclaw dropped on to all four paws.

"Let it go!" Ottersplash called to Beetlepaw.

The broad-shouldered apprentice hung on, like soot against snow. "It'll feed us for a moon!"

"We don't eat heron!" Ottersplash yowled.

Growling, Beetlepaw let go and the heron floundered on to its spindly feet, then heaved itself out of the clearing.

"Why don't we eat heron?" Beetlepaw frowned as he watched the great bird escape.

Rippleclaw padded forward. "If you'd ever tasted heron, you'd know." He looked at Crookedkit. "That was fast thinking."

Ottersplash nodded. "Well spotted."

Brightsky darted toward them. "It's a good thing you saw it!"

The nursery shook as Fallowtail burst out of the entrance.

Trembling with relief, Crookedkit sat up, letting Willowkit and Graykit struggle out from under him. They sneezed and shook snow from their ears.

"What did you do that for?" Willowkit snorted.

Fallowtail slewed to a halt beside them. "What happened?"

"It's okay, they're safe," Ottersplash reassured her.

Hailstar appeared from his den.

"Crookedkit just saved the kits," Ottersplash told the RiverClan leader.

"A heron tried to take them." Rippleclaw shook snow from his paws. "Crookedkit grabbed them just in time."

"He nearly crushed us!" Graykit complained.

Ottersplash flicked the kit's ear with her tail. "He risked his own pelt to protect yours!"

"Thanks for fighting it off." Crookedkit nodded to Ottersplash and Beetlepaw. "I thought I was going to lose my ears."

Fallowtail wrapped her tail around her kits. "Thank you, Crookedkit."

Hailstar circled them, tail high. "How big was the heron?"

"Huge!" Ottersplash gasped.

"*I* didn't see it!" Graykit complained.

Willowkit sniffed. "That's because Crookedkit was sitting on us."

"*Anyone* can sit on a kit." Beetlepaw huffed. "*I* helped fight it off."

Hailstar dipped his head to the black warrior. "Well done." He turned to Crookedkit. "But you stopped it from harming the kits." His eyes glowed. "I should have done this a long time ago, but your Clan needed to see your courage and loyalty for themselves. Today you risked your life for your Clanmates." He raised his muzzle. "It's time I gave you your apprentice name." He lifted his voice to the sky. "Let all cats old enough to swim gather to hear my words," he called.

Crookedkit's heart soared. *At last!* His destiny was beginning to come true! He glanced at Beetlepaw, who was scowling beside him. *You won't just be competing with Oakpaw anymore.*

The elders were already hurrying from their den, disturbed by the commotion. Shellheart, padding into camp, paused. "What's going on?" He stared at his Clanmates who were gathering at the edge of the clearing. Crookedkit proudly met his gaze and nodded. He knew his father would figure out what was happening.

His brother guessed first. Oakpaw raced across the snow. "We can train together at last!" He ran his muzzle along Crookedkit's twisted jaw. "We'll be *warriors* soon. I can't wait! I promise as soon as I'm leader, I'll make you deputy."

Thanks! Crookedkit purred. *But I plan on being RiverClan's leader first.*

Hailstar glanced around his Clan. His gaze stopped at Cedarpelt. Crookedkit's heart sank. Had the brown-striped warrior forgiven him for running away? "Cedarpelt!" he called. "You distrusted Crookedkit when he returned. You will demand more of him than any other warrior."

Even more than Mapleshade? Crookedkit looked at his paws, guilt pricking him as he thought of his secret mentor. "You will mentor him to become the fine warrior I know he can be. One day I hope his honor and bravery will match yours." Hailstar's gaze flicked to Crookedkit. "From this moment on, you shall be known as Crookedpaw."

Crookedpaw broke into a purr so strong that it shook the snow from his whiskers. Oakpaw circled Shellheart excitedly while the RiverClan deputy pawed the ground.

Brambleberry raised her muzzle. "Crookedpaw! Crookedpaw!" The medicine cat's eyes shone with pride.

Beetlepaw, Volepaw, and Petalpaw joined in and Troutclaw's rasping call made the cold air shudder. As his Clanmates called his new name, Crookedpaw looked for Rainflower. Had she seen him become an apprentice? This was just the beginning of his destiny. *Where are you?* His gaze darted among his Clanmates' cheering faces.

There she was! Beside Shimmerpelt.

"Crookedpaw! Crookedpaw!" Shellheart and Oakpaw yowled to the darkening sky.

Crookedpaw stared at his mother, his heart quickening as she stood still and silent. Then, with a rush of relief, he watched her lift her muzzle and call his new name.

"Crookedpaw!"

CHAPTER 11

"Tuck in your tail!" Mapleshade ordered.

Crookedpaw twined his tail around his hind legs as he reared up, slashing with his forepaws. Unbalanced, he staggered, his tail catching between his paws. "Oomph!" He fell with a thud to the dark earth.

"You've got two mentors and you can't even stay on your paws," Mapleshade growled. "Get up."

Crookedpaw was already scrambling to his paws. "What's the point of tucking in my tail?" he mewed crossly.

"The less you give your enemy to grab hold of, the better," Mapleshade explained.

"But I can't balance."

"You'll just have to keep practicing until you can." Mapleshade paced around him. "Now try again."

Concentrating, Crookedpaw shifted his paws, then heaved himself into the air once more. Tucking his tail around his hind legs, he slashed again. His muscles burned. He tried to balance, but the swing of his forepaws sent him staggering forward.

"Frog dung!" He dropped on to four paws before he fell.

"You're getting close," Mapleshade encouraged.

"Not close enough," Crookedpaw grunted through clenched teeth. He tried again and again, each time staying up a moment longer until, aching, he stopped and let his tail droop.

"Keep going!" Mapleshade ordered.

"Don't forget I train all day with Cedarpelt, too," he grumbled.

"You want to be the best warrior in RiverClan, don't you?" Mapleshade circled him impatiently.

"Of course," Crookedpaw snapped. "But I need a rest." He gazed into the shadowy forest. "Why don't you show me around StarClan territory?" He blinked hopefully at Mapleshade. "Cedarpelt showed me around RiverClan territory on my first day as an apprentice."

"Not till you've got this move right."

"I'll practice it tomorrow night." Crookedpaw stood up. "I want to see what's beyond the trees." He padded forward. "There must be more to StarClan's hunting grounds than this smelly old forest."

Mapleshade shot in front of him, her orange-and-white pelt blocking his view.

He peered over her, straining to see through the mist. "Come on," he pleaded. "Just take me to the edge of the trees so I can see what's behind them."

"No!" Mapleshade's command was sharp. She wove around him, steering him back into the dingy clearing. "You're not ready."

Crookedpaw growled. "It's not fair!"

Mapleshade's claws stung his ear.

"What was that for?" he gasped. She'd drawn blood. He could feel it, warm and wet, on his ear tip. He rubbed it with his paw.

She glared at him. "Remember your promise!" she hissed. "You must be prepared to do anything for the sake of the Clan."

"What's that got to do with exploring StarClan territory?" Crookedpaw retorted.

Mapleshade narrowed her eyes. "You're not here to ask questions. You're here to learn. Or you'll have more than a scratched ear to worry about."

"Is that blood on your ear?"

Crookedpaw felt a rough tongue lick the wound Mapleshade had left. He blinked open his eyes. "Get off, Oakpaw." Ducking away from his brother, he sat up. His muscles ached, strained and tired.

Oakpaw was still staring at his ear. "Did you catch it on something? Is there a thorn in your nest?"

Crookedpaw sniffed the chilly dawn air. "I probably did it in my sleep. Scratching a flea." Sometimes he wished he could tell Oakpaw about his StarClan mentor, but he'd promised to obey Mapleshade and she'd sworn him to secrecy. How could he argue with StarClan?

Rain thrummed on the den roof. Beetlepaw, Volepaw, and Petalpaw were still curled in their nests. Stiffly, Crookedpaw stepped out of his nest. "Has the dawn patrol left?"

Oakpaw shook his head. "They're in the clearing."

Crookedpaw pricked his ears. He could hear Cedarpelt's deep mew beyond the den wall.

"Are we going to leave markers below Sunningrocks?"

Lakeshine answered. "I hope not," she sighed. "It'd be like admitting we agree with the changed border."

Crookedpaw listened to Mudfur's throaty growl. "All this fighting over a lump of rock."

"It's our territory!" Cedarpelt snapped. "We can't give it up."

Crookedpaw flexed his aching claws and winced.

"Are you okay?" Oakpaw fretted. "Maybe you should go and see Brambleberry. At least she could put some ointment on your ear."

"I'm fine," Crookedpaw insisted. It hardly stung. Besides, warriors always had nicks in their ears. He licked a paw and rubbed off the dried blood. The cut felt straight and shallow underneath.

Beetlepaw stretched, his black pelt no more than a shadow in the watery dawn light. "Who's coming on patrol?" He sat up. "Hailstar's leading it."

"Me!" Petalpaw hopped out of her nest. "What about you?" She glanced at Crookedpaw as Beetlepaw pushed past her to the entrance. "Cedarpelt's going."

"I hope so," Crookedpaw mewed. If Beetlepaw was patrolling, he didn't want to be stuck in camp. He glanced at Oakpaw. "What are you doing today?"

"Shellheart's taking me fishing with Volepaw and Rippleclaw."

Volepaw sleepily lifted his head. "If it keeps raining like this, the fish will come to us."

"In your dreams!" Purring, Crookedpaw flicked Volepaw's flank with his tail and nosed his way out of the den. Through a haze of rain he saw Shellheart assigning patrols beneath a branch of the fallen tree. Echomist, Timberfur, Brightsky, and Owlfur clustered around him, beads of rain streaming from their glossy coats like water off duck feathers. "I want you to lead the hunting patrol, Echomist," Shellheart ordered.

Cedarpelt paced the sedge wall while Lakeshine and Mudfur huddled next to each other, their gaze fixed on Hailstar's den. Its draping moss quivered as the RiverClan leader padded out. "Petalpaw!"

She was nosing through the soggy pile of prey. She looked up eagerly.

"Don't keep us waiting," Hailstar warned.

Lakeshine snorted. "Waiting indeed! *He's* the one sitting in his den keeping his ears dry," she muttered as Petalpaw fell in beside Mudfur.

"Wait for me!" Crookedpaw raced after Cedarpelt as Hailstar led the way out of camp.

Cedarpelt paused in the entrance. "Next time."

Crookedpaw slithered to a halt. "Why not this time?"

"We're checking the borders," Cedarpelt told him. "We might meet an enemy patrol and I haven't assessed your battle skills yet."

"They're fine!" This could be his chance to use some of the moves Mapleshade had taught him.

Cedarpelt narrowed his eyes. "I'll be the one to decide that!"

"Are you coming?" Lakeshine called from the tunnel.

"I'll assess you this afternoon." Cedarpelt turned and headed through the sedge. "I promise."

Crookedpaw's tail drooped, slapping into a puddle. He heard a squeak behind him.

"Watch out!"

He turned and saw Willowkit rubbing water from her nose. "Sorry!" he mewed. "Did I splash you?"

Graykit stood beside her sister, whiskers quivering. "She was trying to stalk you."

"I nearly got you!" Willowkit puffed out her rain-spiked fur.

Crookedpaw stifled a purr. "Shouldn't you be in the nursery keeping dry?"

Graykit lifted her muzzle. "We're RiverClan cats." She sniffed. "We're supposed to get wet."

"There's wet and there's *drowned*!" Brambleberry's stern mew made Graykit jump. The medicine cat was padding from her den. "I don't think Fallowtail will thank you for traipsing a puddleful of rain into the nursery." The medicine cat halted beside Crookedpaw. "If you've nothing better to do," she caught his eye, "you could fetch me some coltsfoot."

"From the waterfall?"

"You remembered!" Brambleberry sounded pleased.

"We're going to need some fresh stock." She glanced up into the streaming rain. "If this weather keeps up, there'll be coughs spreading through all the dens. Do you remember what it looks like?"

"I'll know it when I see it," Crookedpaw promised.

"Can we come, too?" Willowkit asked.

Crookedpaw shook his head sympathetically, remembering all too clearly what it felt like to be a kit trapped in camp. "Sorry," he mewed.

"We won't get in your way," Graykit promised.

Brambleberry cleared her throat. "That's because you'll be safe and dry in your nest." Fallowtail was at the nursery entrance, staring anxiously through the rain at her soggy kits. Brambleberry shook the rain from her whiskers. "Be careful by the falls, Crookedpaw," she warned as she began to shoo the kits toward their mother. "The path gets slippery and the river will be raging."

"I won't let you down!" Crookedpaw raced for the camp entrance. Brambleberry was depending on him. His paws pricked with excitement.

There was little shelter on the riverbank now that the greenleaf bushes had died back. But the rain was easing by the time the path began to slope up to meet the head of the falls. Unsheathing his claws to get a better grip, he climbed the wet stone track, flattening his ears against the roar of the swollen waters below. Tasting the air, Crookedpaw smelled the first tang of coltsfoot. He shook out his fur, glancing up as the sky brightened. The clouds were thinning, stretching to show patches of blue. He stopped beside a fragrant green clump that clung at the edge of the path. Beyond, the cliff dropped away and Crookedpaw could just see the water swirling below.

The coltsfoot had died back, browned by frost, but a core of richly scented leaves curled at the center. Crookedpaw plunged his paws into the wet leaves. Hooking a bunch with his claws, he hauled out a pawful of sprigs and laid them on the path before turning back for more.

"Are you Brambleberry's apprentice?"

A husky mew made Crookedpaw jump. Heart lurching, he spun around and saw three WindClan warriors standing beside the top of the falls. Crookedpaw backed away, pulling his coltsfoot stems with him. His pelt bristled, embarrassed at being caught off guard. The scent of the coltsfoot and the roar of the water had hidden the WindClan patrol's approach.

The three warriors advanced down the path toward him. Crookedpaw arched his back. "You're on RiverClan territory!" He tried to remember Mapleshade's training. There was no way he was going to try tucking his tail around his hind paws here on the edge of the gorge. Perhaps he should run back to warn the Clan? He eyed the WindClan cats nervously. Their hackles were smooth. The biggest warrior, a brown tom, stared at him levelly while his Clanmates—a tabby she-cat and a small, mottled tom—stood calmly beside him.

The brown tom dipped his head. "I'm Reedfeather and I wish to speak with Hailstar."

Crookedpaw frowned. "Why?"

Reedfeather nodded to his Clanmates. "Go back to

camp," he told them. "I'll be okay."

The two WindClan warriors turned and darted back along the path, disappearing over the crest of the falls.

Reedfeather dipped his head. "What's your name?"

"Crookedpaw."

"Brambleberry's apprentice?"

Crookedpaw shook his head. "Cedarpelt's."

"A warrior apprentice?" Reedfeather narrowed his eyes. "I haven't seen you at a Gathering yet."

"I just got my apprentice name." Crookedpaw shifted his paws. Was he supposed to take an enemy warrior into camp just because he'd been asked?

"You lead," Reedfeather instructed as if he'd guessed what Crookedpaw was thinking. "I'll follow."

Crookedpaw stared uncertainly at the WindClan warrior.

"Don't worry," Reedfeather reassured him. "I only want to talk with Hailstar." He turned his head. "As you can see, I'm alone."

Crookedpaw glanced at the coltsfoot he'd picked.

"Take it," Reedfeather advised. "I'm sure Brambleberry will be pleased to have it."

Crookedpaw snatched it up in his jaws. Ears twitching, he led Reedfeather down the path. *Is this a trick?* The path flattened as the river settled down after its rush through the gorge and began to lap lazily at the shore. Crookedpaw glanced over his shoulder. Reedfeather's gaze was fixed firmly on the distant reed bed where the RiverClan camp sheltered. As the river narrowed and deepened, Crookedpaw jumped down on to the shore. He began to wade into the water. The current here was gentle and it would be easy to swim across.

"Aren't there stepping-stones?" Reedfeather called.

Crookedpaw halted, water tugging his belly fur. "They're farther downstream." The coltsfoot muffled his mew. *How does a WindClan cat know about the stepping-stones?*

"Can we cross there?" Reedfeather asked. "I don't swim."

Crookedpaw backed awkwardly out of the river, the coltsfoot sour on his tongue. He took Reedfeather to the stepping-stones and stood back while the WindClan warrior crossed. Swollen by rain, the river ran fast around the boulders, and Reedfeather's pelt bristled, but he was sure-pawed and didn't hesitate. Crookedpaw bounded after him, paws slapping the wet sand as he landed on the shore. He darted past Reedfeather and led the way through the bushes on to the grassy path.

As he neared camp, his belly tightened. He was leading an enemy warrior into the heart of the Clan. What if all the warriors were out hunting or patrolling? Who would defend the elders, or Fallowtail and her kits? He stiffened. *I will!* Fluffing out his wet fur, he ducked through the sedge tunnel.

"Crookedpaw!" Volepaw's call surprised him.

He dropped the coltsfoot. "I thought you were swimming."

"Shellheart wanted to wait till after the rain." Volepaw trotted across the clearing. "I don't know why—it's probably drier in the riv—" He stared past Crookedpaw, eyes widening. "You captured a WindClan warrior!"

Crookedpaw shifted his paws. "I didn't exactly capture

him," he mumbled. "I sort of found him and he asked to see Hailstar."

"WindClan!" Shimmerpelt charged from her den, nose twitching, fur spiked in alarm. She halted when she saw Reedfeather. "What's he doing here?"

Reedfeather padded calmly to the center of the clearing and looked around. Troutclaw, Birdsong, and Tanglewhisker crowded out of their den and stood bristling at the top of the slope. Ottersplash and Lakeshine stopped stuffing leaves in gaps in the apprentices' den. Piketooth and Whitefang looked up from their fresh-kill, mouths open. Oakpaw scrambled over the fallen tree, a frog dangling from his mouth. He dropped it in surprise and stared at Reedfeather. No one tried to stop the frog as it hopped over the clearing and plopped into the safety of the river.

"Reedfeather?" Shellheart had been lying in the shelter of the willow. He scrambled to his paws and padded toward the WindClan warrior. "Why in StarClan are you here?"

Reedfeather dipped his head to the RiverClan deputy. "I need to speak with Hailstar."

"Hailstar's patrolling," Shellheart told him.

Reedfeather sat down. "Then I'll wait."

"Oh, no, you won't!" Birdsong bustled down the slope, pelt ruffled. "You'll go home to your own camp where you belong." She glanced anxiously at the nursery where Fallowtail peered out, her eyes dark.

Does Reedfeather's visit have something to do with what she was doing in WindClan? Crookedpaw suddenly wondered. He studied

Reedfeather more closely. There was something familiar about the shape of his head and the tone of his voice. Had he been the cat with Fallowtail on the pile of WindClan rocks all those moons ago?

The sedge rustled and Rippleclaw raced into camp. He skidded to a halt in front of Reedfeather, hackles raised and snarling. "I knew I smelled WindClan!" he hissed as Hailstar pounded into the clearing. Cedarpelt followed, Petalpaw and Beetlepaw on his tail.

Shellheart nodded to his leader. "Crookedpaw found him at the border," he reported. "He wants to speak with you."

Reedfeather stood up. "I've come to ask for what is mine."

Willowkit and Graykit tumbled out of the nursery. Fallowtail reached after them but they escaped her paws and bounded into the clearing.

"I've never seen a WindClan cat!" Willowkit gasped.

Graykit screwed up her face. "He smells weird!"

"Hush!" Birdsong wrapped her tail around them and pulled them close as Fallowtail slid from the nursery.

Cedarpelt crossed the clearing and stood beside the queen, a growl rumbling in his throat. Crookedpaw lifted his chin, proud that his mentor was so protective of his littermate and her kits.

Reedfeather dipped his head. "I've come to take my kits home."

Cedarpelt stiffened. "*His* kits?"

Crookedpaw stared. How could a WindClan cat have kits in RiverClan?

"You can't!" Fallowtail's cry was desperate.

There was a gasp from the cats in the clearing. Crookedpaw looked from one face to the other. Slowly images stirred in his mind. Willowkit and Graykit had no father in RiverClan—or at least not one that Fallowtail had named. Crookedpaw had seen Fallowtail in WindClan territory with a tom two moons before the kits were born. Could *Reedfeather* be their father?

Rippleclaw turned his snarl from the WindClan warrior and glared at Fallowtail, who looked as if her world were ending. "You're not even going to deny it? Have you forgotten the meaning of loyalty?"

Fallowtail pushed Birdsong out of the way and gathered her kits close to her belly. "I am loyal!" Fallowtail's eyes sparked with grief. "I haven't seen Reedfeather in moons. I love my kits more than my own life and I planned to bring them up as true RiverClan warriors." She stared at Reedfeather. "How can you even suggest taking them away from me?"

The WindClan warrior returned her gaze. "They are as much mine as yours."

Willowkit stared up at her mother. "He can't be our father," she whimpered. "He doesn't smell like us."

Hailstar padded across the clearing and stopped beside the queen. "Is this true?"

Fallowtail stared at the ground, pulling her kits closer with her tail.

Shellheart sighed. "These kits have a right to be with their father."

Crookedpaw watched, his heart twisting.

Shimmerpelt crossed the clearing and pressed against Fallowtail. "You can't make her give up her kits."

Piketooth lashed his tail. "Kits should be with their mother!"

"We can't give them up!"

"They were born in RiverClan!"

"How can we let strangers raise them?"

A snarl cut dead the Clan's murmuring. "How can we trust them, knowing they are half WindClan?" Rippleclaw's eyes shone.

Tanglewhisker shook his head. "He's right," the elder murmured. "We'll never truly know where their loyalties lie."

Graykit squirmed free of her mother. "We're RiverClan!" she cried. "We'll always be RiverClan."

"You're WindClan, too." Reedfeather spoke up. "They will be well cared for," he promised. "We have plenty of prey." He scanned the clearing, his gaze lingering on the dens crowding the fallen tree. "You have enough mouths to feed. What if there's another flood? Or the river freezes? It's happened before." His gaze returned to the kits. "They'll grow stronger on WindClan prey."

"No." Hailstar padded between Reedfeather and Fallowtail.

Reedfeather's gaze hardened. "If it comes to war, WindClan will fight for them."

Hailstar unsheathed his claws. "RiverClan isn't scared by threats!"

"You should be," Reedfeather meowed. "Don't think the other Clans haven't seen how you gave up Sunningrocks without a fight. RiverClan is weak. My Clanmates will join me to take back what is mine. You should fear us, old cat."

Tension spiked the air. Then Fallowtail's mew broke the silence. "I've caused enough trouble," she whispered. "I don't want bloodshed. Nothing is worth that."

Crookedpaw felt sick. *Don't give up! Fight for them!* He stared in disbelief as Fallowtail backed away from her kits.

"Fallowtail?" Willowkit blinked at her mother.

Graykit spun around. "What's happening?"

Hailstar stared at the queen. "Are you sure?"

She nodded. "Reedfeather is right. Our kits will fare better in WindClan. And we cannot risk war over my . . . my mistake."

Graykit scrambled after her mother, but Hailstar nudged the kit away with his muzzle. "You're going to live in your father's Clan," he meowed softly.

Willowkit stiffened. "How can he be our father? I've never seen him before!"

"He smells horrid!" Graykit flinched away as Reedfeather sniffed each kit gently.

"You'll be well taken care of," he told them. "WindClan is looking forward to meeting you."

Willowkit searched desperately for her mother's gaze but Fallowtail stared at the ground. Crookedpaw wanted to race from where his paws were rooted and beg the queen not to let them go. But, like his Clanmates, he sat in silence as Hailstar nudged the kits toward their father.

"No!" Graykit yelped in terror as Reedfeather scooped her up. "Fallowtail!"

He padded toward the camp entrance.

Willowkit stared wildly around the Clan. "Aren't you going to stop him?"

"Willowkit!" Graykit struggled. "Don't leave me!"

Stumbling, Willowkit followed. "I'm coming, Graykit! I'm coming!"

As they disappeared through the tunnel, Hailstar padded slowly to his den.

Birdsong pressed against Fallowtail. "They won't forget you."

Shimmerpelt rubbed her muzzle against the queen's cheek. "You'll see them again. They'll always be your kits."

Fallowtail tore away from her Clanmates and staggered toward the nursery.

Rippleclaw snorted. "What does she want to go *there* for?"

Ottersplash spun around and hissed at the silver warrior. "Shut up! Just shut up!"

Crookedpaw darted after the grief-stricken queen and squeezed into the nursery after her. He searched for words to comfort her as she collapsed into her nest.

How could anyone let a queen be separated from her kits? His heart ached for Willowkit and Graykit. They'd be terrified without their mother. He crouched down beside Fallowtail and pressed against her trembling flank. "I wouldn't have let him take them," he whispered. "If *I* was leader."

CHAPTER 12

❧

"No, no, no!" Cedarpelt's frustrated yowl made Crookedpaw stop.

He straightened up and blinked at his mentor. "What am I doing wrong?"

A lump of snow dropped from an icy branch overhead and landed on his back. He shook it off. He could see across the meadow and beyond the river to the snow-whitened moorlands. The frosted beeches behind them were stark against the gray leaf-bare sky; the marsh meadow stretching below them sparkled, smoothed by snow, and the small clearing beside the beech copse, where they'd been practicing battle moves all afternoon, was icy underpaw.

Cedarpelt sighed. "How many times do I have to tell you? When you're attacking, bush out your fur! StarClan gave RiverClan thick pelts for a reason. Bush it out and you'll look twice as big as your enemy. And a frightened enemy is already half-beaten."

Crookedpaw flicked his tail. "The other Clans *know* that!" Mapleshade was always telling him to slick down his fur and fool his opponent into thinking he looked weaker than he was. "It's just fur, and fur never hurt anyone."

"In the middle of battle, there's no time to think," Cedarpelt insisted. "If you see a big warrior, you don't wonder how much is fur and how much is muscle." His breath billowed in the icy air. "You just react."

"Okay, okay!" Crookedpaw snapped. "If you want bushed-out fur, you can have bushed-out fur." He fluffed up his pelt. "Big enough?" He couldn't wait for his first battle so he could find out for himself which mentor was right.

Cedarpelt's whiskers twitched.

"What?" Crookedpaw snorted.

A purr rumbled in his mentor's throat. "You never do things by halves." He shook his head. "You look like a pinecone."

Crookedpaw's irritation dissolved. "Make up your mind," he mewed. As he shook his pelt back into place, a sound made his ears prick.

"What is it?" Cedarpelt darted beside him, hackles twitching as he scanned the marsh.

"Look." Crookedpaw flicked his tail toward the dark pelts moving toward them across the snow. He tasted the freezing air. *RiverClan.*

"Piketooth!" Cedarpelt hailed the snaggle-toothed warrior, who was already bounding up the slope.

Beetlenose ducked ahead of his Clanmate and reached the beech copse first. "How's training, Crookedpaw?" he called. "Getting the hang of it?"

Crookedpaw scowled. *You're only a moon older than me!* Beetlenose was acting as though he'd been made deputy instead of a warrior. At least it meant that he'd moved out of the apprentices' den. Crookedpaw wasn't going to miss his boasting, though he missed Voleclaw's fish-brained jokes and Petaldust's quiet encouragement. At least he still had Oakpaw for company.

Crookedpaw sat down. What would happen when Oakpaw became a warrior? He'd be alone again, and now that Willowkit and Graykit were in WindClan, there weren't even new 'paws to look forward to. He'd have to train by himself.

"How's hunting?" Cedarpelt asked Piketooth.

"River's frozen." Piketooth tasted the air. "Any sign of birds up here?"

Cedarpelt shook his head.

"We were just at the WindClan border." Piketooth stared across the snowy marsh. "We saw Reedfeather. He wanted to share news."

Cedarpelt's ears pricked. "How are the kits?"

"Doing well." Piketooth was frowning. Crookedpaw tensed as the warrior went on. "He warned us to watch out for ThunderClan. They raided WindClan's camp."

"The *camp*?" Cedarpelt blinked.

Crookedpaw gasped. "Did they attack the nursery?"

Piketooth shook his head. "They were trying to steal herbs."

"Anyone hurt?" Cedarpelt asked.

"ThunderClan lost a warrior—Moonflower." Piketooth flexed his claws.

Beetlenose growled. "Serves them right."

Cedarpelt scowled at the young tom. "*No* warrior deserves

to die!" He turned back to Piketooth. "Have you warned Hailstar?"

"He was with us," Piketooth meowed. "He's gone back to camp to warn Brambleberry to hide her supplies."

"They won't attack our camp." Beetlenose paced through the frost, lashing his tail. "They don't have the guts to cross the river even when it's frozen!"

Cedarpelt looked thoughtful. "Let's hope so." He beckoned Beetlenose with his tail. "Will you practice some battle moves with Crookedpaw? He knows my moves too well."

Crookedpaw rolled his eyes. "What makes you think I don't know Beetlenose's moves, too?"

Beetlenose flattened his ears, ready for a fight. "We only trained together twice."

"That was enough." Crookedpaw sniffed.

Piketooth wove between the two young toms. "Let's act like Clanmates." He glanced at Crookedpaw. "You still have plenty to learn. Stop complaining. Beetlenose might teach you something."

Cedarpelt shrugged. "Crookedpaw thinks he's learned enough." He nodded to Beetlenose. "Can he try his front paw swipe on you?"

"He can *try*." Beetlenose dropped into a crouch.

Smug frog-face! Crookedpaw ducked down and fluffed out his pelt. Energy surged in his muscles. He unsheathed his hind claws, digging them deep into the snow, then reared up. Black as a crow against the white snow, Beetlenose leaned back and raised his forepaws. Crookedpaw adjusted his balance, wrapped his tail around his hind legs, and swiped at Beetlenose. He blinked with surprise as Beetlenose dropped and darted behind him.

Turning on his hind paws, Crookedpaw saw Beetlenose's jaws snapping where his tail should've been. "You missed!" With a rush of satisfaction he slammed down on the young warrior, knocking him flat on to his belly.

"Ow!" Beetlenose wriggled from under him as Crookedpaw shifted his weight. "My chin!" He rubbed at it with a paw.

"Crookedpaw!" Cedarpelt's mew was sharp. "This is just practice!"

"I had my foreclaws sheathed!" Crookedpaw protested. "And we were supposed to be practicing the front paw swipe! He was going for my tail!"

"So?" Beetlenose squared up to Crookedpaw. "A warrior should be ready for anything!"

"Then why weren't you ready for my counterattack?" Crookedpaw spat back.

"You hid your tail!" Beetlenose hissed. "That's not fair! No cat hides his tail!"

Cedarpelt's gaze darkened. "ThunderClan cats do," he meowed. "Where did you learn to do that?"

Crookedpaw puffed out his chest. "Great, isn't it? Did you see how I balanced even without my tail?" *StarClan warriors must know the moves of every Clan.*

Cedarpelt narrowed his eyes. "It isn't fair to use tricks."

"It wasn't a trick!" Crookedpaw flashed a look at Piketooth. "I taught him a new move."

"Show some respect!" Cedarpelt snapped. "Beetlenose is a warrior. You've been an apprentice less than a moon. You've never even been to a Gathering."

Beetlenose's tail-tip was twitching angrily. "Crookedpaw's always thought he was better than any RiverClan cat."

Cedarpelt marched past the black warrior. "Let's get back to camp," he growled. "It's freezing."

Crookedpaw watched his mentor bound down the slope, following the snow-covered trail back to camp. Guilt tugged in his belly. He hadn't meant to show off. Beetlenose was just so annoying. *I know stuff they don't. Why do I have to hide it?*

No one spoke as they trekked back to camp. Crookedpaw fluffed out his pelt for warmth, pads frozen, breath billowing. The sedge tunnel was half-squashed with snow and Crookedpaw had to duck to squeeze through. Inside, the camp glowed purple in the setting sun. Snow draped the walls and the dens. It had been swept from the clearing but had drifted by the shore. The fallen tree was crisscrossed by trails to the warriors' dens and frosted reeds spiked the frozen river.

Cedarpelt headed for Hailstar's den. Crookedpaw's heart sank. His mentor was probably going to report him for disobedience.

Beetlenose barged past him. "Serves you right!" Sniffing, he headed for the fresh-kill pile, where Petaldust and Echomist were already nosing through the fish. Crookedpaw's belly growled. The fish smelled delicious.

"Don't worry." Piketooth paused at Crookedpaw's shoulder. "You won't be the first 'paw in trouble, or the last."

He bounded across the clearing and touched muzzles with Shimmerpelt, his mate, who was sitting in a hollow dug out of the snow sharing a fat pike with Brightsky and Mudfur. She stood to greet him, then nodded toward the fresh-kill pile. Sighing, Crookedpaw watched Piketooth clamber toward the heap of fish.

"Crookedpaw!" Cedarpelt called from outside Hailstar's den. He beckoned with a flick of his tail. "Hailstar wants to talk to you."

Crookedpaw followed Cedarpelt's snow-trail with heavy paws. "I'm sorry." He reached Cedarpelt. "But—"

Cedarpelt cut him off. "We'll start over tomorrow." The stout brown-striped tom tipped his head toward Hailstar's den as the moss shivered and the RiverClan leader padded out. "He just wants to talk to you."

As Cedarpelt headed away, Crookedpaw turned toward Hailstar, shrinking beneath his pelt. "I didn't hurt Beetlenose on purpose," he began.

Hailstar sat down. "I'm sure he'll recover." His amber eyes glowed in the early evening light. "I realize you're in a hurry to finish your training—"

"I'm trying to be patient. Really! It's just hard . . ." Crookedpaw cut him off, then stumbled into silence as he realized he'd interrupted his leader. He shifted his paws. "Sorry."

"Don't rush," Hailstar began again. "Take your time. Learn what you need to learn, and learn it well."

Crookedpaw clamped his mouth shut as words tumbled

through his head. *But I know more than you think! I'm being trained by StarClan!* Frustration made his claws itch as Hailstar went on.

"You'll be a warrior soon enough." The old cat gazed up at the sky. The clouds had cleared and Silverpelt was beginning to show. "Enjoy your training. Have some fun before the responsibilities of—" Hailstar stopped.

The distant shrieking of Twoleg kits shattered the air. Mudfur darted out of the snowy hollow and scrambled on to the frozen river. Tiptoeing carefully over the ice, he headed out past the reeds and peered along the channel.

"Can you see anything?" Brightsky gingerly followed her mate, while the rest of the Clan watched in silence.

"It's a Twoleg kit!" Mudfur called back. "Upstream. It's fallen through the ice."

Echomist rushed to Brightsky's side and stared upriver. "It'll drown!"

"It has Clanmates with it," Mudfur reported. "They're pulling it out. And there's a full-grown Twoleg on the bank." He backed toward the shore, ducking among the reeds. "The kit's out of the water."

Echomist sighed. "Let's hope that's the last we see of Twolegs this leaf-bare."

Crookedpaw pricked his ears. Paws were pounding through the snow beyond the sedge. Petaldust turned from the river, fur pricking. Piketooth dropped into a crouch and stared at the camp entrance. Crookedpaw tasted the air.

Shellheart.

The RiverClan deputy thundered into camp, eyes bright,

tail bushed. Oakpaw and Owlfur raced in after him, Softwing on their tail.

Softwing's white pelt was bristling with excitement. "Oakpaw saved us!" She skidded to a halt, sending snow spattering over her Clanmates.

"Shellheart?" Hailstar pricked his ears.

Piketooth straightened. "What happened?"

Shellheart lifted his tail. "We were attacked by a dog."

"A dog!" Brightsky bristled. "Where?"

Softwing paced in front of Hailstar. "We were patrolling beyond the marsh, near the Twoleg place," she panted. "It came out from under the fence and went straight for us."

"How big was it?" Hailstar asked.

Shellheart's ears twitched. "Three times my size."

Brambleberry stuck her head out from her den. "Any injuries?"

"None." Shellheart flicked his tail. "Oakpaw was too fast."

"He was so brave." Softwing circled him.

Rainflower crossed the clearing and nudged Softwing out of the way. "Are you sure you're not hurt?" She licked Oakpaw's ears.

Oakpaw ducked away. "I'm fine."

Brambleberry was weaving among the patrol, sniffing their pelts.

"It nearly got me!" Softwing's eyes were round.

Owlfur brushed against the white warrior, curling his tail protectively over her back. "It was a whisker away from her tail!"

Shellheart plucked at the icy ground. "But Oakpaw turned around and distracted it." He gazed proudly at his son.

Owlfur nodded. "He raced right at it . . ."

". . . then reared up and slashed its muzzle," Softwing finished.

"I don't know whether the dog was more surprised or hurt." Shellheart wound around Oakpaw. "But while it was howling and whining, we had time to get up a tree."

Oakpaw looked at his paws. "I decided my claws were sharper than its teeth."

Rainflower's eyes glowed. "You saved your Clanmates."

Oakpaw shrugged. "If I hadn't, Shellheart would have done it." He glanced at the others. "Or Owlfur or Softwing. I just got there first."

Hailstar fluffed out his fur. "You did well, Oakpaw." He paced the clearing. "But if a dog has started targeting warriors, we must be wary." He raised his muzzle. "Let all cats old enough to swim gather to hear my words."

He's going to warn everyone about the dog. Crookedpaw nosed his way between Oakpaw and Shellheart. "Well done," he whispered.

Shellheart was purring. "You'd have been proud if you'd seen him, Crookedpaw."

I'm proud even though I didn't see him! Crookedpaw shot a warm glance at his brother.

Brambleberry brushed against him. "Courage must run in the family," she murmured.

Rainflower touched Oakpaw's muzzle with her own. "I'm

just glad you're not hurt."

Troutclaw padded stiffly down the slope. "What's happening?"

"Dog attack," Softwing called.

Tanglewhisker slid out of the elders' den with Birdsong behind him. "Dog?" His eyes widened. "Where?"

"By the Twolegplace," Owlfur explained. "Oakpaw fought it off."

Fallowtail slid out of the warriors' den. In the moon since Reedfeather took her kits, she'd grown thin and unkempt. "Did it follow them home?" She scanned the snow-covered reeds.

Echomist hurried to her side. "No, it's gone. We're safe," she soothed.

As the Clan gathered, Hailstar padded to the middle of the clearing. "Oakpaw showed bravery tonight that has made him worthy of his warrior name."

Oakpaw gasped. Crookedpaw stared at him in astonishment. He was going to be made a warrior! Right now! *What if he makes it to leader before me, too?*

"Go on, Oakpaw." Shellheart nudged him forward.

"Oakpaw." Hailstar dipped his wide gray head. Oakpaw's glossy pelt glinted red under the round, rising moon. "From this moment on you shall be known as Oakheart," Hailstar meowed. "StarClan honors your courage and your quick wits, and we welcome you as a full warrior of RiverClan." He pressed his muzzle to Oakheart's head. "Serve your Clan well."

Crookedpaw felt a surge of pride as his Clanmates raised their voices to call Oakheart's new name. But as he joined in, his voice caught in his throat. *Why has it been so easy for you?* The thought stung. He pushed it away. *Who cares why? I'll be a warrior soon and we'll hunt and fight side by side!*

"Oakheart! Oakheart!" He raised his voice to the darkening sky.

Purring, Oakheart padded from the clearing and stopped beside Crookedpaw. "Wow!" His eyes shone. "I didn't think it would feel this good!"

"Well done, Oakheart." Shellheart touched his nose to Oakheart's ear.

Rainflower pressed against her warrior kit. "I'm so proud of you."

Oakheart's gaze caught Crookedpaw's. "It's your turn next," he purred.

Rainflower flicked her ears. "Does that matter right now?" she murmured. "He'll never be as good as you." Her words sliced through Crookedpaw's heart like claws.

Shellheart's head snapped around and he glared at his former mate. Rage blazed in his eyes. "Can't you keep your thoughts to yourself, just once?"

Why did she have to spoil it? Crookedpaw fought the anger tightening his throat.

"Ignore her," Oakheart urged, steering Crookedpaw away. His eyes grew bright. "Look!" He glanced up at the round moon. "You know what night it is?"

"Full moon?"

"The Gathering!"

Of course! Crookedpaw felt a surge of excitement. He was an apprentice now. He could go! He glanced anxiously at Hailstar. Couldn't he?

Oakheart nudged him. "Hailstar has to let you come!" he promised. "You're an apprentice and I'm a warrior. Only a frog-brain would stop us from going to the Gathering tonight!"

CHAPTER 13

❧

Crookedpaw's breath billowed in the cold air and turned to ice on his whiskers. Frosted snow cracked underpaw as he followed his Clanmates down the bank toward the river. His pelt pricked with excitement. His first Gathering! He pressed against Oakheart.

"Will we use the Twoleg bridge?"

Hailstar was leading the patrol along the shore toward the wooden crossing. The frozen river shone silver below as it snaked up into the gorge.

"It's the safest way to cross tonight," Oakheart whispered.

Warriors never made use of Twoleg paths if they could help it, but the frozen river was untested, and the stepping-stones were too icy to risk. Hailstar jumped over the low fence on to the bridge and landed in churned snow. Brightsky followed, her paws slithering on the frosty rail. Petaldust ducked under it as Beetlenose scrambled over.

"Hurry up, you two!" Cedarpelt called over his shoulder.

Crookedpaw bounded forward, Oakheart's pelt brushing his as they skidded down the bank. Owlfur and Ottersplash slipped on to the bridge just ahead of them, their pelts sharply outlined against the white ground. Brambleberry, her pelt pale as the snow, followed like a ghost behind them.

Shellheart paused beside Cedarpelt and let Crookedpaw and Oakheart pass. "I hope it's a peaceful Gathering," he mewed.

Cedarpelt sniffed. "Surely even ThunderClan wouldn't break the full moon truce?"

As the two warriors fell in behind, Crookedpaw glanced over his shoulder. "*WindClan* might," he predicted.

"They'll still be angry that ThunderClan attacked their camp," Oakheart agreed.

Shellheart padded on to the bridge. "We're angry they took Graykit and Willowkit," he pointed out. "But we won't fight over them tonight."

Crookedpaw pricked his ears. "When *will* we fight over them?"

Shellheart glanced at Hailstar. "Probably never," he muttered.

Crookedpaw peered over the side of the bridge. Moonlight glared on the ice. He looked up, blinking, and saw his Clanmates streaming up the slope toward ThunderClan territory. "Aren't we going to follow the path beside the waterfall?"

Oakheart shook his head. "There's a truce," he reminded him. "We can cross ThunderClan territory straight to the hollow tonight."

Crookedpaw was out of breath by the time he reached the top of the short, steep rise. Oakheart had already disappeared into the trees crowding on either side. He gazed up at the looming trunks, wrinkling his nose.

"Don't you like it?" Brambleberry had waited for him.

"It smells horrible." Crookedpaw shivered. The bushes growing around the trunks were drenched with ThunderClan scent.

"Are you excited about the Gathering?" Brambleberry asked gently.

"Yeah!" Why wouldn't he be?

"I'm very proud of you," she murmured. "After you broke your jaw I thought you'd never become an apprentice." She glanced at him. "But you've grown so strong, I hardly recognize you." A purr rolled in her throat as she quickened her pace and caught up with the rest of the patrol.

Crookedpaw watched their pelts flashing through the undergrowth. Drifts of snow hemmed the trail even here where the sky was hardly visible.

"No wonder ThunderClan wants Sunningrocks," Crookedpaw muttered to himself. "They must never see the sun in here." He was relieved when they broke out of the forest and wind swept the stink of ThunderClan from his pelt.

As his Clanmates halted, Crookedpaw fluffed out his pelt. The land sloped away at his paw tips, opening into a wide valley. In the middle, four great oaks guarded a clearing. *Fourtrees.*

Brightsky paced the crest of the slope. "We're the last to arrive."

Mudfur tasted the air. "ThunderClan just got here."

"It's very quiet," Petaldust whispered.

Crookedpaw narrowed his eyes. Countless pelts swarmed between the four oaks, shoaling like fish around a huge boulder. *That must be the Great Rock!*

A growl rumbled in Hailstar's throat. "They've started without us." The RiverClan leader plunged down the slope, snow flying in his wake. Owlfur and Shellheart followed, Beetlenose and Mudfur on their tail.

"Come on!" Oakheart bounded after them.

Crookedpaw hesitated.

Cedarpelt's nudged him. "Are you ready?"

To be announced as a RiverClan apprentice? To meet the other Clans as an equal? Yes!

Energy fizzed beneath his pelt. "Let's go!" Crookedpaw leaped over the edge and streamed down the slope with his Clanmates. Moonlight lit their glossy pelts as they raced for the clearing. Crookedpaw pushed harder, catching up with them as they skidded to a halt beneath a gigantic oak. He stared up through the branches, his eyes wide. It was bigger than any tree in RiverClan territory. It was even bigger than ThunderClan's trees. He felt dizzy. Did the top branches touch the stars?

"Come on." Hailstar flicked his tail and pushed into the crowd.

Crookedpaw scanned the sea of pelts, confused by jumbled scents. Oakheart slid among the gathered cats and disappeared as Hailstar jumped onto the Great Rock, where three other cats waited, starlight glinting in their eyes.

Crookedpaw looked at his mentor. "Which way do I go?"

"Follow me." Cedarpelt nudged his way between two tabby toms.

The toms leaned aside to let him pass and Crookedpaw followed, keeping his nose to Cedarpelt's tail until they stopped in the middle.

"It's warmer here," Cedarpelt murmured.

Crookedpaw, hot with excitement, wished it wasn't. He turned on the spot, staring. He'd never seen so many cats. Where were his Clanmates? His heart lurched as he spotted Reedfeather. The WindClan warrior sat among his Clanmates, staring up at the Great Rock, ears flattened against the cold. Crookedpaw stretched up, balancing on his hind legs to get a better look.

"Don't stare." Cedarpelt nudged him and he stumbled forward.

"Watch out!" A pale gray she-cat with ThunderClan scent turned and hissed at him as he fell against her. Her long fur quivered with annoyance. "You nearly knocked me over!" She stopped and stared at him.

For the first time in moons, Crookedpaw remembered his twisted jaw. He shrank beneath his pelt. Why did she have to stare like he was a talking frog? He swallowed and steadied himself with a deep breath. "Hi," he mewed. "I'm Crookedpaw."

"Crooked*paw*?"

Her eyes were round and blue and hid nothing. He could see her thoughts. *She knows it's not my paws that are crooked.* "I'm guessing my warrior name will be Crookedjaw," he joked half-heartedly.

She was still staring at him.

He swallowed back irritation. Were all ThunderClan cats this rude?

"Unless"—he flicked his tail under her nose—"my tail goes the same way. Then Hailstar might have to rethink."

The gray cat shifted her paws. Crookedpaw frowned. *Okay. ThunderClan cats are rude.* "I should have guessed cats would stare at me."

"I'm sorry!" Guilt sparked in her gaze. "You surprised me, that's all."

Crookedpaw lifted his chin. "I'd better get used to it," he mewed. "Until everyone gets used to me." Why bother being upset over something he couldn't change? "At least no one forgets my name," he pointed out. "What's yours?"

"Bluepaw."

Crookedpaw sat back on his haunches and looked at her. "You're not *very* blue."

Bluepaw purred. "I look more blue in daylight."

Crookedpaw glanced around at the Clans. "Is this your first Gathering?"

Bluepaw shook her head.

"Then you know what's going on?" he asked. "What do the leaders talk about?"

"If you listened you might find out!" Cedarpelt hissed sharply.

Crookedpaw ducked forward and whispered in Bluepaw's

ear. "Which one is Pinestar?"

Bluepaw flicked her tail toward a reddish-brown tom on the rock. *Oh, yes!* Crookedpaw recognized him from Sunningrocks. The ThunderClan leader's eyes shone green in the moonlight, his powerful shoulders rippling as he moved to give Hailstar more space.

"Why haven't you come before?" Bluepaw was looking at him curiously. "You must have been an apprentice for moons."

"I was apprenticed late," Crookedpaw whispered. "I was a pretty sickly kit." Why bother giving the details? "Not anymore though." He puffed out his chest. "I think I surprised my Clanmates by growing this big."

Bluepaw's whiskers twitched. Warmth lit her blue eyes.

"Hush!" A pretty tortoiseshell warrior leaned over. "The leaders are speaking."

"Sorry." Crookedpaw waited for her to turn away, then whispered in Bluepaw's ear, "Which one's Heatherstar?" He wanted to know what Willowkit's new leader looked like.

"The small one. Cedarstar's next to her." *ShadowClan's leader.* Bluepaw nodded toward a small knot of cats gathered at the side of the Great Rock. Brambleberry was sitting with them and Crookedpaw guessed they must be the Clans' medicine cats. "That's Goosefeather, our medicine cat. . . ."

Crookedpaw blinked. It was the cat who'd chased him on the stepping-stones, when he'd fallen in. He scowled. *If that fleabag hadn't chased me, I wouldn't have broken my jaw. I'd be Stormpaw now! I might even be a warrior—*

Bluepaw interrupted his thoughts. ". . . and the white cat is

Sagewhisker, the ShadowClan medicine cat." She shuddered as she pointed out a tom beside Sagewhisker. "That's Hawkheart." There was a snarl in her mew.

"Don't you like him?"

"He killed my mother."

Crookedpaw swallowed. *At least Rainflower's still alive.* Without thinking, he touched Bluepaw's cheek with his tail, whisking it away as he remembered she was from another Clan. "Where are the deputies?" he asked quickly.

A bright ginger tom turned his sharp yellow gaze on them. "The *ThunderClan* deputy is right in front of you, and he'll pull out your whiskers if you don't do as you're told and be quiet!"

Crookedpaw rolled his eyes at Bluepaw. Were *all* senior warriors bossy? She stifled a purr as she turned to watch the leaders. Crookedpaw followed her gaze. The Great Rock was sunk deep into the earth, as though dropped from Silverpelt by StarClan.

Heatherstar stood at the edge. "We have restocked our medicine supplies." Her eyes flashed toward the ThunderClan cats. "And all our elders and kits have *finally* recovered from the unprovoked attack by ThunderClan."

A ThunderClan tom growled. "We fought only warriors! No kit or elder was attacked."

"Or *stolen*." Crookedpaw heard Ottersplash's bitter mew. The white-and-ginger she-cat was staring at Reedfeather.

The WindClan warrior turned. "They weren't stolen," he growled. "They were taken home."

A WindClan tom beside him snapped his head around and

glared at Ottersplash. She didn't flinch, meeting the gaze, chin high. Owlfur pushed through the crowd and lined up beside Ottersplash.

"Calm down," Cedarpelt warned through gritted teeth. "Don't forget the truce."

Owlfur narrowed his eyes. "Like Hailstar's forgotten Willowkit and Graykit?"

"I'm glad Fallowtail's not here," Beetlenose hissed over the heads of a knot of ThunderClan warriors.

Reedfeather whipped around and stared at the young tom. "Let her come next time," he snarled. "Then I can tell her how much our kits prefer eating rabbit to fish!"

Crookedpaw unsheathed his claws. Pelts were bristling around him. Growls rumbled ominously. Bluepaw tensed. Crookedpaw smelled her fear scent. He stared at the leaders on the rock. They shifted their paws, as though each was unwilling to be the first to call for calm.

"Great StarClan! It's cold!" Crookedpaw pressed against Bluepaw, hoping to distract her. She flinched at his touch, then relaxed.

Pinestar stepped forward. "ThunderClan is thriving despite the snow."

Beetlenose was pushing through the crowd toward Reedfeather. "No cat with a drop of RiverClan blood could enjoy rabbit," he snarled. Reedfeather's hackles lifted. He showed his teeth as Beetlenose neared him.

"Beetlenose!" Shellheart slid through the crowd, blocking the young warrior's path. "What in the name of StarClan do you think you're doing?" He pressed Beetlenose back, steering him to the edge of the crowd and clamping the black warrior's tail to the ground with one paw. "Stay here!"

Hailstar was padding to the edge of the Great Rock. The RiverClan leader lifted his muzzle. "RiverClan has been free from Twolegs since the snows came."

"Except those Twoleg kits!" Ottersplash called.

Owlfur answered his Clanmate. "They won't be back for a while!"

Crookedpaw purred. "That'll teach them to slide on the ice."

Bluepaw gasped. "Did they fall in?"

"They only got their paws wet," Crookedpaw reassured her. "*Mouse*-brains!" He felt pleased he'd used a ThunderClan word. "Every RiverClan kit knows to stay off the ice unless a warrior's tested it first."

Hailstar flicked his tail. "Fishing is good despite the ice." His gaze scanned his Clan. Crookedpaw leaned forward, excited, as it settled on Oakheart. "And we have one new warrior. Welcome, Oakheart!"

WindClan cheered, ShadowClan's voices joining them in welcoming the Clan's newest warrior.

"That's my brother," Crookedpaw told Bluepaw.

She blinked at him. "Who?"

"Oakheart," Crookedpaw explained. "He's my littermate."

Bluepaw stretched up to get a better view.

"He's great," Crookedpaw purred proudly. "He caught a fish on his first day as an apprentice." *The day I ran away.* He pushed the memory away. "He says that when he becomes leader, he'll make me deputy." *Should I warn him I plan on being leader first?*

"I have a sister," Bluepaw shot back. She nodded toward a snowy she-cat sitting a tail-length away. "She's a brilliant hunter, too."

"Maybe if they both become leader we could be deputies together," Crookedpaw mewed politely.

Bluepaw frowned. "Deputy? I want to be *leader!*"

Yeah! Me, too!

Bluepaw's tortoiseshell Clanmate flicked her ear with a paw. "Hush!" The warrior sounded cross. "How many times do you have to be told?"

"Sorry." Bluepaw dipped her head.

Crookedpaw turned back to the Great Rock. Cedarstar was speaking. "It is with sadness that I must announce our deputy, Stonetooth, is moving to the elders' den."

A thin gray tabby, standing at the foot of the rock, nodded solemnly as his Clan called his name.

"He doesn't look so old," Bluepaw whispered.

The gray tom's teeth curled from under his lip like claws. Crookedpaw choked back a purr. "Just a bit long in the tooth."

Bluepaw nudged Crookedpaw, purring, too. "He can't help it."

"Raggedpelt will take his place," Cedarstar went on.

A dark brown warrior stalked from the crowd of ShadowClan cats into a pool of moonlight below the rock. Crookedpaw noticed the fur lifting along Bluepaw's spine as

Raggedpelt's Clanmates yowled his name. She was watching the ShadowClan cats gathered at the foot of the rock through narrowed eyes. *She doesn't trust them at all.* Was it just because they were ShadowClan? Maybe there would be time to ask her later.

As the leaders jumped down from the Great Rock, he watched the Clans melting into their separate groups. He tasted the air, collecting scents as he memorized as many pelts as he could.

"Come on." Cedarpelt nudged him. "Let's go. It's too cold to hang around and share tongues." He threw a look at WindClan as they climbed the other side of the hollow, heading up to the moors. "And I don't think any Clan would want to share tongues tonight, even if it was greenleaf."

Crookedpaw followed his mentor. "Are the Clans always so angry with one another?"

Cedarpelt twitched his ears. "Leaf-bare makes bellies hungry and tempers short."

Oakheart's mew made Crookedpaw jump. "What did you think?"

Crookedpaw purred as his brother fell in beside him. "It was great," he replied. "I met a ThunderClan apprentice. She's so much like *us*." He lowered his voice. "She wants to be leader, too."

"Doesn't *every* apprentice want to be leader one day?" Oakheart answered airily.

"Does that mean you've changed your mind about wanting to be leader now that you're a warrior?" Crookedpaw teased.

"Never." Oakheart's eyes flashed and he quickened his pace, skimming the snow with long strides as he followed his Clanmates up the slope. "Come on, I'll race you back to camp!"

Crookedpaw blinked open his eyes. He stared into the dark forest, surprised to find himself dreaming. After the Gathering, too excited to sleep, he'd stared for ages through a small crack in the den wall at the moonlight sparkling on the snowy clearing. His mind was whirling with new pelts and scents and possibilities.

"So you've moved among the other Clans." Mapleshade's mew sounded through the mist. She slid from the shadows and faced him. "What did you think?"

Crookedpaw swished his tail. "It was great!" His paws itched with excitement. "I talked to a ThunderClan apprentice. It was like talking to a Clanmate."

Mapleshade's eyes blazed. "Don't ever say that!"

"But she was just like me." Crookedpaw tipped his head to one side. "I wonder what it's like to live in a forest and eat mice?"

Mapleshade's breath bathed his nose. Her muzzle was a whisker from his as she snarled, "RiverClan is the *only* Clan that should concern you! The other Clans are no more than dust and beetles. Did you forget your promise?"

Crookedpaw shook his head, startled by her fury. "Of course not," he mewed. "I'll always put my Clan above everything."

"Then start practicing your moves!" She backed away and

watched as Crookedpaw reared and began to swipe at the air.

"*Reach!*" Mapleshade called.

Crookedpaw staggered as he stretched farther with each swipe.

"Stay up!" Mapleshade growled as he started to falter, his legs aching with effort.

Crookedpaw gritted his teeth and swiped again at thin air. Through the pain, he felt himself growing stronger, perfectly balanced and more powerful than ever before. This was the training he needed to become a leader! He wondered if Bluepaw was being trained in StarClan as well. What about Oakheart? Would he meet them here one night? Or was this his destiny alone? His promise to Mapleshade rang in his ears.

I will be loyal to my Clan above everything. What I want doesn't matter. The Clan must always come first.

CHAPTER 14

❧

"*Let all cats old enough to* swim gather to hear my words!"

Crookedpaw straightened at Hailstar's call. He dragged his numb paw from the water, hooking out the minnow he'd been groping for and dropping it beside two others that he'd caught. He'd been fishing through a narrow ice hole among the reeds. With the river frozen, prey was growing scarce, and he'd promised Cedarpelt he'd find some minnows before he settled down to share tongues with his Clanmates. Leaving his catch, he scrambled, skidding, for the shore. Snow flumped down from the bulrushes as he pushed among the thawing stems.

What did Hailstar want? The sun was sinking, turning the pale sky pink. Crookedpaw ached all over, sore from a night's training with Mapleshade and stiff from spending the day hunting birds in the willow copse with Cedarpelt. At least it looked as though the cold weather was loosening its grip. In the two nights since the Gathering, the air had lost its aching chill. The river would be flowing again soon. He slithered from the reeds and hurried over the softening snow to the edge of the clearing.

Oakheart trotted to meet him. "There you are!"

"What's up?" Crookedpaw glanced at Hailstar. The RiverClan leader paced the head of the clearing, hackles high. His eyes glittered. Shellheart stood behind him, tail flicking stiffly.

Oakheart ducked close to Crookedpaw. "I don't know. Hailstar's been meeting with Shellheart, Rippleclaw, and Timberfur all afternoon."

Rippleclaw and Timberfur sat like rocks at the side of the clearing. Timberfur blinked, his gaze unreadable. Rippleclaw was coolly watching a blackbird flitting from bush to bush on the far bank.

"They even called for Brambleberry," Oakheart whispered.

"Is someone sick?"

Oakheart shrugged. "Birdsong's got a cough and Brightsky's been sneezing since the Gathering, but that's all."

Beetlenose padded lazily from the fallen tree. Petaldust raced past him and stopped beside Crookedpaw. "What's happening?"

Beetlenose caught up. "Maybe he's going to change Crookedpaw's name again," he suggested. "To Scarpaw." He stared at Crookedpaw's muzzle. "You seem to have a fresh scratch every day."

Crookedpaw shrugged. "I train hard."

Voleclaw darted from the dirtplace tunnel. "What did I miss?" he panted.

"Nothing yet," Petaldust reassured him. "The Clan's still gathering."

Troutclaw and Tanglewhisker had reached the clearing. Birdsong peered from the elders' den, her eyes bright with fever. Dens rattled around the fallen tree as Rainflower, Echomist, and Mudfur slid out. Lakeshine, Softwing, and Shimmerpelt clustered together at the edge of the clearing, ears pricked. Piketooth, Owlfur, and Ottersplash paced beside them. Cedarpelt slid from the sedges, his fur ruffled, padded across the clearing, and sat beside Whitefang.

Brambleberry crouched outside Fallowtail's den. "Come on," she coaxed. "RiverClan needs all its warriors."

Fallowtail poked her head out. "What's going on?"

"Come and hear." Brambleberry guided her to the edge of the clearing and nodded to Hailstar.

"We saw ThunderClan at the Gathering," the RiverClan leader began. "Leaf-bare has left them hungry, as usual." Murmurs of satisfaction rumbled around the clearing. "They look weak," Hailstar continued, "while we are strong. At sunset, we take back Sunningrocks!"

Owlfur twitched his ears. "How? Are we just going to move the markers again?"

Hailstar lashed his tail. "We'll do more than that! The only markers we'll leave will be ThunderClan's blood!"

"About time!" Ottersplash called.

Whitefang, hardly visible against the snow, showed his teeth. "I'll shred any ThunderClan cat I get my claws on!"

Hailstar nodded to the white warrior. "ThunderClan won't forget this day."

"What's the plan?" Lakeshine asked.

"A battle patrol will occupy Sunningrocks and wait for ThunderClan."

"What if they don't come?" Shimmerpelt meowed.

"They'll come." Rippleclaw stepped forward. "ThunderClan always acts strong when they're too weak to fight."

Timberfur plucked at the ground. "It'll be an easy victory."

"One we deserve!" Hailstar's eyes blazed. "We've put up with ThunderClan's arrogance for long enough. Sunningrocks is ours."

The Clan's cheer sent Rippleclaw's blackbird panicking into the sky.

Beetlenose reared and swiped at the air. "I'm going to bring home some ThunderClan fur."

Petaldust bristled. "We've never fought before," she mewed.

Crookedpaw nudged her. "But we've trained," he reminded her. "We know what to do."

Petaldust lifted her chin. "I'll fight to the death if I have to."

Cedarpelt turned his head. "Don't be silly," he meowed sharply. "We're fighting to defend *territory*, not our Clan."

Whitefang purred. "I remember my first battle," he sighed. "I was ready to take on every cat in WindClan."

"Were you scared?" Petaldust's eyes widened.

"Of course!" Whitefang wrapped his tail over his paws. "I'm not stupid. Battles are dangerous."

Cedarpelt nodded. "Just remember the warrior code and you'll be fine."

Beetlenose sniffed. "Let's hope *ThunderClan* remembers the

warrior code," he meowed. "They didn't let it stop them from attacking WindClan in their nests."

"Shellheart." Hailstar nodded to his deputy. "Call the names of the cats who will join the battle patrol."

Shellheart lift his chin. "Timberfur, Rippleclaw, Owlfur, Ottersplash." The warriors padded to the head of the clearing. Crookedpaw leaned forward as his father went on.

"Oakheart, Beetlenose, Petaldust, Whitefang, Shimmerpelt, Softwing."

Crookedpaw watched his brother pad away.

"Piketooth, Rainflower, Voleclaw, Cedarpelt, and Crookedpaw."

Crookedpaw lashed his tail excitedly and darted after Cedarpelt.

"Wait!" Brambleberry blocked his path. "Please stay here!" The medicine cat's eyes were dark with worry.

"Why?" Crookedpaw stared at her, bewildered. "I'm strong now! You said it yourself. *Bigger* than Beetlenose! And my jaw is as strong as a pike's!"

She shook her head. "Please stay in camp."

"And miss my first battle?" Beetlenose and Oakheart were already heading out of camp. He had to catch up!

Brambleberry looked away, her fur spiking. Crookedpaw narrowed his eyes. "You don't have to worry about me anymore. I'm ready for this. I'm not staying behind," he growled. He *had* to go. He'd promised Mapleshade he'd fight for his Clan above everything. This was his first chance to prove he had the makings of a great leader. He marched past Brambleberry and ducked through the sedge tunnel.

Outside camp, the patrol was pounding along the shore. As Crookedpaw jumped down the bank he saw them head out on to the ice. He caught up with them as they crossed the frozen river, his claws throwing up a shower of sparkling crystals, and stopped beside them at the foot of Sunningrocks, where snow drifted against the stone.

"Ready?" Hailstar surveyed the patrol, eyes dark.

"Ready," Shellheart answered for them.

Crookedpaw's belly tightened. He flexed his claws as his Clanmates started to climb the rock face.

Cedarpelt ran his tail along Crookedpaw's spine. "Be careful and remember what I taught you."

And everything Mapleshade taught me! He hoped she was watching. He'd show her what a great leader he was going to be.

"Good luck." Cedarpelt swarmed up the rock.

Crookedpaw reached up and hooked his claws into a crack. Pushing off with his hind legs, he swung himself up, catching the next clawhold and the next until he'd reached the top of the rock. The fiery glare of the setting sun lit the stone. Beyond Sunningrocks stood the forest, dark and silent. Crookedpaw hauled himself over the edge and joined his Clanmates. They wove restlessly around one another, their growls echoing on the rock.

Rainflower caught his eye. "I've asked Oakheart to keep an eye on you."

"No need." Crookedpaw turned away, avoiding her gaze, frightened at the coldness he might find there. Then he stiffened. A bush trembled between the trees below the rocks. Had they been spotted?

Hailstar nodded to Shellheart. "Prepare the battle line." His gaze swept over Beetlenose, Petaldust, and Voleclaw. "This is your first battle." He glanced at Oakheart and Crookedpaw. "This won't be the only opportunity you get to prove you are great warriors. Don't take any chances and good luck."

Shellheart flicked his tail and RiverClan spread out along the rock. Crookedpaw backed into place between Oakheart and Shimmerpelt. He glanced down the line, pride rising in his chest. The RiverClan warriors stood, pelts bushed, the setting sun firing their fur till they shone like StarClan warriors. Hailstar walked along the line, which straightened as he passed. Then he took his place in the middle and glared into the shadowy trees. Crookedpaw pricked his ears. Paws were thrumming the forest floor.

Oakheart's claws scratched the stone. "Good luck, Crookedpaw," he breathed.

Shimmerpelt's pelt spiked. "They're coming."

The thrumming grew louder, like wind roaring through branches. Crookedpaw swallowed as the ThunderClan patrol broke from the trees. Eyes blazing, fur spiked, they pulsed rage.

In the middle of battle, there's no time to think. Cedarpelt's words rang in his mind. *You just react.* Now he understood. His fur bushed and a hiss rose in his throat as the ThunderClan patrol faced RiverClan.

Hailstar stepped forward. "An ancient wrong has been put

right!" he yowled. "These rocks are ours again."

Pinestar padded up the sloping rock, his eyes no more than slits. "Never." He drew back his lips. "ThunderClan, attack!"

As ThunderClan surged forward, Pinestar lunged for Hailstar and the two leaders fell, rolling, across the stone. Oakheart plunged into the snarling, spitting mass of warriors, breaking through and turning on a black-and-white tom, a yowl of fury piercing the battle cries. Crookedpaw pressed his ears flat, shocked by the shrieks as fear and rage merged. He spun around as his Clanmates fell tumbling into combat. Confused and scared, he had no idea where to start.

Then paws slammed into him, sending him rolling. Twisting, his claws scraped the rock. He found his paws, but only for a moment. A vicious blow to the cheek sent him spinning. Rage flared in his belly. Mapleshade's mew sounded in his ear.

Fight!

He turned and reared up. A ginger tom spat at him, back arched, paw raised, ready to deal another mighty blow. Crookedpaw knocked his paw aside and swiped the tom's muzzle with such force it sent them both reeling backward. Staggering on his hind paws, Crookedpaw felt the rock disappear from underneath him. With a yelp, he fell, stone scraping his pelt as he tumbled down the side of Sunningrocks and landed in the snow beneath. Stiff with shock, he fought for breath.

Frog dung!

Anger pulsed in his paws. He looked up the sheer rock face.

The pink sky arced above, strangely calm above the shriek of battle. He had to help his Clanmates! He darted along the foot of the rock, skidding around the corner to where he knew he'd find enough paw holds to haul himself up. A blue-gray pelt blocked his way. ThunderClan stench bathed his tongue.

An enemy warrior! He stumbled to a halt as the ThunderClan cat whirled to face him. *Bluepaw!* Was that relief in her eyes?

"Thank StarClan," she sighed.

What would Mapleshade say? *The other Clans are no more than dust and beetles!* This was his chance to prove he was loyal to RiverClan above *everything*. So *what* if he'd spoken to this cat at a Gathering? There was no truce now. "You're on our territory!" Crookedpaw dropped into a crouch, eyes narrowed to slits. "We're enemies now," he hissed.

Bluepaw blinked. She was *surprised!* *Dumb cat!*

Crookedpaw sprang forward and knocked her into the snow. Before she could move, he grabbed her shoulders and churned his hind paws against her spine. Yowling, she twisted her head back, clamping her jaws around his forepaw. She bit down hard. Crookedpaw yelped. He kicked her away, pain searing his paw. Bluepaw tumbled screeching down the shore toward the icy river. Crookedpaw licked at his wound, the fierce sting of it making him feel sick. Then he heard snow swish and saw a flash of blue fur.

Bluepaw crashed into him with a howl of rage. Shocked, he staggered, and Bluepaw spun around and nipped his hind leg.

She turned again and nipped his forepaw, then reared up and lunged at him, sinking her teeth deep into his scruff.

You snake-heart! Energy shot like lightning through Crookedpaw. She was trying to drag him backward. *Stupid furball!* He dug in his claws and thrashed his head from side to side. Flinging her off, he turned and spat. "Don't expect mercy from me!"

Panic lit her eyes and she reared up again, swiping blindly. He had her! Lifting his forepaws, he met her blow for blow. She staggered, trying to balance, while he kept swiping steadily, using the move he'd practiced over and over until it seemed as easy as fishing. She caught his muzzle with a claw but he hit back, slicing her ear, feeling it tear beneath his claws.

Run away!

He knew he could beat her back to ThunderClan land if he wanted. A yowl sounded behind them.

"Snowpaw!" Bluepaw's eyes sparked as her sister darted beside her.

Crookedpaw growled as Snowpaw plunged forward and began swiping alongside her Clanmate. Fielding blows from two pairs of paws, Crookedpaw fought harder. But the blows kept coming, relentless and fast. His hind legs began to weaken. His muscles screamed to stop. Claws raked his muzzle, then his ears, then his cheek. The flurry of paws was too fast to match. He started to back away, his hind paws slipping on the snow. Then Snowpaw ducked and bit his hind leg. It collapsed beneath him.

"Frog-dung!" Crookedpaw dropped on to all fours, growling, and lunged for the two cats, trying to get between them and split their attack. But Snowpaw darted underneath him. Pain ripped his belly as she raked him with thorn-sharp claws. More claws sank into his shoulders. Bluepaw was on his back. Panic rising, he tried to shake her off while scrambling away from Snowpaw. But Snowpaw rolled and knocked out his hind legs. Tumbling, Crookedpaw yowled with rage. Bluepaw was clinging on like a burr. He felt his pelt shredding beneath her churning paws as he rolled down the bank. Agony gripped him, blood roaring in his ears. Flinging Bluepaw off, he dived for the frozen river and hurtled across the ice. Racing for the bank he exploded through the bushes, relieved to smell RiverClan scent bathe his tongue.

A yowl split the air. "Forward, ThunderClan!"

Bluepaw and Snowpaw were staring up at Sunningrocks, ears pricked with excitement. They ducked against the rock as RiverClan warriors began to plunge down the cliff and charge across the river. Crookedpaw watched in shock as Hailstar hurtled past him, leaving blood in his trail. Ottersplash and Shimmerpelt thundered after him, the rest of the patrol at their heels.

RiverClan is retreating?

Shellheart, Rippleclaw, and Timberfur were pounding the ice on the far side of the river, smashing it with their hind paws. As Crookedpaw stared, they broke open a channel of icy water and swam hard for the far shore. ThunderClan streamed down the rocks in pursuit, slithering to a clumsy halt at the edge of the racing water. The broken ice meant there was no way for them to follow.

"Mouse-hearts!" a mottled warrior growled as Shellheart dived through the bushes on RiverClan's side of the river.

"Crookedpaw?" Shellheart pulled up sharply. "Are you okay?" Crookedpaw straightened and lifted his chin. "I'm fine."

Shellheart frowned. "You must have fought like a warrior." He leaned forward and licked Crookedpaw's blood-soaked cheek. Crookedpaw ducked away, wincing.

"Come on." Shellheart nudged him toward camp. "You're going to need some herbs on those scratches."

"You ordered us to retreat!" Rippleclaw stared, dumbfounded, at Shellheart. "How could you do that?"

Shellheart was padding among his Clanmates, checking injuries, doling out praise and encouragement to the battered warriors. Dawn colored the sky and birds were beginning to sing in the bushes outside camp. Crookedpaw crouched beside Oakheart, his pain easing as Brambleberry's herbs soaked into his wounds.

"We had no choice," Shellheart meowed.

Timberfur shifted, wincing, on to his other side. "But Hailstar told us ThunderClan was weak."

"We were *winning*!" Lakeshine paused from smoothing her long gray-and-white fur. It was smeared with blood and fragments of herb.

Whitefang sighed. "If only Stormtail hadn't turned up with a second patrol—"

Rippleclaw cut him off. "Why didn't Hailstar think of that?"

"He's not a mind reader," Shellheart snapped.

Timberfur growled. "But he's a leader. Leaders should know how to win battles." He glared toward the medicine den.

Hailstar's wounds had been deep. When Brambleberry couldn't stop the bleeding in the clearing, Shellheart and Owlfur had carried the half-conscious leader to her den.

"Shut up!" Petaldust's eyes flared. A long scratch traced from her forehead to her muzzle, and her tortoiseshell pelt was clumped with blood. "Hailstar could be losing a life!"

Crookedpaw got to his paws. His wounds burned like fire.

Oakheart looked up. "Where are you going?"

"I want to take fresh-kill to Brambleberry." He glanced at his paws. Truthfully, he was more interested in finding out how Hailstar was so he could reassure Petaldust and Voleclaw. They were clearly worried about their father. Even Beetlenose wasn't boasting for a change. "She's been busy all night. She must be hungry."

"But the fresh-kill pile's empty," Oakheart pointed out.

"I know where there are some minnows." He padded carefully through the reed bed. The ice creaked beneath his paws. It would be gone in a day or so. He quickly caught a few minnows in his jaws. Back on shore, he crossed the clearing.

Rainflower was licking her wounds. She looked up as he

passed. "Well done, Crookedpaw," she meowed, and returned to her washing.

Crookedpaw's fur prickled with surprise. Rainflower had praised him! His heart lifted. Ducking through the sedge tunnel into Brambleberry's den, he dropped the fish at the medicine cat's paws. "How is he?"

Hailstar lay curled in a nest beside the wall of the den. Echomist sat beside him, lapping his pelt. The RiverClan leader's fur was dull and matted, his flanks hardly moving.

"He's stopped bleeding," Brambleberry murmured. "But he lost a lot of blood."

Echomist stiffened. "He's not breathing!"

Brambleberry darted to the nest and pressed her ear to Hailstar's flank. She sat up slowly. Crookedpaw shivered as silence gripped the den. Brambleberry broke it with a sigh as Hailstar took a sudden shuddering gasp. "He lost a life," she mewed softly.

Echomist's eyes glistened. "Then he's on his ninth," she breathed.

Brambleberry touched the she-cat's cheek with her muzzle. "I'm afraid so." She glanced at Crookedpaw. "You'd better go."

Crookedpaw nodded and headed for the entrance.

"Thanks for the fish," Brambleberry called after him.

Crookedpaw squeezed into the clearing. Rainflower was padding stiffly to her den. Oakheart rested his nose on his paws, his eyes closed. Tanglewhisker was carrying a lump of snow in his jaws. He dropped it beside Shimmerpelt, who began lapping at it thirstily. None of them knew that their leader had lost a life in the failed battle for Sunningrocks, just as Petaldust feared. It wasn't Crookedpaw's place to tell them; Brambleberry would do that, or Hailstar himself, once he had recovered.

If only I'd fought better! Mapleshade will never believe I'm worthy of being Clan leader now. Crookedpaw felt a rush of frustration. *Next time I'll fight like a StarClan warrior. Next time, I won't let my Clan down!*

CHAPTER 15

"Stop!" Mapleshade yowled.

"But I haven't done it perfectly yet!" Crookedpaw lunged forward again, his belly brushing the ground. He twisted, thrusting out his hind paws with a grunt of effort. In the days since the battle he'd practiced harder than ever.

Mapleshade ignored him. *"Stop!"*

"I have to get this right." Crookedpaw scrambled to his paws. "I'm never going to be beaten again!"

"You must wake up, Crookedpaw!" Mapleshade hissed. "Something's happening."

Crookedpaw stared at her in alarm. "Is the Clan in trouble?"

"Wake up!"

Crookedpaw blinked open his eyes. He scrambled to his paws, heart racing. The apprentices' den was dark. He could hardly see the walls. Paws pricking, he slipped into the clearing and looked up at the sky. The moon was no more than a claw scratch. Dawn was lighting the distant moorland. The thaw, which had followed the defeat at Sunningrocks, had left the camp muddy. The reeds drooped, feigning death. The snow had melted, revealing moss once more. It squelched underpaw as Crookedpaw padded toward the reed bed. He peered through the stiff stems, tasting the air. Hailstar's scent hung there, Timberfur's, too. Crookedpaw followed their trail, picking out the fresh scent of Ottersplash, Owlfur, and Rippleclaw as he neared a gap in the sedge. They'd left camp recently.

Crookedpaw ducked, ready to follow. Just then, a screech tore the air. Bristling, Crookedpaw spun around. It had come from the other side of the river. A yowl followed it.

Ottersplash!

Crookedpaw darted across the clearing and leaped onto the fallen tree. Weaving past the dens, he headed along the jutting branch until he was above the reeds. His gaze followed the sliding river far upstream to the distant bank. Ottersplash and Owlfur were pelting down the slope from WindClan territory. They skimmed the low bushes with long strides. Rippleclaw and Timberfur followed. Dark bundles swung from their jaws. Crookedpaw's heart skipped a beat as he heard mewling.

The kits! They had the kits!

Hailstar pounded after them, a WindClan warrior spitting at his heels. *Reedfeather!* Crookedpaw recognized the bristling pelt. Four snarling Clanmates sped alongside him. Timberfur and Rippleclaw were nearing the river. Crookedpaw gripped the bark under his claws, as the camp stirred behind him.

"What's happening?"

"Who's yowling?"

Dens rustled and paws hurried over wet moss. Oakheart

scuttled along the branch and crouched behind him. "What is it?"

"Just watch!" Crookedpaw kept his gaze fixed on the fleeing patrol.

"Get into the river!" Hailstar's yowl rang loud in the dawn air. Timberfur and Rippleclaw sprang off the shore and plunged into the shallows.

Willowkit squealed. "It's cold!"

"Help!" Graykit was shrieking.

Hailstar slowed and turned to face Reedfeather. The WindClan warrior stopped a whisker from Hailstar's nose. His Clanmates charged past him to the river's edge. "You can't steal my kits!"

Hailstar glanced over his shoulder, toward Rippleclaw and Timberfur who stood belly deep in the water. His eyes lit with triumph. "We already have!"

Spitting, Reedfeather struck the RiverClan leader with a blow so fierce it sent him crashing against a rock. Crookedpaw's breath stopped. Hailstar lay still. *Get up! Get up!* Had the RiverClan leader given his final life to save the kits?

Reedfeather charged for the shore, following his Clanmates. He paused at the river's edge as the others waded in, snarling. Ottersplash and Owlfur turned in the shallows and met their pursuers with a flurry of vicious swipes. Knocking one WindClan warrior back, Owlfur spun around and sent another floundering out of his depth with a mighty blow. Ottersplash dived under the belly of a dark tabby tom and sent him lurching off balance with a heave of her shoulders.

As their Clanmates held off WindClan, Rippleclaw and Timberfur plunged toward RiverClan, necks stretched as they held the kits above water.

Reedfeather stared wildly as the RiverClan warriors staggered from the river and dropped the kits on the marshy bank. His Clanmates struggled back to shore on the WindClan side and hauled themselves out. Reedfeather turned to them in dismay. "We can't give up! Those are my kits!" Without waiting for an answer, he whirled around and leaped into the river. "Give them back!" he screeched.

Behind him, Hailstar moved. He struggled to his paws and pelted after Reedfeather. With a grunt of effort, he jumped onto the WindClan deputy's back, sending him flailing forward into the river.

As Reedfeather surfaced, spluttering, Hailstar lunged forward with his front paws outstretched and thrust the WindClan warrior beneath the water. His eyes glowed, reflecting the rising sun, as he held Reedfeather down. The other WindClan warriors backed away up the slope, their eyes as round as owls'.

Bubbles rose around Hailstar's paws. Reedfeather was fighting for his life.

Let him go! Crookedpaw leaned forward, trembling. *Don't kill him! The kits are safe!*

"Hailstar? Hailstar! Stop!" Owlfur splashed to his leader's side. "You're killing him."

Hailstar gazed at his Clanmates, dazed. He released his grip and staggered backward. Owlfur tugged at Reedfeather's pelt. "Help me get him out!" he spluttered.

Hailstar darted forward and grabbed Reedfeather's scruff. Together they dragged him to the shore on WindClan's side. Weak with relief, Crookedpaw hurried toward the kits.

Rippleclaw pressed against Willowkit while Timberfur lapped at Graykit's dripping fur. The kits' gaze was fixed on the far shore where Hailstar and Owlfur leaned over their father's limp body.

"Is he dead?" Willowkit wailed.

Owlfur began to rub Reedfeather's chest.

"Should I get Brambleberry?" Crookedpaw offered.

Rippleclaw looked up, his eyes dark. "It'd be too late."

Suddenly Reedfeather coughed, twisting and vomiting river water.

"He's alive!" Willowkit's eyes shone. Then she turned and stared at Crookedpaw. "Is he going to take us home now?"

"This is your home!" Fallowtail exploded out of the reeds. She skidded to a stop and stared, huge-eyed, at her kits. "You've grown," she breathed. "You've grown so big." Her mew cracked.

"Fallowtail!" Graykit ducked away from Timberfur and raced to her mother, rubbing her muzzle along Fallowtail's jaw and purring loud enough to wake the birds. Willowkit rushed to join her, tucking herself under Fallowtail's belly. On the far shore, the WindClan warriors were helping Reedfeather up the slope. His drenched fur clung to his bony shape, and he was limping badly.

Owlfur slid into the water and swam toward home.

Hailstar followed. Crookedpaw shivered. Just for a moment, Hailstar had wanted to kill Reedfeather. Not for his own sake—Reedfeather had done nothing to him personally—but for the sake of his Clan, because Hailstar truly believed the kits belonged to RiverClan. *Will I ever fight like that?*

A voice breathed in Crookedpaw's ear.

Mapleshade!

Her mew was fierce. *One day it will be your turn to show your Clan you are worthy of being their leader, Crookedpaw. I have faith in you, young warrior.*

CHAPTER 16

"Willowpaw! Graypaw!"

The cheers of the Clan rang in the golden morning air as they welcomed their newest apprentices. Fallowtail called loudest of all, her blue eyes misting. Crookedpaw purred. At last he'd have denmates!

Willowpaw stood in the center of the clearing; her amber eyes shone and her pale tabby coat reflected the rising sun. Her mentor, Owlfur, touched his white-splashed muzzle to Willowpaw's head while Brightsky padded proudly around her first apprentice, Graypaw.

Hailstar stepped back, chin high. "WindClan's loss is our gain!"

In the two moons since the RiverClan leader had led the patrol to rescue RiverClan's youngest members, newleaf had furred the stark branches of the willows with soft green buds. The reeds had lifted their snow-crushed fronds and were thick with new growth. And the river was beginning to lose its biting chill.

"What are we going to do first?" As the Clan began to return to its duties, Willowpaw stared excitedly at Owlfur.

Owlfur glanced conspiratorially at Cedarpelt.

"What?" Crookedpaw knew when his mentor was keeping a secret. Cedarpelt's pelt was pricking. Purring, the brown warrior padded toward Owlfur.

Crookedpaw scampered after him. "Is something going on?"

"We're going to the Moonstone to share with StarClan," Cedarpelt told him. "I wanted to take you there before, but I thought you'd prefer to share the experience with denmates."

I have denmates! Crookedpaw circled his mentor excitedly. *And we're going to the Moonstone!*

Graypaw pricked her ears. "*We're* going, too?"

Cedarpelt nodded. "Yes."

"Really?" Willowpaw's gaze glittered anxiously. "It'll mean traveling through WindClan territory," she mewed. "What if they steal us back?"

Crookedpaw cocked his head, surprised. "Would you let them?"

"Of course not!" Willowpaw lashed her tail.

Graypaw fluffed out her fur. "WindClan follows the warrior code, okay?" she reminded her sister. "They'd never stop us from traveling to the Moonstone." She and Willowpaw exchanged a glance and Crookedpaw wondered what memories they were sharing. They'd seemed happy to return to their mother's Clan, but they never criticized WindClan, who had cared for and nurtured them for a whole moon.

"It must have been disgusting," Beetlenose had goaded them, more than once. "Eating rabbit."

Even Voleclaw had joined in. "Weren't you cold?" he wondered. "How could a *heather* den keep out the wind? Especially up on the moorland. It never stops up there."

But Graypaw and Willowpaw had just shrugged. "They treated us well, but we're glad to be home," was all they'd ever say.

Crookedpaw respected their careful silence.

"Ignore him," he told them. "Beetlenose likes to get under other cats' pelts."

He'd settled down beside Willowkit one evening, while the Clan was sharing tongues. Beetlenose had been calling her *rabbit-breath* all afternoon and her pelt was still spiked. "When I was on the farm, I hunted mice," he told her quietly. "I got so used to the taste it was hard eating fish again." He wanted her to know that he understood what it felt like to come back, to have her loyalty questioned. "Even Oakheart teased me about being more like a ThunderClan cat than a RiverClan cat."

She blinked at him. "Really?"

"Really." He purred and touched his muzzle to her ear. "Don't worry. They'll get over it."

But that was last moon. Now, he was just glad they were 'paws—not only because he'd have denmates but because they'd have a chance to show their loyalty to their true Clan.

"When are we leaving?" He paced around Cedarpelt.

"Go to Brambleberry," Cedarpelt ordered. "She has traveling herbs ready for you."

Graypaw screwed up her nose.

"You'll be thankful for them by sunhigh," Owlfur told her.

"We have a long way to go."

Crookedpaw raced for Brambleberry's den, but Willowpaw darted ahead of him and slipped through the entrance first. Three piles of herbs were laid out on the den floor.

Brambleberry was pulling stale supplies from a gap in the reeds. "I'm glad newleaf's here," she muttered. "There's hardly any goodness left in this coltsfoot, and we'll be needing poppy seeds before long."

Crookedpaw sniffed at one of the herb piles she'd prepared. It smelled sour. "Do we have to chew them or can we just swallow them whole?"

Brambleberry dropped a pawful of shrivelled mallow on the floor. "Swallow them whole," she advised. "It'll slow down their effect till you really need it."

Closing his eyes, Crookedpaw gulped down the herbs. He shuddered. Even without chewing they left a bitter taste on his tongue.

"Yuck!" Graypaw made a face as she swallowed hers.

Willowpaw winced but didn't complain. "How far is it to the Moonstone?" she asked Brambleberry when she'd licked her lips.

"You'll be there by nightfall if you keep up a good pace." Brambleberry shrugged. "The journey's nothing once you get used to it." She traveled it every half-moon with the other medicine cats to share tongues with StarClan. "The worst bit is Mothermouth." Her pelt rippled. "It's very dark, and you need to trust StarClan to guide your paws." She blinked at the three apprentices. "Stay close to your mentors."

Willowpaw wrapped her tail tight around her forepaws. "What's the Moonstone like?"

"Are StarClan cats friendly?" Graypaw added. "Even the warriors from other Clans?"

"The Moonstone is beautiful." Brambleberry sighed. "And StarClan is wise." Her gaze fixed on Crookedpaw. "Listen carefully to what they tell you," she warned. "Let them guide your paws onto the right path."

Crookedpaw swallowed. Why had she singled him out? Did she think his paws were on the wrong path?

"Hurry up." Brambleberry began to herd them toward the entrance. "You need to get there by moonhigh."

"Why?" Graypaw mewed as Brambleberry nosed her from the den.

Brambleberry turned back to her supplies. "You'll see."

Cedarpelt, Brightsky, and Owlfur were waiting by the entrance. Crookedpaw hurried to join them. "Don't you need herbs?"

"We had some earlier," Brightsky explained.

Owlfur nodded to Willowpaw. "Are you ready?"

"Yes." Her voice suddenly sounded very small. Was she overwhelmed, traveling all the way to the Moonstone on her first day as an apprentice?

Crookedpaw felt a surge of excitement. He'd traveled part of this journey before, but now he wasn't alone. He was with his Clanmates. And if he had a chance to dream at the Moonstone, he'd probably meet the whole of StarClan and not just Mapleshade.

* * *

The cats kept to the edge of WindClan territory, wary of patrols.

"I know WindClan has honorable warriors," Cedarpelt told Graypaw. "But there's no need to stir up memories by marching you right past their camp."

Crookedpaw couldn't help wondering if it was WindClan's memories or Graypaw's that Cedarpelt was frightened of stirring up. He was relieved when they reached the WindClan scent line. Beyond it, the world seemed to open like a water lily. The wide valley between the moors and Highstones was green with newleaf growth. The sun warmed Crookedpaw's back as they padded along the hedgerows that bordered the Twoleg meadows. From time to time, he recognized a familiar scent on his tongue, and for the first time in moons he longed to taste mouse.

"Crookedpaw!" Cedarpelt's call startled him.

He suddenly realized that he'd veered off the track they'd been following and was staring through a beech hedge into a furrowed field of mud.

"Keep up!" Cedarpelt ordered.

Crookedpaw raced after his Clanmates. Was that Mitzi's cornfield? He glanced sideways through the hedge as he caught up with Willowpaw. Where was the golden corn? Then he remembered the giant corn-eating monster and bristled.

Willowpaw looked at him. "Are you okay? It must be weird, coming back here after so long."

"I'm fine."

She slowed her pace and they fell behind the others. "You're thinking about Fleck, aren't you?"

"Weren't *you* thinking about WindClan when you were traveling through the moorland?" he countered.

Her gaze flicked away. "Is there anything wrong with that?"

Crookedpaw sighed. "It's possible to care about cats outside the Clan and be loyal."

"Is it?"

"Crookedkit!" A loud mew made them both turn.

A black cat stood a few tail-lengths behind them on the track.

"*Soot?*" Crookedpaw gasped.

The young she-cat ran toward him. She was as big as Willowpaw now. "I didn't think you'd come back!"

"We're going to the Moonstone," Crookedpaw explained.

Cedarpelt's growl rumbled behind them. "What's going on?"

Crookedpaw whirled around, heart lurching. Was Cedarpelt going to chase Soot off?

"I-it's just a cat I knew when . . ." He stammered to a halt as Cedarpelt glowered at him.

"Wow!" Soot breathed. "A real warrior!" She stared at Cedarpelt. "You're so big." Her green eyes were wide.

Cedarpelt growled softly.

Crookedpaw stood between his mentor and Soot and met Cedarpelt's gaze. "She's hardly more than a kit." There was a warning in his mew. "She's not doing any harm."

Cedarpelt narrowed his eyes. "Don't be long," he muttered, and stalked back to where Owlfur, Brightsky, and Graypaw were waiting farther up the track. "Leave them alone, Willowpaw!" he called. "It's bad enough having one apprentice hanging out with farm cats."

Crookedpaw ignored the jibe. "How are you?" he purred to Soot. "How are Fleck and Mitzi? And Piper and Magpie and Mist?"

"Fleck's fine!" Soot wound around Crookedpaw, brushing against him and purring. "So are Mitzi and Piper." Then she paused. "I *think* Mist and Magpie are okay. Some Twolegs came and took them away. Fleck says they were going to catch mice on another farm. What about you? Are you a warrior yet?"

Crookedpaw shook his head. "No, but I'm an apprentice. I'm Crooked*paw* now."

Soot blinked. "Is that good?"

"It's *great!*"

"Hurry up!" Cedarpelt called.

"I've got to go." Crookedpaw felt a tug in his chest.

"I'll tell Fleck and Mitzi I saw you," Soot promised. "They'll be pleased you're okay."

"Tell them I said . . ." He reached for the right words, something that would let them know he missed them and he was grateful but he was also happy to be back with his Clan.

Soot's eyes glowed. "I understand," she mewed. "I'll tell them."

Cedarpelt was lashing his tail. "Come *on!*"

Crookedpaw began to back away from Soot. "I'm really glad I saw you."

"Me too!" The young cat waved her tail as Crookedpaw

turned and sprinted to catch up with his Clanmates.

"Everything okay?" Willowpaw asked in a whisper as he fell in beside her.

Crookedpaw nodded, one eye on his mentor's flicking tail. *It's not up to Cedarpelt to tell me who I can be friends with! Those cats made me feel wanted when my Clanmates didn't. I'm never going to forget that.*

Highstones reared above them, the setting sun melting over its peaks. The last Thunderpath had been the hardest to cross, the gaps between monsters so narrow that Willowpaw was still trembling from the mad dash across the slippery stone. Crookedpaw forced his pelt to lie flat even though his heart was still racing. Brightsky led them quickly away from the bitter stench up toward the foot of Highstones. The earth was darker here, the grass coarser underpaw, giving way to bare, rocky soil dotted with patches of clinging heather.

"Look!" Willowpaw tilted her chin.

Crookedpaw screwed up his eyes against the sun sliding down behind the peaks. As it disappeared, the shadowed slope lightened and he could make out a square black hole yawning darkly beneath a stone archway.

Graypaw gasped. "Is that Mothermouth?"

"Yes." Owlfur climbed onto a wide, smooth stone and sat down. "But we have to wait till nearly moonhigh before we go in."

"I'm hungry," Willowpaw complained.

Brightsky shook her head. "No fish or birds here," she meowed sympathetically.

Crookedpaw pricked his ears. "There may be mice." He tasted the air. There was definitely a musky scent worth investigating.

Cedarpelt turned. "Mice?"

"They're easy to hunt," Crookedpaw enthused.

"Not as nice as fish," Brightsky meowed. "But I suppose they'll fill your belly."

"If you can catch one," Cedarpelt snorted.

Is that a challenge? Crookedpaw hurried away across the slope, ears scanning the gravelly earth for the scrabbling of tiny paws. He ducked behind a patch of heather and waited. The sky darkened and stars began to prick the sky. Crookedpaw's nose twitched.

Mouse?

He peered through the shadows. Something was shifting the pebbles farther along the slope. It *smelled* musky but was making a lot of noise for a mouse. Suddenly a pale tabby shape sped past and leaped skidding over the shale, sending pebbles cracking across the slope. Crookedpaw darted out from behind the heather and stared round-eyed as Willowpaw turned and lifted her head. A dead rabbit hung from her jaws. She carried it back to her Clanmates.

Crookedpaw stiffened. What would Owlfur say? RiverClan cats didn't catch rabbits! He followed Willowpaw and climbed up onto the rock where his Clanmates had settled. They sat staring at the dead rabbit, their fur twitching.

Willowpaw shrugged. "It's fresh-kill."

Graypaw's nostrils flared as she breathed in its warm scent.

Brightsky mewed, "I guess."

Owlfur wrapped his tail tighter around his paws. "If we're going to eat it, we should do it now." He looked up at the moon rising, fat and white, in the sky. "It's nearly time."

They shared the rabbit between them, though no one commented on the taste. Crookedpaw secretly enjoyed the rich meaty flavor but he wasn't going to admit it. Graypaw finished eating first.

"You must have been hungry." Brightsky pushed her share toward her apprentice. "You might as well have mine."

As Graypaw gulped it down, Cedarpelt stood and stretched. "Let's go." He began to pad up the slope toward Mothermouth. Owlfur fell in behind.

Brightsky got to her paws. "Come on." She nudged Graypaw, who followed her, noisily chewing her last mouthful. "Doesn't *anything* ruin your appetite?" Brightsky purred, shaking her head. "You *do* realize you're about to meet StarClan, don't you?"

Willowpaw's eyes sparkled with starlight. Crookedpaw flicked his tail down her spine. "Excited?"

Willowpaw nodded and bounded up the steep, stony slope. Crookedpaw's heart quickened as he trotted after her. As he neared the shadowy entrance, he shivered. Cold air iced with the tang of stone rolled from the mouth of the tunnel.

Cedarpelt had paused and the others clustered around him. "Ready?" He gazed at his Clanmates. They nodded but no one spoke. "Stay close." He slid into the night-black shadow.

Crookedpaw trotted after him. The tunnel sloped down

into the darkness and the cold reached through his thick fur and into his bones. This air had never felt the sun. Crookedpaw gave up straining to see anything. He could hear Brightsky's paw steps behind him and feel her breath on his tail. His whiskers brushed stone and he veered away, careful not to crash into the wall. The tunnel bent and the slope under his paws steepened.

Suddenly the dank air freshened. Crookedpaw sniffed, relieved to smell the familiar world above. He could scent earth and grass and heather. There must be a hole in the roof of the tunnel. He looked up, searching for a patch of starlight in the blackness. "Where are we?"

"We're in the Moonstone cave." Cedarpelt halted ahead of him and guided Crookedpaw forward with a flick of his tail. A distant drip echoed against the rock and he could hear his Clanmates breathing. Willowpaw's pelt brushed his and Graypaw's pads grazed the stone as they stood, waiting.

"Where is the Moonstone?" Willowpaw whispered.

Suddenly, in a flash more blinding than the setting sun, the cave lit up. Crookedpaw closed his eyes in surprise. Willowpaw recoiled against him.

"Wow!" Graypaw breathed.

Crookedpaw slowly opened his eyes. A huge rock loomed over him, glittering as though it were made of countless dewdrops.

The Moonstone!

In the cold light reflecting from the stone, he could make out the shadowy edges of a high-roofed cavern. The

Moonstone rose up from the middle of the floor, three tail-lengths high. Far above it, an opening in the roof revealed a small triangle of night sky. The moon was casting a beam of light through the hole, down onto the Moonstone, making it sparkle like a star.

Cedarpelt padded forward, his pelt bleached by the Moonstone's glow. He crouched down beside the rock and touched it with his nose. Brightsky did the same.

"Come on." Owlfur beckoned the three apprentices forward.

Crookedpaw went first. Willowpaw's breath trembled behind him. "It'll be okay," he whispered to her. He lay down beside Cedarpelt and touched his nose to the stone.

The world shifted underneath his paws. Crookedpaw let out a cry as he found himself standing in the dark forest where he trained with Mapleshade. It wasn't the usual place they met; the muddy ground here was more sloping, and the trees were more tightly packed, but it was lit by the same eerie light that came from neither stars nor moon. Crookedpaw strained to see through the shadows.

"Welcome." Mapleshade stepped out of the trees.

"Where are the other StarClan cats?" Hope fluttered in Crookedpaw's chest. He turned his head, scanning the forest.

"Why don't you look for them?" Mapleshade invited smoothly.

Crookedpaw snapped his gaze back. "Do you mean I can explore now?"

Mapleshade nodded. "But stay close to me."

Crookedpaw followed the orange-and-white warrior, his eyes wide. "Is this *really* StarClan's hunting grounds?" He frowned. What did they hunt? There was no scent of prey, only the smell of decay.

"This is where the greatest cats come after they die." Mapleshade padded up the slope. "And if you keep your promise, this is where you'll come one day."

Crookedpaw blinked. "Once I'm RiverClan's leader?"

"Not just RiverClan's leader." Mapleshade turned to face him. "The greatest leader the Clans have ever known. But only if you keep your promise."

A shadow moved between the trees at the corner of Crookedpaw's vision. He whipped his head around and saw a pelt moving through the half-light. Then he saw another, and another. Slowly he realized the forest was filled with cats padding silently through the gloom. Crookedpaw narrowed his eyes. This wasn't exactly how he'd imagined StarClan. Then he recognized a shaggy gray pelt shambling toward Mapleshade.

"Leave us alone." Mapleshade padded in front of the tom, brushing him away with her tail.

It's Goosefeather! Crookedpaw blinked in surprise as he recognized the chewed whiskers and ragged ears of the ThunderClan medicine cat. *What's he doing here? He's still alive.*

Goosefeather stood his ground. "Is this the newcomer?" His growl was rasping and deep.

Crookedpaw stared at Mapleshade. "Is Goosefeather *dead?*"

"Are *you?*" Mapleshade replied.

"I—I guess not." Crookedpaw peered past her but the old medicine cat had disappeared.

"You must go back to your Clanmates now," Mapleshade told him. "They'll be waking from their dreams."

"Is that it?" Wasn't he supposed to share tongues with his ancestors? Learn all kinds of wise stuff about being a warrior, and how to achieve his destiny? "I'm not ready!" He fought to stay, digging his claws into the slimy earth as the forest began to fade around him. "No!" He woke, bristling with frustration. The cave was black. The moon had passed and the Moonstone had faded to dull stone.

Crookedpaw stood up, surprised to find that his muscles felt stiff. Had he been lying here all night? Was that dawn light seeping through the hole in the roof? Graypaw and Brightsky were getting to their paws beside him. Cedarpelt was stretching while Owlfur paced back and forth as if he couldn't wait to leave.

"Willowpaw?" Crookedpaw mewed.

The young apprentice was snoring, her head resting against the Moonstone. Crookedpaw nudged her gently. The long journey must have worn her out. As Willowpaw opened her eyes, Crookedpaw wondered what vision she'd had. Had she met her WindClan ancestors? He shrugged. Even if Willowpaw had met every warrior in StarClan, he guessed none of them had told her she'd be the greatest leader RiverClan had ever known.

CHAPTER 17

"How was your trip to the Moonstone?"

Crookedpaw looked up from his meal as Hailstar stopped beside him. He scrambled to his paws. He felt rested after a good night's sleep though his pads were still sore. "It was great." *If only he knew! I'm going to be—*

Hailstar cut into his thoughts. "Walk with me." He led Crookedpaw out of camp and into the willow grove.

"What is it?" *Did Hailstar want to know about his vision?*

"I just thought we should talk." Hailstar stopped beside a mossy log. Soft evening light filtered through the rustling leaves. Bees hummed sleepily among the wildflowers and a blackbird was calling from the branches above their heads. "Are you enjoying your apprenticeship?" he asked.

Crookedpaw nodded. "It's great!" He guessed the RiverClan leader must have asked Oakheart, Beetlenose, Voleclaw, and Petaldust the same question when they were still 'paws.

"Your journey to becoming a warrior has taken longer than most."

"Four seasons," Crookedpaw reminded him.

"Yes." The RiverClan leader padded on, nodding. "That must seem a long time to a young cat."

"Yeah," Crookedpaw sighed.

"Are you jealous that your brother's already a warrior?"

"Jealous?" Crookedpaw blinked. "No. Oakheart's a great warrior. And I'll be a great warrior, too." He fluffed out his fur. "One day."

"Is that all you want?" Hailstar asked softly. "To become a great warrior?"

"What else is there?" Crookedpaw wondered where these questions were leading. Was Hailstar about to make him a warrior? Excitement pricked beneath his pelt. "I want to look after my Clan. That's the most important thing in the world."

"Really?" Hailstar halted and stared hard at Crookedpaw.

Crookedpaw shifted his paws. "Of course!" Did Hailstar doubt him? He'd trained harder than any apprentice!

Hailstar looked away. "Brambleberry's worried."

"What's she worried about?" What did she have to do with his apprenticeship? She mixed herbs. She didn't train warriors! Crookedpaw swallowed back his anger. "I'll do any task you want, any assessment, fight any battle to show you I can be a great warrior!"

"I'm sure you would." Hailstar narrowed his eyes. "Without doubt. But being a warrior isn't just about courage and skill and being ready to fight battles. . . ." His mew trailed away.

What is it about then? Crookedpaw stared at his leader, but the old gray cat was padding away. "What can I do to prove myself?" Crookedpaw called after him.

Hailstar didn't answer. He was slowly shaking his head, lost in his own thoughts.

What did Brambleberry tell him? Crookedpaw raced back to camp.

"Whoa!" Shellheart ducked out of his way as he charged through the sedge tunnel. "What's up?"

"Nothing." Crookedpaw stormed into the medicine den.

Brambleberry looked up from the herbs she was mixing. "Crookedpaw? Is something wrong?"

"Hailstar doubts I can be a warrior!" Crookedpaw snapped. "You told him there's something wrong with me! Is it because of my jaw?"

Brambleberry dusted the herbs from her paws. "It has nothing to do with your jaw."

"Then why did you tell Hailstar you were worried about me?"

The medicine cat glanced at her paws. "I worry about all the apprentices," she mumbled.

"Really?" Crookedpaw's tail lashed. "Is Hailstar going to ask *Willowpaw* if she's jealous of Graypaw or if she thinks there's more to being a warrior than fighting?"

Brambleberry didn't answer.

"I didn't think so," Crookedpaw growled. "So what is it? What's different about me? I always trusted you! I thought we were friends!" His belly tightened. "What am I doing wrong? You tried to stop me from fighting in the battle and you told me to listen to StarClan when I went to the Moonstone. You think there's something wrong with me, don't you?" He sat down, baffled. "Have you had an omen about me?"

He was half joking but the flash of fear in Brambleberry's eyes made him stiffen. "What was it?" he demanded. "What have you seen?"

"You wouldn't understand," she answered quickly. "Y-you have the chance to be a great warrior. . . ." She was searching for words. "Like all RiverClan cats. You just have to follow the right path."

"And I'm not following it now?" He stared at her. *But I'm training every day! And every night! I'm being taught by StarClan!* "You don't know anything!" he snapped. "If you *did* see an omen, you must have misread it! I *am* going to be a great warrior!"

He turned and stalked out of the den. He barged past Graypool, who was dragging a fish across the clearing, and raced away from the camp, hurtling blindly along the shore. Why did he bother training so hard for his Clan when they doubted him? He'd prove them wrong.

A moon passed and the days grew longer and warmer. The river had begun to teem with fresh prey and the Clan feasted in the rosy glow of the setting sun. Shimmerpelt and Piketooth were sharing tongues beside the reed bed, grooming each other's fur on the back of their necks. Whitefang was tucking into a fat carp beside them while Cedarpelt lay beside Lakeshine, his tail wrapped protectively across her swollen belly. She was expecting his kits and had given up warrior duties and moved to the nursery.

Birdsong stretched. "This would be a perfect evening for

warming my bones on Sunningrocks." The old she-cat looked wistfully out over the reed bed.

Oakheart rolled on to his back. "You can have what's left if you like." He pushed the remains of his fish toward Crookedpaw.

"I'm not hungry." Crookedpaw sat hunched, watching his Clanmates share tongues in the late-afternoon light.

Softwing was stripping flesh from a bony trout. She called to Brambleberry, who was padding from her den. "Do you want some?"

Fresh herb scent wafted around the medicine cat as she crossed the clearing. "Thanks." She settled beside Softwing. "Let me wash this water-mint off my paws first." She began nibbling at the green-tinged fur between her claws.

Crookedpaw scowled. Hailstar was lying beside Echomist, eyes half closed. Neither he nor Brambleberry had mentioned the omen again, but Crookedpaw guessed they were keeping an eye on him. He had to make them trust him. He had to prove he was loyal to RiverClan.

A dog barked in the distance. It was getting to be a familiar sound in the RiverClan camp. The dog lived on the farm beside the meadow where Twolegs came in greenleaf to live in little pelt dens, and it seemed to know that the cats were close by, almost within reach of its snapping jaws.

Crookedpaw's whiskers twitched. "Are Willowpaw and Graypaw back from training?"

"Not yet." Fallowtail padded to the entrance and peered through. "Do you think they're okay?"

Shellheart, sitting beside his den, flipped over his carp. "They're training by the beech copse."

Oakheart sat up. "The dog won't stray that far from its Twoleg nest."

"Brightsky and Owlfur are with them." Timberfur was sharing fresh-kill with Rippleclaw beneath the willow. "They'll be fine."

Crookedpaw scrambled to his paws. "Why don't we chase the dog away?"

Hailstar sat up.

Crookedpaw padded across the clearing. "We could scare it." He lashed his tail. "Shimmerpelt's fast!" His mind was whirling. "So's Softwing. They could lure it from Twolegplace into the marsh meadow. We'd be waiting for it. We'd give it a shock that it won't forget in a hurry."

The dirtplace tunnel rustled and Beetlenose padded out.

"Saving the whole Clan on your own?" he muttered as he passed Crookedpaw.

"Yeah," Crookedpaw shot back. "What've you been doing?" He ignored Beetlenose's growl. "I think it could work."

"So do I." Whitefang jumped to his paws.

Hailstar pushed away his fish and sat up. "Let's do it now."

"Now?" Cedarpelt's pelt fluffed up.

"Now." The RiverClan leader tasted the air. "Before dark." He turned to Shimmerpelt. "Are you quick enough to lure the dog toward the attack line without being caught?"

Shimmerpelt nodded. Softwing sprang to her paws. "I am, too."

"Good." Hailstar glanced around his Clan. "I'll head the attack patrol. Shellheart, you shadow Shimmerpelt and Softwing."

Shellheart showed his teeth. "If the dog gets within a whisker of them, I'll claw its eyes out."

Hailstar nodded. "Cedarpelt, Whitefang, Rippleclaw, Beetlenose, Oakheart, Ottersplash, Rainflower, and Pike-tooth, you'll join Crookedpaw in my patrol."

Fallowtail stood up. "I want to come, too."

"Fine." Hailstar swished his tail as his Clanmates gathered by the entrance; then, with a nod, he pelted out of camp.

Crookedpaw's heart was racing as they pounded along the track through the reeds. Hailstar led them up the slope and around the camp, doubling back toward the marsh meadow. They skirted the beech copse, which topped a hillock arching from the meadow like a pike's spine. Brightsky was calling instructions to Graypaw, and Crookedpaw could just see Willowpaw's ears as she peered over the top of the slope.

"Where are you going?" Her call faded behind them as they crossed the meadow, weaving between the clumps of marsh grass and sedge, their paws splashing over the boggy ground.

Crookedpaw felt Oakheart's pelt brush his. "Nice plan, Crookedpaw," he puffed, matching Crookedpaw paw step for paw step as they raced after Hailstar.

"I just hope it works." Crookedpaw saw Hailstar pull up and swerved to a halt behind him. A Twoleg fence, separating two meadows, was a few tail-lengths away. Beyond it the dog's fur flashed against the bright green grass as it darted from side to side, barking excitedly.

Hailstar weaved between Shimmerpelt and Softwing. "Are you sure you're up to this?"

Softwing flicked her tail. "Of course!"

Shimmerpelt nodded.

Shellheart padded around them. "I'll run alongside, keeping up as much I can," he promised.

Hailstar turned to Crookedpaw. "Have you thought about where the attack party should be?"

Beetlenose flexed his claws. "Why are you letting an apprentice tell *warriors* what to do?"

"It was *his* plan." Hailstar silenced the young tom with a growl.

And if it works, I won't be an apprentice for long. Crookedpaw pointed to a thicket of young willow trees behind them. "We could climb those. The leaves will hide us."

"Hide in *trees*?" Beetlenose narrowed his eyes. "Do you think we're squirrels?"

"It won't be for long," Crookedpaw urged. "And willow's soft enough to sink your claws in."

Piketooth was already heading toward the thicket. He leaped smoothly up a slim trunk and clung to one of the branches. It swayed beneath his weight, but he managed to hang on and the lush leaves hid his dark tabby pelt. "It'll work!" he called.

Fallowtail and Cedarpelt bounded after him.

"Give us time to get ready," Hailstar told Shimmerpelt and Softwing. "Then lure the dog toward us."

Crookedpaw raced to the thicket and scrambled up a willow. He sank his claws into the trembling branch. Through the leaves, he could just see the Twoleg fence. As Hailstar scrambled into place, Oakheart teetered along a wobbly branch and leaped across the small gap into Crookedpaw's tree.

"I hope this works," he muttered, swaying to keep his balance.

Crookedpaw dug his claws in harder. "It'll work." Heart in his throat, he stared at the Twoleg fence and waited for Shimmerpelt and Softwing to begin.

• Shimmerpelt slunk forward and slid under the lowest bar of the fence. Softwing's white fur flashed beside her. Keeping low, the two warriors crept up the field. Beyond them, the dog charged back and forth. Slowing to a halt, Shimmerpelt rested her tail on Softwing's spine and gave an earsplitting yowl.

Crookedpaw leaned forward, energy bursting beneath his pelt, as the dog skidded to a halt and stared down the field. Its bark faltered, then turned to a menacing growl.

Run!

The dog hurtled down the field. Shimmerpelt spun on her haunches and raced away, Softwing at her side, flying over the grass, their paws hardly touching the ground. Ducking, they shot under the fence and pelted for the willow thicket.

Come on!

The willows shivered as the attack patrol tensed. The dog squeezed under the fence and exploded into the meadow. Shimmerpelt and Softwing ran like rabbits ahead of it.

Crookedpaw glimpsed his father's gray pelt slipping like a shadow through the long grass, keeping pace alongside. A growl rumbled in Rippleclaw's throat.

"Hush!" Hailstar ordered.

Shimmerpelt and Softwing closed on the thicket, their paws thrumming the ground.

"Take him!" Softwing yowled as they shot beneath the waiting patrol.

"Ready!" Hailstar hissed as the dog neared. "Attack!"

Crookedpaw dropped and landed on his toes, back arched, pelt bushed, lips drawn back as he hissed at the dog. His Clanmates lined up beside him, a wall of spitting rage. The dog yelped and stumbled to a halt. It stared at the cats for a moment. Then, with a yelp of terror, it hurtled away, streaking across the meadow.

Fallowtail shrieked, "It's heading for the beech copse!"

Willowpaw!

Crookedpaw broke away from the warriors and pelted after the dog. It was taking a line straight for the beeches. Why wasn't it barking? Crookedpaw willed it to give some warning to Willowpaw and the others. What if they didn't hear its paw steps? He pelted after it, gaining ground as it jumped over a patch of marshy grass and bolted for the trees.

Crookedpaw's pads hit the slope. "Willowpaw!"

"Dog!" Owlfur's panicked yowl sounded from the top. Paws scrabbled on leaves and the copse exploded with shrieks and hisses.

Crookedpaw crested the slope. Graypaw, Owlfur, and

Brightsky clung halfway up the beech trunks, staring helplessly down. With a jolt of horror, Crookedpaw spotted Willowpaw. The dog had her cornered, backed up against the roots of a tree. Her eyes were wild as she flailed with her forepaws, hissing in panic.

Crookedpaw dived at the dog. He landed square on its back and sank his teeth deep into its fur. As the dog bucked, howling, beneath him, he leaped off and growled. The dog turned on him, its eyes blazing with fury. Crookedpaw backed away, pelt bushed up. *Come on, you fish-brain. Follow me!* He swiped at its muzzle, then turned and ran.

The dog pelted after him, barking with rage. Crookedpaw sped down the slope. He could see Cedarpelt and Piketooth racing toward the beech copse as he dived into the long marshy grass. The ground trembled under his paws as the dog pounded after him. Teeth snapped at his tail; hot breath bathed his heels. Pulling at the ground with his claws, Crookedpaw pushed harder, his mind blank as he hurtled blindly on. Suddenly he broke through a wall of fear scent. He'd reached his Clanmates!

"Keep running!" Hailstar screeched.

As Crookedpaw shot past them, the patrol closed ranks behind him and met the dog with a frenzy of claws and teeth. Crookedpaw pulled up, his lungs screaming as he fought to get his breath. Turning, he saw the dog flee. Oakheart led the charge after it. The patrol was driving it toward the fence, back to its home. Yelping in alarm, the dog scrabbled under the lowest bar and fled whimpering up the field.

"You saved my life!" Willowpaw's yowl made Crookedpaw spin around.

The pale tabby was racing toward him with Graypaw at her heels. She stopped in front of him, purring loudly. "I thought that dog was going to kill me!" Eyes shining, she rubbed her cheek along his twisted jaw.

Crookedpaw's pelt pricked, hot with embarrassment. "Th-that's okay," he stammered.

Suddenly Oakheart, Hailstar, and the others were crowding around.

"He saved me!" Willowpaw told them.

Her mentor Owlfur was still wide-eyed with shock. "It all happened so quickly," he explained. "I thought Willowpaw had made it up a tree and then I looked down and there she was. . . ." He trailed off, lost in thoughts of what might have happened.

"I've never seen anything braver," Brightsky cut in. "Crookedpaw actually jumped on its back!"

Fallowtail pushed past her Clanmates and pressed her muzzle against Crookedpaw's. "Thank you," she breathed. "I'd die if I lost her again."

Overwhelmed, Crookedpaw stared at his paws. "Any warrior would have done the same," he insisted. He stole a look at Hailstar. Surely he'd managed to impress the RiverClan leader this time?

Of course you have. Mapleshade's mew sounded in his ear. *Look what happens when you put your Clan first.*

* * *

"Are you sure you don't need more ointment for your paws?" Oakheart mimicked Willowpaw's mew as he followed Crookedpaw along the shore.

"Shut up." Crookedpaw fluffed out his pelt, hoping it would cool him down. The newleaf sun was hot.

Oakheart took no notice. "But they must be sooooo sore after chasing that dog and rescuing me."

Crookedpaw waded into the river, ignoring his brother.

"Graypaw says she's going to move her nest next to yours," Oakheart persisted.

Cool water flooded his ears as Crookedpaw dived under the surface. He swam strongly, following the dip of the riverbed, using his tail to balance him against the buffeting current. Eyes open, he could see a fat trout basking on the bottom. With a kick of his hind legs he shot forward, snapping his teeth around the trout and pushing upward toward daylight. He broke the surface with a splash, the trout flapping between his jaws. With a flick of his head, he snapped its spine and the fish drooped instantly.

"Nice catch." Oakheart was sitting on the shore, washing his face.

Crookedpaw climbed out and dropped the fish beside his brother. "Aren't you fishing?"

"I thought I'd let you get the best catch first," Oakheart teased.

Crookedpaw nudged him playfully, unbalancing him. Tumbling on to his side, Oakheart purred, "It's not *really* serious between you and Willowpaw, is it?"

"Who said it was?" Crookedpaw stared at him in surprise.

"The whole Clan's been gossiping since sunhigh," Oakheart told him.

Crookedpaw snorted. "They're like a bunch of elders." He shook out the water from his fur. "Willowpaw's just a denmate."

"Nothing more?"

"No!" Willowpaw was nice. And there was something special about her. But it was embarrassing to talk about it. "I just like her as a *den*mate! That's not against the warrior code, is it?"

Oakpaw padded into the water. "I guess not."

Crookedpaw watched his brother dive in and disappear. He frowned. Even if he did like Willowpaw, why would she like him? He had a twisted jaw that made other cats stare. Growling irritably, Crookedpaw dived back into the river. *Who cares?* Learning to be a great warrior was far more important.

CHAPTER 18

❧

"Hey, you two!" Cedarpelt called to Crookedpaw and Willowpaw as they padded along the sun-drenched riverbank. "Slow down!"

"You don't have to keep up with us," Crookedpaw called over his shoulder. "We know where we're going and we know how to fish!"

Owlfur sighed. "Let them be."

"Why did I have to get an apprentice who thinks he knows everything?" Cedarpelt grumbled loud enough for Crookedpaw to hear over the chattering of the river.

Willowpaw brushed against Crookedpaw. "Ignore him," she whispered.

But Crookedpaw was tired of being treated like a bothersome kit. He trained as hard as any cat and if he argued with Cedarpelt over some of the moves, it was only because Mapleshade had shown him a better way. And she, after all, was a *StarClan* warrior. "Why do I have to have a mentor who thinks I'm a fish-brain?" he called back.

"Don't answer him," Owlfur advised Cedarpelt. "All apprentices think they know everything until they become warriors. He'll grow out of it."

Crookedpaw quickened his pace.

"We can't leave them behind," Willowpaw fretted.

"Why not?" Crookedpaw was bristling.

Willowpaw looked back. "It's okay," she meowed. "They sat down." She padded into the water. "Let's fish here."

"There's a deep pool in the river just past the stepping-stones," Crookedpaw told her. "It'll be full of carp hiding from the sun."

Willowpaw licked her lips. "Sounds good."

They padded downstream, side by side.

"Did you hear the news?" Willowpaw mewed.

"What?"

"Shimmerpelt's moved to the nursery."

"Shimmerpelt?" Crookedpaw nearly tripped over a stone. "But she agreed to chase the dog!"

Willowpaw twitched her tail. "I know! What if the dog had got her? She swore she didn't know then. Brambleberry's furious."

"I bet Piketooth's pretty cross."

"He'd *never* be cross with Shimmerpelt," Willowpaw purred. "He still can't believe a cat like her would look twice at an old snaggletooth like him." She brushed her muzzle against Crookedpaw's jaw. "Have you seen Lakeshine's kits yet?" The gray-and-white queen had kitted in the night.

"What?" Crookedpaw was still lost in her scent.

"Lakeshine's kits." Willowpaw nudged him. "Have you seen them?"

Crookedpaw shook his head. "Has she named them yet?"

"Sunkit and Frogkit," Willowpaw purred. "They're so cute. She let me wash one."

Crookedpaw leaped over a shallow pool among the pebbles. "It's good news for all of us. RiverClan always needs new warriors."

"They're still *kits*!"

"They'll be warriors soon enough," Crookedpaw pointed out. "Just like us."

Willowpaw rolled her eyes. "Is that *all* you think about?" She bounded ahead and raced along the shore, her paws splashing in and out of the shallows as she veered past clumps of water-mint and mossy rocks.

Crookedpaw chased after her.

"Is this the pool?" Willowpaw leaped over the first stepping-stone, splashing down in the shallows, and pointed her nose to where the water dipped into a smooth, rolling current.

"That's it." Crookedpaw waded toward it. "You have to be careful," he warned. "It sucks you down near the bottom."

"I'm a strong swimmer," Willowpaw reassured him.

"I know." Crookedpaw glanced at her smooth, strong shoulders and purred. "But if it does grab you, don't fight it. Just go limp. The river will wash you downstream where it's shallower."

Willowpaw took a deep breath and plunged in. Crookedpaw watched the broken water close over her and waited. Even though he trusted her skills, he couldn't help worrying. The thought that anything bad might happen to her made his chest tighten. He was relieved when her ears broke the surface and she popped up holding a juicy carp.

"There's loads down there!" she mewed happily. "And they're too dumb to swim away!"

Crookedpaw dived in, feeling the water suck at his fur, pulling him down into the school of carp. He grabbed one, swam up, flung it on to the bank, and dived down for another.

"I want to go next!" Willowpaw called as he came up for the third time.

Crookedpaw tossed the fresh carp on to the shore. "Dive in with me!"

Willowpaw plunged in and swam down beside him. Her fur clouded around her as she reached the carp pool. She hooked one with her claws and dragged it to her mouth for a killing bite before she turned and began to pull herself up to the surface. Crookedpaw watched, impressed by her grace, before realizing that his lungs were aching. Quickly he ducked down, grabbed a carp, and swam for the surface.

Jeering mews welcomed him back to the air. A patrol of ThunderClan warriors was strutting on the edge of Sunningrocks.

"What's the difference between a RiverClan warrior and a fish?" one yowled.

"A fish is hard to catch!" his Clanmate answered.

Another warrior, his fur thick and white, leaned over the edge. "Enjoy the river while it's still yours."

Willowpaw's pelt bushed, her eyes blazing. "How dare they?"

Crookedpaw tossed his fish to the shore and bounded on

to the stepping-stones. Spitting with rage, he leaped halfway across the river. "Come down here and say that, you worm-ridden fish-brains!"

"We just might!" the white warrior yowled. "Why don't you run home before we do?"

"Come on then!" Crookedpaw unsheathed his claws. "I'll rip your ears off!"

"You couldn't climb down if you tried!" Willowpaw piped up behind him. "The only way ThunderClan can get down from Sunningrocks is to fall down! Go on! Try it! I wouldn't mind if a few of you broke your flea-bitten necks!"

"Crookedpaw!" Oakheart's mew made them both jump. "Come here."

Prickling with frustration, Crookedpaw turned and leaped back to shore.

The ThunderClan warriors yowled with amusement. "Go back to the nursery, Wetkit!"

Crookedpaw growled.

Oakheart was pacing with excitement. "Save it for your next battle," he meowed. "Hailstar wants *everyone* back at camp."

"What for?"

"Come on!" Oakheart charged away.

Willowpaw stared. "What's going on?"

Crookedpaw shrugged. "Let's find out!"

They each scooped a carp from the pile they'd made and raced for camp. The fish tail flapped in Crookedpaw's face as he ran.

He skidded through the sedge tunnel, Willowpaw at his

heels. Their Clanmates were already gathered in the clearing. Oakheart stood panting beside Shellheart while Hailstar paced in the middle, tail swishing.

Crookedpaw dropped his fish on the fresh-kill pile beside Willowpaw's. She'd already slid in beside Graypaw.

Crookedpaw nosed his way between Shellheart and Oakheart. "What's going on?"

"Listen!" Shellheart silenced him.

Hailstar was mid-speech. ". . . so on the darkest night of the moon we will reclaim Sunningrocks!"

At last! Oakheart lashed his tail and Shellheart clawed the ground as the whole Clan cheered.

"What if we lose again?" Rippleclaw's question was almost lost in the noise but he repeated it, louder. "What if we lose again?"

The cheers faltered and faded.

"There will be no battle this time," Hailstar announced. He looked up at the fat, waxing moon. "Next claw-moon, when it's no more than a scratch on the sky, we'll reset the boundaries."

Timberfur leaned forward. "Won't ThunderClan just set them back again?"

Worried murmurs rippled through the Clan.

"We'll keep resetting them until ThunderClan gets the message," Hailstar answered. "And if it comes to a battle—" The RiverClan leader glanced at Crookedpaw. "We'll fight it and, this time, we'll win!"

As the Clan broke into another cheer, Crookedpaw tipped

his head to one side. Why had Hailstar looked at him? Didn't he trust him to fight?

"Yesterday an apprentice saved the life of a Clanmate." Hailstar silenced the cheers.

Crookedpaw straightened.

Oakheart purred. "I'm guessing he means you."

Hailstar's eyes shone. "Crookedpaw." He beckoned Crookedpaw forward with a flick of his tail. "This apprentice has not yet completed his six moons of warrior training."

Heart racing, Crookedpaw padded into the clearing. Brambleberry watched him, her eyes dark. Rainflower wrapped her tail tightly over her paws. Beetlenose whispered something in Voleclaw's ear.

Hailstar padded to meet him. "But I see no point in delaying his warrior ceremony any longer."

Crookedpaw's heart jumped. *My warrior ceremony!*

"I want Crookedpaw to be in the patrol that resets the borders beyond Sunningrocks." Hailstar paused. "No," he meowed. "I want *Crookedjaw!*"

The Clan took up the call: "Crookedjaw! Crookedjaw!"

Crookedjaw stared at his leader. Joy fizzed like stars beneath his pelt. "Well done!" Cedarpelt walked forward and touched his muzzle to Crookedjaw's head.

Crookedjaw detected relief in his mew. "Glad to get rid of me?" he murmured, half-joking.

"It's hard work teaching a cat who already knows everything," Cedarpelt answered.

Crookedjaw stepped back. "I'm sorry." He stared at his paws.

Cedarpelt broke into a purr. "I like to believe I taught you something."

"You taught me so much!" Crookedjaw insisted.

"And I'm sure you still have plenty to learn." Shellheart's voice made Crookedjaw turn. His father was gazing at him proudly.

Oakheart dashed past the RiverClan deputy and wove around Crookedjaw. "We're warriors together at last! Will you share my den? Whitefang won't mind. There's room for an extra nest."

"Congratulations." Beetlenose crossed the clearing, tail flicking. "You *finally* made it."

Crookedjaw met his gaze. "Now you've got more competition than just Oakheart." As he spoke, he spotted a familiar pelt moving in the shadows by the reeds. Mapleshade was watching, her gaze slitted.

A soft muzzle nudged his shoulder. Willowpaw was purring loudly in his ear. "I'm going to miss sleeping beside you."

Crookedjaw twined his tail around hers. "Then hurry up and become a warrior!"

Rainflower hadn't moved. She sat as still as a rock, on the far side of the clearing. Lifting his chin, Crookedjaw squeezed past Oakheart and approached his mother. She didn't move as he neared, only narrowed her eyes.

"I'm sorry I can't make you proud of me," Crookedjaw meowed. "But I haven't finished yet. I'll do everything I can to make you glad I'm your son."

Rainflower stared silently at him. Crookedjaw fought back

the hurt tightening his throat. He lifted his chin, refusing to hide his twisted jaw. "You'll never make me ashamed of who I am or what I look like." Turning away, he saw Oakheart and Willowpaw staring at him.

Oakheart dashed over and ran the tip of his tail along his brother's spine. "Good for you, Crookedjaw." He glanced past Crookedjaw, his gaze hardening as it reached Rainflower. "If our mother can't be proud of you, it's her loss."

"We believe in you." Willowpaw's eyes shone at him, reflecting starlight.

Feeling as if the bubble of happiness inside him might explode, Crookedjaw pressed his muzzle to hers and purred.

CHAPTER 19

A night heron called from the far bank, its wings pulsing as it lifted into the air. Crookedjaw saw the flash of its belly as it flew over the reed bed and disappeared upstream. He'd been listening to the bird fishing—the plop as it dived, the splash as it dragged a fish struggling from the river. He tucked his tail tighter over his paws and gazed around the camp. Sitting vigil on his first night as a warrior, Crookedjaw felt the weight of responsibility for his sleeping Clanmates. He glanced up at Silverpelt. *Thank you for helping me to become a warrior. Thank you for helping me to keep my Clan safe.*

"Crookedjaw."

Crookedjaw twisted his head. "Who's that?"

A pale shape twined around him. He barely felt the wraith-like pelt as it brushed his. "Have you forgotten me so quickly?"

"Mapleshade!" Crookedjaw blinked in surprise. "What do you want?"

"I've been waiting for you to come and train," she growled. "But if you won't come to me, I'll come to you."

"I can't train tonight! I'm sitting *vigil.*"

"Do you think you've learned all there is to learn?"

230 WARRIORS SUPER EDITION: CROOKEDSTAR'S PROMISE

"No! I'm sitting vigil!" The fur ruffled along his spine. He was a warrior now. Just like Mapleshade. She had to respect that. She couldn't boss him around like an apprentice anymore. "I can't talk now," he whispered. "I'll visit you when I can."

Suddenly he was alone. He glanced over his shoulder, just to make sure, then shifted his weight and went on with his vigil.

Crookedjaw was shivering by the time dawn began pushing back the darkness. The apprentices' den rustled and Willowpaw slipped out. She crossed the misty clearing and sat beside Crookedjaw. "You're cold." She pressed against him, warm and soft from sleep. Crookedjaw felt his eyes begin to close.

"Hey!" Willowpaw poked him. "The Clan will be waking any moment."

Crookedjaw snapped awake, his heart lurching. He pulled away from Willowpaw. He needed the fresh dawn chill to keep him alert.

"Hi, Crookedjaw!" Whitefang padded from his den with Oakheart on his tail. "How was the vigil?"

"Long!" Crookedjaw stood up, shaking each numb paw in turn. "And chilly."

"You should try doing it in leaf-bare," Oakheart joked.

Hailstar padded from his den. "How's our newest warrior?" he called.

"Ready for patrol!" Crookedjaw stretched his stiff muscles.

Shellheart ducked out of his den. "Owlfur! Brightsky! Are you ready?"

Willowpaw flicked her tail. "Oh, I'd forgotten!" She circled Crookedjaw excitedly. "We're going on dawn patrol! Then Owlfur's going to show me a new move and we're going to try a mock battle." She darted to the apprentices' den, calling for Graypaw. "Wake up! We're leaving!"

Graypaw stuck her head out of the den and yawned. "Already?"

Willowpaw rolled her eyes. "It's called the dawn patrol for a reason." She led a sleepy Graypaw to where Brightsky was stretching beside Shellheart. Owlfur was picking through the remains of the fresh-kill pile.

"Take something to Lakeshine," Shellheart ordered. "She'll be hungry."

"And thirsty." Brambleberry padded from her den. She signaled to Echomist, who'd followed Hailstar out of the leader's den. "Will you sit with the kits while she goes for a drink?"

Echomist purred. "I'd love to."

"Come on, Graypaw!" Brightsky called to her apprentice, who was lapping water at the edge of the river. "Those borders won't mark themselves." Shellheart was already leading Owlfur and Willowpaw out of camp. Graypaw scampered across the clearing and caught up with her mentor as she ducked out of the tunnel.

Crookedjaw felt a tug of disappointment as he watched the apprentices leave, but suddenly excitement thrilled through him. He didn't have to train! He was a warrior now. He glanced at the space where the fresh-kill pile should be. He'd hunt. By the end of the day the fresh-kill pile would be heaped with fish.

"Good catch, Crookedjaw!" Shimmerpelt called across the clearing, her mouth full. The setting sun made her pelt glow as she leaned down for another bite of the fat trout glistening at her paws.

Shellheart purred. "I don't know if he left any fish in the river for tomorrow!" The RiverClan deputy sat with Timberfur and Whitefang, sharing a pike. Crookedjaw glanced proudly at the fresh-kill pile. He'd caught nearly every fish there.

Brightsky rolled on to her back. "The rest of us might as well move to the elders' den, now that Crookedjaw's a warrior," she teased.

Crookedjaw stretched, his muscles aching from hunting. "Newleaf fishing is fun."

Willowpaw nudged him. "Even without me?" she whispered.

"It's better," he teased. "You steal all the best fish."

"You snake-heart!" She pushed him with her head and he fell back, pretending to be beaten.

"No more, please!"

"That's just the start!" She leaped on him and they tumbled across the mossy ground. Willowpaw's claws tickled his ribs.

"Hey!" he yelped, squirming. "That's not fair!"

She paused. "Really?" She blinked down at him innocently, then tickled him again. "You should have thought of that before you started teasing me!"

Birdsong padded down the slope toward the fresh-kill pile. She glanced at the two young cats, her whiskers twitching. "They start younger every year." She began to rummage through the fish, pulling a plump gray perch from the bottom. "Tanglewhisker!" She called up to the elders' den. "Are you coming or are you going to spend the evening pulling ticks?" She shook her head, muttering half to herself, "He can't even reach most of them."

Willowpaw leaped to her paws. "I'll help him." She nuzzled Crookedjaw's ear and headed up the slope.

Crookedjaw straightened and yawned. The sun had disappeared behind the willow, and the camp was turning blue in the twilight.

"Your nest is ready." Oakheart nodded toward his den. "It's the one with fresh moss."

"Thanks." Crookedjaw was looking forward to a good night's sleep. He padded to his den and ducked inside. The cocoon of woven reeds rested against the crumbling bark of the fallen tree. It was just big enough for three nests. Crookedjaw could tell by sniffing which was Whitefang's and which was Oakheart's. He padded past them and climbed into his own, grateful for the soft, clean moss that lined the carefully threaded reeds. Oakheart must have been working on this for ages. Crookedjaw felt a jolt of affection for his brother; Oakheart had never lost faith in him. A purr rumbled in his throat as he curled down into his nest and closed his eyes.

"Wake up!" A snarl wrenched him from sleep.

Crookedjaw leaped to his paws. He was in the shadowy forest.

Mapleshade's eyes blazed in the gloom. "Have you forgotten your promise?"

Crookedjaw, still half asleep, stared at her. "What?"

"Your promise!"

"Is this because I didn't come training last night?" He struggled against the tiredness fogging his thoughts.

"No, you mouse-brain! I heard you talking to Willowpaw. I've *seen* you, acting like mates-for-life. What did I ask you to do?"

"To look after my Clan?" Crookedjaw backed away. Mapleshade's breath was rank.

She lunged for him, swiping his twisted jaw so viciously that he staggered, pain shooting through his face. "I asked you to put your Clan before *everything*!" She stood over him as he crouched down, stiff with shock. "That includes any feelings you might have for that pathetic ball of fur you've been mooning over!"

He stared up at her. "Do you mean Willowpaw?"

"You want to be a great warrior, don't you?"

"Of course!" Crookedjaw could scent rage pulsing from her, hot and sharp.

"Then forget about love and friendship and what *you* want, you selfish mouse-brain, and put your Clan first like you promised!"

"I have put my Clan first." Anger surged beneath his pelt. "Don't tell me that I haven't!" He squared up against her. Mapleshade stared back as vicious as a fox. Why was she suddenly so mean? StarClan cats weren't supposed to be mean! Crookedjaw had become a warrior. She should be proud. Confused, he turned and fled.

Swerving between the dark trees, he raced through the tangled, slippery undergrowth. Mist swirled around him and he slipped and staggered as he ran, fighting to keep his balance as trunks loomed from the fog, and the undergrowth seemed to grab for his paws. Heart pounding, he slowed. He was tired and he didn't want to be here. He wanted to sleep. He wanted to be back in his nest. He stumbled to a halt, hanging his head as he caught his breath.

"You're back."

The croaking mew made him jump. Crookedjaw squinted and made out a shape in the shadows up ahead. It shambled toward him and he recognized the pelt. "Goosefeather?" The ThunderClan medicine cat was here again. He must share his dreams with StarClan a lot.

Goosefeather dipped his head. "Mapleshade's apprentice." He padded closer and sniffed Crookedjaw's pelt. "I've been hearing rumors about you."

Crookedjaw backed away. "From who?"

"Don't forget I share with StarClan."

"Is that why you're here?" Crookedjaw's paws pricked. Were the old cat's whiskers twitching?

"I suppose you could say that."

What did he mean? "What does StarClan say about me?"

Goosefeather circled Crookedjaw slowly. "That you could be a great warrior."

Crookedjaw sensed the old tom's gaze flicking over his pelt. "Really?" He brightened.

"Don't take any notice of that old fool." Mapleshade's mew made him turn. She'd caught up to him. She must have run fast, yet she looked as cool as ever and her breath was slow and steady.

Goosefeather glanced at her, amusement lighting his gaze. "I may be an old fool," he rasped. "But at least my heart is true." He padded past Crookedjaw and stopped in front of Mapleshade. "My heart isn't soured by bitterness or guided by revenge."

Crookedjaw padded closer. "What do you mean?"

Goosefeather ignored him. "You should tread the path you're following with care, Mapleshade. A destiny shouldn't be played with like prey."

Mapleshade barged past the old ThunderClan medicine cat. "Ignore him, Crookedjaw. His mind has been addled by too many visions."

Crookedjaw met her gaze. "At least he speaks to me like an equal," he challenged.

Mapleshade broke into a purr. "You're not upset because I reminded you of your promise, are you?" She pressed against him, guiding him forward, away from Goosefeather. "Maybe I was a little harsh, but I was frightened that you were forgetting your destiny. I want you to be the greatest warrior RiverClan has ever known—the greatest *any* Clan will ever know. Willowpaw is a sweet, pretty cat and I'm not surprised you're fond of her. But the sweetest traps are often the most dangerous. She will soften you and sway you from your course." She halted. "You do still want to be a great warrior, don't you?"

"Yes!" Crookedjaw cried.

"Very good." Mapleshade stopped him with a flick of her tail. "That is all I ask." She padded on into the mist, her voice trailing after her. "Everything I do, Crookedjaw, I do with your best interests at heart."

CHAPTER 20

❧

A warm wind set the four great oaks whispering above the Clans. Thick with foliage now, they'd lost their leaf-bare starkness. After moons of going to Gatherings, Crookedjaw had learned the names and pelts of most of the other Clans and, with the truce, he felt comfortable moving among them. Besides, the warmer weather had smoothed tempers. He followed his Clanmates into the clearing where they melted into the chattering flock of cats. Owlfur and Brightsky joined a group of warriors who were comparing apprentices loudly.

"It's been a good batch in ThunderClan this year," Adderfang boasted.

Crookedjaw watched as Brambleberry hailed the medicine cats gathered below the Great Rock. "Featherwhisker!" She greeted Goosefeather's apprentice first, touching her muzzle to his head before turning to the others.

Ottersplash headed straight for Patchpelt, a ThunderClan warrior. "Has Leopardfoot kitted yet?" she asked.

Seeing Ottersplash's round belly, Crookedjaw wondered if she wouldn't beat Leopardfoot to it. She hadn't moved to the nursery yet but surely she *had* to be expecting kits?

Even in newleaf, no RiverClan cat got that fat. He stopped beside Oakheart. "Why do she-cats always put off going to the nursery till the last minute?" Both Shimmerpelt and Lakeshine had waited a moon.

Oakheart shrugged. "You'd think they'd like lying around all day having fresh-kill brought to them."

Paws scuffed the ground behind him. Crookedjaw smelled Rainflower's scent. "Has it occurred to you that they might enjoy helping their Clan?" she pointed out. "Wouldn't you find it hard to give up being a warrior?"

Oakheart sniffed. "I'm just glad I don't have to sleep in the nursery," he meowed. "I had to stick my paws in my ears last night. Sunkit and Frogkit were mewling their ears off."

"Hi, Poppydawn." Crookedjaw nodded to a dark red ThunderClan she-cat as she passed. "Are Sweetpaw, Rosepaw, and Thistlepaw here?"

"No." Poppydawn sighed. "Thistlepaw's in trouble with Smallear again."

Windflight, her mate, shook his head. "Sweetpaw and Rosepaw stayed behind to cheer him up."

Crookedjaw purred. "They sound loyal."

Poppydawn dipped her head as Crookedjaw praised her kits. "They are," she meowed proudly.

Tanglewhisker trotted past them. "Mumblefoot!" he called to the ThunderClan elder.

"Wait for me!" Birdsong hurried after him as her mate greeted Mumblefoot and Whiteberry, a WindClan elder.

Oakheart watched the old cats. "They'd talk the night

away if they could," he joked. He caught Crookedjaw's eye. "So, how does it feel to be a warrior instead of an apprentice at the Gathering?"

Crookedjaw flicked his tail happily. He was the equal of any cat here. "It feels great."

Willowpaw broke away from a knot of apprentices demonstrating their latest moves. "Graypaw can be such a show-off!" She glanced sharply back at her sister, who was twisting in the air like a salmon trying to climb a waterfall.

Crookedjaw fizzed with mischief. "Why don't you go and show them how she snores?"

"I'm not sure they're ready for that," Willowpaw returned, purring.

Rainflower beckoned Oakheart. "Have you met Talltail yet? He'll be WindClan's leader one day. You should get to know him." As she led him away, Crookedjaw spotted Bluepaw. He hadn't seen her since the battle. His nose stung as he remembered the wounds she'd inflicted. Not bad for a ThunderClan cat. He padded toward her. "You fought well."

She flattened her ears. "I fight even better now that I'm a *warrior*. My name is Bluefur."

He broke into a purr. "I've got my warrior name, too!"

"Crookedjaw?"

He purred. "How did you guess?"

"Because your tail's still straight."

As she joked with him, he felt a prick of guilt. She had no

idea that RiverClan planned to reclaim Sunningrocks as soon as the moon had waned. He pushed away the thought. She was a rival, pure and simple.

A yowl sounded from the Great Rock. "Let the Gathering begin."

Pinestar stood at the edge of the stone, moonlight gleaming in his pelt. Hailstar was silhouetted behind him with Heatherstar and Cedarstar. Crookedjaw was swept forward beside Bluefur as the Clans crowded around the rock. Pinestar stepped back and Cedarstar took his place.

"Newleaf has brought prey and warmth, but also more kittypets straying across the borders," the ShadowClan leader announced.

Ottersplash lifted her muzzle. "They hide in their cozy nests all leaf-bare and forget that the woods are ours," she agreed.

Just like Twolegs. Crookedjaw sighed. The field downriver was already filling up with their pelt-dens.

The ThunderClan leader stepped forward. "We intend to increase patrols." He glared at Hailstar. "To warn off any intruders!"

Did he know about RiverClan's plan to reset the boundaries? Growls rumbled uncertainly among the RiverClan cats.

Raggedpelt, ShadowClan's deputy, responded first. "No ShadowClan cat has crossed your border in moons."

Hawkheart called from the cluster of medicine cats. "WindClan has stayed to our side of Fourtrees!"

Hailstar's hackles lifted. "Are you accusing RiverClan of crossing your scent line?"

Crookedjaw lashed his tail. In less than a moon it would be RiverClan's scent line!

Pinestar shrugged. "I'm not accusing any cat of anything. But ThunderClan will be stepping up patrols from now on." He flexed his claws. "Better safe than sorry."

Why was Pinestar stirring up trouble at such a peaceful Gathering? Crookedjaw felt Bluefur stiffen beside him. "Why start accusing the Clans of trespassing?" he called. "We were talking about kittypets!"

Oakheart's growl sounded behind him. "ThunderClan cats always were a bunch of kittypet friends!"

Adderfang whipped his head around, eyes blazing. "Who are you calling kittypet friends?"

Oakheart met the ThunderClan warrior's gaze steadily. "Have you got something to say, fish-breath?"

Heatherstar called from the Great Rock. "In the name of StarClan, stop!" She looked up at the wisps of clouds streaking Silverpelt. Some of the stars were already hidden. Muttering, the Clans fell into a prickly silence.

The WindClan leader raised her muzzle. "Kittypets rarely reach our borders."

Talltail called from below. "They're too slow to chase rabbits anyway."

"And squirrels," Smallear added.

Murmurs of agreement rippled through the Clans but pelts were still ruffled. Crookedjaw felt Bluefur shift her paws.

ThunderClan must suspect that we're planning something.

He was relieved when Hailstar padded to the front of Great Rock again. "Enough of kittypets," he yowled. "RiverClan has a new warrior." He nodded to his Clan. "Crookedjaw!"

Crookedjaw looked up. He'd forgotten he was going to be introduced formally to the Clans. He puffed out his chest as the Clans chanted his warrior name, and joined in to welcome Bluefur as Pinestar called out hers. But the cheers were halfhearted. The warmth of the Gathering had evaporated and it broke up in frosty silence.

Crookedjaw joined his Clanmates milling at the bottom of the slope. He paced around his brother while Tanglewhisker and Birdsong caught up. "Do you think Pinestar suspects we're going to take back Sunningrocks?"

Oakheart narrowed his eyes. "He was acting strange, but how could he know?"

"Perhaps Goosefeather's had a sign?"

Shellheart cut in. "Pinestar's a wily old cat," he murmured. "He's up to something, but no cat's crossed his borders. He's just stirring up trouble for his own reasons."

"What did Bluefur say?" Oakheart asked.

"Bluefur?" *Why did he want to know about Bluefur?*

"You were talking to her." Oakheart shrugged. "I just wondered if she gave anything away."

"No."

"Didn't you feel weird talking to her, knowing we're planning an attack?" Oakheart prompted.

"My loyalty's to RiverClan, not Bluefur."

"I guess." Oakheart's eyes darkened. "But I kind of felt sorry for her."

Crookedjaw bristled. "Don't be soft on our enemies!" He felt a rush of pride. *I hope Mapleshade's listening.*

As they approached camp, Crookedjaw guessed that something was wrong. They usually returned from Gatherings to a sleeping camp. But tonight anxious mews sounded from beyond the reeds.

A shadow moved on the path. "Have you seen Beetlenose and Voleclaw?" Petaldust was pacing outside the camp.

"Why? What's wrong?" Hailstar pulled up sharply, the patrol stumbling to a halt around him.

Petaldust looked frantic. "They went to fetch you!"

Hailstar shook his head. "We came back by the waterfall." He turned and nodded to Shellheart and Owlfur. "Go and find them before they run into a ThunderClan patrol. After tonight's speech, Pinestar will shred them if he catches them on ThunderClan territory, truce or no truce."

As Shellheart and Owlfur dashed away, Brambleberry pushed through the entrance to the clearing. "Is it the kits?" she called.

Crookedjaw raced after her. Mudfur was pacing in front of the nursery. Echomist and Softwing were huddled near him in urgent, whispered conversation.

"You're back!" Echomist leaped to her paws.

Troutclaw sat bleary-eyed at the bottom of the slope. "So much fuss over a kitting."

Brambleberry's ears twitched. "Shimmerpelt's kitting already?"

Echomist circled the medicine cat. "She started just before moonhigh. Lakeshine and Piketooth are with her." The pale she-cat shook her head. "It's too early, isn't it?"

Brambleberry didn't answer. "Has there been any bleeding?" she asked calmly.

"No."

"Good." Brambleberry padded past her toward the nursery.

"Do you need herbs?" Echomist called after her.

Brambleberry shook her head. "Only StarClan can help her, I'm afraid." She hopped into the round reed den.

"I hope she's all right." Willowpaw was pacing around Softwing.

Lakeshine popped her head out of the nursery. "She needs water."

"I'll get it!" Willowpaw dashed to the reed bed. Brightsky raced to join her and together they pulled up a clump of dripping moss from the river's edge. They carried it back to the nursery and passed it to Lakeshine waiting at the entrance.

"I need honey!" Brambleberry called from the nursery.

"Okay!" Birdsong headed for the medicine den.

Crookedjaw exchanged glances with Oakheart as Willowpaw passed him, her jaws dripping with another mouthful of moss. *"Honey?"*

"It'll give her energy."

Willowpaw's mew was so muffled he could hardly make out her words. Crookedjaw turned to Oakheart, feeling helpless.

"We could start collecting bulrushes to make a training wall for the kits?" he suggested.

Oakheart purred. "It's a bit early for that."

"There must be something we can do!"

Timberfur caught his eye. "The warrior code doesn't cover kitting," he meowed sympathetically. "We can just wait and hope."

"Unless you want to go in and help," Rippleclaw muttered.

Crookedjaw shuddered. "No thanks."

Paws sounded outside camp and Shellheart ducked through the entrance, leading Owlfur, Beetlenose, and Voleclaw. "They made it to Fourtrees and back without meeting anyone."

Crookedjaw's whiskers twitched. "You should work on your tracking skills, Beetlenose."

"Finding cats is different from finding prey." Beetlenose sniffed. "Cats are smarter than prey—at least *some* are."

"How's she doing?" Echomist called into the nursery.

A low groan answered.

"She'll be fine," Brambleberry yowled. "Where's that honey?"

"Coming!" Birdsong was trotting stiffly across the clearing, a lump of honeycomb oozing between her jaws.

Beetlenose flicked his tail. "Hey, Crookedjaw, why don't you help Brambleberry deliver the kits? You always like to be the center of attention."

"Why don't *you*?" Crookedjaw retorted.

Beetlenose wrinkled his nose. "I'm a warrior, not a medicine cat."

Willowpaw wove between them. "Why are you so squeamish?" she chided. "Every cat has kits sometime."

Voleclaw stared at her. "I won't!"

Beetlenose walked in a circle around Willowpaw. "You just want to have kits with Crookedjaw," he taunted.

Crookedjaw nudged the black warrior away indignantly. "That's not true!"

A mewl sounded from the nursery. Lakeshine slid out. "Two kits!" Her eyes shone in the moonlight. "A tom and a she-kit."

"Come on, Crookedjaw!" Willowpaw raced for the nursery. Reluctantly he followed, sensing Beetlenose's mocking gaze. Brambleberry's face showed in the entrance.

"Can we see them?" Willowpaw begged.

"Okay, but you can't stay long and don't lick them. They're still getting used to their mother."

Willowpaw squeezed inside.

"Come on." Brambleberry motioned Crookedjaw in with a flick of her muzzle.

"Um . . ."

She rolled her eyes. "Toms!" she sighed. "It's no scarier than a battle, I promise."

Crookedjaw heaved himself through the entrance, suddenly aware of how much he'd grown. It was hard to believe he was ever small enough to hop in and out of the nursery without effort. Inside it was stifling. The air was dark and heavy with a strange scent. He could hardly see Shimmerpelt's crow-black pelt in the shadows, but the mewling of tiny kits filled his ears.

"Look!" Piketooth was crouching beside Shimmerpelt, his eyes shining.

"They're our new denmates!" Frogkit was peering proudly over the side of his nest.

"We're going to be the first ones to play with them *ever*," Sunkit squeaked beside him.

Willowpaw was staring into Shimmerpelt's nest. Crookedjaw peered in nervously. Two tiny kits wriggled against Shimmerpelt's belly. One was as brown as her father. The other had a black pelt as smoky as mist on the river at night.

"Here are Blackkit and Skykit," Shimmerpelt murmured.

Skykit raised her muzzle, eyes closed, pink mouth opening to cry. She looked so tiny and helpless, Crookedjaw wanted to wrap his tail around her.

Willowpaw pressed against him, purring. "Welcome to RiverClan, kits."

Crookedjaw shifted his paws. "They are kind of cute," he muttered grudgingly. *Will I have my own one day? Is that part of my destiny? No.* He sighed. *Mapleshade would tell me I'm putting myself ahead of my Clan.*

Crookedjaw curled wearily into his nest. Whitefang was already snoring. Oakheart was giving his paws a final wash. Crookedjaw tucked his paw under his nose and closed his eyes. He was desperate for sleep but he couldn't relax. What if Mapleshade had seen him mooning over the kits with Willowpaw? She'd claw him for sure. He could imagine her hissing that he was a warrior not a queen; that he should be out hunting for his Clan, not huddled in the nursery imagining what it'd be like to sit next to Willowpaw as she cared for their kits.

He pushed away the thought. *I'm doing it again! The Clan comes first. The Clan comes first!* But why did that mean he couldn't dream of having a mate and kits? The Clan needed kits. Kits became warriors and his kits would be strong and brave. Why couldn't he like Willowpaw? *I'm allowed to be friends with my Clanmates. More than friends, if I want! It can't hurt the Clan!* His pelt shivered with indignation. How dare Mapleshade tell him how to feel!

"Are you okay?" Oakheart prodded him with a paw.

Crookedjaw kept his nose tucked under his paw. "Fine."

"Stop fidgeting then," Oakheart complained. "Some of us are trying to sleep."

Slowing his thoughts, Crookedjaw felt himself drift toward sleep.

When he blinked open his eyes, sunshine was streaming through the entrance to the den. He hadn't dreamed of Mapleshade! He sat up, a purr rising in his throat.

"What are you so cheerful about?" Oakheart was stretching in his nest. "Have you been dreaming about Willowpaw?"

Crookedjaw hopped out of his nest, flicking Oakheart's ear with his tail as he passed. "Actually I didn't dream at all." Perhaps he'd scared Mapleshade by telling her off before he went to sleep. It felt good to wake up with no scratches or aching muscles. He hadn't felt so rested in moons.

Shellheart was already organizing patrols beneath the willow when Crookedjaw padded out of the den. The RiverClan deputy beckoned him with a flick of his muzzle. Crookedjaw crossed the sunny clearing and nosed his way between Timberfur and Brightsky. Owlfur and Cedarpelt were fidgeting, eager to be out on such a fine morning. Mudfur was still yawning while Voleclaw picked mud from between his claws. Beetlenose was watching the tip of Petaldust's tail flick back and forth, his eyes bright. Crookedjaw could tell he was fighting back the urge to pounce on it. He scanned the camp for Willowpaw, pricking his ears. Gentle snoring was coming from the apprentices' den. Graypaw and Willowpaw were probably worn out after the Gathering and then the excitement of Shimmerpelt's kitting.

"Ottersplash moved to the nursery this morning," Shellheart announced. "Which means we're another warrior down. But the river's full of fish, and still deep enough to keep the other Clans at bay."

"Unless they've learned to fly," Voleclaw joked.

Petaldust stifled a purr. "WindClan is more likely to learn how to fly than to swim. They hate water more than ThunderClan!"

"Crookedjaw." Shellheart nodded at his son. "Take Oakheart, Mudfur, Brightsky, and Voleclaw upstream and check the Twoleg bridge for WindClan scent. Timberfur will be leading a patrol to check the stepping-stones for any trace of ThunderClan." *I'm leading a patrol!* Crookedjaw clawed at the ground.

"And Crookedjaw?"

Crookedjaw snapped to attention as Shellheart went on.

"Check the Twoleg fence on your way back. See if that dog's been straying again."

As Crookedjaw headed away, Shellheart called after him. "Be careful. If we didn't manage to scare him last time, the dog may be out for revenge."

Crookedjaw poked his head into his den. Oakheart was cleaning stale moss from his nest. "Come on. We've got a mission." He glanced at Whitefang. The warrior was still sound asleep in his nest; his whiskers were twitching furiously and he was chirruping like a nervous moorhen. "Should we wake him?"

"And ruin his dream?" Oakheart shook his head. "What's the mission?" He followed Crookedjaw outside.

"We're checking the bridge." Mudfur, Voleclaw, and Brightsky were already waiting by the entrance. "And the Twoleg fence." Graypaw was there, too, flicking her tail.

"Can Graypaw come with us?" Brightsky called.

"Of course." Crookedjaw fluffed out his fur with importance. He ducked through the gap in the reeds and set a fast pace along the grass path. The sound of paws thrumming behind him filled him with joy. The sun was shining and a warm breeze wafted across the sparkling river. Crookedjaw had to fight to keep himself from purring out loud. He veered off the path, following the trail up through the alders and doubling back around the camp, keeping up the pace until the patrol swerved back down to meet the river again. The shore was sandy on the edge of the marsh and soft on his paws. His pads sprayed dirt behind him as he slowed and the patrol fanned out around him. Walking now, Crookedjaw led the way upstream.

Graypaw scampered through the shallows. "Can we fish?"

Oakheart shrugged. "If you want to carry what you catch for the rest of the morning."

Graypaw sighed. "We could eat it now," she mewed hopefully. "Just a little minnow wouldn't be breaking the warrior code, would it?"

"Yes, it would," Mudfur answered sternly. "Besides, we should check the bridge. Then look for the dog."

Graypaw bounded ahead, her tail swishing. As they rounded a bend in the river, Crookedjaw glimpsed the Twoleg bridge. Trees crowded the bank beyond it. Their leaves whispered in the breeze. They could fish from there and eat, shaded from the hot sun.

"Wait." He signaled to the patrol with his tail and called Graypaw back. They were approaching the path that crossed the bridge. "Can anyone detect Twolegs?"

Brightsky was already tasting the air. "The wind's blowing upstream."

Mudfur pricked his ears. "I can't hear anything."

Crookedjaw stalked forward, keeping low. "Follow me."

He crept up the bank where the legs of the bridge dug into the shore and padded on to the wooden pathway. The river splashed beneath as he sniffed the warm timber. His Clanmates crept after him, padding from side to side of the bridge and checking for scents.

"Come back!" Brightsky's alarmed call made Crookedjaw look up. Graypaw had crossed the bridge and was sniffing the bank on the far side.

"But it's our territory!" Graypaw called back. "Right up to the waterfall!"

A growl rumbled in Brightsky's throat. "I don't know why Fallowtail didn't raise that kit to do as she's told!"

Mudfur purred. "Apprentices never do as they're told." His eyes sparkled as he glanced at Crookedjaw. "Do they?"

Crookedjaw whisked his tail. "Only fish-brains follow rules without question!" With a lurch, he suddenly realized that Oakheart had dropped into a crouch and was growling.

"What?" Crookedjaw followed his brother's gaze and felt his hackles lift.

A flash of white showed between the trees on the other shore. Then a flash of red. Then green and blue.

"Twolegs!" Crookedjaw froze, heart racing. Twoleg kits were scampering between the trees on the other side of the bridge, only a few tail-lengths from Graypaw.

Brightsky had already darted forward, hissing to her apprentice. "Run!"

Graypaw was staring at the Twoleg kits, her fur bushed up, eyes glittering.

"Run!" Mudfur yowled.

The kits turned. With a whoop, they spotted Graypaw.

Crookedjaw's heart rose in his throat. "Run!"

The dumb 'paw was rooted to the spot. Crookedjaw charged forward, darting past Brightsky. "Come on!"

The bridge trembled as she dashed after him. One of the Twoleg kits was holding out a paw. Graypaw stared at it, stiff with terror. Crookedjaw raced between the Twoleg kit's paws, spitting with fury. The Twoleg yelped and hopped away. Brightsky raced past Graypaw, grasping her scruff and dragging her along until the apprentice squealed and struggled free.

"Run!" Brightsky yowled.

Shaken from her moment of terror, Graypaw hurtled back across the bridge. Brightsky pelted after her. Crookedjaw ducked back past the Twoleg. With a jolt of horror, he felt its paws grasp his pelt. Struggling wildly, he broke free, yowling with pain as the Twoleg ripped out a clump of fur. His paws slipped on the wood as he hit the bridge. Unsheathing his claws, he dug them deep and pushed hard. He crossed the bridge in two breaths.

"Come on!" he called to his patrol as he raced past them. Glancing over his shoulder, he made sure his Clanmates were following, then leaped on to the shore. He slowed to let them pass and fell in behind as they raced downstream. There was no way he was going to let any of them out of his sight till they were back in the safety of camp.

The cries of the Twoleg kits faded as they neared camp.

Spotting the reed bed, Crookedjaw slowed. His lungs were splitting. He slowed to a stop and hung his head, gulping air. Brightsky pulled up, too, alongside Oakheart and Mudfur. Graypaw kept running until she reached the reed bed and she plunged in, splashing through the river as she pushed her way home.

Brightsky watched her go. "Don't worry," she mewed. "She's a strong swimmer."

Crookedjaw nodded, too winded to speak.

Oakheart was still bristling and Mudfur paced, catching his breath and letting his pelt smooth. As they slowly recovered, paw steps sounded beside the shore. Crookedjaw looked up the bank as Graypaw led Hailstar and Echomist out of the marsh grass.

Hailstar's fur was pricking. "Graypaw told us what happened."

Fallowtail pressed her cheek to Crookedjaw's. "Thank you for saving my kit," she whispered.

Crookedjaw twitched. "She could have done more to save herself," he muttered as he followed the she-cat into the clearing.

It looked like the whole Clan was waiting for them, their eyes bright with worry. Graypaw had clearly told them about her near-capture.

"Why can't Twolegs stay on their own territory?" Troutclaw protested. "When I was a kit, we hardly ever saw one. Now they're here every greenleaf, making a nuisance of themselves."

Hailstar shook his head. "It's just the way it is," he sighed.

"We must be more cautious."

Echomist wrapped her tail over Graypaw. "Perhaps we should shrink our borders, just while the Twolegs are around?"

"Shrink our borders!" Whitefang was awake now and spitting with anger. "Why should we? We're not scared of Twolegs!"

Crookedjaw paced beside the reed bed lashing his tail. *I'm not scared of anything that threatens my Clan!*

CHAPTER 21

❧

"*Brambleberry!*" *Mudfur yowled as he hurried* past the reed bed.

Crookedjaw hauled himself out of the river, water streaming from his pelt. He tipped his head on one side. The brown warrior's call had been edged with worry.

Brambleberry poked her head out of her den. "Is Brightsky still uncomfortable?"

Mudfur's tail trembled. "She keeps saying she's thirsty and then she won't drink."

Brambleberry ducked back into her den. "Wait there."

Crookedjaw knew they were worried about Brightsky. She'd moved to the nursery half a moon ago, expecting Mudfur's kits. But fever had struck and she'd been sick for days. Crookedjaw picked his way across camp. The clearing was littered with his Clanmates stretched out in the bright sunshine, too sleepy to move. It was pointless hunting with the sun so high. It was too hot to eat and any fish caught now would be stinking by evening. Even the reeds were drooping under the scorching greenleaf sun.

Crookedjaw hopped over Rippleclaw, who was fast asleep, and landed beside Graypaw. The gray apprentice was huddled in the shade of the fallen tree. "Where's Willowpaw?"

"She's out training with Owlfur." Graypaw gazed wistfully at the nursery. "I shouldn't have crossed the bridge." She tucked her tail tighter. "Then Brightsky wouldn't have had to rescue me."

"That didn't make her ill," Crookedjaw reassured her. "She knew she was expecting kits. It was her choice to carry on with her warrior duties as long as possible."

"Why didn't she tell me?" Graypaw sighed. "I would have come back when she told me."

Are you sure? Crookedjaw bit his tongue, remembering his own days as an apprentice. "When are her kits due?"

"Claw-moon."

"That soon?" Crookedjaw was surprised. It was only a few days away. "She'll be fine," he meowed.

Rippleclaw lifted his head and looked at Graypaw, sympathy lighting his gaze. "Are you still worrying about Brightsky?" He got sleepily to his paws. "Can't Piketooth take you training?" Piketooth had been made Graypaw's mentor when Brightsky had moved to the nursery. "It'll take your mind off things." Rippleclaw glanced across the clearing to where Piketooth and Voleclaw were playing moss-ball with Sunkit and Frogkit. "I could teach you some moves while he's busy."

Graypaw blinked gratefully at the black-and-silver warrior. "Yes, please."

Rippleclaw led Graypaw to a shaded spot at the edge of the clearing and started showing her a battle crouch. The sedge rustled as Brambleberry nosed her way from her den. With a bundle of herbs clasped in her jaws, she led Mudfur across the clearing and into the nursery.

Crookedjaw closed his eyes. *Please, StarClan, make Brightsky healthy again.* A bundle of dark gray fur darted between his paws and pressed against his belly.

"Hide me!" Blackkit squeaked. "Don't tell them where I am."

Crookedjaw stifled a purr and drew his forepaws closer together. Skykit was leading the search party. Ottersplash's kits, less than half a moon old, were following her as though she were Clan leader.

"Can you see him?" Loudkit mewed, his dark brown pelt pricking.

"What if he fell in the river?" Reedkit fretted.

"Don't be silly!" Sedgekit rolled her eyes at her brother. "The warriors would be rushing around flapping like herons if he'd fallen in the river!"

"He's not here." Skykit sniffed her way around the sedge wall.

"Wait!" Loudkit tasted the air. "I can smell him."

"Where?" Reedkit fluffed out his long, stiff tail. He darted past Skykit, nose to the ground, and sniffed his way between the lounging warriors, heading for Crookedjaw.

"Watch out," Crookedjaw whispered to the wriggling bundle beneath his belly. "I think they've found you." He jumped out of the way as the kit patrol launched itself at him. They dived onto Blackkit, squeaking with triumph.

"Found you! Found you!" Loudkit crowed.

"Now it's my turn to hide," Sedgekit squeaked.

Skykit flicked her brown tabby tail. "I want to play something different." She glanced at Piketooth. He tossed the moss ball high over Sunkit's and Frogkit's heads. They leaped to reach it, but Voleclaw raised a paw and plucked it from the air. "I want to play that." Skykit scampered away, her patrol following.

Whitefang grumbled as they clambered over him, and Troutclaw opened an eye and flicked his tail out of the way.

"StarClan bless them." Birdsong dragged her gaze from the kits and called to Crookedjaw. "Is Shellheart back yet?"

Shellheart was leading Beetlenose, Petaldust, Cedarpelt, and Timberfur on border patrol. They'd been out since sunhigh.

"Not yet." Crookedjaw shrugged. "They'll be back soon unless they've found somewhere shady to rest."

"I don't know why they bother." Troutclaw sat up. "There's hardly any border left for them to patrol."

Whitefang heaved himself to his paws and shook out his white pelt. "Has Hailstar decided when we will re-mark Sunningrocks?" He glanced toward the leader's den, hidden in shade under the roots of the willow.

Lakeshine lifted her gray-and-white head. She was lying beside the nursery with Shimmerpelt and Ottersplash. "It's too hot to talk about battles."

Willow leaves fluttered as Oakheart jumped down from the lowest branch. "It's never too hot to talk about battles." He padded across the clearing. "Hailstar said claw-moon, which is any day now." He glanced up to the wide blue sky. "The moon was no more than a sliver of trout skin last night."

Rainflower stretched. "He isn't planning a battle," she reminded them. "He just wants to restore the proper boundary."

Crookedjaw scratched an itch behind his ear. "I'm ready whenever Hailstar decides."

Piketooth looked up from his game with the kits. "I hope I'm in the patrol," he meowed. Every warrior wanted a chance to leave his or her scent.

"Me too!" Rippleclaw was adjusting Graypaw's crouch with a paw. "Just reach a little farther," he advised. "And you'll have it perfect."

Piketooth glanced at his apprentice. "Sorry, kits. Game's over. I have to train Graypaw now."

Sunkit's tail drooped.

Frogkit leaped on to Piketooth's tail. "Don't go!"

Sedgekit raced around him. "Can we come?"

Loudkit leaped on his sister, tumbling her to the ground. "You can't even swim!"

"Neither can you!" Sedgekit pushed him off.

"Stay away from the water!" Piketooth leaped over the squabbling kits, beckoning Graypaw with his tail. "Do you want to practice fishing?" he asked her as she followed him out of the camp.

Crookedjaw leaned down to wash his damp belly. Tiny paws scurried toward him.

"Attack!" A flurry of tails, paws, and noses battered his

flank. Crookedjaw staggered dramatically and fell on to his side. "You've killed me!" he groaned as the kits swarmed over him.

Paw steps padded into camp.

"The patrol's back!" Skykit squeaked.

Crookedjaw looked up to see Shellheart, Cedarpelt, Beetlenose, and Petaldust staring at him, whiskers twitching with amusement.

"Has Lakeshine made you leader of the nursery?" Shellheart teased.

Crookedjaw jumped to his paws, wincing as Skykit and Frogkit stuck in their claws and hung on like burrs.

"Sorry, Crookedjaw," Cedarpelt purred. "I forgot to teach you how to fight off kits!"

"Let me help." Beetlenose rolled a clump of moss between his paws and tossed it across the clearing. The kits squeaked with delight and darted after it like a shoal of minnows.

"Thanks." As Crookedjaw followed Shellheart into the shade of the willow, the branches at the entrance to Hailstar's den shivered.

"You're back." Hailstar padded into the clearing, his pelt shining in the sun. "Let all cats old enough to swim gather to hear my words."

"Loudkit! Sedgekit! Reedkit!" Ottersplash called to her kits. "Come out of the way." Dragging their paws, the kits headed toward their mother.

"And you two!" Shimmerpelt called to Skykit and Blackkit. Frogkit and Sunkit ducked behind Beetlenose, but the black warrior nosed them toward the nursery. "But we can swim!" Frogkit complained.

"Really?" Beetlenose picked Frogkit up by his scruff and dangled him over the edge of the river.

Lakeshine jumped to her paws. "No!" she shrilled. "Put him down! He'll drown!"

Beetlenose purred. "Don't panic." He dropped the wriggling kit at his mother's paws. "I'll teach you to swim as soon as your mother says you're ready," he promised.

"I'd rather be taught to swim by a snake," Crookedjaw muttered as Oakheart joined him at the edge of the clearing.

Oakheart didn't answer. His attention was fixed on Hailstar. "I bet he's going to announce the retaking of Sunningrocks."

Crookedjaw flexed his claws. "Good."

Timberfur paced the edge of the clearing. "At least you already know you'll be part of the patrol."

Hailstar waited for the Clan to settle, then lifted his muzzle. "We re-mark the Sunningrocks boundary tonight."

Tension pricked the air. Oakheart leaned forward. Timberfur stopped pacing.

"Who are you taking?" Rippleclaw demanded.

"Shellheart, Owlfur, Echomist, Timberfur, Softwing, and Rippleclaw . . ." the RiverClan leader began.

And? Crookedjaw's heart quickened. Surely Hailstar would keep his promise? Oakheart tensed beside him.

"Whitefang and Crookedjaw . . ."

Crookedjaw swallowed a purr of relief.

"Oakheart," Hailstar went on. "And Voleclaw." He sat down and curled his tail over his paws.

"Is that it?" Beetlenose lashed his tail.

Hailstar turned his gaze on the young warrior. "The new boundary will need re-marking for many moons to come," he reminded him. "You'll get your turn to leave your scent soon enough."

"Retaking an old boundary's not the same as marking an existing one!" Beetlenose glared at Crookedjaw. "Why does *he* get to go when he's been a warrior for less than a moon? He didn't even have an assessment. How do we know he can even climb the rocks?"

Crookedjaw leaped forward, bristling. "I climbed Sunningrocks when I was still an apprentice," he growled.

Shellheart stepped between them. "Not every warrior can be on every patrol," he soothed.

Beetlenose darted around Shellheart and squared up to Crookedjaw.

Shellheart leaned close. "It might be better for you to meet Beetlenose's disappointment with words rather than claws," he whispered in Crookedjaw's ear.

Crookedjaw narrowed his eyes. *You must put your Clan first.* Mapleshade's words rang in his ears. He smoothed his fur. "I'm lucky to have been chosen," he confessed. "I'm sorry you won't be with us tonight, Beetlenose." The words nearly stuck in his throat but he forced them out for the sake of the Clan. Rainflower was glowering beneath the willow. She hadn't been chosen, either. "I wish I could have the whole Clan beside me." Crookedjaw nodded to Piketooth and Cedarpelt. "You taught me everything I know." His paws pricked. He wasn't used to making speeches. But if he was going to be leader one day, he'd better to get used to it. He met Beetlenose's gaze. "And I learned lots just watching you train. Your courage gave *me* courage and your skill sharpened mine." *Not as much as Mapleshade's.* He dipped his head low. "When I leave my mark tonight, I shall be leaving it in your honor." He looked up, hoping desperately that his words had soothed his Clanmates' ruffled pelts.

Beetlenose's eyes glittered. "Okay," he conceded.

Oakheart padded past Crookedjaw and halted. "That's right, Crookedjaw," he purred. "We are a Clan and when one cat fights, he fights for the whole Clan."

"Well said, son," Shellheart meowed.

Crookedjaw felt a surge of pride. Was that a glimmer of respect flashing in Rainflower's narrowed gaze?

Hailstar flicked his tail. "We leave at moonhigh."

As the gathering broke up, Crookedjaw headed for the nursery. Joy fizzed beneath his pelt. This would be his first warrior mission. But before he left, he had time to help out with some nursery duties.

He called to the kits, sulking behind their mothers. "Who wants a game of hunt the frog?"

The night heron spiraled up and whirled away downstream as the patrol padded on to the shore. Crookedjaw paused at the water's edge. The river flowed black and smooth past his paws, lit only by stars and the thinnest scratch of moon. Sunningrocks stood on the far bank, dark against a dark sky, timeless as Highstones.

Hailstar slid into the river. As the water closed silently over his back, his Clanmates followed him in. Crookedjaw let the cool water wrap itself around him, relishing the chill after a long day's wait. Quieter than trout, the patrol swam the river, hardly disturbing the surface of the water. No ThunderClan lookout would have seen or heard them. They probably would be watching the stepping-stones, alert for a flash of pelt or the sound of paws on stone.

Crookedjaw pushed ahead with long, smooth kicks and reached the shore first. Here the river's edge was little more than a rock shelf jutting out below Sunningrocks and dropping straight down to the bottom of the river. Crookedjaw pulled himself noiselessly from the water, hopping up onto the stone. Oakheart climbed out beside him while Hailstar and Whitefang waded on to the bank a tail-length downstream. Voleclaw flung a paw over the edge of the rock shelf and hauled himself out with Rippleclaw and Softwing on his tail. Echomist and Owlfur followed and Shellheart brought up the rear. They stood dripping on the bank while Hailstar launched himself up the rock.

"Wait here," he hissed down. "I'll check for patrols."

Crookedjaw gazed up at the starlit sky. He remembered last time he was here, fighting Bluepaw and Snowpaw. This time he wasn't going to be chased from his own territory.

Hailstar's head appeared over the top. "All clear."

With a nod Shellheart leaped up the sheer rock face. His Clanmates swarmed after him. Crookedjaw followed, hooking himself up one clawhold at a time, and landing easily on the smooth, flat stone. The rock sparkled with starlight.

Hailstar waved his tail toward the trees crowding the far edge of Sunningrocks. ThunderClan's territory, every last branch and twig. "You begin that side, Shellheart." He nodded toward the top of the cliff. "Owlfur, Softwing, Voleclaw, and Rippleclaw, join him." He glanced at the others. "You come with me."

As Crookedjaw followed the RiverClan leader over the rock, he let the cool night air bathe his tongue. *ThunderClan scent.* His pelt pricked.

Stale.

They hadn't been here for days. He guessed glaring sun was too hot for cats used to forest shade.

Hailstar sprayed the first tree they reached. Crookedjaw winced at the stench. It was strong enough for ThunderClan to smell long before they reached the tree line.

"I want every bush and tree sprayed," Hailstar ordered.

Crookedjaw crossed the narrow strip of grass and stopped beside a bramble. He marked it, growling. *Smell that, ThunderClan!* By the time they met back at the cliff top, the forest was drenched in RiverClan scent.

"I want four warriors to stay," Hailstar announced. "If a ThunderClan patrol comes, challenge them. If there's a fight, we'll hear from the camp and send reinforcements."

Timberfur stepped forward. "I'll stay."

"Me too." Crookedjaw lined up with him.

Hailstar nudged him away. "I want my most experienced warriors to take the first watch." He glanced at Shellheart. "You stay with Timberfur, Echomist, and Owlfur."

Crookedjaw's itched with frustration as he followed Oakheart down the cliff face. He lowered himself paw hold by paw hold until he felt the ground brush his tail-tip. Then he let himself drop and landed lightly beside Whitefang.

The white warrior's eyes shone. "That was as easy as swallowing a minnow."

Hailstar nodded. "Let's go and tell the Clan."

Their Clanmates were waiting in the starlit clearing. Beetlenose paced beside the reed bed. Lilystem stared expectantly from beneath the willow. Even the queens had slid from the nursery and were lined up, their eyes filled with hope.

"Did you do it?" Lakeshine called.

"Sunningrocks belongs to RiverClan again!" Hailstar announced.

The Clan's cheers sent roosting birds flapping into the still night air.

Willowpaw hurried over to Crookedjaw. "Did you have to fight?"

"It was easy," he told her. "There wasn't a single patrol."

Beetlenose snorted. "That's because all of ThunderClan is asleep!"

"They hadn't been there for days," Voleclaw added.

"It's too hot for their delicate forest paws," Petaldust crowed.

Crookedjaw looked around at his jubilant Clanmates. Was he the only cat who felt that this victory had been too easy?

"I can't believe they haven't tried to fight for it." Oakheart hauled himself onto the topmost boulder of Sunningrocks. "It's been two days. We'll be able to bring the elders up here soon to enjoy the warmth."

Crookedjaw followed his brother over the edge and surveyed the wide stretch of stone, white now beneath the fierce morning sun. "They might still be waiting to catch us off guard." He nodded to the RiverClan patrol they'd been sent to relieve. Petaldust and Cedarpelt flicked their tails in welcome. Beetlenose stretched while Mudfur hurried toward them.

"Brightsky's doing fine," Crookedjaw told the brown warrior. Had Hailstar hoped to distract Mudfur from Brightsky's illness by sending him for guard duty? Clearly it hadn't worked. Mudfur was frowning as he disappeared over the edge of the rock, fast as a fish, and splashed into the river. Why hadn't StarClan healed Brightsky by now?

Fallowtail and Whitefang clambered onto the rocks as Beetlenose, Cedarpelt, and Petaldust began to climb down.

"Mudfur was in a hurry," Whitefang panted.

Fallowtail sighed. "I just hope Brightsky's fever breaks before her kits come." She called after Petaldust, "Send word if there's any change."

"Even if it's bad news?" Petaldust's mew echoed up the rock.

"Yes."

Beetlenose yowled from the foot of the cliff face. "Call if you need help."

Crookedjaw turned away. "We won't need help." Not one marker had been replaced by ThunderClan scent in the two days since they'd set them. ThunderClan seemed to have given in without a fight. Crookedjaw padded across the rock and lay down on its hot, smooth surface.

Oakheart sat beside him, staring into the woods while Fallowtail and Whitefang sniffed along the rim of the rock plateau. White clouds drifted across the sun, sending shadows over the rocks. Crookedjaw stretched, enjoying the sunshine and shade sweeping his pelt. Oakheart began washing.

"I can't believe it was so easy." Whitefang sounded as if he'd wanted a battle.

Crookedjaw rolled over. "They may still make us fight for them."

Below them, bushes rustled at the tree line.

Crookedjaw sat up, bristling. "Did you hear that?"

Fallowtail tasted the air. "ThunderClan," she whispered.

The patrol was on its paws in a moment, hackles up, staring into the trees. Crookedjaw took a long breath, letting the air wash his tongue. There were definitely ThunderClan cats moving among the undergrowth, but not enough to make an attack patrol. He detected one familiar scent.

"Bluefur." Oakheart was already bounding down the rocks.

"Careful!" Fallowtail warned.

Crookedjaw shook his head. "They won't attack," he reassured her. "It's just a border patrol."

Oakheart was peering through the trees. His ears pricked as though he'd spotted prey. Then Crookedjaw heard a vicious hiss and the yowl of a ThunderClan warrior calling to her Clanmate. "Bluefur!"

Oakheart turned away, pelt smooth, eyes glittering.

Whitefang jumped down the rocks to meet him. "Did you see anything?" he called.

"Just a young ThunderClan warrior being nosy." Oakheart climbed back up the rocks and sat down to lick his paws.

"Just a young warrior?" Crookedjaw remembered Oakheart talking about Bluefur at the Gathering. "It was Bluefur, wasn't it?"

Oakheart ran his wet paw over his ear. "So?"

"Was she upset about losing Sunningrocks?"

"I guess so." Oakheart sniffed. "I didn't ask. Why would I want to speak to a ThunderClan cat?"

"You seemed like you were really interested in finding out all about her after the last Gathering."

His brother stopped washing. "It's not me who moons over she-cats!" Oakheart shot back. "You follow Willowpaw around like a kit following its mother."

Crookedjaw flushed. "I do not!"

Oakheart nodded. "Yeah, right." He sounded unconvinced.

Crookedjaw narrowed his eyes and leaped on his brother. "I'm just helping her with her training!"

Oakheart grabbed his shoulders and rolled him over. "That's one way of putting it!"

They tussled, squawking, on the warm rock.

"Hey!" Fallowtail grabbed Crookedjaw's scruff and pulled him off. "We're supposed to be guarding our territory," she growled. "Not showing ThunderClan how we play fight!"

Crookedjaw sat up, his fur ruffled. "Sorry."

"Fallowtail!" Whitefang was calling from the forest's edge. "More ThunderClan warriors are coming!" He dropped into a crouch as Fallowtail, Oakheart, and Crookedjaw leaped down Sunningrocks to join him.

Crookedjaw squinted into the green shadows. He could see pelts flashing between the trunks. Anger flared in his chest. No ThunderClan cat was going to set a paw on his territory. Now that RiverClan had reclaimed it, he'd fight to the death to keep it. He curled his lip and hissed into the forest. The undergrowth swished and the pelts melted away.

Fox-hearts!

Crookedjaw felt power pulsing in his paws. He was ready to beat any cat who threatened his Clan. Mapleshade was right: Being loyal to his Clan felt better than anything else in the whole world!

CHAPTER 22

❧

"Keep your tail down!" Crookedjaw pressed Willowpaw's tail to the ground and nudged her forepaws forward. "Reach as far as you can."

"Oomph." The breath puffed out of Willowpaw as he adjusted her ribs, flattening them to the ground.

"Now, leap!" Crookedjaw ordered.

"Leap?" Willowpaw was splayed like a dead frog. She twisted her head around and stared at him. "I can hardly *move*."

Crookedjaw sat up. "I'm only trying to help." The sun was rising over the trees on the far side of the river. Willowpaw's assessment was due to start any moment.

She struggled to her paws. "Thanks," she mewed, shaking out her legs. "But I'm not sure if you're cut out to be a mentor."

"Don't say that!" Crookedjaw's pelt rippled with dismay. He really wanted to help her pass the first time. "I'm just trying to make you see how important it is to stay low if you're stalking birds."

"Owlfur won't make us stalk *birds*," Willowpaw argued. "I'm training to be a RiverClan warrior, not ThunderClan."

"When the river freezes, birds are all we can catch,"

Crookedjaw reminded her.

"But I've never caught a bird!" Willowpaw's eyes sparked with sudden panic. "You don't think he'll actually test me on that? Owlfur only covered basic land-hunting techniques. He doesn't like catching leaf-bare prey when the river's full of fish! He said it was a waste." She dropped back into a crouch. "Let's try again!" She flattened her tail and pressed her muzzle into the grass, then sat up wailing. "I can't do it! I'm going to fail!"

"No, you're not!" Crookedjaw circled her, trying to remember what Mapleshade had taught him. His pads itched with frustration. Mapleshade had concentrated on battle moves. He thought harder. Had he caught birds with Cedarpelt?

Oh, yes!

"I know!" He realized in a flash what was wrong with her crouch. "Your forepaws should be tucked under your shoulders, not stretched out. That way you'll get a better jump."

Willowpaw dropped again, drawing her paws beneath her. "That feels better." With a sharp push, she shot forward and stretched up, skimming a clump of marsh grass.

"Excellent!" Crookedjaw purred.

"Willowpaw!" Graypaw's mew sounded from the other side of the reeds. "Owlfur's ready!"

Willowpaw's eyes stretched wide. "Oh, StarClan!" Worry clouded her gaze. "I hope I pass."

"Hurry up!" Graypaw urged. "Piketooth's started my assessment!"

"You'll be great!" Crookedpaw promised, but Willowpaw

was already dashing away. "Good luck!" he called after her.

As she disappeared into the rattling stalks, he headed for the river, too restless to go back to camp. It was too early to fish, but he could swim. It'd cool him down. He slid into the water and let it carry him downstream, rolling on to his back as he drifted past the camp. Through the reeds he could see flashes of pelt and hear squeals as the kits charged across the clearing. He felt a prick of sadness. He remembered playing with Oakkit and Beetlekit, Volekit and Petalkit. Things had changed so much since then.

He pushed away the thought. He was a warrior now. And one day he'd be the greatest leader RiverClan had ever known. What more could he possibly want? He struck out and swam for the bank. Climbing out near the stepping-stones, he could hear Birdsong's mew drifting down from Sunningrocks. Hailstar had decided it was safe for the elders to start visiting them again.

"It's so good to feel the warmth of the stone on my pelt," she rasped.

Tanglewhisker answered, purring. "There's nothing like it for reaching every ache."

Crookedjaw padded up the shore and followed a narrow trail into the spindly trees. The sun was shining but he could taste a change in the wind. It was scented with heather from the moors. Rain was on the way.

The grass swished ahead of him. Crookedjaw froze. A pelt was moving between the trees, keeping low.

Owlfur.

Crookedjaw crouched and held his breath as the brown-and-white warrior passed. He must be assessing Willowpaw! Was she nearby? Darting behind a trunk, he crouched down, out of sight. Paw steps scampered toward him. Crookedjaw's heart quickened as he waited for Willowpaw's pelt to come flashing past. But it was Graypaw heading toward the river, scowling with concentration.

Crookedjaw hid as she passed, then pulled himself up the tree, straining to see over the grass. There! Willowpaw's pale tabby pelt was pushing through a clump of ferns. The feathery green fronds curled over and trailed along her spine. Her eyes were fixed on the ground. She must be stalking something.

A blackbird!

She padded closer as the bird struggled to pull a worm from the ground.

Pounce! Crookedjaw willed her on but Willowpaw was taking her time. She dropped into a crouch, flattening her tail, tucking her forepaws under her shoulders, and pressing her belly against the ground. Crookedjaw felt a flicker of pride. *I taught her that.* He tensed as the blackbird plucked the worm free.

Now!

Willowpaw leaped as the blackbird lifted into the air. With a deft paw she hooked it and brought it plummeting to the ground. She held it fluttering beneath her forepaws and looked around hopefully.

Owlfur's head appeared from behind a bush. "Very good," he meowed. "You can let it go."

Eyes shining, Willowpaw released the blackbird and it fled, squawking, into the branches above her head.

Well done! Crookedjaw's heart soared.

"What in the name of StarClan are you doing?" A voice sounded from the bottom of the tree.

Guilt flooded his fur. *Mapleshade!* She'd caught him watching Willowpaw again. Crookedjaw whirled around, ready with an excuse, and saw Shellheart staring up at him, puzzled.

"Why are you hiding in a tree?" Shellheart asked.

Crookedjaw slithered headfirst down the trunk. "I was just—er—just watching—er—just seeing if the assessments were g-going okay. . . ." He stammered to a halt.

Shellheart's ears twitched. "Really?" He didn't sound convinced.

Crookedjaw shrugged. "I wanted to see how Willowpaw was doing."

Shellheart looked at him with amusement. "I guessed." He purred. "And how *is* Willowpaw doing?"

Crookedjaw couldn't stifle his purr. "Great!"

"Good." Shellheart nosed him away from the tree. "Why don't you come back to camp with me? We don't want to distract her when she's doing so well." He steered Crookedjaw on to a trail that led away from the apprentices.

In the clearing, Mudfur was pacing outside the nursery. *Something's wrong!*

Ottersplash trotted after the brown warrior, calling, "I'm sure she'll be fine. They'll all be fine."

Crookedjaw stopped and looked around. Echomist

crouched beneath the willow, her anxious gaze fixed on the nursery. Rainflower growled softly to herself as she padded along the edge of the reeds.

Crookedjaw blocked her path. "What's wrong?"

Rainflower closed her eyes. "Brightsky's kitting."

"Why can't we go to the nursery?" Sunkit complained.

"We just can't!" mewed Shimmerpelt, who was helping Lakeshine shoo the kits up the slope toward the elders' den.

"But why not?"

"Come on, dears!" Birdsong called from the top. "Come and explore our nests. Have you been inside the elders' den before, Reedkit?"

"I don't want to go in there." Reedkit stopped at the entrance. "It's stinky."

Shimmerpelt nudged him forward with her nose. "Don't be rude."

Loudkit scowled. "It's too hot to be inside!" he complained. "Can't we practice swimming in the reed bed?"

Lakeshine shook her head. "Later, little one. We just need to be quiet for a while."

A shriek sounded from the nursery.

Sunkit bristled. "What was that?"

Shimmerpelt nudged her inside. "Brightsky's kitting."

Crookedjaw stared at Rainflower. "When did she start?"

"Just after dawn." Rainflower's gaze was dark. "Brambleberry's worried. Brightsky's still weak from fever."

"But she's a tough warrior," Crookedjaw pointed out.

"Sometimes that's not enough," Rainflower warned over

her shoulder as she padded away.

Crookedjaw joined Ottersplash and Mudfur. "Does Brambleberry need anything? Water? Honey?"

Ottersplash halted. "She's tried all that, and raspberry leaf, too." She lowered her voice as Mudfur carried on walking. "Nothing's working."

Another long, desperate moan sounded in the nursery.

"She's exhausted," Ottersplash murmured.

Birdsong dashed down the slope. "Troutclaw's keeping the kits busy playing hunt the tick." Her eyes turned to the nursery. "How is she?"

Ottersplash just shook her head.

"I'm going inside." Birdsong heaved her wide white belly through the nursery entrance and disappeared.

Oakheart padded, yawning, from his nest. "Is it over yet?" He caught Ottersplash's gaze and stopped.

Birdsong slid out again. Her amber eyes were round and misted with grief. "Three kits." Her mew was husky. "All dead."

Mudfur was at her side in an instant. "And Brightsky?"

Birdsong stared at him blankly. "You'd better go in."

Mudfur lowered his head and turned toward the nursery. He stepped slowly inside, as if he had suddenly grown very old. A moment later a low moan drifted through the reed wall.

Crookedjaw stared at Birdsong. "Is she dead?"

Birdsong nodded. Crookedjaw stared at the ground, not knowing what to say or do. Then a thin mewl drifted across the clearing.

Crookedjaw looked up. *A kit?*

Brambleberry poked her head out. "There was a fourth," she mewed quickly. "She's weak, but she's breathing." She ducked back inside.

Hailstar pushed his way out of his den and stood beside Echomist. He dipped his head. "Thank StarClan for this precious life."

"Get Shimmerpelt," Birdsong told Crookedjaw. "The kit will need warmth and milk."

Crookedjaw dashed up the slope and called into the elders' den. "Shimmerpelt!" She darted out at once. "Come with me." Crookedjaw escorted her down the slope. "One kit survived. It'll need your milk."

Shimmerpelt stopped. *"Survived?"*

"Hurry up!"

"How's Brightsky?" Shimmerpelt's gaze pierced him.

Crookedjaw's paws froze. He stared at her.

"Is she *dead?*"

"I'm sorry!" he burst out. "I should have warned you. I—I—I . . ."

Shimmerpelt padded past him, silencing him with a flick of her tail. "It's okay," she murmured. "It's okay."

Crookedjaw watched her pad to the nursery and disappear inside. A moment later Mudfur squeezed out. He staggered blindly across the clearing. Timberfur hurried to his side and propped him up as he guided his denmate to a shady space under the willow. The grief-stricken warrior collapsed, muzzle on paws, staring into the distance. Timberfur crouched beside him as though sitting vigil, and Rippleclaw crossed the clearing to join them. Crookedjaw's heart twisted in his chest.

The kits were streaming out of the elders' den, squealing as they chased one another down the slope. The reeds swished as Graypaw and Willowpaw charged into camp.

"We passed!" Willowpaw's eyes shone. "We passed our assessment!"

Graypaw paced around her sister, tail high. "Willowpaw caught a blackbird!"

"And Graypaw caught the biggest trout Owlfur's ever seen!" Willowpaw charged across the clearing to Crookedjaw. "Thank you, thank you!" She licked his cheek. "I did everything you told me. You should have seen me!" She paused and tilted her head to one side. "What's wrong?" She stepped away from Crookedjaw. "What's happened?"

Rainflower looked up from the bottom of the slope. "Brightsky died," she meowed. "And three of her newborn kits." Crookedjaw was surprised by the grief in his mother's gaze.

He pressed his muzzle against Willowpaw's cheek. "I'm proud of you," he whispered.

"Let all cats old enough to swim gather to hear my words," Hailstar called from outside his den. Brambleberry stood beside the RiverClan leader, back straight, fur smooth. Willowpaw's eyes glistened.

"You'll be getting your warrior name," Crookedjaw murmured.

Willowpaw sighed. "I never imagined it would be like this."

She padded into the clearing as the Clan gathered. Mudfur seemed unaware of what was happening and stayed beneath the willow. Timberfur and Rippleclaw didn't move from his side.

The kits hung back beside the reed bed, quiet now. Even they realized something terrible had happened.

"Brightsky is dead," Hailstar announced. "And three of her kits." He waited for murmurs of grief to pass through the Clan before he went on. "But one kit has survived." He glanced at Mudfur. "She has not been named yet, but she will always be treasured by the Clan—a reminder of a warrior worthy of StarClan. We will make sure Brightsky's kit grows up to honor and love her mother's memory." He lifted his muzzle, his eyes fixing on Fallowtail. "RiverClan never forgets the sacrifice of its queens. Fallowtail once sacrificed her kits so that the Clan could live in peace. We are lucky to have them back and I consider it a blessing from StarClan that they have grown into such fine warriors." He dipped his head. "Willowpaw, Graypaw, come forward."

As the apprentices padded into the clearing, Hailstar went on. "Willowpaw, you have the swiftness of a WindClan cat but the heart of a RiverClan warrior. In honor of your speed, courage, and cleverness, I give you the name Willowbreeze!"

Crookedjaw lifted his voice, solemnly chanting the new warrior name with his Clanmates. Clouds had covered the sun and were quickly darkening as Hailstar went on. "Graypaw, you have your mother's determination, bravery, and warmth. From this moment you shall be known as Graypool."

"Graypool! Graypool! Graypool!"

As Crookedjaw lifted his muzzle to join in, a raindrop splashed on his nose. In a few moments, the storm broke and rain pounded the camp as though StarClan itself was mourning for Brightsky and her lost kits.

CHAPTER 23

❦

Crookedjaw padded, yawning, from his nest. Dawn was just starting
to brighten the horizon. The river gurgled beyond the reeds
and snores rumbled from the other dens as he nosed his way
into the clearing. He'd noticed the Clan had been sleeping
more since the death of Brightsky and her kits. They crawled
later from their dens, their old enthusiasm for the day's duties
drooping like sedge beneath a heavy frost.

"Ow!"

A squeak made him pause.

"You're treading on my tail!"

The sedge was rustling on the far side of camp. Crookedjaw
strained to see through the half-light. A tiny tail was
disappearing among the green fronds. He padded noiselessly
across the clearing, pricking his ears.

"Which way are we going?"

"I don't know!"

He recognized the squabbling mews of Frogkit and Skykit.

"Why didn't we just go out the entrance?"

"We might have been caught."

Crookedjaw plunged his head into the sedge and grabbed Frogkit by his scruff. Dragging him out, he dropped him on the ground and reached in for Skykit.

"Hey!" She struggled as he pulled her out of the stalks.

"Where are you going?" he asked sternly, depositing Skykit beside her denmate.

The two kits exchanged glances. Crookedjaw guessed they were working out whether to tell the truth or not. Fur brushed the sedge wall behind him.

Brambleberry.

She was yawning. "I was just heading out to fetch herbs," she mewed sleepily.

"I'm glad you're here," Crookedjaw greeted her. "I caught these two trying to sneak out of camp."

Brambleberry's whiskers twitched. "What? Kits! Trying to sneak out? That's never happened before!" She stared in mock surprise at Crookedjaw.

Crookedjaw swallowed back a purr. He was trying to stay stern for the kits' sake. Besides, he knew better than any cat the dangers waiting beyond the camp wall for adventurous kits. "Where were you going?" he asked them again.

Frogkit glanced at Brambleberry, then at his paws. "We wanted to see where Brightsky's kits were buried," he mumbled.

Brambleberry frowned. "Why in the name of StarClan would you want to do that?"

Skykit shuffled her paws. "We wanted to see if it was true they were dead."

Crookedjaw leaned closer. "Why wouldn't it be true?"

"StarClan doesn't really let kits die, does it?" The kit's pale brown fur rippled.

Frogkit twitched his striped tail. "Ottersplash wouldn't let us see the vigil."

Crookedjaw tucked his tail tight over his paws as he remembered the long, heartbreaking night, less than half a moon ago, when Mudfur had chased his Clanmates away from Brightsky's body and cradled his three dead kits against his mate's stiff flank.

"StarClan does take kits," Brambleberry told them. "And keeps them safe." She crouched beside the wide-eyed kits. "They'll be allowed to hunt there. StarClan has the clearest rivers and fastest fish. And they'll be with Brightsky."

Frogkit stuck out his tail. "Birdsong says StarClan took them as an omen."

"Rainflower and Echomist say that more bad things are going to happen," Skykit added.

Frogkit went on. "Piketooth thinks StarClan is angry with us."

"And Troutclaw says that's why you couldn't save the kits or Brightsky."

Brambleberry flinched. "It wasn't an omen." Her mew was steady. "Sometimes bad things happen. I did everything I could, but Brightsky was too sick and it made her kits sick, too."

Crookedjaw drew closer to the medicine cat. "If StarClan was angry with us, why did they leave us Leopardkit?" he reminded the kits. Mudfur had named his daughter after the ancient Clan, hoping it would give the tiny kit all the strength she would need to survive without her mother.

"I guess they want *us* to look after her," Skykit conceded.

"Exactly," Brambleberry agreed. "And why would they leave her with us if they thought we were bad or that bad things were going to happen?"

Frogkit flexed his claws. "Can we go and see where they're buried anyway?"

"No." Crookedjaw nosed them toward the nursery. "Shimmerpelt and Lakeshine will be wondering where you are."

Skykit sniffed. "Shimmerpelt's always too busy feeding Leopardkit."

Brambleberry smoothed the kit's ruffled fur with her tail-tip. "Why don't you take your mother some wet moss?" she suggested. "Feeding Leopardkit will make her thirsty. She'll be so proud of you for being helpful to Brightsky's kit."

Skykit's eyes brightened. "Okay!" She dashed away toward the reed bed.

"Don't fall in!" Crookedjaw warned as Frogkit hurtled after her. He turned back to Brambleberry, hesitating. "Are you sure it wasn't an omen?"

"I'm sure."

Crookedjaw narrowed his eyes. "How can you tell what's an omen and what isn't?"

"An omen feels different," Brambleberry told him.

"Can omens change things or do they just tell you what's

going to happen?" He knew Brambleberry would understand that he wasn't just talking about the kits' gossip.

Brambleberry met his gaze. "Sometimes they tell you what's already happening."

"So that you can change it?"

"So that you're prepared for it."

Frustration clawed at Crookedjaw's belly. She wasn't giving anything away. "Why don't you just tell me about *my* omen— the one that worried you?"

"There's nothing to tell," she answered softly.

"You mean there wasn't an omen?"

"I mean it's up to you."

"*What's* up to me?" Crookedjaw couldn't keep the growl from his voice.

"The path you choose is in your paws," Brambleberry meowed. "Only you can know your own heart, and that will decide whether you choose the right path or the wrong path."

"My heart is as true and loyal as any RiverClan cat!"

"Good."

"Let me prove it!"

"How?"

Crookedjaw searched desperately for ideas. "I don't know! Let me help you gather herbs!" Perhaps if he spent time with her, he'd be able to persuade her he was good.

"I've already asked Beetlenose to help me."

Crookedjaw swished his tail. "Okay!" he snapped. "But don't blame me if I choose the wrong path. You're the medicine cat! You're supposed to help your Clanmates, not make them suffer because you won't tell them everything." Ears hot with fury, he stalked away.

The first light of dawn was showing behind the willow tree. Beetlenose padded from his den and greeted Brambleberry with a yawn. "I'm ready," he muttered. He brightened as Hailstar ducked out of his den. "Can't you get Willowbreeze to help you?" he begged Brambleberry. "This is an apprentice's job and she's the closest to an apprentice we've got."

Brambleberry scowled back. "Stop fussing and hurry up."

Beetlenose sighed and, casting a final, rueful look at Hailstar, followed her out of camp.

"Let all cats old enough to swim gather to hear my words." The RiverClan leader padded to the center of the clearing.

Crookedjaw frowned. What was the leader planning now? Whatever it was, he hoped it would cheer up the Clan. The kits weren't the only ones who believed StarClan was punishing them.

Dens rustled and paws scuffed the ground as his Clanmates climbed from their nests and padded to hear what Hailstar wanted.

Rippleclaw's fur was ruffled and unwashed. Piketooth sat askew, his whiskers crumpled. Even Shellheart's shoulders drooped.

Oakheart squeezed next to Crookedjaw, his gaze bleary with sleep. "What's going on?" He sighed. "It's hardly dawn."

Hailstar turned slowly, eyeing his Clan. "We took Sunningrocks back and ThunderClan didn't even retaliate. Today we will take more of their territory."

More? Crookedjaw looked past Hailstar to his father, who was sitting behind the RiverClan leader. He tried to read Shellheart's gaze, but it was clear and unblinking.

Cedarpelt stepped forward. "Do we need more of their territory?" he asked.

"We need the river," Hailstar countered. "We should control both banks beyond Sunningrocks. Which includes the forest that runs along the far side of the river."

Owlfur tipped his head. "You want to capture *forest*?"

Hailstar nodded.

Troutclaw shook his graying head. "What would RiverClan do with trees?"

Rippleclaw answered the elder with a growl. "It means we'll be able to fish the river above Sunningrocks without fear of attack."

Willowbreeze was looking puzzled. "ThunderClan would never attack us in the water," she pointed out. "They're terrified of it."

Ottersplash padded forward, her kits trotting after her. "But what if they learned to swim?" She shooed them away with her tail. "It'd give them prey all year round. As long as they control that stretch of river, there's a chance they may learn to use it like we do."

Troutclaw snorted. "ThunderClan is more likely to learn how to fly!"

Birdsong nodded. "RiverClan has never owned that piece of territory!"

"Patrolling it would be hard work," Fallowtail added.

Timberfur lashed his tail. "Are you scared of hard work?"

Fallowtail flattened her ears. "Of course not!"

"It would show ThunderClan we're strong," Whitefang put in.

"They wouldn't try taking Sunningrocks again," Piketooth growled. "They'd be too busy trying to hold on to what's left of their forest."

"Then it's decided." Hailstar flexed his claws.

Whitefang circled the RiverClan leader, pelt bristling. "When do we attack?"

"Now!"

Crookedjaw stared at Hailstar in astonishment. Whitefang's gaze shone with excitement. Rippleclaw's, too. Timberfur clawed at the ground impatiently. But Cedarpelt watched through narrowed eyes. Fallowtail was frowning and Owlfur turned his head away, sighing.

Why isn't he satisfied with Sunningrocks? Crookedjaw didn't understand Hailstar's plan. How in the name of StarClan could they win a battle fought on ThunderClan's land? He'd seen the thick ferns and clawing brambles that choked the trees around Sunningrocks. His thick pelt rippled as he imagined getting it tangled in a thornbush.

Oakheart's mew shook him from his thoughts. "Does Hailstar think a battle will cheer us up?"

"I guess he's got to try something." Crookedjaw shrugged. "Even the kits have been worried about Brightsky's death." Out of the corner of his eye, he noticed Ottersplash whispering to her kits. "But a battle is risky and we don't need more grief."

"I want to be in the attack patrol." Ottersplash's mew rang across the clearing.

Shimmerpelt gasped. "What about your kits?"

"Will you look after them till I return?" Ottersplash dipped her head to her denmate.

"O-of course," Shimmerpelt stuttered. "But what if you—"

Ottersplash cut her off. "Timberfur takes that risk," she answered sharply. "Why shouldn't I?"

Hailstar padded across the clearing. "I'd be proud to have you fight beside me." His eyes glowed as he surveyed the rest of his Clan. "Timberfur, Rippleclaw, Shellheart, Piketooth, and Whitefang." He nodded to each warrior. "You'll join us."

For once, Crookedjaw was relieved he hadn't been chosen. "An impressive patrol," he commented.

Oakheart sniffed. "They believe in this battle."

"At least someone does," Crookedjaw growled under his breath. He felt a flash of guilt. "Can I lead a border patrol on this side of the river?" he called to Hailstar. "We haven't checked the bridge or fence in days."

Hailstar was already leading his Clanmates toward the reeds. He glanced back. "Okay," he answered. "Take anyone you like."

Loudkit was chasing after Ottersplash. "When are you coming back?" he whimpered.

She stopped and leaned down. "I told you," she murmured softly. "I'll be back before sunhigh."

"Promise?"

Ottersplash pressed her muzzle to Loudkit's head.

"StarClan willing," she breathed.

Loudkit stared after her as Ottersplash followed the patrol out of camp. "Will StarClan want her like they wanted Brightsky?" he whispered.

Crookedjaw opened his mouth to reassure him, but Shimmerpelt had already darted forward and was sweeping him away with a soft swish of her tail.

Crookedjaw skirted the Twoleg bridge and headed away from the river, into a line of willow trees. He glanced over his shoulder. Voleclaw, Oakheart, Petaldust, Willowbreeze, and Graypool were following him through the straggly grass, ducking behind the slim gray trunks at the edge of the meadow.

"I don't see why we couldn't hunt," Voleclaw grumbled.

"We're patrolling, not hunting," Crookedjaw told him.

"Just because you suggested the patrol doesn't make you Clan leader." Voleclaw sniffed.

Petaldust nudged her brother. "It does make him patrol leader, though," she pointed out.

"Sssh!" Crookedjaw paused and glanced through the willow trees. The sun was lifting into the sky, and all around the meadow Twolegs were beginning to stir from their pelt-dens. The field was dotted with the brightly colored mounds. They rustled and flapped in the breeze.

"Get down!" Crookedjaw warned as a Twoleg crawled out of his den and padded, coughing, up the field. A Twoleg kit tottered out after him, carrying a bright yellow ball. It tossed the ball and stood watching as it rolled across the grass and bumped into another den.

"We're better get past here before they're all awake," Oakheart whispered.

Crookedjaw glanced at the knotted gray fence that bounded the field beyond the trees. They'd have to creep up through the willows and around the top of the field to reach the dog fence. "Come on." He began to pad forward, tail down. Sunlight streamed through the shivering leaves and dappled the grass. Crookedjaw trod lightly, keeping one eye on the pelt-dens.

Suddenly a shadow flashed between them. Crookedjaw paused. The shadow flashed again and with a jolt he recognized the shape. A cat. With shoulders and tail that were familiar.

Mapleshade? He hadn't trained with her for a moon. Why was she here?

Oakheart halted beside him and tasted the air. "What's up?"

"Can you see that cat?" Crookedjaw nodded to the gap between pelt-dens where Mapleshade's outline was showing clear as day.

"What cat?" Oakheart frowned at him. "Do you think the Twolegs have started taking their kittypets out with them?"

"It's not a kittypet," Crookedjaw whispered. "It's a warrior."

Oakheart twitched. "Where?"

"There."

Mapleshade returned his gaze, then flitted behind a pelt-den as the Twoleg kit toddled past.

"I can't see anything."

"What's holding us up?" Voleclaw hissed from behind.

Willowbreeze crept past him and stopped beside Crookedjaw. "Is anything wrong?"

Crookedjaw shook his head. "I'm seeing things," he joked. As he began to move off, Mapleshade appeared again, padding around the edge of the pelt-den. *What is she doing?* He kept walking. His patrol was depending on him to get them away from these Twolegs and safely back to camp.

"You *definitely* can't see any cats with the Twolegs?" he checked with Oakheart.

"Definitely." Oakheart flicked his tail over Crookedjaw's spine. "I think you should get Brambleberry to check your eyes when we get back." He purred. "And I can tell Beetlenose he's missed two patrols. He's going to be spitting mad. He's picking mallow leaves while Hailstar's invading ThunderClan and we're stalking a dog *and* an invisible cat!"

"Wait!" Crookedjaw interrupted, his heart tightening.

Mapleshade was nudging the yellow ball toward them.

Go away! Panic flared in him. *The Twolegs will see us!*

Oakheart bristled beside him. "Is the wind making that ball move?" His gaze was fixed on the slowly rolling ball.

"No." Crookedjaw stared pleadingly at Mapleshade as she tapped the ball closer. She held his gaze but did nothing to stop the ball from trickling within a reed-length of the warriors.

"Twoleg!" Willowbreeze's hiss snapped his attention from Mapleshade. The Twoleg kit was running after the ball, mewling.

Graypool stiffened, a growl rumbling in her throat. "It's heading straight for us."

"Duck down!" Crookedjaw ordered. "And stay still! It won't see us through the long grass. It's just a kit."

The patrol crouched, fear sparking around them. Crookedjaw peered through the green stems. Mapleshade's eyes glittered as she rolled the ball closer. With a final push she sent it spinning toward the edge of the meadow. The Twoleg kit stumbled after it, paws outstretched. With a thump, the kit fell over and started to wail.

A huge Twoleg darted from a pelt-den and raced toward the kit, yowling. It scooped it up and held it, its gaze drifting toward the ball and then the willow trees.

"StarClan help us!" Willowbreeze's hiss barely made it through her gritted teeth.

The Twoleg let out a yelp of surprise.

"It's seen us!" Oakheart growled.

"Hide!" Crookedjaw backed deeper into the long grass. He darted behind a trunk and held his breath as the Twoleg put down its kit and headed into the willows. The Twoleg kit was pointing straight at them! Voleclaw darted behind a fern. Petaldust crouched beside him. Graypool flattened herself beneath an arching strand of bramble and Oakheart ducked behind a rock. Crookedjaw scanned the trees. Where was Willowbreeze?

The Twoleg was wading through the long grass now, ducking under a low branch. *Willowbreeze!* Crookedjaw's heart lurched as he spotted her backed against the gray knotted fence where it extended into the trees. The Twoleg was leaning down toward her. With a grunt, it reached out with one pink hairless paw and grabbed her scruff.

Crookedjaw swallowed back a cry of rage and fear and watched helplessly as the Twoleg carried Willowbreeze back toward its pelt-den. Its kit followed, yelping happily.

Oakheart was beside Crookedjaw in an instant. "What happens now?"

Crookedjaw stared at Willowbreeze, her paws churning the air as she dangled in the Twoleg's grip. "We've got to rescue her!"

"How?" Voleclaw stared at him, eyes blazing. "Why did you bring us here, you fish-brain?"

Petaldust leaped from her hiding place and circled her Clanmates. "What are we going to do?"

"We've got to get out of here before they find the rest of us," Voleclaw hissed.

Crookedjaw noticed Graypool staring after her sister in horror. "We'll rescue her, I promise."

"Not now, though." Oakheart nodded to the Twolegs, who were crowding to see their catch. Some of them turned and pointed to the willow trees.

Crookedjaw straightened up. "Let's get back to camp and organize a rescue patrol. We'll take the quickest route. Just make sure no one slows down enough to get caught as well." He raced out of the trees and pelted across the meadow. The Twolegs stared in surprise as the patrol streamed past them.

"Willowbreeze!" Crookedjaw yowled to her as he passed.

"Don't fight them! Stay calm! I'll come back to rescue you!" He pounded into the marshes, twisting his ears to make sure he could hear his patrol at his heels. Weaving among the tussocks of spiky grass, he hurtled toward camp. He raced through the entrance so fast that reeds whipped his back. "They've got Willowbreeze!"

The words froze on his tongue. The clearing was littered with injured cats. Ottersplash lay panting, her ear torn, her pelt clumped with blood. Her kits pressed against her, wailing with fear as Brambleberry draped cobwebs over her wounds. Whitefang crouched beside her, his muzzle bleeding, while Piketooth limped back and forth, growling under his breath. Hailstar sat huddled in conversation with Shellheart, Timberfur, and Rippleclaw.

Crookedjaw stared in dismay.

They lost the battle!

But what about Willowbreeze? He had to get her back.

StarClan help me!

CHAPTER 24

Petaldust and Graypool skidded to a halt behind Crookedjaw.

"They lost!" Petaldust gasped.

Voleclaw stopped beside them. "What happened?"

"We'll worry about that later!" Crookedjaw raced toward Hailstar. "Twolegs took Willowbreeze!"

Shellheart looked up, his eyes dark. Hailstar's pelt bushed up.

Timberfur flexed his bloodstained claws. "Where?"

"When?" Rippleclaw leaned forward.

"In the pelt-den field. Just now."

"Did they hurt her?" Hailstar demanded.

Crookedjaw shook his head. "They just carried her to their den."

"They didn't harm her at all?" Hailstar pressed. "Did they seem angry?"

Crookedjaw frowned. What difference did that make? They'd *taken* her. She'd be terrified and alone.

Hailstar sighed. "This has been a bad day." He called to Brambleberry. "How's Ottersplash?"

Brambleberry peeled another cobweb from the wad beside

her. "No deep wounds," she reported. "She'll be okay."

Timberfur shrugged. "The brambles did more damage than ThunderClan."

Rippleclaw's pelt was smeared with blood. "They knew what they were doing when they drove us deeper into the forest."

Crookedjaw leaned forward. "What about Willowbreeze?"

Hailstar shifted his paws. "From what you say, it seems like the Twolegs don't want to hurt her. She'll be okay until tomorrow. We'll send a rescue party then."

"Tomorrow might be too late! What if they leave in the night and take her with them?" *Don't you care?*

Shellheart ran his tail down Crookedjaw's spine. "We've taken quite a beating today," he explained.

Crookedjaw ducked away.

Fallowtail pounded toward them. "Graypool says Willowbreeze has been taken!" Her blue eyes darted frantically from one warrior to another. "We have to save her!"

"We'll rescue her tomorrow," Hailstar meowed gently. "Once we've recovered from our wounds."

"You're leaving her there?" Fallowtail stared at him. "Is it because she's half WindClan?"

Hailstar shook his head. "That has nothing to do with it."

"Really?" Fallowtail curled her lip. "You gave her up easily last time. Are you giving her up again?"

"*You* gave her up last time," Hailstar corrected.

"And you *let* me!"

"I rescued her from WindClan," Hailstar reminded her.

"You just wanted to win your Clan's respect!" Fallowtail hissed.

Hailstar's eyes glittered. "I wanted your kits to be with their true Clan."

Timberfur stood and nudged Fallowtail away. "Hailstar will rescue her." He steered her toward the clearing.

Crookedjaw followed. "She'll be okay." He nodded to Timberfur. "I'll look after her."

As Timberfur returned to Hailstar and Shellheart, Crookedjaw felt Fallowtail tremble beside him. "You have to save her!" Her blue eyes were clouded with fear. "I can't lose her again!"

Graypool joined them. "We can't leave her there," she agreed. She leaned against her mother. "Who knows what the Twolegs will do with her?"

Crookedjaw nodded. "I'll rescue her," he promised.

"Now?" Graypool prompted.

"After dark." Crookedjaw was already planning his mission. He'd never get past the Twolegs while it was light, but they slept at night. He'd be able to find Willowbreeze in the dark by following her scent.

"Can I come?" Graypool asked.

Fallowtail bristled. "No!"

Crookedjaw gazed sympathetically at the gray warrior. "You stay with Fallowtail," he ordered. "I can do this alone."

Why had Mapleshade pulled such a stupid trick? Did she hate Willowbreeze that much? Where was her loyalty to the Clan?

* * *

The day dragged on. As the sun slowly eased toward the horizon, Crookedjaw's heart seemed to beat his chest hollow. Fallowtail paced along the edge of the reeds, muttering to herself, while Graypool trotted after her. Brambleberry moved from injured warrior to injured warrior, treating wounds, while the kits raced around the clearing acting out the battle.

"It's your turn to be ThunderClan!" Sunkit poked Frogkit with her paw.

"I don't want to be stinky ThunderClan!" Frogkit growled.

Owlfur and Cedarpelt had restocked the fresh-kill pile, but Crookedjaw wasn't hungry. As the river slid past, the air pressed hot against his pelt. Crookedjaw longed for a breeze. He glanced at the horizon, hoping for clouds to signal a change in the weather. But the sky was clear, blossoming stars as it darkened around a pale half-moon.

Brambleberry got to her paws. It was time for her meeting at the Moonstone with the medicine cats from the other Clans. Crookedjaw watched her head out of the camp, wondering how Goosefeather would welcome her after today's battle.

It was time he left, too.

"Aren't you eating?" Shellheart called as Crookedjaw padded past the fresh-kill pile.

"Later." Crookedjaw headed for the entrance. "I want a swim first," he mumbled. "It's hot." He ducked through the entrance and hurried along the grassy path.

"I know where you're going." Brambleberry's mew surprised him. She bounded down the bank and blocked his path.

"How?"

The medicine cat's eyes were wild, as though something had startled her.

"Are you okay?" Crookedjaw shifted his paws. What was wrong with her?

Brambleberry ignored his question. "You're going to get Willowbreeze." She circled him, tail flicking.

"Someone has to."

"Yes, yes," she agreed distractedly. "And that someone must be you. You must do it. It is part of your destiny."

Crookedjaw pricked his ears. *My destiny!* That must be why Mapleshade had been in the field. "What do you know about my destiny?"

"I know what I need to know. This is it. This is part of it." Brambleberry paused and stared at him. "You're going to rescue Willowbreeze? Is that the path you're choosing?"

"Is that the path I should choose?" Crookedjaw's belly twisted at the alternative: to let Willowbreeze stay with the Twolegs.

"You know your own heart." Brambleberry started pacing around him again. "I just hope StarClan is right."

"Right about what?"

Before he had finished speaking, Brambleberry darted back up the bank and disappeared into shadow. Crookedjaw swallowed. *Am I doing the right thing?* He pushed away the thought. *Of course I am! I can't abandon Willowbreeze. She's my Clanmate.*

He bounded up the bank, following Brambleberry's trail around the camp and into the marshes. The medicine cat must have moved fast because her scent was already growing stale.

Crookedjaw headed down to the shore and followed the river upstream. The water looked black and deep beneath the stars. Behind him the reeds rattled and the night heron swooped low across the water before soaring away.

Crookedjaw veered away from the river and followed the shore past the first meadow, skirting the Twoleg field right up to the bridge. He paused there, ducking down in its spiky shadow, catching his breath. *I'm not scared,* he told himself. He flexed his claws and peered through the willow trees. The pelt-dens glowed with yellow light, throwing wildly misshapen shadows across the field as the Twolegs moved around inside.

Pebbles shifted on the shore downstream. Crookedjaw froze. Something was stalking him. He crouched deeper into the shadow, tasting the air, scenting nothing but Twoleg smells. Keeping low, he crept out from beneath the bridge and stalked forward. He ducked beneath the longest grass and crept along the shore.

A shadow skirted the water. Crookedjaw flexed his claws and crouched down, ready to attack.

"Crookedjaw?"

Graypool?

He straightened up. "What are you doing here?"

She dashed forward to greet him. "It's spooky out here at night!" Her eyes were glittering.

"I thought I told you to stay behind and look after Fallow-tail."

"Echomist's with her," Graypool mewed.

Crookedjaw's paws pricked with irritation. "It's bad enough

that I lost Willowbreeze!" he growled. "I don't want to lose you, too!"

"You won't!" Graypool's claws scraped the pebbles. "I'm here to help get her back!"

"Go home!"

"No!"

Crookedjaw hissed with frustration. "Fine. Follow me."

Graypool jumped up the bank into the willow trees.

"What did I just say?" Crookedjaw yanked her back down by her tail. "Follow me! And stay close."

He padded quietly back to the bridge, leaped up onto the shadowy timbers, and tasted the air. The pelt-dens were noisy with Twolegs mumbling and yowling.

Graypool snorted. "Don't they ever go to sleep?"

Crookedjaw beckoned her on with a flick of his muzzle. "At least they're inside," he whispered. "Let's see if we can figure out which one Willowbreeze is in."

Heart pounding, Crookedjaw padded across the field, the soft grass stroking his belly fur. Graypool followed, her paw steps no more than a faint whisper on the grass. They halted beside the nearest pelt-den and began sniffing the edge. Ducking down, Crookedjaw caught a glimpse inside. It was chaotic, with brightly colored piles heaped everywhere and Twolegs squatting in the small space between. Countless scents bathed his nose, strong and startling.

"Here!" Graypool hissed from the next pelt-den.

"I thought I told you to stay close!" He darted over to her and sniffed the edge of the den. Hope flared in his belly.

Willowbreeze! Her scent was thickly laced with fear, but it was fresh.

Suddenly a Twoleg moved in the den, its shadow engulfing them as it swept over the grass. Crookedjaw froze, feeling Graypool trembling against him. Then the shadow swooped away as the Twoleg settled down.

"We've got to go in there," Graypool whispered shakily.

"Yes." Crookedjaw poked his head under the stretched pelt and peered inside. It was more chaotic than the last den, the colorful piles bigger and brighter. *Good.* They'd be able to hide easily. He squeezed under the pelt and crouched behind a heap of Twoleg clutter. Graypool slid in after him. Her breath was fast, her hackles high.

"I won't let them catch you," Crookedjaw promised. He nosed his way around the edge of the den, squeezing through the narrow channel between the clutter and the den wall. The Twolegs were chattering and hooting, crouched around something in the middle of the den. Crookedjaw stretched up and peered over the nearest pile, his ears flat, eyes wide.

The Twolegs were dangling a thread into a square brown nest. Familiar pale tabby paws flapped frantically at the thread, trying to catch it as the Twolegs twitched it and pulled it out of reach.

"I can see her!" Crookedjaw dropped down and whispered in Graypool's ear. "They've got her in some sort of trap and they're teasing her."

Graypool flexed her claws. "Is she okay?"

"I think she's playing along," Crookedjaw guessed.

Graypool opened her mouth. "I don't smell blood."

"They haven't harmed her, then." Crookedjaw felt a rush of relief. "Now we have to wait."

"Here?"

Crookedjaw nodded. Now that he had Willowbreeze in sight, he didn't want to lose her again. He flattened his belly against the floor. Graypool settled beside him.

"It'll be okay," he promised her.

She swallowed and nodded.

Crookedjaw began to grow stiff as the Twolegs played with Willowbreeze. He glanced over the pile again and again, itching with frustration, until suddenly the Twolegs started moving clumsily around the den, rummaging in the muddled pelts that were scattered on the floor.

Crookedjaw tensed. "Look out!" Twoleg paws plunged into the heap they were sheltering behind. He ducked under the edge, out into the field, dragging Graypool after him. "That was close!"

They crouched in the grass. The earthy scent of it soothed Crookedjaw's jangled nerves. The light disappeared from the pelt-den. Murmuring and rustling, the Twolegs gradually settled down.

"Can we go back in?" Graypool's round eyes reflected the moon.

"Let's wait a bit longer," Crookedjaw whispered. "Until they're asleep."

On the other side of the willow trees, the river glided past, rolling pebbles along the shore, and an owl screeched far away.

One by one, the pelt-dens grew dark and silent.

"Now." Crookedjaw slid under the stretched pelt once more. Ears pricked, he listened for movement. The Twolegs were still, lying under pelts at the far side of the den. He sensed rather than saw Graypool beside him as he crept over a heap of pelts and padded across the den. He could just make out the brown trap near the Twolegs' hind paws. Fur swished inside it. Claws scrabbled quietly against its walls.

"She's trying to get out." Crookedjaw darted toward it, hissing. "We're here, Willowbreeze. We've come to get you."

A low purr of relief sounded inside the box. "I can't get the flaps open at the top."

Crookedjaw reached up and saw the top of the trap was folded, flap over flap. He tugged at one, but it wouldn't shift.

"Let me help." Graypool stretched up beside him and hooked her claws under a flap. Together they tugged, but the strange hard substance wouldn't give.

"Push!" Crookedjaw hissed to Willowbreeze.

"I am!" she snapped back.

"Together!" Crookedjaw gave a fierce heave.

The trap rocked wildly and tumbled over on to its side. Graypool squawked as it fell on top of her. The Twolegs sat up, yelping, as Graypool struggled to escape. Crookedjaw whipped his head around. The Twolegs were flailing in the dark. They hadn't spotted the extra cats yet, but it wouldn't be long. Panic surging inside him, Crookedjaw turned back to the trap. A gap had opened between the flaps. Willowbreeze's paws were stretching through.

"Pull!" he yowled to Graypool. He didn't care if the Twolegs heard. They were thrashing around in their pelts, slapping the darkness with lumbering paws. As one brushed Crookedjaw's tail, he yanked desperately at the trap. It gave way and Willowbreeze shot out like a rabbit from a foxhole.

A light flashed over them. Crookedjaw caught the full glare and staggered, blinded. The Twolegs screeched.

"This way!" Graypool pushed him forward.

Crookedjaw hurtled headlong into a heap of pelts, his paws tangling with StarClan knew what. Terror clawed at him as he struggled free. Blurred shapes moved around him as he adjusted to the light. Willowbreeze was disappearing over the wall of pelts with Graypool on her tail. Crookedjaw shot after them, Twolegs shrieking behind him. He dived under the stretched pelt and out into the field.

Willowbreeze was standing in the grass staring at him. "That was close!"

Graypool grabbed her scruff and dragged her forward. "Run, you fish-brain!"

They pelted away through the dewy grass. Crookedjaw glanced over his shoulder. Twolegs were bursting out of the dens all over the meadow, flashing lights and howling. Crookedjaw stretched his claws and dug them deeper with every stride, racing after his Clanmates with the blood roaring in his ears.

CHAPTER 25

☘

"Psst!"

A hiss stopped Crookedjaw in his tracks.

The reed bed was in view, pale under the moon, the Twoleg pelt-dens far behind. Willowbreeze scrambled to a halt and turned. "What's wrong?"

Crookedjaw whipped his head around, tasting the air.

"Pssst!"

A cat was signaling from the riverbank. Straining to see in the light of the half-moon, Crookedjaw spotted an orange-and-white pelt.

"Go on without me!" he called to Willowbreeze. "I want to check something out."

Graypool had doubled back and was pacing around her sister. "What's the holdup?"

"Crookedjaw's seen something." Willowbreeze gazed at him curiously.

"Nothing important," he assured them. "Get back to camp. Fallowtail will be waiting."

Graypool frowned. "Are you sure you don't need help?"

Crookedjaw flicked his tail impatiently. "Just get

Willowbreeze safely back. She's gone through a lot in one day."

Graypool nodded and steered her sister down the path.

"What do you want, Mapleshade?" Crookedjaw padded angrily toward the clump of sedge she was hiding behind. "Haven't you caused enough trouble?"

The she-cat flew at him, spitting. Shocked, Crookedjaw rolled on to his back and heaved her off with a sharp kick of his hind legs. Scrambling to his paws he faced her, bristling.

Her eyes blazed. "You mouse-brain," she snarled.

"What?" He couldn't believe his ears. "You betray us to the Twolegs and then you're angry?"

"I was testing you, idiot!" A sneer curled her lip. "I knew you were weak. I knew you wouldn't keep your promise! When your mate was stolen, you should have left her!"

"She's not my mate!"

"She will be." Mapleshade stalked around him. "I can see it in the way you look at her."

Crookedjaw growled. "So what?"

"So what?" Mapleshade echoed with a sneer. "If she can't keep herself safe then she's of no use to you! Your loyalty should be to your Clan, not her! Your Clanmates are lying injured in camp yet you sneak off and risk your life to save a warrior who can't even outrun a Twoleg! She should be ashamed that she caused so much trouble. *You* should be ashamed that you deserted your Clan on a fish-brained mission! Did Hailstar say you could go?" She didn't wait for an answer. "No! He told you to wait. Your disloyalty makes me sick. Cats who betray their Clan should be banished. They should live as rogues and loners because that's all they are!" Hissing, she reared and slashed at Crookedjaw's muzzle with both paws.

He knocked her away, suddenly aware that he was bigger than her and stronger. "Who *are* you?" He swiped at her, his paw catching her cheek and sending her tumbling to the ground. He was on her in an instant, digging his claws into her shoulders and pinning her down. "No StarClan warrior would turn on its Clanmate. You mentored me and now you *attack* me?"

Mapleshade went limp in his grip. Crookedjaw recoiled, suddenly afraid he had hurt her. The she-cat struggled to her paws, shrinking into a huddled crouch. She looked elderly and frail. Guilt seared Crookedjaw. Her blood was wet on his claws. Beating an old cat like that was no measure of strength.

Groaning with the effort, Mapleshade lifted her muzzle. "I saw greatness in you the moment you were born," she croaked. "You don't remember the storm, but I saw it. I saw how the skies heaved and roared at your birth." She dropped on to her belly, panting. "You have a wonderful destiny, Crookedjaw. You're not just going to be the greatest leader of your Clan, you're going to be the greatest leader of *any* Clan." She stopped to catch her breath. "But you have to keep your promise to me."

He crouched beside her, pity sweeping over him. "Of course I will."

"You'll have to make sacrifices," she warned. "Your life is not your own; it belongs to your Clan. Don't be distracted from all the wonderful things you can achieve."

The greatest leader of any Clan? Excitement flashed though Crookedjaw as Mapleshade went on. "And you will achieve so much! As long as you have me to guide you." She seemed to be gaining strength with each word. "I have chosen to help you. No one else. Just you. Never forget that the Clan is greater than its cats. Even if you sacrifice every cat who ever loved you, it will be no more than shedding raindrops from your fur because, even if they go, the Clan will still be there and relying on you. Do you agree?"

She lifted her gaze to meet his. It sparked with hope.

Sacrifice every cat who loved me? Crookedjaw frowned. *Why would I have to?* "But why—" He started to argue, but shadow was swallowing Mapleshade as a cloud swept across the moon. Fat raindrops splashed on Crookedjaw's pelt. Wind tugged the branches above his head.

"Don't go yet!" he begged. "Tell me more!" With a jab of disappointment, he found himself staring at bare earth. She had gone. He straightened up and stared across the marsh. The reeds beside the camp were rattling as the rain hardened.

I'm going to be the greatest leader any Clan has ever known!

The words sang in Crookedjaw's heart. He broke into a run, heading for home. Strength pulsed in his paws. He'd saved Willowbreeze from Twolegs. He'd been chosen by StarClan.

I can do anything!

CHAPTER 26

Leaf-fall had reddened the willow and darkened the sedge. Crookedjaw shivered as a cold wind swept through the camp. "Come on!" he called to the kits. "Let's warm up with a game." His charges—who were close to becoming 'paws now that they were five moons old—padded disdainfully around him.

Skykit sniffed. "We want to learn battle moves."

"The camp may be invaded by Twolegs any moment!" Reedkit flicked his long, reed-straight tail.

Crookedjaw purred. "I don't think a patrol of kits doing forepaw slashes is going to drive them off."

Blackkit growled. "Just you wait!"

"We'll shred them!" Frogkit barged past his denmate and squared up to Crookedjaw. "Show me that move you talked about, the forepaw slash."

Crookedjaw started to feel trapped. He glanced toward the nursery where Shimmerpelt and Lakeshine were busy clearing out their greenleaf nests. Ottersplash had just delivered a bundle of fresh reeds from the river to weave into sturdier leaf-bare nests that would keep out the cold wind.

"Hey, Ottersplash, I could fetch reeds if you like!"

Crookedjaw called. *And you can watch your kits!*

"Thanks, Crookedjaw." Ottersplash dropped her bundle and turned back for more. "But they'd much rather hang out with a warrior than with their mothers."

Crookedjaw scanned the entrance to the camp, hoping Cedarpelt, Piketooth, or Timberfur would return and take over kit duty. Willowbreeze was taking them on a hunting patrol—her first as patrol leader. They were fishing below Sunningrocks where the fish lurked in the cool shadows. He wondered how she was doing.

"Go on!" Sunkit interrupted his thoughts. "Show us a forepaw slash."

"Lakeshine says you're too young to learn battle moves," Crookedjaw told her.

Sunkit glowered at her mother, who was pulling wisps of stale moss out of the nursery. "*Ottersplash* doesn't think we're too young."

Ottersplash called from the reed bed. "They're never too young to start training!"

Lakeshine reproached her with a sharp look. "I don't want them to get hurt."

"You can't wrap them up in feathers," Ottersplash argued.

Shimmerpelt sat back from her work and shook her head. "There's no hurry. They'll be 'paws soon," she reminded both queens. "It won't be long till they can learn all the battle moves they want."

Loudkit flexed his claws. "What if the Twolegs *do* invade the camp?"

Crookedjaw sat down. "They won't." There had been plenty of pelt-dens in the field this green-leaf, but as the colder weather set in, fewer Twolegs came. "Hey, Oakheart!" He called across the clearing to his brother, who was organizing a fresh border patrol. "The Twolegs won't invade the camp, will they?"

Oakheart shook his head. "We've kept a close eye on them for moons," he reassured the kits. "They rarely stray as far as the marsh meadow." Oakheart had taken on responsibility for patrolling the Twoleg field in the moons since Willowbreeze had been stolen. He made a daily check on the pelt-dens, monitoring their arrival and disappearance, he'd invented patrol strategies for distracting Twolegs should they ever wander near the camp, and he could get a patrol of warriors right around the field without being spotted.

Leopardkit brushed against Crookedjaw. Younger than her denmates, her pelt was still soft as duck down. "*Please* teach us a battle move?" She gazed up at Crookedjaw with round, dark eyes.

His whiskers twitched. The whole Clan had spoiled the motherless kit, especially her father Mudfur, who doted on her, and she could wrap almost any Clanmate around her tail.

Leopardkit blinked sweetly and purred, "Please?"

"Don't you dare teach her anything!" Shimmerpelt bustled over and shooed Leopardkit away. "Mudfur would be horrified if he came back and found her fighting!" Though the night-black queen was fiercely fond of her adopted kit, she wasn't as easily swayed as the rest of the Clan by Leopardkit's wiles.

"Come on!" Sunkit bounced around him. "Tell us what to do!"

"We could stalk Oakheart!" Crookedjaw proposed. "First one to creep up on him wins."

Oakheart flicked his tail. "Sorry, Crookedjaw. We're leaving." He headed for the gap in the reeds with Petaldust and Whitefang at his heels.

Blackkit clawed the ground. "Why don't we stalk you instead?" He sprang and landed on Crookedjaw's back.

Crookedjaw staggered dramatically, wincing as the other kits joined in. Collapsing under a storm of churning, flailing paws, he sank grunting to the ground and writhed like a captured pike. The kits squealed as he flung them back and forth, tugging his fur in an effort to cling on.

"Look!" Skykit's excited squeak caused a fresh flurry of paws.

Frogkit yowled with delight. "The hunting patrol's back!"

The kits scrambled off Crookedjaw and charged for the fresh-kill pile.

"I want carp!" Leopardkit pattered on the ground as she raced to keep up.

Crookedjaw sat up, sighing. "Thank StarClan."

Willowbreeze, Cedarpelt, and Timberfur were stacking their catch beside the reed bed. Piketooth dropped his trout and turned in surprise as the kits surged past him, knocking the pile of fish flying.

"Careful!" Cedarpelt yelped, grabbing for a trout as it skidded toward the river. "We just got them out. Don't put them back!"

Willowbreeze crossed the clearing, eyes shining as she neared Crookedjaw. "It looks like I got back just in time," she purred. "You were about to be devoured by a school of starving kits." She touched her muzzle to his affectionately.

Crookedjaw ducked away.

"What?" Willowbreeze's eyes flashed with hurt.

"Not here."

He could feel Shimmerpelt's and Lakeshine's eyes on them—storing up gossip. He'd grown closer and closer to Willowbreeze since he'd rescued her from the Twolegs, but he hated the way the Clan watched them. He knew they were waiting for them to announce they were mates. He could picture Hailstar yowling the news from the Great Rock next Gathering. He snorted crossly. Why couldn't his Clanmates mind their own business?

"Okay." Willowbreeze briskly smoothed his fur with her tail and sniffed.

Crookedjaw shrugged apologetically. "Let's go for a walk," he suggested. Now that Cedarpelt and Piketooth were back, there was no need to watch the kits.

Willowbreeze flicked her tail past his nose and turned and headed for the entrance. They padded in silence along the grassy path.

"I don't see why you have to be so embarrassed," Willowbreeze meowed.

Crookedjaw stared at his paws. "I don't want my Clanmates to think I'm soft."

"It's not soft to have feelings for another cat!" Willowbreeze challenged. "Do you think Hailstar's soft? Or Cedarpelt? Or Timberfur? They all have mates!"

"I'm sorry," Crookedjaw murmured. He ducked under a hawthorn bush and padded into the alder grove. It was bright under the trees now that leaf-bare had begun to strip the leaves.

"Do you remember your assessment?" Crookedjaw changed the subject.

"Of course." Willowbreeze nosed her way after him. "You watched me catch the blackbird." Her mew softened.

"I could have watched you all day," Crookedjaw mewed.

"And now you can't?"

He looked at her, blinking. "Oh, I still could. But I'd get nothing useful done." He flicked her muzzle playfully with the tip of his tail. "That would get us both into trouble!" Crookedjaw darted forward and scrambled up an alder trunk. Digging in his claws, he hauled himself onto the lowest branch. "Come on!"

Willowbreeze narrowed her eyes. She climbed the alder beside his, scooted along a low branch, and leaped into the next tree. The bough swayed under her weight. Crookedjaw purred. If she could climb like a squirrel, so could he! He flung himself into the branches of the next alder, clinging tight with his claws as it shivered beneath him. Willowbreeze lifted her chin and raced onward, leaping from branch to branch alongside him, light as a blackbird. Crookedjaw matched her tree for tree until they'd crossed the whole grove without touching the ground.

"Can you do this?" Crookedjaw jumped onto a higher branch, then higher, till he was at the spindly top of the tree.

Willowbreeze gasped. "Watch out!"

The branches slumped under his weight. Bark splintered and wood cracked. Squawking with surprise, Crookedjaw slithered through the tree like a stone dropping through water. Heart lurching, he stretched out his claws and grabbed hold of a branch. He hung for a moment, his hind paws churning the air before finding a hold on the trunk. Catching his breath, he lowered himself carefully and dropped to the ground.

"You frog-brain!" Willowbreeze jumped down and glared at him. "I thought you were going to hurt yourself!"

"Impossible." Crookedjaw whisked his tail.

"How can you be so sure?" Her eyes glittered with worry.

She really cares! "I'm sorry I scared you," he meowed softly. "But you don't have to worry about me."

"I worry every moment you're out of my sight," Willowbreeze confessed.

Crookedjaw touched his nose to her cheek. She was trembling. "Please don't," he begged. "I'll be fine."

"Stop saying that!" She circled him, bristling. "You don't know that for sure!"

Crookedjaw blocked her path. He wondered for a moment whether to tell her about Mapleshade and his destiny. *No. She'll think I'm crazy.* Why tell her when he could just show her by becoming the greatest leader any Clan had ever known?

"You're right." He pressed against her flank. "I don't know for sure. But I'm so happy just being with you, it feels like nothing can hurt me."

"Really?"

"Really," he promised. "Everything will be fine. I love you." She softened against him. "We'll have a great life together," he murmured. "Surrounded by our Clanmates." He pulled away and looked deep into her eyes. "And our kits."

A purr rumbled in her throat. "I love you, Crookedjaw." She touched her muzzle to his ear. Her warm breath made him weak.

Suddenly a cold breeze lifted his fur. For a moment, Mapleshade's scent drifted in the air and her voice echoed around him. *Don't forget your promise!*

Crookedjaw closed his eyes and let the soft scent of Willowbreeze bathe him. Mapleshade was wrong. Having a mate wouldn't stop him from being a great leader. Hailstar had Echomist, and their kits Petaldust, Beetlenose, and Voleclaw. It didn't distract him from his loyalty to the Clan or his readiness for battle.

"What's that?" Willowbreeze jerked away, ears pricking.

A dog was yapping upstream. Hisses and yowls exploded nearby. It sounded like it had encountered a patrol.

"I'll go and help!" Crookedjaw raced down the slope.

"Be careful!" Willowbreeze called after him.

Diving through the hawthorns, Crookedjaw spotted Whitefang and Petaldust at full pelt, chasing a small white dog. He charged after them. "Steer it past the camp!" he yowled.

Whitefang veered away, outflanking the dog and driving it onward, away from the camp entrance. They chased it up the slope and around the top of the camp. Crookedjaw's heart thudded with excitement as he whipped around bushes and ducked under branches, keeping the dog in sight. Ahead, Whitefang and Petaldust matched each other step for step, steering it toward the marsh. As they broke from the trees the dog glanced over its shoulder. Its eyes gleamed white around the edges. It was terrified. Pounding the earth with desperate paws, it fled past the beech copse and hurtled into the long grass.

"Keep going!" Crookedjaw called.

Whitefang leaped over a clump of sedge as Petaldust swerved around it. The ground flashed beneath Crookedjaw's paws as he hared after them. They crossed the marsh and drove the dog down onto the shore. Petaldust splashed into the shallows, keeping pace with the dog as it hurtled forward, sending stones cracking from under her paws. Whitefang pelted along the bank, hissing every time the dog tried to swerve up onto the grass.

Crookedjaw stayed at the rear, blocking the dog with a snarl if it tried to turn. "Twoleg!" he warned, spotting a figure on the bridge. He pulled up, pebbles clattering beneath his feet.

Whitefang and Petaldust slewed to a halt as the dog flung itself on to the bridge and bounded around the Twoleg, yapping with relief.

Crookedjaw circled his Clanmates as they flopped down on the shore. "Nice chase," he puffed.

"Thanks." Petaldust clambered to her paws once she had caught her breath.

Whitefang lifted his head. "We'd better carry on with our patrol." He stood up and shook out his pelt.

"Where's Oakheart?" Crookedjaw suddenly realized his brother was missing.

"Didn't you see him?" Petaldust blinked at him in surprise. "He was heading your way. He thought he saw ThunderClan warriors on the shore below Sunningrocks. He went to investigate."

Crookedjaw frowned. "Alone?"

"That's what he wanted." Whitefang shrugged. "He told us to check the Twoleg field and that he'd catch up."

"I'll check on him." Crookedjaw flattened his ears. It was risky to check for intruders single-pawed. What was his brother thinking?

He found Oakheart near the alders, emerging from long grass. "What are you doing here?"

Oakheart looked startled. His pelt was wet.

"Are you okay?" Crookedjaw meowed. "Whitefang said you saw cats from ThunderClan."

"Just one warrior." Oakheart's voice was casual as he padded past, heading for the camp. "I chased her off."

Crookedjaw picked up a trace of familiar scent on his brother's pelt. "Was it Bluefur?"

Oakheart whipped around. "How did you know?"

"I recognized her scent." Crookedjaw searched Oakheart's gaze. Was he hiding something? Was Bluefur causing trouble? "Did you fight? Did she beat you?" He remembered with a shudder what a fierce opponent Bluefur could be.

Oakheart turned toward camp. "I drove her back into the forest." He shrugged. "It wasn't much of a fight. Nothing worth mentioning. Why start a battle over something so small?"

Crookedjaw watched his brother pad away. "What about your patrol? They chased a dog as far as the bridge. They're waiting for you."

Oakheart paused. "The patrol!" He swerved to head upriver.

Crookedjaw tipped his head on one side. It wasn't like Oakheart to be so reserved, especially about an encounter with another Clan. Perhaps the fight had been tougher than he wanted to admit. But he didn't seem to have any injuries.

Crookedjaw shrugged. Oakheart was a great warrior. He'd be fine. He tasted the air, wondering if Willowbreeze was still near or if she'd given up waiting for him and returned to camp. He wanted to spend as much time with her as he could.

CHAPTER 27

❧

"Mapleshade!"

Dreaming, Crookedjaw raced through the forest. Dark earth sprayed behind him as he barged through the tangled undergrowth.

"Mapleshade?"

Where is she? He had so much to ask her. Questions that had been churning in his belly for days, nagging and nagging till he had to have answers. Why had she put Willowbreeze's life at risk? Why had she clawed him for saving a Clanmate? What about his destiny? When was he going to get his first apprentice? How long till he became deputy? Would he follow Hailstar? Or Shellheart?

Shellheart?

Crookedjaw stumbled to a halt. Who, if he became leader, would have to die over and over before Crookedjaw took his place? Crookedjaw felt sick. It was bad enough waiting for Hailstar to lose his last life. He didn't want to count off his own father's deaths while he waited for his destiny to come true.

"Higher!"

A sharp growl sliced through the mist.

"Faster! Do you want to die at the paws of a common warrior?"

Crookedjaw heard a grunt and the thud of hard muscle hitting earth. Did Mapleshade have another pupil? He crept forward, ears pricked. Ducking behind a thornbush, he saw two shapes moving in a narrow clearing. As the mist swirled away, two pelts showed: one ragged, one sleek.

The ragged mentor wasn't Mapleshade. It was a cat he'd never seen before. But who was the sleek tom? Crookedjaw searched his memory. There was something familiar in the wide, muscled shoulders and the dark tabby pelt.

"Do it again!" the ragged cat snarled. "Do it better!"

The sleek tom took a short run up and leaped, higher than Crookedjaw had seen any cat jump. With a flick of his tail, he twisted in the air, kicking out his hind legs, claws splayed while he punched the air with his forepaw. He hit the ground with a thump, landing on his side. Crookedjaw felt the jolt, gasping as though the breath had been knocked from him instead of from the tom.

The ragged cat was on his apprentice in an instant, battering his head with a flurry of swipes. Crookedjaw flinched as blood sprayed from the torn fur. The tom struggled free and met his mentor's blows with vicious, slicing jabs.

The ragged cat ducked away. "That was better!"

Blood welled on both cats' muzzles and, as Crookedjaw peered closer, he could see the tom's pelt was laced with slash marks.

"Let me try it again, Shredtail," the tom growled.

Again? Crookedjaw swallowed. He thought his training sessions with Mapleshade had been brutal, but they were never this violent. These cats acted as though shedding blood meant nothing.

In a flash, Crookedjaw recognized him. *Thistleclaw!* He'd seen the ThunderClan warrior at Gatherings.

Thistleclaw took another run up, leaping once more and twisting. This time he finished the move before landing on his paws. Yowling with triumph, he reared and slashed the air. "This is it!" He faced his mentor. "My time is coming."

Shredtail nodded. "You've worked hard for it, Thistleclaw."

"And I'm going to get it. I'll be deputy before the next full moon."

"Are you sure Sunstar won't soften and choose Bluefur instead?" Shredtail snarled.

Thistleclaw narrowed his eyes. "He'd be a fool if he did," he growled. "Bluefur is weak. I bet she's whimpering for Snowfur right now."

"Grief can bring strength," Shredtail warned.

"But Snowfur's body is hardly cold," Thistleclaw pointed out. "Bluefur will be breaking her heart for moons. Which will give me a chance to make Sunstar see that I'm the only one capable of following him."

"Snowfur was your mate." Shredtail narrowed his eyes. "Aren't you grieving, too?"

"Of course!" Thistleclaw slashed at a moss-coated tree. "Snowfur shouldn't have died! It should've been Bluefur on the Thunderpath instead!"

"What about your kit?" Shredtail pressed. "Your son?"

Thistleclaw curled his lip. "He takes after his mother," he spat. "There's no fire in his belly, no hunger for battle." He swung his gaze around to his mentor. "Why are we talking?" he snarled. "I came to train, not to talk." Rearing up, he strode forward on his hind paws, slicing the air with his tail tucked in tight.

Crookedjaw backed away, cold to his bones. He'd never seen a hunger for blood like this, not in the battle for Sunningrocks, not even when Hailstar nearly killed Reedfeather. He turned and ran, scanning the trees as they flashed by, hoping to catch a glimpse of Mapleshade. He skimmed bushes and swerved around trees, running faster and faster, praying he found her.

"Crookedjaw!" Paws shook him awake.

"What?" He lifted his head.

Willowbreeze sat beside him, her pelt still ruffled by sleep. "You kicked me!" she mewed. "Were you having a bad dream?"

"Kind of." He stretched in his nest. The small den they had woven into the crook of the tree was warm and cozy.

Willowbreeze leaned down and touched her muzzle to his. "Well, you're awake now." She padded out of the den and Crookedjaw sat up. Why couldn't he find Mapleshade? He flexed his claws. Had something happened to her? This was StarClan! Cats lived forever there, didn't they? He ducked out of the den, looking around the clearing, relieved when he saw Oakheart picking sleepily through the frosty remains of the fresh-kill pie. Poor Bluefur. Losing a littermate must be heartbreaking.

Shellheart was beneath the willow, organizing the day's patrols. Cedarpelt, Timberfur, Mudfur, and Petaldust crowded around him. Beetlenose was washing, but his ears pricked when he heard his name. Voleclaw was staring wistfully at the fresh-kill pile while Rippleclaw murmured in Graypool's ear.

Crookedjaw called across the clearing. "Can I hunt this morning?" His breath billowed in the air. He wondered if there'd be ice on the river.

Shellheart nodded. "Take Mudfur and Petaldust." He waved the two warriors toward Crookedjaw with a flick of his tail.

"Can Oakheart come, too?" Crookedjaw asked.

Oakheart looked up. "Come where?"

"Hunting."

"Great!" Oakheart picked up a fish and headed for the nursery. "I'll just deliver this."

Willowbreeze ducked out of the elders' den and padded down the slope. Her paws suddenly slid on the frost and she skidded clumsily to the bottom. "The kits will be happy." She joined Crookedjaw. "They've got an ice slide to play on."

"Ice?" Frogkit was already tearing across the clearing. He bounded up the slope, then half-ran, half-slid down it, squealing with delight.

Crookedjaw purred at Willowbreeze. "I'm taking Oakheart, Petaldust, and Mudfur hunting," he told her. "Do you want to come?"

She shook her head. "I promised Birdsong I'd help her find

moss for her nest. She nearly froze last night."

"Come on, Crookedjaw!" Mudfur was pacing the entrance in a cloud of his own breath.

"See you later." Crookedjaw brushed muzzles with Willowbreeze and hurried after Petaldust and Oakheart as they made for the gap in the reeds. Outside camp, the air was even colder.

"I hope this is just a snap," Petaldust sighed. "It's still leaf-fall."

They passed the stepping-stones and followed the shore downstream, past the alder grove and along the bank where ferns and hawthorns grew right up to the water's edge. Splashing through the shallows, Crookedjaw led the way to a rocky outcrop that jutted out into the river. The rocks smoothed into a flat stretch of stone only a whisker higher than the water.

Crookedjaw sat close to the edge and peered down into the river as it swirled past. Deep and clear, he could see through the brown water right down to the weed streaming on the riverbed. A fish slid past, too deep to reach, but he waited and another followed soon after, closer to the surface. Excitement flashed in his belly as he darted a paw into the water, gasping at the chill. He hooked out the fish and flicked it on to the stone. With a quick lunge he gave it a killing bite and turned back for another, anticipation tingling in his paws.

"Nice catch." Oakheart crouched beside him, ready for his own. He stared at the water speeding below his nose, muscles bunched in anticipation. Then, with a mew of satisfaction, he plunged in a lightning-fast paw and snatched out a trout.

Mudfur leaned over the water. "I want to catch a carp for Leopardkit," he murmured, eyes fixed on the water. "It's her favorite."

Petaldust plunged in both her front paws. Crookedjaw turned in time to see her lift a struggling pike from the water. It was a tail-length long and thrashing wildly. He sprang over to help but as he grasped the fish, Petaldust lost her balance. With a yelp of surprise she tumbled into the water. As she bobbed, gasping, to the surface, the pike struggled in Crookedjaw's paws. He pinned it to the stone and killed it with a bite.

Petaldust swam for shore. Padding on to the bank, she shook out her dripping pelt. "Did you get it?" she called.

"It's fresh-kill now," Crookedjaw assured her.

Oakheart's whiskers twitched. "I didn't know you wanted a swim," he teased.

Petaldust paced the shore, trying to get warm. "I didn't realize it was so big!"

Mudfur gave a triumphant mew as he fished a carp from the water.

"Let's take these back to camp," Crookedjaw suggested. "Then we can come and catch more."

Petaldust stared across the river into ThunderClan's forest. "I wonder why they never catch fish like us?"

Mudfur shrugged. "They're scared of water. They'd drown if they fell in."

Oakheart tasted the air. "No fresh markers on their border."

He leaned forward. "I wonder where they are today? There's usually a warrior or two yowling at us while we're fishing."

Crookedjaw's dream flashed back to him. "They're probably mourning Snowfur."

Oakheart snapped his head around, eyes glittering. "What?"

Crookedjaw shrank beneath his pelt. *Fish-brain! How am I going to explain this?*

"Are you sure?" Petaldust blinked.

Crookedjaw's thoughts whirled.

Mudfur sniffed his carp absently. "Who told you?"

"I—I heard a border patrol the other day when I was guarding Sunningrocks," Crookedjaw stammered.

Oakheart tipped his head. "Why didn't you mention it?"

Crookedjaw glanced at Mudfur. "It—it seemed too sad." There was at least truth in that.

Petaldust padded along the outcrop and joined them on the stone. "How did she die?"

Crookedjaw glanced at his paws. "On the Thunderpath, I think."

"The Thunderpath?" Oakheart echoed.

Crookedjaw looked up. His brother's thoughts seemed to have drifted into the forest. "It's okay," he reassured him. "There's no Thunderpath on our territory."

Oakheart watched a fallen leaf swirling downriver. "I'm sorry for Bluefur," he murmured. "She must be so sad."

Crookedjaw sighed. "Yeah." He picked up his fish in his

jaws and clambered over the rocks. Beckoning the patrol with his tail, he headed toward the camp.

Fourtrees was lit by a cold white moon. Crookedjaw gazed up through the rattling leaves. Silverpelt stretched across the night sky. *Which one is Snowfur?* It had been a quarter moon since his dream and Crookedjaw was surprised to see that Bluefur had come to the Gathering.

"I hear fishing is still good." Hollyflower's mew snapped him back to the conversation. He'd been sharing news with a group of mixed Clan warriors.

"Yes."

Foxheart shivered. "It's bad enough getting wet, but in this weather?"

"I guess." Goldenflower, ThunderClan's newest warrior, didn't seem to be listening. She was staring across the clearing, her eyes dark. Crookedjaw followed her gaze. She was watching Bluefur. The gray warrior was talking to Oakheart. He must be offering his sympathies.

Goldenflower stood up. "I'll just make sure Bluefur's okay." She weaved through the gathered cats.

"Crookedjaw!" Hailstar was approaching. "Where's Oakheart? I want him to tell the Gathering about the pelt-dens. Some of his tactics are worth sharing. The Twolegs may start building dens on the other Clans' territory." He dipped his head to Hollyflower. "Pray StarClan they don't."

Oakheart's going to address the Gathering? Crookedjaw felt a flash of worry. Was Hailstar grooming his brother to be RiverClan's next deputy? "He's over there." He flicked his tail toward Oakheart.

"Thanks." Hailstar padded away. "I'd better warn him."

As the leaders made their reports, Crookedjaw huddled among his Clanmates. He hunched his shoulders against the cold night air, studying Oakheart through narrowed eyes. As his brother waited calmly at the foot of the Great Rock, Crookedjaw swallowed back jealousy.

"RiverClan, too, has enjoyed plenty of fresh-kill recently." Hailstar began his report. "The river has been full of fish and its banks stocked with prey." The RiverClan leader glanced down at Oakheart. "Only one cloud has darkened our horizon." He beckoned with a nod. "Oakheart has more information."

Murmurs of surprise rippled around the Clans as Oakheart bounded onto the Great Rock.

"The Great Rock's for *leaders*," growled a ShadowClan warrior. "Not junior warriors!"

Crookedjaw stuck out his chin, suddenly defensive of his brother. "Listen to him!" he snarled. "He has important news to share."

The ShadowClan warrior's claws scraped the frosty earth. Crookedjaw flexed his own. No one criticized Oakheart!

"I am sorry," Oakheart began, his voice carrying clearly across the hollow. "I do not belong here, but with so many cats I was afraid you wouldn't be able to hear me from down there." He nodded to the shadowy base of the rock. "I hope

you will forgive my boldness. I do not mean to offend."
Crookedjaw felt a glow of pride as the murmuring ceased.
The cats were pricking their ears and raising their muzzles,
eager to hear what Oakheart was about to share. He glanced
around, basking in his brother's success. Then he spotted
Bluefur, ruffled and scowling. Beside her, a pretty Clanmate
was staring at Oakheart, her eyes shining as though she were
watching a StarClan warrior speak.

He did look like a leader up there among the other cats.
Crookedjaw shifted his paws, worry rushing back. *But I'm the
one with the great destiny!*

The journey home seemed to take much longer than usual.
Petaldust was bouncing around Oakheart. "Everyone was
listening to you!" Her eyes shone. "Weren't you scared?"

Voleclaw snorted. "What was there to be scared of?" he
muttered. "There's a truce."

"But he had to speak to so many cats!" Petaldust shuddered.
"I'd hate it."

Crookedjaw slowed his pace, falling behind his Clanmates
as they crossed the tree line into ThunderClan forest. He
didn't want to hear how great Oakheart had been.

A pelt brushed beside him.

Brambleberry.

"You wish it had been you on the Great Rock," she
murmured.

Crookedjaw bristled. "No, I don't!"

She snorted. "Don't worry. It'll be your turn soon enough

and there's plenty to keep you busy until then." There was an edge in her mew.

"How do you know?" Crookedjaw narrowed his eyes. "Have you had another omen?" Why did he bother asking? Even if she had, he wouldn't tell him what it was. But curiosity kept pricking, sharper and sharper. Brambleberry was silent as a fish. There was clearly something on her mind.

"How do you know it'll be my turn soon?" Crookedjaw repeated.

Brambleberry jumped onto a fallen tree that blocked the trail. She paused on top and stared down at him. "Nothing's for certain." Her eyes were darker than the shadows surrounding her. "The power is within you to be a fine warrior." She slid down the other side and Crookedjaw followed, heart quickening. She went on as he fell in beside her. "Every cat knows that you're going to be great, just from watching you." Her gaze flashed up through the overlapping branches. "The stars don't have to decide everything for us."

Really? Crookedjaw flexed his claws. Brambleberry knew nothing! *Then why am I being trained by StarClan?*

CHAPTER 28

Fine snow drifted down from a wide gray sky and settled on the camp. Crookedjaw winced. His twisted jaw was aching with cold. But he didn't care. Excitement sparked in his pelt. He sat with his Clanmates, lining the edge of the clearing, pelts dusty with snow as Hailstar called forward the next apprentice. Crookedjaw swished his tail.

"Sedgekit." The RiverClan leader beckoned the brown tabby she-kit forward with a nod. Blackpaw, Skypaw, Loudpaw, and Reedpaw fidgeted behind him, eyes shining, their apprentice names still fresh on the tongues of their Clanmates. Hailstar's decision to wait until Leopardkit had reached six moons before he made any new apprentices had been welcomed by the Clan. The young cats had been born so close together that they'd formed a strong bond.

"Why split them up?" Shellheart had argued. Hailstar agreed. Crookedjaw was just pleased that Leopardkit wouldn't be alone in the nursery—even for a moon. He knew how painful it was to be left behind. Then he reminded himself that Leopardkit would have had Shimmerpelt to keep her company. Even though the night-black queen wanted to return to her warrior duties, Crookedjaw knew she wouldn't abandon Leopardkit. She loved the golden-spotted kit too much.

Shifting his paws, he scowled at Rainflower. She sat apart in a chilly cloud of her own breath. If only she'd been able to see past his broken jaw and remember how much she had loved him at first. His accident had changed nothing about him except the way he looked—but for Rainflower, that had been everything. Crookedjaw pushed away the thought. The past couldn't be changed. His own kits—if he had any—would be loved. The mate he'd chosen would never desert them, no matter what they did.

He pressed closer to Willowbreeze. "Thanks," he whispered.

She glanced at him, surprised. "What for?"

"Just because . . ." He stared at her fondly, lost for words.

She purred and brushed the snow from his pelt with a paw. "Go on," she whispered. "Hailstar's calling you."

Crookedjaw realized the eyes of the Clan were on him. Hailstar beckoned him forward with a nod. "May you share with Sedgepaw your courage, skill, and loyalty."

Crookedjaw padded into the clearing and pressed his nose to his new apprentice's head. She was trembling. "Don't worry," he whispered. "You'll be great."

He looked up and saw Oakheart standing beside his apprentice, Loudpaw. The young tom was fidgeting, tail up, clearly desperate for the ceremony to finish so he could start training. Oakheart whisked his tail over his restless apprentice's ear and twitched one ear at Crookedjaw.

They were mentors at last.

Hailstar cleared his throat. "We have one more kit to welcome into RiverClan as an apprentice," he announced.

At the edge of the clearing, Mudfur licked Leopardkit's head, holding her back with a paw while she struggled.

"Stop it, Mudfur!" she squeaked. "It's my turn!"

Eyes misting, he let her go, and she dashed into the clearing before Hailstar had even called her name.

"Leopardkit." Hailstar purred as she skittered to a halt at his paws.

She blinked up at him. "Yes?"

"Until you earn your warrior name, you will be Leopardpaw."

She stared eagerly around the clearing as Hailstar went on. "Your mentor will be Whitefang."

Leopardpaw's eyes widened as the huge white tom padded toward her. He pressed his muzzle to her head.

"I hope I grow as big as you," she breathed.

Whitefang purred. "Perhaps not *quite* as big."

Hailstar flicked his tail. "Whitefang, share with her your courage, discipline, and compassion."

The Clan cheered, not just Leopardpaw's name, but the names of all the new apprentices. Sedgepaw and Loudpaw raced to Ottersplash and bounced around her while Timberfur nuzzled Reedpaw. Shimmerpelt wrapped her tail around Skypaw while Piketooth tumbled across the clearing, play fighting with Blackpaw. Leopardpaw raced straight to Mudfur, nuzzling his cheek with her muzzle.

Mudfur's eyes were dark with worry. "I pray you'll never

have to fight in a battle." He flicked his tail protectively around her.

"Don't be silly!" She skipped away. "I can't *wait* to fight in my first battle!"

Crookedjaw backed away from the mayhem.

Willowbreeze nudged him. "Scared?" she teased.

"Never."

"A 'paw is a big responsibility." Her gaze suddenly clouded. "I wish I had one."

"What? A kit or a 'paw?"

She shoved him hard. "An apprentice, of course!"

"You'll get one soon," he promised.

Owlfur was teasing Softwing about her new apprentice, Skypaw. "She'll wear out your whiskers," he joked.

Softwing sniffed. "I can handle her."

Owlfur glanced at the little brown tabby running rings around Cedarpelt. "You think?"

"Can we go out now?" Sedgepaw's mew made Crookedjaw jump. The young she-cat was standing, tail high, pelt fluffed against the snow. Crookedjaw felt a surge of excitement. "Sure! I'll show you our territory."

Sedgepaw bounced back to her denmates. "*I'm* going out!" she boasted.

"I want to go!" Frogpaw mewed.

"Me too!" Blackpaw stared hopefully at his mentor, Hailstar.

Sunpaw flicked her tail. "I'm going to be the first to cross the stepping-stones!"

"Try getting there before *me*!" Skypaw dared.

Loudpaw barged past both of them. "I'm going to be first to climb Sunningrocks!"

Reedpaw purred. "We are totally going to *rule* this Clan!"

Beetlenose padded toward Reedpaw. "You'll rule every Clan when I've finished training you." He glanced at Crookedjaw. "Do you think Sedgepaw will make it to warrior?"

Crookedjaw rolled his eyes. "If you want to compete, Beetlenose, go ahead. I'm just going to make Sedgepaw into the best warrior she can be."

Sedgepaw flicked her tail. "Should I check the elders for ticks before we go?"

Crookedjaw shook his head. "I think the ticks will be there when we get back." He called to Oakheart. "Do you want to come, too?"

"Yes, yes, yes!" Loudpaw skidded toward Crookedjaw. "Can we, *please*?" He looked desperately at Oakheart.

"Yeah," Oakheart purred.

Reedpaw was gazing hopefully at Beetlenose. "You're not going to let them go without me, are you?" he mewed wistfully.

"Do you want to come, too?" Crookedjaw asked Beetlenose.

Beetlenose sniffed. "I suppose so."

Ottersplash sat down, eyes shining as she watched her kits pelt toward the sedge tunnel. "You'll look after them, won't you?" she meowed.

"As if they were my own," Crookedjaw promised. He hurried to catch up before the young cats made it to the stepping-stones. Oakheart puffed beside him as they raced along the grassy path, Beetlenose at their heels. They caught up with the kits on the shore. Snow was piling against the bank, turning Sunningrocks white on the far shore. But there was no ice on the river yet.

"Can we swim?" Loudpaw asked. "We've only swum around the reed bed before. Never in the proper river."

"It's much too cold!" Crookedjaw snorted. "I don't think your mother would thank us for bringing you home with whitecough."

Sedgepaw bounded on to the first stepping-stone. "Are we going to cross?"

Oakheart shook his head. "Let's stick to the shore today," he decided. "We'll take you downstream and then through the willows to the marsh."

Reedpaw skipped around Beetlenose. "Will we see pelt-dens?"

"And Twolegs?" Sedgepaw's eyes were huge.

"Let's find out." Beetlenose headed along the shore, flicking snow from each paw as he went. Loudpaw, Sedgepaw, and Reedpaw bounded after him.

"Were we like that?" Oakheart fell in beside Crookedjaw.

Sedgepaw turned, ears twitching. "Like what?"

"Like excited squirrels," Crookedjaw teased.

Sedgepaw's attention flitted to the trees. A bird was hopping from branch to branch, sending down showers of snow. "What's that bird?"

"A mistle thrush," Crookedjaw told her.

"Do we hunt it?"

"Yes, if the river freezes."

"What else do we hunt?" Sedgepaw didn't wait for an answer. "Do we hunt mice like ThunderClan or rabbits like WindClan? Have you eaten rabbit? What does it taste like? Did Willowbreeze eat it when—"

Oakheart cut her off. "Look!" He nodded at her littermates, who were disappearing after Beetlenose around a bend in the river. "You'd better catch up. You don't want to miss anything."

"Oh!" Sedgepaw tore away after Loudpaw and Reedpaw.

Crookedjaw's whiskers twitched. "We're not going to be bored for a while." He followed Oakheart downstream. Sedgepaw was going to be fun to mentor.

"Is this how I stalk?" Sedgepaw was waiting just past the bend, crouching on the grassy bank, her tail down and her legs bent. She looked like a frog.

"Not bad," Crookedjaw meowed.

Oakheart headed on to catch up with Loudpaw, who was racing Reedpaw up and down the shore while Beetlenose padded steadily on.

"When will I learn to catch a fish?" Sedgepaw hopped down the bank and joined Crookedjaw. "What's the best fish to catch? What was your first fish?"

Crookedjaw's head was spinning. "Slow down," he meowed.

"Sorry!" Sedgepaw flattened her ears. "I know I talk too much but I just want to be the best apprentice. I'm so glad you're my mentor. You're the strongest cat in RiverClan, except Rippleclaw, but he's old—not an elder or anything—but you're younger and you remember what it's like to be a 'paw. And I'm going to listen to everything you tell me—"

Crookedjaw felt a twinge of guilt. He'd never been this enthusiastic with Cedarpelt. He'd valued his mentor's training; it had been useful. But it was Mapleshade who'd taught him the most about courage and skill in battle. He gazed at Sedgepaw. She was still chattering like a blackbird. Would she have a StarClan mentor, too?

No. Surely there wasn't room in the Clan for more than one warrior with a great destiny?

Crookedjaw yawned. Most of the Clan had gone to their nests for the night. The moss draping Hailstar's entrance twitched behind him as the RiverClan leader disappeared for the night. Ottersplash, Lakeshine, and Shimmerpelt were shaking the dusty moss from their nests. The elders were murmuring in their den.

The wind had already dropped and the night was silent and still.

Willowbreeze nudged him toward their den. "Let's go to sleep."

Curled in their nest, Crookedjaw closed his eyes. Willowbreeze wriggled closer, tucking her nose into his fur. Crookedjaw sighed happily. *I'm a mentor.* There was nothing to stop him from becoming deputy now. Purring, he drifted into sleep.

"So you're a mentor." Mapleshade's rasping mew woke him into a dream. The forest loomed dark around him.

He puffed out his chest. "Yes."

"With an apprentice of your own." Her amber eyes glowed. "Do you think you've got nothing left to learn?"

"No!" Crookedjaw gasped. "I know I'm not ready to be leader. I'm not even ready to be deputy!" Didn't she realize how relieved he was to see her again? It had been such a long time since he'd dreamed of her. He was worried he was losing his edge over the other warriors in the Clan. Beetlenose had caught more fish than him yesterday. "I want you to teach me everything you know. I want to become the best leader I can. My Clan deserves that."

Mapleshade narrowed her eyes. "Good," she murmured. "You're still worthy of my teaching." She circled him, her gaze unwavering.

"Look!" Crookedjaw ran, leaped, and twisted in the air, kicking out with his hind legs and jabbing with his forepaws. He landed skillfully on all four paws. He'd been practicing the move since he'd seen Thistleclaw do it. He was sure he'd gotten it right.

"Not bad, I suppose," she conceded.

"Not bad?" He stared at her. *It was brilliant.*

"Tell me your promise," she demanded.

"Again?"

"Tell me that there's nothing as important as looking after your Clan, no matter what it costs you!" Her eyes burned.

Crookedjaw frowned. "Okay." He gritted his teeth. "There's nothing as important as looking after my—"

"Say it like you really mean it!" Mapleshade thrust her face into his.

Straightening, Crookedjaw tried again. "There's nothing as important as looking after my Clan, no matter what it costs me!" he meowed loudly.

"Promise?"

"I promise." His ear twitched. Why did she keep insisting he promised over and over again? And was this promise the reason Mapleshade had led the Twolegs to Willowbreeze?

CHAPTER 29

❧

Greenleaf had taken hold. The sun shone from a wide blue sky and the beech copse swayed in the breeze. Sedgepaw crouched beneath the whispering leaves, chest pressed to the grass.

"Quietly now." Crookedjaw dropped a leaf a tail-length in front of her. "Pretend this is a bird. It has better hearing than you. It's faster than you." He leaned closer. "And it's much more frightened than you."

Sedgepaw narrowed her eyes. She pulled herself forward, silent as a snake. *Good.* Crookedjaw willed her on. One paw at a time, she crept up on the leaf. Then, in a sudden flurry of paws, she jumped.

"Did I get it? Did I get it?" she squeaked.

Crookedjaw's heart sank. She'd landed half a tail-length past it.

Oakheart shrugged. "It was a good try."

"You could do better, though." Beetlenose padded from the trees, while Reedpaw and Loudpaw snuffled with amusement behind him. He silenced them with a flick of his tail. "Sedgepaw," he meowed gently. "You've got a lot of strength in your hind legs." He glanced at Crookedjaw, making sure that it was okay to offer advice to his apprentice.

Crookedjaw nodded. "Go ahead." He could use all the help he could get with Sedgepaw. She had so much enthusiasm; it was painful watching her fail at every task by a whisker.

Beetlenose hooked the leaf in his paw. "You need to adjust your jump to take all that strength into account." He dropped the leaf in front of her. "Don't push so hard and keep your eye on your target."

Sedgepaw crouched again. "I'll get it this time."

"If it doesn't get you first," Reedpaw teased.

Sedgepaw wriggled her hindquarters and jumped. She landed square on top of the leaf and sat up, ears twitching as she stared at the ground around her. "Where did it go? Did I miss it again?"

Reedpaw rolled his eyes. "Can we go fishing now?" he mewed. "It's getting hot."

"You need to learn how to hunt birds as well as fish," Crookedjaw reminded him.

Loudpaw sniffed. "I want to learn battle moves. We need to win back Sunningrocks!" ThunderClan had reset the scent markers, making Sunningrocks theirs again just after leaf-fall, and Hailstar had refused to risk lives seizing it back during the hardest moons.

Oakheart sighed. "Perhaps we should just give ThunderClan leaf-bare hunting rights there," he suggested. "That's always when they take it. They must need the prey."

"What?" Beetlenose stared at him. "They'll take over our whole territory if we start making promises like that."

"Yeah!" Reedpaw lined up beside his mentor. "They've got a whole forest! If they can't find enough prey they must be bad hunters."

Crookedjaw flicked the end of his tail. "Shellheart's been trying to persuade Hailstar to reclaim Sunningrocks for a moon. I don't know why he's hesitating. It was easy last time."

Loudpaw ripped at the grass. "Are we going to learn battle moves or not?"

Sedgepaw flattened her ears. "My shoulder's still sore from last time we tried."

"You should move quicker," Reedpaw snapped.

"I move quicker than you!" Sedgepaw retorted.

Yes, but always in the wrong direction. Crookedjaw swallowed back a sigh. He padded to the edge of the beech copse and looked across the meadow. "Let's try some of the moves Oakheart invented for distracting Twolegs." Sedgepaw could practice her hunting skills later, when Loudpaw and Reedpaw weren't around to tease her.

Reedpaw pricked his ears. "Do you mean the ones where we lure them away from camp?" He collapsed into a convincing limp, moaning like an injured kittypet and dragged his hind legs over the grass. "Help me, help me. I'm hurt!"

"Great!" Oakheart pointed at Loudpaw. "Now, what should you be doing?"

Loudpaw hesitated.

"I know! I know!" Sedgepaw was bouncing with excitement. "We race back to camp as fast as we can and hide the elders and kits in the reeds or carry them downriver."

"Exactly!" Oakheart glanced at the slender beech trees. "Let's try climbing."

Beetlenose coughed in surprise. "Tree climbing?"

Oakheart hopped over a jutting root. "It's the best place to watch for Twolegs." He unsheathed his claws. "Remember how Echomist spotted those Twolegs bringing their dog through the marsh last moon?"

Sedgepaw bristled. "It was the first dog I'd ever seen."

Crookedjaw smoothed her fur with his tail. "It could have found the camp if Echomist hadn't spotted it and lured it away."

"Okay." Beetlenose padded to the base of a trunk. "We'll practice tree climbing." He beckoned Reedpaw closer. "You go up first. I'll be on your tail."

Reedpaw raced to the tree and squatted between its roots. With a grunt, he jumped and grabbed hold of the trunk, then hauled himself up till he reached the lowest branch. He wobbled and clung on as it shivered beneath him.

"Your turn." Crookedjaw picked out another beech and nudged Sedgepaw forward.

She stared up at him, wide-eyed. "Really?"

"You can do it," Crookedjaw encouraged. "Keep your claws out and you'll be fine."

She leaped and hung on to the bark.

"Go on!" Crookedjaw urged. "Remember how you could climb up my back in three hops when you were a kit?" He remembered her spiky claws with a wince.

Sedgepaw pulled herself up, gaining confidence with each

jump until she was scooting up the tree like a squirrel.

"That's great!" Crookedjaw climbed after her, his claws sinking easily into the soft greenleaf bark. He paused and leaned back. Peering up through the fluttering leaves, he could just make out Sedgepaw's tabby pelt among the branches. "Stop on the next branch," he called.

"Okay." Her mew sounded a long way off.

"I hope she hasn't gone too high," Crookedjaw muttered.

"It's okay," Beetlenose called from a branch of the next tree. "I can see her. There's plenty of branch for her to hang on to."

Reedpaw crouched next to his mentor. "Can I climb that high?"

"No."

Oakheart was still on the ground, trying to persuade Loudpaw to climb.

"But I'm a RiverClan cat!" Loudpaw complained. "We're not supposed to climb; we're supposed to swim!"

"We need to learn new skills," Oakheart coaxed. "You've got claws strong enough to fight. They'll be strong enough to climb."

"Crookedjaw!" Sedgepaw suddenly wailed from above.

He looked up, pelt pricking. "Are you okay?"

"Crookedjaw!" she wailed again.

Oh, StarClan! Panicking, Crookedjaw scrambled higher. "I'm coming!" Had she climbed too high and lost her nerve? Perhaps she'd found a bee's nest and got stung? *Please don't fall!* The ground was hidden below leaves and branches, far below.

"I can see a dog!" Sedgepaw's wail was suddenly clear.

"It's huge!" Leaves fluttered down around Crookedjaw. "It's heading this way."

Crookedjaw's fur bushed up. *The camp!* He peered out through the branches. The meadow stretched far below them. Then he saw it. A wide brown shape swerving through the sedge like a fish slipping through river weed. He opened his mouth. Dog-scent bathed his tongue. He glanced back toward the camp. It was well hidden by willow and reeds, but if the dog kept charging this way, he'd burst straight through it. Thinking fast, Crookedjaw scrambled down the tree.

"Stay up there!" he yowled to Sedgepaw. "Don't come down till I tell you!"

"Did you see it?" Beetlenose was flat against the branch of his tree, ears pricked.

"Yes," Crookedjaw told him. "Heading this way. We have to lure him away from the camp."

"What about the apprentices?"

"Tell Reedpaw to stay in the tree."

Reedpaw was clinging to the next branch. "Can't we help?"

Crookedjaw hissed. "You're too small." There was no time for argument. He dropped to the ground.

Oakheart was still trying to persuade Loudpaw to make his first jump.

"Get him up there," Crookedjaw ordered. "Fast! There's a dog heading this way. It's a big one, too fast for apprentices to outrun. We need to steer it away from the camp."

Loudpaw scrabbled at the bark while Oakheart nudged him from behind. With a yelp of triumph, the brown apprentice

WARRIORS SUPER EDITION: CROOKEDSTAR'S PROMISE 353

hooked in his claws and began to grapple his way up the slippery trunk.

"Keep going!" Oakheart urged.

Loudpaw fought his way up till he reached a thick branch. With a grunt he threw himself on to it and clung with his forepaws.

Oakheart faced Crookedjaw. "Which way do we go?"

"Into the meadow to get its attention." Crookedjaw flexed his claws.

Beetlenose was beside them. "Then?"

"We lead it uphill, away from the camp," Crookedjaw decided. "Right out of our territory." He stiffened. "One of us needs to get to the camp and warn them!"

"I'll go!" Reedpaw slithered down the tree.

Beetlenose spun around. "I told you to stay where you were!"

But Reedpaw had already hared away, throwing up clawfuls of grass in his wake.

"He's fast," Beetlenose muttered. "He'll make it."

"Good." Crookedjaw scanned the meadow. The dog was pounding closer. "Come on." He pelted down the slope and dived through the long grass. The dog's position was fixed in his mind. He raced toward it, seeing nothing but marsh grass. Oakheart was on his tail, Beetlenose at the rear. Swerving through the narrow channels between tussocks, Crookedjaw hurtled blindly on. He opened his mouth, his breath fast, and tasted dog-scent. It bathed his tongue. Heavy paws pounded ahead.

"Ready?" he called to his Clanmates.

As he skidded around a solid clump of grass, dog-stench filled his nose. The dog flashed black and bristling at the edge of his vision. He swerved and headed back toward the beeches. Oakheart's pelt flickered through the grass beside him. He'd turned and was keeping pace. As Crookedjaw scanned the sedge for Beetlenose, a black pelt burst through a clump of spike-rush and shot past him, taking the lead. The dog yelped with excitement.

"Let's take him around the top of the beech copse," Beetlenose yowled.

"Is he following?" Crookedjaw screeched.

"Look behind you!"

Crookedjaw glanced over his shoulder and saw the dog a tail-length behind. It was huge, jaws slavering, teeth glinting. Its shoulders were wide and hard with muscle. Beetlenose pushed ahead and Crookedjaw pelted after him. The dog yowled and pounded more loudly on the ground.

Crookedjaw weaved, quicker on the turns than the dog. Fur spiked, he rounded the top of the beech copse. He prayed that Sedgepaw and Loudpaw had stayed put and that Reedpaw had made it to camp. The ground hardened underpaw as marsh gave way to willow trees. Bursting from the long grass, Crookedjaw saw Oakheart already zigzagging between the spindly trunks. Ferns loomed over them and hawthorn bushes grew in tangled clumps, making it impossible to run in a straight line. As Beetlenose's paw steps thrummed behind him, Crookedjaw dug his claws against the springy earth and pushed harder. The dog tore the air with a howl as it charged out of the long grass.

"Split up!" Crookedjaw yowled.

Oakheart veered up the slope, Beetlenose shot straight ahead. Crookedjaw swerved toward the river, taking a path around the top of the camp. He glanced back and saw the dog thumping behind him. Flying past the camp, he skimmed a patch of withered bluebells. Blood roared in his ears as he weaved between the blurring trees. The dog thundered behind him, saliva flicking from his muzzle. Crookedjaw skidded on wet moss and lurched sideways, fighting to keep his footing. He could feel the dog's sharp, hot breath on his tail. His lungs screamed, but terror drove him on.

The camp was behind them now. Crookedjaw swung sideways and headed downhill, hoping to gain speed. The dog tried to follow, but its clumsy paws slid on the grass and it crashed on to its side. Crookedjaw bounded down the slope. The river glittered through the willows. If he could just make it to the water, he could catch his breath. The dog was back on its paws and pounding after him. With a grunt, Crookedjaw broke through the swath of ferns edging the bank and burst onto the shore.

Rainflower was standing among the rocks at the water's edge, drinking from the river. She spun around, her eyes wide, and stared at him in horror.

"Dog!" Crookedjaw turned and raced back up the slope. The dog couldn't be allowed to reach the shore. He spotted it hurtling toward the ferns and screeched to get its attention.

The dog tried to turn when it saw him, but its weight carried it down through a long, skidding arc that crashed through the bushes onto the shore. A terrified shriek split the air.

Rainflower!

Crookedjaw whipped around, claws throwing up earth as he ran for the shore. He shot through the ferns in time to see his mother hit the water. The dog stopped, its eyes glittering with surprise, and glanced back at the cat thrashing among the rocky shallows. Its gaze lit up.

Crookedjaw growled and leaped for the dog. Slashing its nose, he turned and ran. The dog howled, rattling stones as it gave chase. Crookedjaw gulped for air as he hauled himself up the hill. He felt the ground shake beneath his paws. The dog was gaining on him.

Oakheart burst from the hawthorn ahead. "Go and save Rainflower!"

Beetlenose skidded out beside him. "We'll take the dog!"

Crookedjaw dived into the prickly branches and crouched, trembling, as paws pounded away through the willows. Gasping, he struggled out of the bush and bounded downhill. He scrambled through the ferns and scanned the shore.

Rainflower?

His mother lay in the water, pressed by the current against a jagged rock while the river slid silently around her, tugging at her soft gray fur. Crookedjaw darted down the bank and splashed into the shallows. Leaning forward, he grabbed her scruff and dragged her from the water.

Leave her! Mapleshade's scent enveloped him. *Save your Clanmates!*

The water drenching Rainflower's pelt tasted of blood. She must have hit a rock when the dog knocked her into the river. With a jolt of horror, Crookedjaw realized her eyes were open and blank. He let her body fall on to the pebbles and backed away. *I have to fetch Brambleberry!*

Mapleshade's outline appeared in front of him, her orange-and-white fur almost transparent so that he could see the reeds and water behind. "Get back to the chase! You have to be there! Remember your promise!"

Crookedjaw hesitated.

Mapleshade hissed in his face. "You want to be great, don't you?"

Crookedjaw glanced once more at his mother. Her body lay limp and still with water streaming from her pelt. What else could he do for her now? Taking a deep breath, he turned and ran up the bank. He caught up with his Clanmates on the other side of the hawthorn bushes. The dog was tiring, tongue hanging, lumbering clumsily through the undergrowth. Crookedjaw pelted past him and fell in beside Oakheart. Oakheart glanced at him out of the corner of his eye and kept running.

The trees were thinning and the land flattened out as they approached the farm. The warriors broke through the RiverClan scent line, leaving their territory. A wooden fence loomed ahead and they squeezed under it, racing into a wide field. Cows moved slowly across the grass. The dog yelped behind them. It couldn't get under the fence and was venting its fury in snarls.

Triumph flared in Crookedjaw's belly. "We did it!" He came to a halt beside his Clanmates. They turned, panting, and stared at the dog. Its eyes burned with rage as it scrabbled at the dirt beneath the fence.

Crookedjaw arched his back and hissed. "Dumb dog!"

Oakheart circled him, bristling. Beetlenose was panting, white rims showing around his eyes.

A shout rang through the willows. Crookedjaw crouched in the grass as a Twoleg strode up behind the dog and grabbed it by the neck. Cursing and yelping, the Twoleg dragged it away. Relief flooded Crookedjaw.

"Is Rainflower okay?" Oakheart's question hit him like a stone.

Crookedjaw stared at his brother. "I was too late," he whispered.

"She's *dead*?" Oakheart's eyes glittered. "Was it the dog? Did it bite her?"

"It knocked her in the water." Crookedjaw lowered his gaze. "She must have hit her head on a rock as she fell."

Oakheart stiffened. "Maybe she was just stunned. Did you get Brambleberry? She might be awake by now." Hope edged his mew.

"I—I left her by the river."

"You left her?" Oakheart blinked at him. "You didn't get Brambleberry?"

"There wasn't time. I had to stop the dog."

Oakheart bristled. "We were taking care of the dog. I left you to take care of Rainflower."

The hardness in his brother's mew turned Crookedjaw's blood cold. Had he made the wrong decision? He closed his eyes. *No! I promised to save my Clan, and that's what I did! Rainflower was dead. She was definitely dead.*

Wasn't she?

Crookedjaw blinked open his eyes. Oakheart was racing away under the fence and into the willows. Crookedjaw headed after him, skidding down the slope and bursting on to the shore.

Oakheart was crouching beside Rainflower. Her eyes had clouded. Blood stained the rocks around her head. "She's dead." Oakheart turned and stared at Crookedjaw. "Our mother is dead."

CHAPTER 30

Rainflower's body lay stiff in the moonlight. Oakheart had dragged it to the clearing, warning Crookedjaw away with a snarl each time he'd tried to help. Crookedjaw crouched outside his den and watched his Clanmates file past his mother.

Echomist touched her nose to Rainflower's pelt. "You were a loyal warrior."

Piketooth leaned down to her ear. "We'll miss you."

Crookedjaw's eyes stung. Now he'd never have a chance to make Rainflower proud of him. Pain jabbed his heart like thorns.

Oakheart sat on the far side of the clearing, Petaldust and Voleclaw pressing close. Oakheart stared ahead as Shimmerpelt padded away from Rainflower's body and murmured something to him. Timberfur dipped his head in respect to the grief-stricken warrior.

Anger flashed through Crookedjaw. Rainflower loved Oakheart more than she had ever loved Crookedjaw. *Well, let them fuss.* Crookedjaw turned his head away. *I don't care.* His heart twisted in his chest.

"It's okay." Willowbreeze walked away from the body and

settled beside Crookedjaw. She leaned into him gently. "She'll be watching over you from StarClan."

Crookedjaw swallowed back a wail of grief. *Would she care that much?*

"You were very brave," Willowbreeze told him. "Facing that dog and leading him out of the territory."

I should have been saving my mother. The thought pounded in his head but he couldn't bring himself to share it, even with Willowbreeze.

As the Clan melted into the edges of the camp, Shellheart emerged from beneath the willow. His eyes glazed as he stared at the mate he'd turned his back on. Crookedjaw could see the pain in them, and realized that Shellheart had never stopped loving her. The RiverClan deputy settled stiffly beside Rainflower and closed his eyes. He looked old. Crookedjaw blinked. He'd never noticed that his father's pelt was growing ragged and gray whiskers had begun to speckle his muzzle.

Oakheart slid out from between Petaldust and Voleclaw and joined his father. He touched Shellheart's head with his cheek, then settled beside him and pressed his nose into Rainflower's matted pelt. Clouds covered the moon, draping the three silent figures in shadow. Crookedjaw tucked his paws tighter beneath him and closed his eyes.

I'm sorry. Was Rainflower in StarClan by now, listening to him? *I shouldn't have left you on the shore. I should have fought the dog and saved you.* Would Mapleshade explain it to her? He felt a rush of hope, but grief washed it away instantly. *I'm sorry for everything, Rainflower—for sneaking out of camp and breaking my jaw; for letting you die. I've missed you so much. I wish I could have gotten you to forgive me.* He snapped open his eyes and stared up at Silverpelt. "Please forgive me," he whispered.

Willowbreeze turned her head and licked his cheek. They slept curled up together in the warm greenleaf breeze, at the edge of the clearing. The sound of paws scuffing the sun-hardened ground woke Crookedjaw. Dawn lit the camp. The elders were taking away Rainflower's body for burial. Shellheart and Oakheart watched, their eyes bleary with tiredness and grief. As Birdsong and Troutclaw lifted the body onto Tanglewhisker's wide, graying back, Oakheart trailed to his den and disappeared inside. Shellheart ducked in beside Tanglewhisker, sharing the weight of the body.

Brambleberry slipped from her den, dipping her head as the burial party passed. She crossed the clearing and stopped in front of Crookedjaw. He got to his paws, careful not to disturb Willowbreeze, who was still dozing beside him.

"She didn't suffer," Brambleberry murmured. "The wound to her head would have knocked her unconscious. She wouldn't have known what was happening."

Crookedjaw hung his head. "You're just trying to comfort me."

"No!" Brambleberry stepped back. "I wouldn't lie!"

Crookedjaw winced. Now he'd hurt her feelings. Why couldn't he say or do anything right? "I—I'm just—"

Brambleberry stopped him. "We need to talk, Crookedjaw."

"Let all cats old enough to swim gather to hear my words!"

Hailstar's call interrupted her.

Willowbreeze scrabbled to her paws. "What's going on?"

"I don't know." Brambleberry ducked away, leaving Crookedjaw staring after her, puzzled. What was she going to tell him?

Dens rustled and whispers murmured around the camp as the Clan collected to listen to their leader. Crookedjaw followed Willowbreeze to the back of the crowd.

Mudfur moved aside to make room for them. He dipped his head to Crookedjaw. "I'm sorry for your loss."

"Thanks," Crookedjaw mumbled.

"We have been united in grief," Hailstar began. "Now let us unite in victory. There is a piece of territory that rightfully belongs to RiverClan. It brings us warmth. It brings us shade. Now it's time to let those mangy squirrel-eaters know it is ours!"

"Sunningrocks!" Timberfur yowled. "Yes!"

Crookedjaw scanned the clearing for Shellheart and Oakheart. Wouldn't they want to be part of this? They were nowhere to be seen. Crookedjaw's tail drooped. Weariness ate at his bones.

"Crookedjaw!" Hailstar called. "I'd like you to be in the patrol to re-mark Sunningrocks." He scanned the rest of the Clan. "Voleclaw and Mudfur, I want you to come, too."

Crookedjaw felt Mudfur stiffen beside him as the RiverClan leader called his name. Crookedjaw glanced at his Clanmate. Mudfur's forehead was furrowed in a scowl.

364 WARRIORS SUPER EDITION: CROOKEDSTAR'S PROMISE

Sedgepaw scrambled forward. "Aren't any apprentices going?' she mewed.

Hailstar shook his head. "I want my strongest, most experienced warriors. I hope we can re-mark the borders without resistance, but if we meet a ThunderClan patrol, I want them to feel the sharpness of our teeth and see the glint of our claws."

Blackpaw whisked his tail. "I have sharp teeth!"

"We need battle practice!" Sunpaw called from beside Voleclaw. "If my mentor's going, why can't I?"

Hailstar dipped his head. "There will be other battles," he meowed. "This one will be clean and quick. Not a place for training." He turned his head. "Owlfur, Softwing, Piketooth!" he called. "You'll form a second patrol. Mine will swim across. I want you to cross by the stepping-stones. Wait at the base of the rocks. If we meet resistance, we'll lead ThunderClan to fight there."

Crookedjaw's interest pricked. If they fought the battle on the ledge below Sunningrocks, the river would give them an advantage. While ThunderClan was struggling not to fall in, RiverClan could take bigger risks and fight far more fearlessly.

Hailstar went on. "I pray there will be no bloodshed. We have already lost a brave and noble warrior in Rainflower."

Whispers of agreement spread through the Clan. Then Mudfur stepped forward. He lifted his voice above the murmuring. "Is it worth risking our lives yet again for these rocks?"

Hailstar's gaze snapped to the old warrior, shock clear in

his eyes. "Mudfur?" He didn't seem to understand. "Why would you object now? You've always been at the front of the fight."

Crookedjaw narrowed his eyes. Mudfur was known for his strength and bravery. He could hold a warrior underwater till he surrendered. The other Clans whispered to their apprentices at Gatherings not to take him on in battle.

Mudfur dipped his head. "I don't know if it's worth fighting the same battle over and over again." His voice was steady and he met the gaze of his Clanmates without flinching.

Rippleclaw hissed. "It is a matter of honor that we don't let ThunderClan take rocks that were given to us at the dawn of the Clans."

Hailstar tipped his head. "Does this mean you refuse to join the patrol, Mudfur?"

"I'll join it," Mudfur rasped. "If you give me the order, I will fight."

Crookedjaw lifted his muzzle. "When do we leave?"

"Now." Hailstar headed for the entrance. Voleclaw raced after him. Crookedjaw fell in beside Mudfur. He wanted to ask the old warrior why he was fighting if he thought it a waste of time.

Mudfur glanced sideways. "Don't worry," he growled softly. "I'll fight as hard as anyone. I'm no minnow-heart and Hailstar is still my leader, just as he is yours."

At the shore, Softwing, Owlfur, and Piketooth hurried away to the stepping-stones. Hailstar waded into the water and started swimming across the river. The sun was hardly over the willow trees. Sunningrocks looked rosy in the early-morning light, dew already drying fast on the top stones. Crookedjaw padded into the river, refreshed by its cool tug as he swam to the far bank. He pulled himself out and shook his pelt, then followed Hailstar, Voleclaw, and Mudfur up the rock face.

His heart quickened as he reached the summit and saw the sweep of smooth stone and the dark forest beyond. Energy pulsed beneath his pelt, pushing away his grief. He had a chance to fight for his Clan. Was Rainflower watching him from StarClan? This could be his chance to make her proud.

Hailstar signaled toward the forest's edge. Crookedjaw knew what to do. He bounded down the far side of the rocks and followed the path Shellheart had taken last time. While Hailstar led Voleclaw to the other end of the Sunningrocks boundary, Crookedjaw headed for the first oak towering at the cliff edge and left his mark. Mudfur marked the bush beside it and they followed the border along the foot of the stones, taking turns to mark until they met Hailstar at the middle.

"Is that it?" Voleclaw stared into the shadowy trees. "Why does ThunderClan want Sunningrocks anyway? They're used to the dark."

"Perhaps that's why they want Sunningrocks, to give them a chance to see some sun." Crookedjaw paused. Bushes rustled beyond the tree line. He smelled ThunderClan. He backed away from the border, hissing. Hailstar's tail bushed. Mudfur held his ground, baring his teeth. Voleclaw's hackles lifted.

"Don't forget," Hailstar whispered. "If they challenge us, we lead them to the shore and fight beside the river."

Suddenly Adderfang burst, bristling, from the forest. Crookedjaw tensed, ready to race for the edge of the rocks.

"We knew you'd try and take them again." Adderfang curled his lip as Swiftbreeze, Smallear, and Speckletail barged out of the bushes behind the dark tabby. "How many times do we have to beat you before you stop trying to take what's *ours*?"

Voleclaw arched his back. "We'll beat you this time!" He glanced at Hailstar. Crookedjaw knew he was waiting for the signal to retreat and lead the unsuspecting ThunderClan patrol to the riverbank. Hailstar raised his tail, ready.

Mudfur stepped forward. "Enough!"

Hailstar's head snapped around. "What?"

Adderfang's yellow gaze sharpened with interest. Swiftbreeze glanced uneasily at her Clanmates.

"Too much blood has been shed already over these stones," Mudfur declared.

Swiftbreeze flattened her ears. "That sounds like surrender."

"No." Mudfur's gaze flicked over the ThunderClan warriors. Crookedjaw could see Hailstar's muscles tightening, but the RiverClan leader held his ground as Mudfur went on. "These rocks belong to RiverClan and always will."

Adderfang lashed his tail. "Never!" He crouched down, ready to spring. Crookedjaw unsheathed his claws.

"Wait!" Mudfur stepped between them. "We'll settle this

now." He glared at Adderfang. "If you have the courage."

Adderfang thrust his face, growling, into Mudfur's. "Oh, I have the courage!"

"Then fight me." Mudfur moved his muzzle a whisker closer to the bristling ThunderClan warrior. "Alone."

Adderfang drew back, eyes wide. "Just you and me?"

"We will each stand for the rest of our Clans."

Adderfang snorted. He glanced back at his Clanmates. "This is too easy." His gaze flicked to Hailstar. "Are you happy with this?" There was disbelief in his mew, as though Mudfur had just dropped a freshly caught mouse at his paws.

Hailstar shifted his paws and glanced at Mudfur. Then he stepped forward. "Yes," he growled. "Do you want to check with Sunstar before we do this?"

"I'm acting as deputy now and I say it's fine." The ThunderClan warrior's yellow eyes glowed as though victory was already his.

Mudfur backed into the middle of the tumbled rocks. Adderfang paced after him, his muscles rippling under his mottled brown pelt. Swiftbreeze, Smallear, and Speckletail spread out to watch. Crookedjaw joined Hailstar and Voleclaw as they lined up behind Mudfur. Fear flickered beneath Crookedjaw's pelt. This was worse than going into battle because he could only watch. *What if every battle was fought this way?* He pushed away the thought. This was no way to fight. He felt helpless, his heart pounding, his paws uncomfortably still.

Mudfur circled Adderfang. Adderfang folded his ears

flat and let out a hiss. He reared and slammed his paws down on Mudfur's spine. Mudfur rolled over, heaving the ThunderClan warrior to the ground. Wrestling him close, he sank his teeth into Adderfang's shoulders. Adderfang screeched and struggled free, turning like a snake and darting forward. Mudfur sprang on to his paws. Adderfang snapped at his forelegs. Mudfur reared up, batting him away, but Adderfang had glimpsed his enemy's pale belly. He lunged, claws swiping. Mudfur shrieked and fell back.

As Swiftbreeze and Smallear hopped out of the way, Mudfur landed with a grunt. Adderfang lunged again, but Mudfur was on his paws and rearing to meet the tabby warrior. In a flurry of claws they slashed at each other. Blood sprayed the rock. Shrieks filled the air and sent a flight of starlings fluttering up from the forest.

Claws scraped against stone at the top of the rocks. Crookedjaw looked up to see Softwing, Owlfur, and Piketooth swarm over the edge.

"Stay back," he warned before they could plunge into the fight.

Piketooth blinked at him.

"Adderfang's fighting Mudfur alone," Crookedjaw explained.

Adderfang was on his hind paws now, striking out fiercely, one swipe after another, driving Mudfur back. The RiverClan warrior's face welled with blood that ran into his eyes.

How can he see? Stop!

Adderfang drove forward, forcing Mudfur toward the

edge of the space. Crookedjaw had to force himself to stay still. Every muscle screamed to attack. Then Mudfur struck back. With a yowl he plunged forward, rearing up at the last moment and meeting Adderfang head on. He sank his teeth into Adderfang's shoulder and pushed him down, his wide shoulders rippling. Adderfang squirmed beneath him, shrieking, but he couldn't fight free. Mudfur pressed his paws to the ThunderClan warrior's throat, pinning Adderfang to the rock as though he were a trout.

"Give in?" Mudfur growled.

Adderfang stared up at him, eyes blazing.

"Give in?" Mudfur repeated, louder.

"Yes." Adderfang's gasp was barely audible.

Mudfur let go and staggered back, panting. Blood ran off his pelt. Adderfang crouched on the sandy ground, his fur hanging in clumps.

Hailstar lifted his muzzle to the sky. "Sunningrocks is ours!" he yowled.

The ThunderClan warriors gathered around Adderfang and steered their wounded Clanmate toward the trees. Crookedjaw watched them disappear into the undergrowth, feeling a prickle of satisfaction. Adderfang had underestimated Mudfur. He glanced at the old RiverClan warrior, expecting to see triumph light his gaze. But Mudfur just turned away and began to limp slowly home.

CHAPTER 31

❧

"Why did you fight alone?" Rippleclaw hissed at Mudfur as Brambleberry bustled around the injured warrior, trying to smooth ointment into his wounds.

Mudfur shook Brambleberry away. "Why risk hurting more warriors? Too much blood has been spilled for those rocks already." He glanced across the clearing to Leopardpaw. "Battles only seem to lead to more battles. It is bad enough we fight, but we teach our kits to fight and then we watch them get hurt."

Crookedjaw watched his Clanmates through narrowed eyes. They'd hurried to hear Hailstar's battle report, clustering beneath the willow, faces puzzled, paws shifting. Crookedjaw was relieved that he wasn't the only one worried by the idea of a single warrior fighting a battle for a whole Clan. Mudfur refused to go to the medicine cat's den so Brambleberry was treating him out here, muttering as she tried to close up the deeper scratches.

Timberfur scowled at Hailstar. "Why did you let him?"

Hailstar met his gaze. "I trust him the same way that I trust all my warriors."

"He did win Sunningrocks for us," Softwing pointed out.

Tanglewhisker sank his claws into the dusty ground. "But RiverClan has never fought that way."

"And we shouldn't start now," Troutclaw put in.

Crookedjaw lashed his tail. "It's cowardly."

Mudfur snapped his head around.

"You're not a coward," Crookedjaw added quickly. "But I felt like a coward watching a Clanmate fight without helping him."

Shellheart stepped forward. His paws were muddy from burying Rainflower. "No warrior wants to feel like he can't help his Clan."

Hailstar gazed uneasily at Mudfur. "Did you doubt the courage of your Clanmates?"

"Never!" Mudfur bristled. "But I'd rather spill my own blood than theirs."

"It mustn't happen again!" Cedarpelt shouldered his way to the front of the crowd. "We're a Clan. We must fight as a Clan."

"Cedarpelt's right." Hailstar dipped his head. "Fighting beside our Clanmates gives us all strength."

Ottersplash pushed forward. "Letting one warrior fight makes the rest of us look weak!"

Hailstar signaled for silence with a flick of his tail. "Mudfur showed great courage today, and RiverClan thanks him. He returned Sunningrocks to us. But from now on, we fight as a Clan. No warrior will go into battle alone. Where one fights, we all fight!"

"RiverClan! RiverClan!" The Clan burst into cheers. Relief washed Crookedjaw's pelt. Mudfur closed his eyes, letting Brambleberry tend to his wounds.

"Can we go to Sunningrocks *now*?" Reedpaw begged Beetlenose.

Skypaw excitedly circled Softwing. "I've never been there!"

"Later," Softwing told her. "When you've cleared out Birdsong's nest."

Sunpaw crouched behind Frogpaw. "Watch out, ThunderClan!" She leaped on her littermate. "No one takes Sunningrocks and gets away with it!" They fell, tumbling, to the ground.

Crookedjaw padded to Shellheart's side. "Are you okay?" He glanced at his father's torn and dirt-filled claws.

Shellheart nodded. "I'm fine."

Crookedjaw glanced at Oakheart's den. "I don't know if Oakheart will speak to me again." His brother was still sleeping, oblivious to the victory at Sunningrocks.

Shellheart ran his tail along Crookedjaw's flank. "He's just angry. It'll pass with the grief." His eyes glistened. "You probably don't remember how loving she could be."

I do. Pain jabbed Crookedjaw as, for a moment, he was a kit again, with Rainflower watching him play, pride lighting her eyes.

Shellheart went on. "She wasn't—"

"Hailstar!" Mudfur's call interrupted them.

Brambleberry was wrapping cobwebs around the injured warrior's hind leg. "Hold still! Do you want to fall apart next time you go into battle?"

"That won't happen," Mudfur meowed calmly. "I don't

want to be a warrior anymore."

What?

Tanglewhisker and Troutclaw turned back from the bottom of the slope, ears pricking. Timberfur paused from sorting through the fresh-kill pile and glanced over. He beckoned Rippleclaw and Owlfur with his tail.

Hailstar blinked. He was still sitting under the willow tree, watching his Clanmates drift back to their duties. "Really, Mudfur? But you're too young to move to the elders' den. You didn't become a 'paw till after me."

Mudfur shook his head. "I don't want to become an elder," he explained. "I want to be a medicine cat."

Brambleberry sat back on her haunches, cobweb trailing from her paw. "A medicine cat?"

Mudfur dipped his head. "If you're willing to train me."

Brambleberry stood. "I was hoping one of the 'paws would take an interest," she admitted. "There's always so much to do, I could use an apprentice."

Hailstar stared at his old friend. "Are you sure about this?" The fur twitched along his spine.

Mudfur held his gaze. "I've lost the taste for battle. I'm no use to my Clan as a warrior now."

"But you fought for the whole Clan this morning."

"I fought to save them from fighting," Mudfur meowed. "But they *want* to fight." He sighed. "I've unsheathed my claws too many times." He turned to Brambleberry. "I want to save lives, not destroy them."

Brightsky. Crookedjaw guessed the warrior was still

mourning his mate. *Watching her die, he must have felt as powerless as I did on Sunningrocks today.*

Softwing leaned toward Timberfur. "Can he do that? Change his mind about what he wants to be?"

Timberfur shrugged. "I don't know. It hasn't happened in RiverClan before, as far as I know."

"He trained as a warrior!" Beetlenose was frowning.

Hailstar met the young tom's gaze. "And he's served his Clan well. Now, if he wishes, he can train as a medicine cat and serve his Clan in a different way."

"Thank you." Mudfur nodded and began to pad away.

"Wait." Shellheart stopped him. "I have an announcement to make, too."

Crookedjaw tensed. *What now?*

"I wish to move to the elders' den."

Hailstar blinked, startled.

Rippleclaw darted forward. "What in the name of StarClan is going on? Is every warrior deserting us?"

Mudfur weaved around Shellheart. "We're not deserting anyone. Hailstar will choose another deputy, as brave and loyal as Shellheart. RiverClan is like the river. Always flowing, yet never changing."

Hailstar sat down, suddenly looking old. "Shellheart, I respect your decision. You have spent many seasons serving your Clan. Of course you may join the elders."

Wasn't the RiverClan leader going to argue? Crookedjaw stared at his father. Why hadn't Shellheart warned him? Did Oakheart know?

Shellheart dipped his head. "Thank you, Hailstar," he mewed formally. "A younger deputy will make RiverClan stronger."

Willowbreeze brushed against Crookedjaw. "Your father has to do what he thinks is right."

But what if he's wrong?

"He's been looking thin and tired for a while," she went on.

Has he?

"I thought you'd noticed." Willowbreeze wrapped her tail around him.

Crookedjaw felt sick. "Is he ill?"

Willowbreeze shrugged. "Probably just slowing down."

Tanglewhisker padded forward and nudged Shellheart. "There's plenty of room in the den," he croaked.

Troutclaw beckoned the old deputy with his tail. "Come and see." He limped toward the slope, his hind leg refusing to bend properly as usual. "You're going to have to get used to Birdsong snoring, mind you."

"I think I can cope with that," Shellheart purred as he followed his new denmates.

"Timberfur, Rippleclaw, Owlfur, Ottersplash, Piketooth, Cedarpelt." Hailstar called to his senior warriors. "Come. I need to hear your advice before I decide who's to be the next deputy." He turned and headed to his den.

"Crookedjaw! Crookedjaw!" Sedgepaw was hurtling across the clearing.

Crookedjaw jumped to his paws.

"Troutclaw says there's going to be a new deputy! And

Mudfur's going to be a medicine cat." Sedgepaw rolled her eyes. "Why does all the good stuff happen when I'm in dirtplace?"

Voleclaw padded past. "I wouldn't call it good stuff," he muttered.

"Oh." Sedgepaw sat down.

Willowbreeze touched the young she-cat lightly with her muzzle. "Change is difficult," she meowed. "But it'll be okay." She gazed at Crookedjaw and he guessed the words were meant more for him than Sedgepaw.

Reedpaw and Loudpaw were bundling toward their littermate. "Has he told you yet?" Loudpaw demanded.

"I haven't asked," Sedgepaw mewed.

"Then I will!" Reedpaw plucked at the ground. "What was the fight with Adderfang like?"

"Did Mudfur totally shred him?" Loudpaw couldn't keep still. "I'm going to fight like that one day."

Voleclaw stilled him with a flick of his tail. "No cat will fight like that," he told the young tom. "It's not part of the warrior code, and Hailstar's forbidden it."

Sedgepaw was nodding. "I'd rather fight beside my Clanmates," she announced.

"Can we practice some battle moves?" Reedpaw begged. "We didn't get a chance yesterday because of the dog."

Loudpaw scanned the clearing. "Where's Oakheart?"

Willowbreeze pointed to his den with her nose. "Resting," she told him. "He sat vigil for Rainflower."

Voleclaw circled the apprentices. "I'm taking Sunpaw

training," he told Loudpaw. "You can join us." He glanced at Crookedjaw. "Do you and Beetlenose want to bring Sedgepaw and Reedpaw?"

Beetlenose was trotting over to join them and overheard. "Yes, please." He glanced at the warriors huddled around Hailstar's den. "Everyone's so serious here."

"They're picking a new *deputy*," Crookedjaw reminded him.

Sedgepaw peered around Beetlenose. "I wonder who they'll choose."

Beetlenose shrugged. "Probably one of the senior warriors." He headed toward the gap in the reeds. "The warrior code says he's got to decide by moonhigh, which gives them ages. We might as well get on with training."

The willows smelled of dog. Though the stench was stale it made Crookedjaw's pelt bristle. He followed Beetlenose and Voleclaw up the slope to a grassy glade above the camp. Sunpaw, Sedgepaw, Loudpaw, and Reedpaw squabbled as they tried to guess who Hailstar would pick as deputy.

"It's got to be Timberfur."

"Why not Rippleclaw?"

"Rippleclaw's too old. He'll pick Ottersplash."

Beetlenose stopped in the middle of the glade. "Why don't you let Hailstar decide and concentrate on your hunting skills?"

Crookedjaw shifted his paws. Did the new deputy definitely have to be a senior warrior?

Voleclaw flicked his tail at Sunpaw and Loudpaw. "Come

on, let's see if we can find some birds."

"Birds?" Loudpaw flattened his ears. "It's not leaf-bare."

"Which means they'll be easy to find." Voleclaw bounded away, leaping a mossy log rotting at the top of the glade.

Sunpaw shrugged and followed her mentor. "We've got to be able to catch land prey as well as river prey," she called over her shoulder.

As Loudpaw charged after her, Beetlenose nudged Reedpaw toward the roots of a gnarled willow. "Let's practice climbing," he meowed. "The trees here should be easier than the beeches."

Willow branches were thinner and felt a lot less stable, but dipped closer to the ground, making it easier to start and less frightening if a cat fell off.

"Okay." Reedpaw scrambled up the trunk and started to pick his way along one of the thickest branches.

"Are we going to climb?" Sedgepaw asked Crookedjaw.

"Not now." Crookedjaw rubbed his nose with a paw. With the other apprentices busy, this would be a great time to help Sedgepaw with her stalking. Beckoning her with his tail, he led her to a gap in the trees, dappled by sunshine filtering through the slender, silvery leaves. He halted and pricked his ears.

"What are we listening for?" Sedgepaw asked.

"Birds."

"Can't you hear them already?" Birdsong chattered from every tree.

"I'm listening for one we can stalk." Crookedjaw crouched.

"Get down!" He flicked his tail. A finch was hopping from branch to branch above them. He could hear its wings fluttering between the leaves. He backed under a fern. "Hide."

Sedgepaw scooted in beside him and peered out from under the fronds. "How do you know it's going to come down from the tree?" she whispered.

"There are some blueberries over there." Crookedjaw nodded toward a shrub of soft leaves hung with dark, round berries. "The bird has its eye on them." As he spoke, wings fluttered and the finch landed among the berries, making the twig dip under its weight.

Sedgepaw gasped. "How did you know?"

"Cedarpelt taught me." And Fleck. He wondered how his old friends were doing. *I bet Soot is as big as a warrior by now.* Crookedjaw watched the finch hop among the leaves for a moment before nudging Sedgepaw forward. "Go on."

"You want *me* to catch it?" He felt her pelt bristle.

"Just give it a try," he encouraged.

Her breath quickened as she stalked forward, pressing her belly to the ground.

"Slow down," he whispered. "You'll be okay."

She paused and steadied her breathing. Crookedjaw saw her flanks relax. Then she moved forward again. She was remembering to keep her tail off the ground, making hardly a sound as she crept across the grass. Crookedjaw tensed. Sedgepaw stopped beside the berry patch. Her tail twitched but she stilled it. Her gaze was fixed on the finch. Crookedjaw held his breath.

Then Sedgepaw leaped, smooth as a fish, and grabbed the finch between her paws. It fluttered in panic but she leaned forward and nipped its neck. Mewing in triumph, she turned and faced Crookedjaw, the finch limp in her jaws.

"Well done!" Pride surged through Crookedjaw as he padded to congratulate her. "Great catch." As he spoke, something gray shot across the clearing.

Squirrel?

Crookedjaw hared after it. Squirrels rarely strayed this side of the river. It raced fast as lightning over the grass. Crookedjaw jumped, soaring through the air, and landed on top of the squirrel. With a bite, he killed it.

Sedgepaw came puffing up behind him. "You got it!" She'd dropped her finch. "I've never tasted squirrel!"

"It's not bad for land prey." Crookedjaw sniffed it, enjoying the warm, musky scent; it couldn't be more different from fish and he wasn't sure the older warriors would approve. But thinking about his time with the farm cats had reminded him of the squirrels they had caught in the hedges, and he wanted to bask in his memories for a little longer.

As slender reed shadows lengthened across the clearing, Willowbreeze stretched. "They must have decided by now." She glanced at the huddle of senior warriors below the willow. "The sun's nearly set."

Crookedjaw shrugged. "They've got till moonhigh." He'd been trying not to think about who would replace his father. He wanted to be deputy more than anything in the world, but surely it was too soon for him? He hadn't even finished training Sedgepaw and there were plenty of warriors with more experience. Even Oakheart had more experience. Anxiety flared in his belly. Hailstar wouldn't choose Oakheart, would he? He had asked him to speak at the Gathering. He pushed away the thought.

Willowbreeze purred.

"What?"

"Sedgepaw's been staring at her finch for ages."

Sedgepaw sat outside the apprentices' den, eyes fixed on the fresh-kill pile.

Crookedjaw's whiskers twitched. "She's wondering who'll choose it."

"Doesn't *she* want to eat it?"

"I think she likes the thought of feeding her Clan." He moved closer to Willowbreeze. "It's her first catch."

"You told me."

"I was starting to think she'd never get the hang of it."

"Land prey's never easy." Willowbreeze yawned. "Your squirrel looks impressive."

It hung over the pile of fish that Shimmerpelt and Lakeshine had caught. Crookedjaw shrugged. "I don't know who'll eat it."

"I think Graypool's got her eye on it."

Crookedjaw didn't reply. Hailstar was walking into the middle of the camp. Rippleclaw and Timberfur followed, with Ottersplash, Owlfur, and Cedarpelt at their heels. Crookedjaw sat up. Dens rustled and fur brushed the ground as the Clan padded from dens and eating places to hear their leader.

Hailstar shook his head, forestalling any questions. "We haven't decided yet," he meowed. He sounded tired.

Echomist swished her tail. "You must be hungry." She nodded at the fresh-kill pile. "There's plenty to eat."

"Good." Hailstar licked his lips. "We'll decide after we've all had a chance to eat."

He headed toward the fresh-kill pile. As he neared it, he froze. The fur lifted along his spine. "Brambleberry!" he yowled, keeping his eyes fixed on the pile of prey.

Crookedjaw darted across the clearing. For a wild moment he wondered if the sight of a squirrel among the fish had startled the old leader. Brambleberry shot from her den and skidded to a halt beside Hailstar. She followed his gaze, her pelt spiking up.

"What does this mean?" Hailstar whispered.

Crookedjaw stared at the prey on the fresh-kill pile. The jaws of the squirrel had been wrenched wide and hung open, dangling by sinews so that its mouth gaped unnaturally. Its broken, twisted face seemed to stare out at the horrified cats.

"That was Crookedjaw's prey," Echomist breathed.

Hailstar sniffed at the pile, then looked up. "It's an omen!" he growled, his eyes flashing. His gaze swung to Crookedjaw. "It's you!" he growled. "You are the new RiverClan deputy!"

CHAPTER 32

Birdsong pushed her way through the stunned cats. "He's too young!"

"He's been a warrior for moons!" Willowbreeze retorted.

Hailstar silenced them with a look. "StarClan knows best." He dipped his head to Crookedjaw. His voice was flat. "I cannot change the will of our ancestors."

Crookedjaw felt ghostly fur slide around his flanks. The scent of Mapleshade hung in the air. Had she left the omen? His heart soared. It truly *was* an omen from StarClan.

"Go to Hailstar!" Willowbreeze nudged Crookedjaw forward. "Go and accept! Tell him you want to be deputy."

Sedgepaw blocked his path. "I'm going to be the deputy's apprentice." She puffed out her chest.

Voleclaw nodded to Crookedjaw. "Well done!"

Beetlenose sniffed. "Who'd believe you were once the smallest kit in the nursery?"

"Now he's the biggest cat in the Clan," Cedarpelt purred. "Congratulations, Crookedjaw. You deserve it."

Do I? Crookedjaw stared numbly at his Clanmates.

"He doesn't have any experience," Troutclaw whispered to Birdsong.

Timberfur's tail was twitching. "He's only fought in one real battle."

Shimmerpelt was staring at the fresh-kill pile. "Are we allowed to eat an omen or should we catch more fish?"

Graypool slid past her. "Why not ask our new deputy?" Her eyes glinted. "Congratulations."

"Crookedjaw!" Oakheart's mew made him turn. His brother weaved through his Clanmates. "You will make a fine deputy and a great leader." He touched his muzzle to Crookedjaw's cheek. "You will always have my loyalty."

Crookedjaw's numbness melted. There was real warmth in Oakheart's gaze. *He's forgiven me for Rainflower's death! Thank StarClan!* "Thank you," he whispered.

Shellheart padded forward. "I'm proud of you."

Crookedjaw looked up at Silverpelt. *Are you proud of me, too, Rainflower?*

A sharp paw prodded him. "You have to tell Hailstar that you accept," Willowbreeze reminded him.

Crookedjaw padded into the shadow of the willow. The moss at the entrance to Hailstar's den quivered in the breeze. Crookedjaw paused, steadying his paws.

"You don't understand!" Brambleberry's urgent mew sounded from inside the den.

Hailstar answered. "What is there to understand?"

"It wasn't an omen from StarClan!"

Crookedjaw's heart seemed to stop.

"Who else would send omens?" Hailstar rasped.

Brambleberry's mew was frightened. "Just let me go to

the Moonstone," she pleaded.

"The Moonstone?" Hailstar sounded puzzled. "An omen is an omen, wherever it comes from. Is there something you're not telling me?"

Crookedjaw burst through the moss. He stared accusingly at Brambleberry. "What is it? What's wrong? Don't you want me to be deputy?"

Brambleberry's eyes glistened. "Of course I do!" She was trembling. "It's just . . ." She trailed off.

"Just *what*, Brambleberry?" Hailstar was sitting at the back of his den, his gray pelt hardly visible. "If you've heard something from StarClan, tell me." He glanced at Crookedjaw. "Tell *us*."

"Not yet." She closed her eyes. "Everything might be all right." She blinked them open and stared at Crookedjaw. "You're as strong and as skilled as any other warrior. As long as you make the right choices, it might still be okay." She slipped out of the den before Hailstar could speak. Crookedjaw wanted to follow her. He wanted to make her tell him what was worrying her, what had been worrying her for so long.

"Do you accept, then?"

"Huh?"

"Do you want to be deputy?" Hailstar's mew snapped Crookedjaw back from his thoughts.

He shifted his paws. "Do you still want me?" Had Brambleberry put him off?

"Of course I do." Hailstar heaved himself to his paws. "The omen of crooked jaws surprised me," he meowed. "But it was an omen. I know you're still young. But you have great potential. You've overcome a lot, Crookedjaw, and you've become a warrior your Clan can be proud of. I always thought you'd become deputy one day—even leader." He shrugged. "Maybe not so soon, but if you want it—"

"*Want* it?" Crookedjaw blinked at his leader. "Of course I want it. More than anything else."

Hailstar narrowed his eyes.

Crookedjaw tumbled on. "My Clan means more to me than anything in the world. I know I'm young, but I promise to learn. I promise to grow wiser and stronger and do everything I can to help my Clan." His promise to Mapleshade rang in his ears. *I will be loyal to my Clan above everything. What I want doesn't matter. The Clan must always come first.* Excitement surged under his pelt as Hailstar brushed past him and nosed his way outside.

"Come on." The RiverClan leader beckoned him with a flick of his tail.

The green reeds glowed almost blue beneath the rising moon, and the willow branches whispered overhead. The air was warm and Crookedjaw could taste the river. His Clanmates lined the clearing, watching silently as Hailstar led him to the middle of the camp.

"Shellheart!" The RiverClan leader called the former deputy forward.

Shellheart padded to join them. His spine showed beneath his ragged pelt as he stood before Hailstar.

Hailstar dipped his head low. "Shellheart, RiverClan thanks you for your loyalty and wisdom. You have never flinched from your duty or shown anything but courage. You've served your Clan well and we wish you peace and comfort in the elders' den. You have earned a long rest."

Sedgepaw bounded forward. "I promise I'll keep your nest clean and pull out all your ticks."

Timberfur tugged his daughter back by her tail. "Shhh!"

Crookedjaw stifled a purr as Hailstar went on solemnly. "I hope you will share your stories with all of us and with the kits yet to be born. We still have much to learn from you."

"Shellheart! Shellheart!" As the Clan called his name, Crookedjaw cheered loudest of all for his father and mentor.

"Crookedjaw." Hailstar touched Crookedjaw's shoulders with his tail-tip. "From this day forward you will be RiverClan's deputy. StarClan has given you its blessing, and I pray you live up to its hopes and to ours."

Crookedjaw glanced at Brambleberry, sitting in shadow outside her den. She was staring at her paws.

Hailstar's eyes darkened. "I am on my ninth life. You are young to be so close to leadership. I pray that StarClan gives you all the strength and wisdom you'll need in the coming moons."

"Crookedjaw! Crookedjaw!" He heard warmth in his Clanmate's cheers, in Oakheart's above all. There was no hint of jealousy, nothing but pride. Willowbreeze watched him from the edge of the clearing, her eyes reflecting the wide, starry sky. Breathing deeply, Crookedjaw tasted the scents of the river and the reeds and the willows. These were all his now, more than ever before. Straightening his back he looked up at the stars. *Thank you, StarClan. I promise I won't let you down.*

* * *

The long day had left Crookedjaw bone-tired. After the ceremony, his Clanmates had crowded around him, sharing tongues until the moon rose high in the sky.

"Should we build you a bigger den now?" Petaldust called as Crookedjaw padded wearily to his nest.

Oakheart swallowed the last of his meal and licked his lips. "Perhaps I should line your nest with swan feathers?" he teased.

Crookedjaw purred with amusement, but he was relieved to creep into the darkness of his den and curl into his nest beside Willowbreeze.

"Good night," he murmured as Willowbreeze snuggled in. He closed his eyes. He was jerked awake almost at once by a paw jabbing his side.

"Mapleshade?" He staggered to his feet.

The orange-and-white cat paced across the gloomy clearing, sending mist swirling as she lashed her tail. "See?" Her eyes glowed with triumph. "I told you I'd keep my promise! You didn't let the death of your mother distract you from your loyalty to the Clan. You chose to save your Clanmates over her! And now you're deputy."

Crookedjaw narrowed his eyes. *I didn't choose anything.* His mother's death had nothing to do with him becoming deputy. He opened his mouth to argue but Mapleshade was too busy crowing.

"I told you I'd reward you! Never underestimate my power!"

"So, you did leave the omen?"

She didn't answer. "Come on! There's someone I want you to meet."

Rainflower? His heart pricked with excitement. She'd be here now, in StarClan's hunting grounds. He raced after Mapleshade as she headed into the mist. She led him to another clearing, little more than a gap between the slimy gray trees.

"Where is she?"

"*She?*" Mapleshade snorted. "What are you talking about?" She nodded toward two toms who were emerging from the withered ferns on the far side of the space. Crookedjaw recognized one of them at once.

Thistleclaw!

The ThunderClan warrior stopped beside his mentor—the same ragged, pale gray tabby who'd been training him last time—and stared at Crookedjaw.

"Is this him?" the ragged tom grunted.

"Just get on with your training session, Silverhawk," Mapleshade ordered.

Crookedjaw darted in front of her. "Why are they here?"

She snorted. "To help you learn, of course!" She whipped her tail across his ears. "Watch!"

Silverhawk crouched, growling at Thistleclaw. Thistleclaw stretched his claws and hissed. They circled each other, eyes like slits. Suddenly Silverhawk darted forward. Thistleclaw ducked away from his mentor's jaws and Silverhawk's teeth snapped at thin air.

"Did you think you'd get me that easily?" Thistleclaw hissed.

Silverhawk crouched lower. "Say that again."

"Did you think—"

Before Thistleclaw could finish, Silverhawk leaped on him and dug his claws deep into Thistleclaw's shoulders. Crookedjaw gasped when he saw the blood welling up in the spiky gray-and-white fur. Thistleclaw yowled, scrabbling at the ground, trying to get a grip, but Silverhawk heaved him on to his back and kicked his churning hind paws away. Crookedjaw's breath stopped in his throat as Silverhawk lunged for Thistleclaw's neck. Opening his jaws wide, he gripped his apprentice's throat in his teeth.

No! He was going to give a killing bite. Crookedjaw started to rush forward, but Mapleshade knocked him back with a vicious blow.

"Wait," she growled.

Silverhawk let go of Thistleclaw

The ThunderClan warrior leaped to his paws, ignoring the drops of blood that flew off his pelt. "Let me try that on you!" he begged. "I think I know what to do now."

Crookedjaw stared in horror. "You're teaching him how to *kill?* But that's against the warrior code!"

Thistleclaw's gaze flashed at him. Contempt lit his eyes. "If you want to be more than just a warrior," he snarled, "you have to be prepared to look beyond the warrior code!"

Silverhawk padded closer. "Victory is everything," he hissed. "There's no glory in surrender."

Thistleclaw tipped his head to one side. "Do you want me to show you how the killing bite's done?"

Crookedjaw recoiled. "No!"

"No?" Thistleclaw narrowed his eyes. "What do mean, *no*? Why wouldn't you want to learn such a powerful move?" He looked puzzled.

Crookedjaw took two steps back. The fur along his spine was standing on end. "I didn't know StarClan was like this!"

"StarClan?" Thistleclaw blinked. "You mouse-brain! This isn't StarClan! Those smug, toothless fools won't teach you anything as useful as this."

"This isn't StarClan?" Crookedjaw's mind whirled. "Then . . . where am I?"

Silverhawk pushed past Thistleclaw. "This is the Dark Forest," he snarled. "This is where you go if StarClan won't take you."

Crookedjaw whipped around. Trees loomed over him on every side, mist swirled, and the shadows moved as though they were alive. Voices sounded from the darkness, cries and whispers that he didn't understand. Breathing fast, the blood roaring in his ears, he turned back and stared at the three warriors. Their eyes were fixed on him, glittering with menace. Crookedjaw stiffened, rage giving him courage. "You lied to me!" he spat at Mapleshade.

"I never told you this was StarClan," she meowed smoothly. She took a step toward him. "Why are you so angry? You're the deputy of RiverClan. You have everything you want. And you got it because I trained you and encouraged you. I did more for you than your own mother."

"Shut up!" Crookedjaw unsheathed his claws.

Mapleshade circled him, pelt smooth, tail swishing behind her. "Your mother never sent an omen telling your Clan to make you deputy, did she?"

"So it *was* you!"

"Of course it was me!" Mapleshade's mew sharpened. "Do you think Hailstar would make you deputy without an omen? You've never even won a fight!"

Thistleclaw hissed. "He's deputy already?" He glared at Silverhawk. "Are you going to do the same for me?"

Silverhawk clouted his apprentice with a lightning-swift forepaw, sending him staggering back. As Thistleclaw struggled to keep his balance, Silverhawk thrust his muzzle in his face. "You still have much to learn!" he spat. "Your time will come when I say so, *apprentice!*"

Crookedjaw shook his head. "I don't want to learn how to kill," he whispered.

Mapleshade's gaze blazed on his fur. "But you promised to do as I say," she reminded him softly. "You promised to sacrifice everything to be the greatest warrior in RiverClan."

"I know, and I will always put my Clan first." Crookedstar knew he had to get away from here. "Thank you for making me deputy." His pelt brushed a slippery tree trunk as he backed out of the clearing. "But I think I'm okay now. I don't need any more training."

Mapleshade's eyes darkened to empty hollows. "What do mean, you don't need more training? You can't break free, Crookedjaw. It's too late for that. You've made me a promise and I'll make sure you keep it."

CHAPTER 33

The hollow around Fourtrees brimmed with moonlight. It silvered the Clans and bathed the Great Rock. Crookedjaw shifted his paws as he stood between the other deputies, his shadow huge on the stone behind him.

"Why did Hailstar make you deputy?" Adderfang hissed in his ear. "You're not even ready to fight for your Clan."

Crookedjaw swallowed back fury. He didn't want his first Gathering as deputy to begin with a fight. Stonetooth, ShadowClan's deputy, glanced at him from the corner of his eye. Reedfeather turned his back. Clearly the WindClan deputy still had not forgiven RiverClan for the theft of his daughters.

Crookedjaw scanned the crowd, looking for Oakheart. Where was he? He'd seemed so eager to come. Didn't he want to see his brother named deputy in front of the other Clans? Disappointment sat in his belly like a stone. Willowbreeze had stayed in camp, unable to make the journey to Fourtrees because of a deep cut on one of her pads. She'd slipped off a rock while fishing for an oversized trout. The wound was healing well, thanks to Brambleberry, but she wouldn't have been able to walk all the way to the Gathering. Shellheart hadn't come, either. He was confined to the elders' den, sick with a swelling in his belly. He'd begged Brambleberry to give him strengthening herbs so he could attend, but she had insisted he rest. Crookedjaw glanced up at Silverpelt. Perhaps Rainflower was watching.

Hailstar raised his voice above the swishing of the great oaks as he addressed the Gathering. "Shellheart retired to the elders' den this moon." The Clans murmured as the RiverClan leader paused. Crookedjaw lifted his chin, his heart racing. "Crookedjaw is RiverClan's new deputy."

"Crookedjaw! Crookedjaw!"

As his Clanmates called his name, Crookedjaw pricked his ears, praying the other Clans would join in. Relief washed over him as he heard ShadowClan join the cheer, WindClan and ThunderClan following.

"Crookedjaw!"

Joy fizzed beneath his pelt. They were cheering for him!

A pair of amber eyes flashed in the crowd. Thistleclaw was staring silently at him. Crookedjaw stiffened. He hadn't been back to the Dark Forest since he'd realized it wasn't StarClan's hunting grounds, waking cold with horror every time he drifted close to a dream. How could he have been so dumb? He'd never go there again. He'd never talk to Mapleshade.

Why did she help me become deputy? The question had burned in his mind since that night. *She can't make me do anything I don't want to do.* He dug his claws into the warm earth. *I'm going to be*

*the best deputy RiverClan's ever known. I'll protect my Clan with my life
if I have to.*

Thistleclaw's gaze still burned into his. *He knows I was there.*
Thistleclaw nodded as if he knew what Crookedjaw was
thinking. *Does he think we're allies?*

Never!

Crookedjaw turned to Adderfang. Did ThunderClan's
acting deputy know that one of his warriors was training in
the Dark Forest? Did Sunstar know? Perhaps the whole of
ThunderClan was learning how to kill!

As the cheering died away, the leaders scrambled down
from the Great Rock.

"Well done." Hailstar landed beside Crookedjaw. He
beckoned with a flick of his tail. "Come and meet—"

Crookedjaw interrupted him. "I want to find Oakheart."

Hailstar cocked his head. "Is everything okay?"

"Everything's fine. I'll join you when I've found him."

Crookedjaw pushed through the cats lingering at the foot
of the Great Rock. The night was warm and the Clans seemed
in no hurry to go home.

"Congratulations!" Hollyflower from ShadowClan ducked
away from a knot of warriors. "One moment you're a 'paw, the
next you're a deputy."

Fallowtail stopped beside Crookedjaw. "I guess StarClan
knows best," murmured the RiverClan she-cat.

Hollyflower pricked her ears. "Was there an omen?"

"It was quite—"

"Not really." Crookedjaw interrupted sharply, silencing

Fallowtail. He didn't want StarClan brought into this.

"What's this about omens?" Talltail of WindClan joined Hollyflower.

Fallowtail narrowed her eyes. "Crookedjaw's so young, everyone's gossiping about StarClan and how they chose him." She glanced at Crookedjaw, clearly picking up his hint. "I don't see what the fuss is about. He's our strongest warrior."

Adderfang slid from the crowd. "Really?" He sniffed. "I thought he'd never fought a battle."

Hollyflower flicked her tail. "You're still smarting after being beaten by a medicine cat."

Adderfang scowled. "He wasn't a medicine cat *then*." He shot a furious glance at Mudfur.

Brambleberry was introducing her new apprentice to the other medicine cats. He'd been working hard in the half-moon since starting his training, padding around camp muttering herb names under his breath as he tried to memorize them all.

The ShadowClan warriors Crowtail and Archeye stopped beside Crookedjaw. "Congratulations." Archeye dipped his head.

"It's good to see such a young cat getting on so well," Crowtail added.

"Thanks." Crookedjaw looked past them, searching the crowd for Oakheart. "I really need to find someone." He excused himself and shouldered his way into the crowd.

Oakheart was pacing the edge of the clearing.

"There you are!" Crookedjaw hailed him with a flick of his tail.

Oakheart blinked at him. "Where else would I be?"

"I couldn't see you in the crowd." Crookedjaw noticed his brother's ruffled fur. "Are you okay?"

"I'm fine. Why wouldn't I be?"

Is he jealous that I'm deputy? Crookedjaw had been keeping that thought at bay since the ceremony in the camp. Oakheart had *seemed* happy for him, but tonight he was definitely avoiding Crookedjaw's gaze. "Did you see Hailstar announce me as RiverClan's new deputy?" He watched Oakheart closely.

Oakheart glanced back at the bushes that lined the hollow. "Yeah! It was great."

Crookedjaw wasn't convinced. "Are you jealous of me?" he blurted.

Oakheart twitched his tail. "Jealous? No!" He straightened up. "I'm proud of you, Crookedjaw. You wanted this so much. You deserve it. You're going to be a great deputy and a great leader."

"Really?"

"Really," Oakheart purred. "I never wanted to be deputy."

"But you said you wanted to be leader one day!"

"*All* apprentices say they want to be leader one day."

Relief flooded Crookedjaw.

"The others are leaving," Oakheart commented. The RiverClan patrol was heading for the slope. "I'll catch up," he promised. "There's something I have to do first."

Crookedjaw hurried to join his Clanmates, falling in beside Brambleberry and Mudfur as they reached the top of the hollow.

"That was an interesting night," Mudfur meowed. "RiverClan now has the youngest deputy and the oldest medicine cat apprentice."

Crookedjaw purred. "What did you think of the other medicine cats?"

"I like Featherwhisker," Mudfur replied.

"Did you ever meet Goosefeather, the previous Thunder-Clan medicine cat?" Brambleberry asked. "He's moved to the elders' den now."

"Oh yes. I always thought he looked like he'd just been pulled through a bramble."

"Mudfur!" Fallowtail was calling him from the head of the patrol. "Come and test out your new skills on Beetlenose. He's got hiccups."

Mudfur hurried away, leaving Brambleberry and Crookedjaw alone. Silence walked between them like a third warrior. He could see her pelt bristling as they headed into the shadow of ThunderClan's forest. He wanted to clear the air, but now that he knew where Mapleshade came from, he was terrified of asking Brambleberry about the omens. What if she *knew* he'd been meeting a warrior from the Dark Forest?

But I'm loyal to my Clan! I've got nothing to hide! Then why did his pelt prick with shame at the thought? Crookedjaw broke the silence, unable to bear it. "Are there any other herbs that might help Shellheart?" It was a dumb question. He knew she'd tried everything already.

"I'm going to start giving him more poppy seeds,"

Brambleberry meowed. "He's in more pain than he'll admit to."

"How long before he gets better?"

She didn't answer.

Crookedjaw felt a small hard lump gather in his belly, as if he'd swallowed a stone. "He's not going to get better, is he?"

"No." Brambleberry's mew was as soft as the breeze. "I've seen lumps like this before. The cat never survives. A lump like this brings pain and sickness and withers a warrior like frost withers a flower."

Where's Oakheart? Part of Crookedjaw wanted to share his grief, part wanted to protect his brother from knowing for as long as he could. First Rainflower and now Shellheart.

He felt Brambleberry's pelt brush his. "I'm sorry you have to go through this," she murmured.

For a moment it felt as if there had never been distance between them. Then Crookedjaw pictured the squirrel with the broken mouth, an omen sent not by StarClan but by a cat from the Dark Forest. If there was any way he could stop Brambleberry from learning the truth—if she didn't already know—he had to find it. He stepped away from her, suddenly worried she might pick up signals through his fur, and walked on alone.

Crookedjaw squeezed through the camp entrance, weary from the Gathering. Sedgepaw and Sunpaw were waiting in the shadows.

"What happened?" Sedgepaw squeaked.

402 WARRIORS SUPER EDITION: CROOKEDSTAR'S PROMISE

"Can we come next time?" Sunpaw begged.

Crookedjaw brushed past them. "Ask Hailstar."

Willowbreeze padded from their den. "Did it go okay?" She yawned.

"Go back to sleep," he called. "I'll tell you in the morning." He hurried across the clearing and climbed the slope. Ducking his head into the elders' den, he peered through the shafts of moonlight streaming through the woven roof. "Shellheart?" he whispered.

"Crookedjaw." Birdsong heaved herself to her paws. "He'll be so glad you came. He's been wondering how you got on at the Gathering." Brushing against him, she guided him past Troutclaw's nest.

"Perhaps he'll stop talking and go to sleep now he's seen you," the old tom muttered.

"Take no notice of him," Birdsong whispered. "He loves listening to Shellheart's stories."

Shellheart lifted his head. "Crookedjaw?"

"He's come to tell you about the Gathering." Birdsong nuzzled Crookedjaw's cheek before padding back to her nest.

Shellheart looked small in his moonlit nest, his fur flat, his ribs showing though his pelt. "Come lie next to me," he croaked. "It's cold."

Can't he feel the warm greenleaf breeze? Crookedjaw climbed into his father's nest and curled beside him. "Hailstar told them I was deputy," he reported.

Shellheart broke into a rattling purr. "I'm so proud of you. Rainflower would have been proud, too."

No, she wouldn't. She'd have found some reason he'd failed her.

He felt his father's breath on his cheek. "I'm sorry she judged you so harshly, Crookedjaw."

I was her son, for StarClan's sake. Bitterness rose in his throat.

"She was wrong." Shellheart's mew was soft. "Ever since I've known her, she's always found it hard to admit when she was wrong." He paused, as though remembering old arguments, in the days when they were both still young and headstrong. "She *will* come to see that. I bet she's watching you now from StarClan, regretting how much she missed."

A chill ran along Crookedjaw's spine. *Rainflower may be watching me from StarClan, but who is watching me from the Dark Forest?*

CHAPTER 34

The willows flailed their branches helplessly while the wind stripped their leaves. Reeds rattled and swayed as the river raged past, skidding up the banks and snatching pebbles from the shore. Crookedjaw watched the water race past his paws. Behind him, the wind moaned through the cracks and hollows of Sunningrocks. Ducking back against the cliff, out of the rain, he shivered and pulled his tail tighter around him. He spotted a head bobbing toward him through the swirling river.

Willowbreeze.

She hauled herself out of the water and shook out her pelt. "There you are." She touched her muzzle to his. "I was worried about you."

"I'm okay." Crookedjaw blinked. "He liked to sit here and watch the river, you know."

"Shellheart?"

He nodded, fresh grief piercing his heart. "Perhaps his spirit still comes here to fish." It'd been three moons since he'd lain beside his father in the elders' den. Two since he'd died.

"Even when he's got the warm rivers of StarClan?"

Crookedjaw swallowed. "But he'll miss his old river, surely?"

Willowbreeze settled beside him and leaned into him. "I'm sure he's always watching from StarClan." She flicked the tip of her tail. "He'll want to see what his sons are up to."

A purr rumbled in Crookedjaw's throat.

Willowbreeze stiffened against him. "Ottersplash?"

The white-and-ginger she-cat was plowing across the river. She hopped out, eyes glittering. "ThunderClan warriors are crossing the stepping-stones!"

"Now?" Crookedjaw strained to see around the bend in the river.

"They'll be in the camp any moment," Ottersplash urged. "Hailstar wants you."

Crookedjaw was already diving into the water. He swam expertly, navigating the swirling current with ease, and climbed out. Looking back to make sure Ottersplash and Willowbreeze were okay, he raced for camp. Through the drizzle, he could taste ThunderClan scent. They were headed this way. He swerved along the grassy path and raced into camp.

Hailstar was pacing the clearing, his pelt spiked. Sedgecreek and Frogleap puffed out their chests, clearly eager to prove themselves worthy of their new warrior names. Softwing stood wide-eyed outside the nursery, her tail wrapped around her two young kits. Her mate Owlfur crouched beside her, his eyes merely slits as he watched the entrance, then stood as Willowbreeze and Ottersplash dashed in. "Did you see them? How many?"

"Where are they?" Hailstar asked Ottersplash.

"Headed this way."

Echomist hissed. "How dare they invade our territory?"

Rippleclaw lashed his tail. "I want to be in the battle patrol!"

"Me too!" Timberfur hurried forward with Cedarpelt on his tail. Sedgecreek and Frogleap darted after them, their eyes shining.

Hailstar waved them back. "Wait," he growled. "This might not be an invasion."

"It can't be." Fallowtail circled her leader. "They wouldn't invade in broad daylight!"

"Then why are they here?" Timberfur growled.

Crookedjaw glanced at the entrance. "I'll try to head them off before they reach camp."

Hailstar flattened his ears. "Take Rippleclaw and Ottersplash with you."

"Where's Oakheart?" Crookedjaw scanned the camp.

"Fishing," Echomist told him. "He went out with Lakeshine and Shimmerpelt just after dawn."

"Find him and tell him what's going on," Crookedjaw ordered.

Echomist nodded and headed for the entrance.

"Not that way!" he hissed. "I don't want you bumping into ThunderClan. Go out through the reed bed."

Echomist slid into the water and disappeared among the reeds. Crookedjaw signaled to Ottersplash and Rippleclaw with his tail. "Let's go meet our visitors." He led the way through the tunnel.

Behind them, Hailstar started snapping orders. "Tell the elders to stay in their den," he growled. "And guard it. I want three warriors by the nursery."

Crookedjaw narrowed his eyes against the drizzle. The next bend might lead them into a bristling ThunderClan patrol. He unsheathed his claws. No ThunderClan cat would get past him.

"I hear them!" Ottersplash halted.

Crookedjaw pricked his ears. The invaders were chatting as though they were visiting Clanmates! He growled and darted around the corner with his hackles up. He skidded to a halt in front of Sunstar. The ThunderClan leader signaled to his patrol with his tail.

Crookedjaw unsheathed his claws. "What are you doing on RiverClan territory?"

Bluefur, Whitestorm, Thrushpelt, and Lionheart fanned out behind their leader, but Crookedjaw kept his gaze fixed on Sunstar.

"We want to talk with Hailstar." The ThunderClan leader sounded as though he were asking a Clanmate for a piece of fresh-kill.

"About what?" Ottersplash thrust her muzzle forward.

Sunstar narrowed his eyes. "You expect me to share words that are meant for your leader?"

Ottersplash snarled. *Keep calm.* Crookedjaw waved the she-cat back with his tail. "You expect me to lead you straight into our camp?" he countered.

"Do we look like a battle patrol?" Sunstar glanced back

at his warriors. Their pelts were smooth, their gaze curious. Bluefur was whispering to Whitestorm.

Crookedjaw tilted his head. "It would take more than this to overrun our camp," he agreed. *Unless there's a second patrol hidden somewhere.* He tasted the air but scented nothing.

Sunstar lifted his chin. "We only wish to share words."

Crookedjaw nodded. His Clan was prepared. "Follow me." He turned and headed toward the camp, uncomfortable with ThunderClan warriors at his tail, but forcing his hackles down. The rain pattered around them as they followed the path through the reeds. Crookedjaw entered the clearing first, leaving Ottersplash and Rippleclaw to escort the patrol behind him.

Timberfur and Owlfur were prowling beside the reed bed, their hackles raised. Cedarpelt stood guard by the elders' den. Loudbelly, Sunfish, Sedgecreek, and Reedtail clustered protectively around the nursery. Softwing huddled between them with her kits.

Lionheart stared around the camp as though it were filled with walking fish. "Why do they live in such uncomfortable-looking dens?"

Crookedjaw growled. "They float if it floods." *Where's Hailstar?* He tasted the air. The RiverClan leader's scent pooled in his den. Crookedjaw understood. Hailstar clearly didn't want ThunderClan to think they were worried. "Wait here," he told Sunstar. He padded to the willow and ducked into Hailstar's den.

Hailstar was sitting in his nest, his eyes sharp in the gloom. "Well?"

"They're here. Only a pawful of warriors. No sign of another patrol."

"Good." Hailstar nodded. "Come on." He led the way into the clearing and stood beneath the willow looking at Sunstar, his gaze more curious than anxious. Sunstar watched him and, when Hailstar didn't speak, dipped his head.

"Sunningrocks belong to ThunderClan. We are taking them back."

Sunningrocks belong to RiverClan! Crookedjaw fought to keep his pelt smooth, praying his Clanmates would stay calm. The camp was no place for a battle.

Hailstar unsheathed his claws. "You'll have to fight for them."

"We'll fight if we have to," Sunstar meowed. "But we thought we'd give you fair warning."

Timberfur padded forward, pelt bristling. "Are you threatening us in our own camp?" he growled.

"We're not threatening you," Sunstar answered calmly.

Crookedjaw steadied his breathing. This was a contest of nerves, not claws.

"We're giving you a choice," Sunstar went on. "If you keep off Sunningrocks, we'll leave you alone. But any cat who sets paw there will be shredded."

Hailstar took a step forward. "Do you really think we'll give up the rocks so easily?"

"If you prefer a battle, then we'll fight," Sunstar repeated. "But are the rocks worth it?" He tipped his head on one side. "You have the river to fish in. Your paws are too big to reach far into the cracks of Sunningrocks; your pelts are too clearly marked to stalk prey there. It is no use for RiverClan's ways of hunting. Is it worth fighting for?"

Mudfur's brown pelt flickered at the edge of Crookedjaw's vision. It was what the medicine cat apprentice had argued all along, that Sunningrocks were not worth the number of RiverClan lives that had been lost. But would Hailstar agree this time?

The RiverClan leader opened his mouth to scent the air. "I smell fear," he snarled.

"Then it comes from your own warriors," Sunstar snapped.

"You actually expect us to give up Sunningrocks?" Hailstar hissed.

Sunstar shook his head. "I expect you to fight for them," he meowed. "Even though you will waste warriors and blood. You will lose, and it will be thanks to your decision."

Hailstar took a step toward the ThunderClan leader. "RiverClan warriors fight with claws, not words."

"Very well." Sunstar nodded. "Sunningrocks are ours. We will set the new markers tomorrow. After that, any RiverClan cat found there will face a fight that he will not win." He gazed around the camp and raised his voice. "Let all of RiverClan know that the warning has been given. Any blood spilled now will be on Hailstar's paws." He turned and headed for the entrance.

Crookedjaw stared after them, stunned by their arrogance.

Timberfur shot forward. "How dare they?" He growled at the disappearing patrol.

"Make sure they leave the territory!" Hailstar nodded at Ottersplash and Timberfur. "Escort them to the border."

The two warriors raced out of camp.

"When are we going to fight?" Sedgecreek appeared beside Crookedjaw, dancing from paw to paw.

Frogleap trotted up behind her. "It'll be our first battle!"

Loudbelly and Sunfish crowded around, with Leopardfur and Skyheart trying to push past them.

"Stand still!" Crookedjaw tried to think. They needed a battle strategy. With so many eager young warriors, victory would be easy. He looked at Hailstar. "We should fight with two patrols," he meowed, remembering his first battle at Sunningrocks. "If not three."

"Wait." The RiverClan leader slowly swished his tail. "This may not be a battle worth fighting."

"What?" Sunfish stared at him.

"Of course it's worth fighting!" Frogleap gasped.

"Quiet!" Crookedjaw flicked his tail. "Your leader's speaking."

"We'll discuss this in my den, Crookedjaw." Hailstar cast a thoughtful gaze over the young warriors, then he headed for his den.

"Why's he hesitating?" Loudbelly growled.

Crookedjaw silenced him with a look. "He's had eight lives of experience to guide him." He followed Hailstar beneath the willow and ducked into his den.

"What good is Sunningrocks to us in leaf-bare?" Hailstar was sitting in the shadowy recess at the back of his den. "Sunstar was right; they can find prey there that we can't reach."

"Surely that's all the more reason to keep them from it," Crookedjaw reasoned.

Hailstar blinked at him. "Do you want to starve another Clan?"

"It would weaken them."

"If we didn't have to battle over Sunningrocks, would we care if they were weak or strong?"

"What if we gave them Sunningrocks and they tried to take more territory?"

"Do you really think that's what Sunstar wants?" Hailstar's gaze was steady.

Perhaps we should just give them leaf-bare hunting rights there. Crookedjaw remembered what Oakheart had said after the latest border challenge. *That's always when they take it. They must need the prey.*

He shrugged. "I guess Sunstar just wants to be able to feed his Clan during leaf-bare."

Hailstar nodded. "We have the river and the willows," he pointed out. "They have only the forest."

Crookedjaw hesitated. "They'll think they've won." The fur rippled along his spine. He didn't want any Clan to think RiverClan was weak.

"They'll think we prefer peace over war," Hailstar

murmured. "Some will see that as a sign of weakness, others will see it as a sign of strength."

Crookedjaw thought of Rippleclaw and Ottersplash. And Sedgecreek and the other new warriors. How would they see it? He dug his claws into the soft earthen floor of the den. "ThunderClan will think they can change borders any time they like!"

Hailstar's whiskers twitched. "Isn't that what we've done?"

"That's different! Sunningrocks is ours! It was given to us by StarClan."

Hailstar tucked his tail over his paws. "I admire your loyalty," he meowed. "StarClan chose well in making you deputy."

Crookedjaw shifted his paws uncomfortably as Hailstar went on.

"You'll make a great leader."

The moss twitched at the entrance to the den. Timberfur poked his head through. "Have you decided on a battle plan yet? The Clan is restless."

Hailstar nodded. As Timberfur ducked out, the RiverClan leader glanced at Crookedjaw. "I want you to tell them."

"That we're giving up Sunningrocks?"

Hailstar nodded. "The young warriors are an excitable bunch. You might as well learn how to handle them sooner rather than later."

Crookedjaw steadied himself with a deep breath. "Okay." He pushed his way out of the den and padded to the center of the clearing. Hailstar halted beside him.

The Clan grew quiet as Crookedjaw lifted his chin and gazed around the camp. "We won't be fighting," he announced. "We'll let ThunderClan have Sunningrocks till newleaf."

Mudfur was the first to speak. "Thank StarClan!"

"But we have to fight!" Timberfur growled.

Loudbelly paced around his denmates. "How can we not?"

"We'd beat them!" Owlfur snarled.

"They'll think we're weak!" Cedarpelt warned with a flick of his tail.

Reedtail flexed his claws. "We'll go anyway," he muttered.

"We can't let them win," Sunfish agreed.

"If you won't defend our territory, we'll do it for you!" Loudbelly yowled.

Crookedjaw bared his teeth at him. "No patrol will cross the river." He glared at the bristling young warriors. "If any one of you sets paw on Sunningrocks, you needn't worry about ThunderClan because *I'll* shred you." He gaze flicked back to Loudbelly. "Got it?"

Loudbelly flattened his ears. "Yes, Crookedjaw," he muttered.

Crookedjaw snapped his head around to survey the rest of the Clan. Rippleclaw was watching him through narrowed eyes but didn't speak. Owlfur stared at his paws. Timberfur sheathed his claws. Crookedjaw felt a surge of triumph but pushed it away. These were his Clanmates; he was leading them, not fighting them. "We don't need Sunningrocks until newleaf," he told them. "Let ThunderClan scavenge for mice in the cracks. We have the river and as much fish as we can eat."

Cedarpelt stepped forward. "I can take out a hunting party now if you like," he offered.

"Thank you." Crookedjaw dipped his head to his old mentor. "Take Sunfish, Frogleap, and Loudbelly." It would keep them busy. As the Clan drifted back to its duties, Crookedjaw scanned the camp for Oakheart. His brother still wasn't back.

"Crookedjaw?" Ottersplash heaved herself out of the water beside the reed bed. Her eyes glittered as she hurried over and leaned close. "Can I speak with you?" She beckoned him toward the sedge wall and crouched beneath the arching fronds. Puzzled, Crookedjaw ducked beside her.

"Have you noticed at the Gatherings if Oakheart is friendly with any of the ThunderClan warriors?" Ottersplash whispered.

Crookedjaw shrugged. "No cat in particular."

"Not even Bluefur?" Ottersplash glanced at him uneasily.

"He's spoken to her one or two times."

Ottersplash frowned.

"Why?" Crookedjaw stiffened.

"While we were escorting the ThunderClan patrol, I saw him . . ." She floundered.

Crookedjaw leaned forward. "Saw him *what?*"

"Saw him talking to Bluefur."

"So?"

"They were alone," Ottersplash reported. "She dropped back from the patrol and he came from the river. He'd been fishing. He couldn't have known what they were doing here."

"That's probably why he stopped her." Crookedjaw

wondered why Ottersplash was making such a big deal out of it. "He just wanted to know what she was doing on RiverClan territory."

"Yes." Ottersplash nodded. "Of course." She straightened up. "Sorry, I shouldn't have troubled you."

Crookedjaw ran the tip of his tail over her flank. "No problem," he meowed. His pelt rippled uneasily. *I wonder if she believes what I just said. I'm not sure if I do.*

The rain had cleared by the next day. Crookedjaw stretched, yawning in the chilly leaf-fall sunshine. The river slid past, deceptively quiet, as if it was just waiting for the first storm to stir up its surface and make fishing impossible. Beetlenose and Reedtail were hunting downstream. Crookedjaw had brought Oakheart to his favorite pool, hoping there'd be carp. He waited on the bank while Oakheart dived for his first catch.

His brother's tawny head broke the surface, a fish between his jaws. He hopped onto the bank and dropped it beside Crookedjaw. "Your turn."

"Are there many down there?"

"Loads."

Crookedjaw waded into the shallows as Oakheart sniffed his carp. "Oakheart?" *Whatever the truth is, I have to know.* He kept his tone casual. "Did you see the ThunderClan patrol yesterday while you were out fishing?"

Oakheart flipped the carp over. "I saw Timberfur and Ottersplash escorting them over the stepping-stones."

Why wouldn't he mention talking to Bluefur? "And they went quietly?" Crookedjaw prompted.

Oakheart shrugged. "As far as I could tell."

Was the fur on his spine twitching? Crookedjaw shifted his paws on the stones.

"What's with all the questions?" Oakheart waded past him. "If you're not going to catch anything, then I will." He dived into the water and disappeared.

Crookedjaw narrowed his eyes. Was he worrying for no reason? Perhaps Oakheart didn't think talking to Bluefur was important enough to mention. Any loyal warrior would have stopped to question an intruder. *Besides, he wouldn't keep secrets from me, would he?* Crookedjaw padded to a flat gray rock and lay down to wait for Oakheart's return. He wasn't the only cat who was loyal to his Clanmates. There was no way his brother would betray RiverClan.

CHAPTER 35

Icy rain dripped through the roof of the den. Crookedjaw shivered. His nest was damp.

Beside him, Willowbreeze rolled over and stretched. "Is it leaking again?" A large drop thudded on to her belly. She jumped to her paws, ears flicking. "When will this rain end?" she snapped. Cold leaf-bare squalls had been battering the camp for days.

Crookedjaw licked her cheek. "I'll ask Brambleberry to have a word with StarClan." He heaved himself to his paws, yawning.

"Very funny!" Willowbreeze called as he squeezed out of the den.

The dawn was dull, the sky gray as a squirrel's pelt. Petaldust, Leopardfur, and Sedgecreek were outside, stuffing the nursery walls and roof with leaves to keep out the weather. Their pelts were spiked with rain, their ears flat against the wind.

Hailstar stood in the clearing, staring at the river.

Crookedjaw stopped beside him. "Is it any higher?"

Water was already lapping over the shore beside the reed

bed. Dawnkit and Mallowkit had been forbidden to go near the river. A swell might sweep through the reed bed at any moment and wash away an unsuspecting kit.

"The banks are holding," Hailstar murmured. "But we need to keep checking."

Oakheart peered from his den, then darted out to join them. "There's not a dry spot in camp." He eyed the river. "Looks higher to me."

Beyond the barrier of reeds the water swirled, brown and fast. It was too dangerous for fishing.

"Should we move Softwing and Graypool up to the elders' den?" Oakheart suggested.

Hailstar glanced at the nursery. "Not yet."

Softwing's kits, Dawnkit and Mallowkit, were peering out of the entrance, blinking at the rain. Three moons old, they looked more like 'paws every day.

"How's Graypool?" Hailstar meowed.

Crookedjaw shook his head. "Still sick."

Graypool had recently moved from her den to the nursery, expecting Rippleclaw's kits. Brambleberry had been treating her nausea for days but the queen had little appetite.

"We'll need to move them if the water comes any higher," Crookedjaw advised.

"I've got an idea." Oakheart tugged a reed from the apprentices' den and stuck it into the muddy earth, marking where the water had reached. "Now we'll be able to see how quickly it's rising." He sat back on his haunches. "I'll check it regularly and let you know if it starts moving more quickly."

420 WARRIORS SUPER EDITION: CROOKEDSTAR'S PROMISE

"Clever plan." Crookedjaw shook out his pelt, pleased that his brother was back to normal. Two moons ago, he'd wondered what was making the tawny warrior so distracted and anxious, and if it'd been Bluefur after all. But Oakheart was his old self now, focused on warrior duties and training the new apprentices, and Crookedjaw had pushed away his worries.

Mudfur trotted toward the elders' den with a bundle of leaves in his jaws.

Crookedjaw hailed him. "Are those for Birdsong?" The old she-cat had been coughing for days.

Mudfur nodded. Crookedjaw hurried after him. As they reached the den, Crookedjaw waited for Mudfur to squeeze inside, then followed.

"Brambleberry." He greeted the medicine cat crouching beside Birdsong. "How is she?"

Birdsong scowled through the shadows. "*She's* still got her hearing and a tongue in her head."

Tanglewhisker rolled his eyes. "She's definitely got a tongue in her head," he muttered. "When Troutclaw joined StarClan I thought I'd get some peace."

Crookedjaw picked his way past the two empty nests beside the entrance. They still carried the very faint scents of Shellheart and Troutclaw. He settled down beside the elderly tabby-and-white she-cat.

Brambleberry was shredding some herbs on the dark earthen floor. "This nest is damp," she hissed. "Everything's damp."

Birdsong started coughing. Tanglewhisker flattened his

ears. "If she's not talking then she's giving me earache with her coughing!"

Birdsong swallowed painfully. "You'll miss me when I'm gone," she rasped.

"You're not going anywhere." Brambleberry finished ripping up the herbs and thrust them under the old she-cat's nose. "Eat these. They'll soothe your throat." She glanced up at Crookedjaw. "I've sent Loudbelly, Frogleap, and Skyheart to look for dry moss, but StarClan knows where they'll find any."

Mudfur tipped his head. "Perhaps ThunderClan would give us some," he suggested. "There are plenty of sheltered spots in the forest and they owe us for giving them Sunningrocks."

Tanglewhisker snorted. "We can't ask ThunderClan for anything! They already think we're weak. And if this damp gets into all our bones, we won't be able to fight off a minnow, let alone those mangy warriors."

Birdsong munched her herbs. "When I was younger, we used to hunt in the big nest by the Twoleg meadow."

Crookedjaw looked anxiously at Brambleberry. The old cat was rambling. Was it a sign that she was getting a fever?

"Before there were so many dogs." Birdsong's eyes misted as she went on. "There was a black-and-white mutt." She purred at Tanglewhisker. "Do you remember it? The scrappy one, always barking. It attacked me once?"

"I remember." Tanglewhisker's whiskers twitched. "It looked very surprised when you turned and swiped it on the muzzle."

"It kept its distance the next time we went hunting there!" There was amusement in Birdsong's wheezy mew.

Tanglewhisker tucked his paws tighter under him and fluffed out his damp fur. "What made you think about the Twoleg nest? Do you want to go and hunt mice?"

"No, frog-brain!" She flicked her tail at him. "The Twolegs used to store dry grass there. That would keep our nests dry. No use putting in more moss; it just soaks up the wet from the ground."

Tanglewhisker's eyes gleamed. "Of course!"

Brambleberry was on her paws. "Do you think you could fetch some?" She stared hopefully at Crookedjaw. "Birdsong's cough won't get any better so long as she's sleeping in a damp nest."

"Of course." Excitement fizzed in his paws. Perhaps Birdsong's mind wasn't so addled after all. It was a brilliant idea. "I'll go ask Hailstar." He squeezed out of the den and hurried down the slope.

Hailstar was crouching beneath the willow. He stood up to greet Crookedjaw. "You look cheerful."

"Birdsong's been telling me about a Twoleg nest where dry grass is stored."

"The barn!" Hailstar lifted his tail. "Of course. She took me hunting there when I was just a 'paw."

A barn?

Crookedjaw instantly pictured Fleck's home. He hadn't thought of his old friend in moons. "Where is it?" The old warriors obviously weren't talking about Fleck and Mitzi's barn, which was much too far for regular hunting patrols.

"Beyond the dog fence," Hailstar told him. "Past the field there's a huge nest. No Twolegs in it, just dry grass and mice." He lifted his muzzle. Even in the cold rain, his pelt sodden, he looked as strong as a warrior half his age. "Petaldust, Sedgecreek, Leopardfur!" He called to the three cats weaving leaves into the nursery walls. "You can finish that later. We have a special mission."

Oakheart, guarding his reed, looked up. "What is it?"

Crookedjaw flicked the rain from his tail. "We're going to fetch dry bedding."

"Where from?" Petaldust dropped her bundle of leaves and raced across the clearing. Sedgecreek leaped down from the nursery roof and followed, Leopardfur on her tail.

"There's a barn just past the dog fence," Hailstar explained, his eyes shining. "I used to hunt there when I was a 'paw. I haven't been there for years."

Crookedjaw paced around the RiverClan leader. "We can catch some mice while we're there."

Sunfish darted out of her nest, ears pricking. "Did someone say hunting?"

"Hunting?" Softwing peered from the nursery. "Isn't the river too fast?"

"We're hunting mice," Hailstar told her.

"I want to come!" Dawnkit tumbled out of the nursery and raced clear of her mother's front paws. Her ginger-and-white fur was drenched in an instant.

"Dawnkit!" Softwing called crossly.

"How come she's allowed out and I'm not?" Mallowkit squeaked indignantly from between her mother's paws.

Hailstar headed for the gap in the reeds. "We'd better get going before we have the whole Clan trailing after us."

Crookedjaw raced after him with Petaldust, Leopardfur, and Sedgecreek pounding at his heels. Rain rattled the beech copse and splattered on to the marsh. Crookedjaw screwed up his eyes against the downpour, relieved when he spotted the dog fence looming ahead of them. "Wait!" He signaled the patrol back with a flick of his tail while he sniffed along the bottom of the fence. "No fresh dog-scent," he called back to his Clanmates. "It must hate rain more than we do."

He slid under the fence. The sour tang of mud and wet grass bathed his tongue as the patrol crept past a horse, munching grass at the edge of the field. Crookedjaw felt exposed in the short grass and quickened the pace. Peering through the rain he saw a huge nest at the far side of the field. It rose squarely from behind a low gray wall, its black wooden sides dark and forbidding against the rain-filled sky. "Is that it?" he asked Hailstar.

Hailstar nodded. Crookedjaw darted forward, racing for the shelter of the low wall. As the patrol caught up, Petaldust tasted the air. "No fresh scents," she reported.

Leopardfur sniffed. "I can't taste anything but rain."

"Wait there." Hailstar jumped onto the wall and, keeping low, scanned the open space on the other side.

Crookedjaw sprang up beside him. Bare cream stone stretched from the wall to the barn, just like the yard at

Fleck's farm. "All clear?"

Hailstar nodded. Crookedjaw glanced down at Petaldust. "Come on."

Sedgecreek was first over the wall.

"Be careful," Crookedjaw whispered as she dropped to the ground below him. He hopped down after her, checking the yard warily as Hailstar led them over the knobbly stone. There was a small ragged hole in the bottom of the huge wooden barrier that blocked the entrance to the barn.

Hailstar slid through first. "All clear," he whispered.

Leopardfur followed, Sedgecreek and Petaldust on his tail. Crookedjaw ducked in after them. Inside, the roof soared as high as Silverpelt. Dim light seeped in through slits in the walls and great shadows stretched across the smooth stone floor. Looming piles of golden dry grass were stacked at the edges.

"We'll collect grass first," Hailstar decided. "Then hunt." He waved Crookedjaw and Sedgecreek toward one bundle and led Petaldust and Leopardfur toward another.

"It smells dusty," Sedgecreek whispered. She gazed up at the far roof, her fur pricking along her spine. Then she sneezed.

Crookedjaw's whiskers twitched. "Come on." He led her to one of the huge grass bundles. Reaching up, he ripped out a clawful and rolled it around his paws before dropping it on the floor. Sedgecreek copied him and they worked quietly until they'd made a pile of fat, prickly bundles, smelling strongly of sunshine and dried leaves.

Crookedjaw dusted grass seed from his ears with a paw

and peered into the shadows at the back of the barn. His pelt tingled. The smell of grass and mouse was stirring old memories. He dropped into a crouch. "Follow me," he hissed to Sedgecreek.

Together they stalked past Hailstar, Petaldust, and Leopardfur, who were still busy bundling dried grass, and slipped into the shadows. Crookedjaw stilled Sedgecreek with a flick of his tail and pricked his ears. Tiny feet were scrabbling at the bottom of the wall. He nodded toward the sound but Sedgecreek was already creeping across the stones, her tail lifted a whisker off the ground, her belly taut.

Crookedjaw selected a wider angle of approach, coming in from the side as Sedgecreek closed in on her prey. Suddenly she pounced, springing forward with her forepaws outstretched. She missed—but the plump brown mouse fled straight toward Crookedjaw. He scooped it up as it shot past and gave it a quick killing bite.

"Very good." Hailstar was sitting back on his haunches, with grass hanging from his paws. He rolled a final bundle and padded across the barn.

Sedgecreek was already crouching down, ready for her next catch.

Hailstar pricked his ears. "A big one!" His eyes widened with delight and he dropped down beside her.

Crookedjaw tasted the air.

He stiffened. That wasn't mouse. That was rat! Fleck had taught him to be wary of rat-scent. One rat was okay. A swarm could be deadly. "Watch out!"

As he yowled a warning, four huge rats raced squealing from the shadows. Sedgecreek squawked with surprise. "They're attacking us!" She hopped into the air as a rat hurtled at her, but it grabbed her hind paw with its teeth and held on.

Crookedjaw pounced squarely on the rat's back, killing it with a bite to its neck. "Are you okay?"

Sedgecreek whimpered with pain as blood welled thick and scarlet from her hind paw. Leopardfur raced over to help. She clawed another rat and sent it squealing away.

"There's more!" Sedgecreek gasped.

Countless rats were streaming from the side of the barn. Their eyes burned and their sharp teeth glinted in the half-light.

"Get help!" Crookedjaw yowled at Petaldust.

"But—" Petaldust began to argue.

"Now!"

As the tortoiseshell warrior tore out of the barn, Crookedjaw braced himself. Trapped by her wounded hind leg, Sedgecreek was batting at the flood of rats with her front paws. Hailstar lunged wildly, rats on every side of him. Leopardfur shrieked as one bit her tail. She turned and sunk her teeth into its neck. Instantly another rat leaped on her back. "Help!"

Crookedjaw darted forward and hooked it off. Leopardfur wailed as it ripped out fur.

"Hailstar!" Sedgecreek's screech made Crookedjaw whirl around.

Two rats were attacking the RiverClan leader, one clinging to his spine, the other dragging at his hind legs with its teeth.

Crookedjaw hauled off the biggest rat and flung it to the edge of the barn.

"*Wait!*" A snarl came from the shadows.

Mapleshade! Crookedjaw recoiled. "What are you doing here?" he growled.

"*This is your chance.*" Her voice rang inside his head. "*Leave him to the rats. You can be the leader of RiverClan today, if you have the courage!*"

"No!" Crookedjaw lunged at the rat clinging on to Hailstar's pelt and clawed it away from the RiverClan leader. "I won't let you kill my leader!" Crookedjaw hooked another rat and slapped it to the floor.

Mapleshade hissed. "*But this is your destiny!*"

Crookedjaw growled under his breath. "I decide my destiny, Mapleshade. Not you!" As Hailstar staggered to his paws, Crookedjaw knocked away another rat. Behind him, Sedgecreek had made it to her feet, leaning on Leopardfur. Crookedjaw glanced at the injured she-cat. She looked as if she could stand on her own for a short while.

It was too dangerous to race for the entrance. The moment they stopped fighting, the rats would overwhelm them. Their only hope was to work together.

"Warriors! Tail-to-tail!" he ordered.

The patrol backed toward one another and pressed their spines together. Rearing up on their hind paws and swiping with their front legs, they met the rats with a circle of flashing claws. Hailstar was gasping for breath, but he jabbed mercilessly at the flood of brown creatures. Leopardfur yowled in triumph at each rat she sent flying. Sedgecreek slammed her paws down again and again on writhing, squealing bodies. Crookedjaw's nose and mouth filled with the musky tang of blood. Panic started to rise in his chest. Sedgecreek was starting to wobble on her injured leg, and Leopardfur sagged against his flank. They couldn't hold out much longer. "Try and get to the entrance!" he yowled. As they edged back toward the hole, a pelt flashed at the corner of Crookedjaw's vision.

"I've brought help!" Petaldust yelled across the barn.

Rippleclaw and Timberfur streaked toward them. Sunfish, Blackclaw, and Owlfur followed. They dived on to the sea of rats, hooking them with their claws and hurling them across the barn. Timberfur cracked a spine in his jaws. Rippleclaw grabbed a rat with each forepaw and smashed them both against the hard stone floor. The rats scattered, shrieking, to the edge of the barn and flowed back into the shadows and disappeared.

Crookedjaw dropped on to all fours. Leopardfur crouched beside him. She was panting, her pelt streaked red, but her eyes were bright. "We did it!" she gasped.

Crookedjaw lapped blood from between her ears. "Yes, we did."

A weak groan sounded beside them.

"Sedgecreek!" Crookedjaw ran to her side and searched her glittering eyes. "How badly are you hurt?"

She groaned. Paws pounded across stone and a white pelt

knocked Crookedjaw away. "Give me room!" Brambleberry snapped. The medicine cat crouched beside Sedgecreek. "Fetch cobwebs!" she ordered. Rippleclaw and Timberfur streaked away and leaped onto the huge piles of grass, stretching up to snatch cobwebs from the wall behind.

"Hailstar!" Owlfur's shocked mew made Crookedjaw freeze.

Hailstar? Horror dropped like a stone in his belly. The RiverClan leader was lying stretched out on the stone floor. Blood pulsed from his throat.

"Brambleberry!" Crookedjaw yowled.

"Hold on!" she called back. "Sedgecreek's bleeding badly."

Crookedjaw dropped down beside Hailstar and felt for the wound in his neck. He found the tear in the skin and pressed his paw against it, desperately trying to stop the blood. "I'm sorry," he whispered. "I let you down."

"No, you didn't." Hailstar drew in a rattling breath. "You fought as bravely as I expected. Now you must lead the patrol home safely."

"Get away from him!"

Crookedjaw gasped as he felt Mapleshade charge into his flank and knock him away from Hailstar. The Dark Forest warrior's pelt was little more than a faint gleam in the half-light, but her eyes burned fierce and yellow.

"No!" Crookedjaw shoved past her and raced back to Hailstar, reaching again for the wound. No blood pulsed beneath his paw. It still seeped out, but no life force throbbed behind it. Hailstar's head had rolled to one side and his eyes were glassy and dull. Crookedjaw felt something snap inside his heart.

"Brambleberry," Crookedjaw mewed hoarsely. "He's dead."

Collapsing to the cold earth floor, Crookedjaw rested his head on Hailstar's matted pelt and closed his eyes.

CHAPTER 36

"Crookedjaw!" Brambleberry was whispering in his ear.

Crookedjaw forced his eyes to open. It hadn't been a dream. He was still in the barn, still covered in Hailstar's blood, his claws still clogged with rat fur. Trembling with shock, he pushed himself to his paws. "How's Sedgecreek?"

Brambleberry rested her tail on his flank. "She'll be okay." She stared down at Hailstar, her eyes glistening.

"I tried to stop the bleeding," Crookedjaw told her. *Maybe I could have if Mapleshade hadn't stopped me.* Guilt scorched through him.

Brambleberry checked the wound on Hailstar's neck. "There was nothing you could do," she meowed. "This wound was too deep to heal."

Crookedjaw looked around. The barn seemed very still and empty. "Is Leopardfur all right?"

"I'm fine." Leopardfur limped to his side and touched her nose to Hailstar's pelt.

Crookedjaw padded to where Sedgecreek was struggling to her paws. Cobwebs swathed her pelt. "You fought like a true warrior." He brushed her cheek with his. "Are you going to be able to make it home?"

Sedgecreek nodded. Her eyes were dull.

Crookedjaw signaled to Timberfur. "Help her."

The brown tom pressed against Sedgecreek and began to guide her toward the entrance. Sunfish darted over and propped her up on the other side.

Rippleclaw dipped his head. "Should I carry Hailstar back to camp?"

Crookedjaw shook his head. "I will."

Brambleberry raised one paw to stop him. "You can't. You're hurt."

"It's only a few nips." Crookedjaw was too numb to feel anything. He crouched down while Rippleclaw and Owlfur dragged the RiverClan leader onto his back, then forced his legs to straighten to begin Hailstar's final journey home.

Crookedjaw hated dragging Hailstar's body through the hole. He flinched as the leader's fur snagged on the splintering wood but he refused to pause for breath. All he could think of was the grief that lay in wait for the Clan.

"Let me carry him a while," Rippleclaw begged as they crossed the rain-soaked meadow.

Crookedjaw was panting beneath the weight, the pain from his wounds beginning to bite. "No. I'm okay."

As they passed the beech copse and neared the camp he became dimly aware of Rippleclaw pressing against him, shouldering some of Hailstar's weight. He staggered into the clearing and stood long enough for Owlfur to slide Hailstar from his back. Then he sank on to his side in the mud, feeling it seep into his fur.

"Crookedjaw!" Willowbreeze frantically licked his cheek. "Are you okay?"

Exhausted, Crookedjaw closed his eyes where he lay and let darkness enfold him.

He woke in his nest, his wounds stinging.

Willowbreeze ducked down beside him. "You're awake?"

Crookedjaw scrambled to his paws. "The vigil for Hailstar!"

"It's okay, you haven't missed it." Willowbreeze's voice was hoarse with sadness. "He's in the clearing."

Crookedjaw hurried out of the den.

"Are you okay?" Oakheart raced over to him.

"I'm fine." Crookedjaw stared past his brother at his wretched, leaderless Clanmates.

Birdsong was pacing the edge to the clearing, wailing in distress. "Why did I suggest going to the barn? I sent him to his death!"

Tanglewhisker padded after her. "How could you know what would happen? You can't blame yourself, frog-brain."

Beetlenose sat, hunched, underneath the willow with Petaldust and Voleclaw beside him. The three warriors stared blankly across the clearing at their father's body. The rain had stopped and the clouds were clearing. A shaft of late-afternoon light illuminated the clearing, sparkling on Hailstar's rain-drenched pelt.

Echomist huddled beside him. She looked up as Crookedjaw approached. "I should never have let him go."

Crookedjaw touched his muzzle to her head. "He fought like a StarClan warrior right to the end."

The entrance to Brambleberry's den swished and the medicine cat padded out.

"How are Sedgecreek and Leopardfur?" Crookedpaw called.

"Resting," Brambleberry reported. "I've put ointment on their wounds to stop them getting infected." She studied Crookedjaw's matted, bloodstained pelt. "I should treat yours, too."

"Later," he growled. "When I've sat vigil for Hailstar."

Brambleberry shook her head. "You have to travel to the Moonstone with me," she reminded him.

He blinked at her.

"To receive your nine lives."

Nine lives. He was the leader of RiverClan! The realization hit him like a wave of cold water.

"We should leave now," Brambleberry prompted. "Mudfur can look after Sedgecreek and Leopardfur."

Crookedjaw glanced at Echomist. "Will you be okay?"

"I have my Clanmates," she murmured.

Crookedjaw dipped his head. His pelt burned and he looked up to see Timberfur staring at him. Graypool peered from the nursery, her eyes wide. Frogleap and Loudbelly padded beside the reed bed, splashing through the shallows overflowing the bank. Their pelts were spiked, their ears flat. They were depending on him now. His heart ached. He'd never felt less like a leader. He'd only just become deputy.

He felt Willowbreeze's warm pelt brush against him. "You should go." Her gaze flicked toward Brambleberry waiting at the entrance. "You'll be fine," Willowbreeze whispered. "Hailstar made the right choice when he chose you as deputy."

No, he didn't. Crookedjaw felt sick. *Mapleshade decided my destiny—a cat from the Dark Forest!* Panic fluttered in his chest. *What have I done?*

"Let's go." Brambleberry's call from the other side of the clearing was gentle but urgent.

"I'm coming."

Brambleberry kept a little way ahead as they leaped the stepping-stones and followed the path beside the waterfall. Crossing the WindClan scent line, Crookedjaw caught up to her. He didn't want her to walk into a WindClan patrol without him at her side. Was she going to say anything about him becoming leader? She had been worried about Hailstar making him deputy; she must be horrified that he was to be RiverClan's leader. He halted.

Brambleberry turned and stared at him in surprise. The heather swayed around her, touched with a pink glow as the evening sun bled into the pale blue sky. "Are you coming?"

"You have to tell me!" Crookedjaw dug his claws into the peaty earth. "I can't face StarClan until I know what you know." A StarClan omen had warned her that he was not to be trusted. If she knew about Mapleshade, so must StarClan. What if they refused to give him his nine lives?

Brambleberry blinked. "What I *know*?"

"Don't pretend you're not worried they won't make me

leader," Crookedjaw growled. "Or is that what you're hoping for?"

"Why would I hope for something like that?"

"Because of the omen! The omen that warned you not to trust me. What was it? You've hidden it long enough. You have to tell me what you've seen!"

Brambleberry's shoulders drooped. "Yes. Yes, I do. But it's not what you're thinking." She sat down and held his gaze with her sky-colored eyes. "I've seen you with her."

Crookedjaw's pelt burned. "Do you mean Mapleshade?"

"Is that her name?" Brambleberry's ears twitched. "I didn't know. I just knew she was training you in a place that was dark and cold and smelled of death." Her fur pricked. "I watched you choose to walk with cats who would never be loyal to you or your Clan."

"I didn't know she was bad," Crookedjaw whispered. "I was so dumb. I thought she was a StarClan cat."

Brambleberry flicked the tip of her tail. "StarClan? You thought that?" Her pelt smoothed. "Now I understand! When it came to your Clanmates, you've always been so brave and loyal—so determined to do your best. I couldn't understand why you were training with that monster."

"I thought she was on my side." Crookedjaw looked at his paws. "I wanted to be the best warrior I could be, and she said she'd help me."

Brambleberry shook her head. "You would always have been a great warrior."

"How could I have known that?" His mew caught in his

throat. "After I broke my jaw, no cat seemed to want me. Everyone treated me like I was useless."

Brambleberry's eyes clouded. "We let you down."

"No!" Crookedjaw shook his head. "The past is over. Everything I love is in RiverClan!"

"But you have walked with a dark warrior."

"I told her I didn't want her help anymore." Crookedjaw flexed his claws. "Is that enough to make StarClan trust me?"

"StarClan sees all." Brambleberry looked down at her paws for a moment. "Far more than me." She turned and began to pad through the heather. "They'll decide for themselves."

Crookedjaw's belly churned. What if his warrior ancestors refused to give him his nine lives as punishment for training in the Dark Forest? He trotted after Brambleberry, his wounds aching as they climbed the slope onto the high moor.

Night fell as they followed tiny trails through the heather. The wind whistled around their ears, and Crookedjaw didn't hear the approaching patrol.

"What are you doing here?" Reedfeather's eyes blazed on the shadowy path.

"We're traveling to the Moonstone," Crookedjaw told him.

Dawnstripe and Talltail flanked the WindClan deputy. Dawnstripe padded forward and pushed past Brambleberry.

Crookedjaw growled. "You must let us pass. I'm going to receive my nine lives."

Reedfeather's gaze sharpened, hard as flint. "Hailstar's dead?" There was no grief in the tabby tom's mew, but he signaled to his Clanmates with his tail. "Let them pass."

The WindClan patrol stood aside and let Crookedjaw and Brambleberry pass.

Beyond the moors, the Thunderpath was silent. They crossed it and headed along the tracks and paths of Twoleg territory. Beneath the glittering stars, they trekked on. Crookedjaw fought the ache in his wounds, pushing himself on though his legs were shaking with tiredness. They gave Fleck's farm a wide berth. Crookedjaw had seen enough barns for one day, and they reached Highstones as the moon was still rising.

"We've made good time," Brambleberry panted as they trudged up the slope toward Mothermouth.

Please give me my lives, Crookedjaw prayed as he followed her into the crow-black tunnel. He'd forgotten how cold it was. The icy tang of stone bathed his tongue. Last time he was here Willowpaw had been with him; it had been an adventure. This time he felt older than the moon. Who would be waiting for him at the Moonstone? Cats from StarClan, or cats from the Dark Forest?

"Brambleberry!" He could hear her pads scuffing the stone ahead, but he suddenly needed to hear her voice, to be sure that it was her he was following and not some other cat sent by Mapleshade.

"I'm here."

Light flared in the tunnel ahead.

"Hurry!" she urged. "The moon's already lit the stone!"

Heart racing, Crookedjaw dashed after her, blinking against the glare as they burst into the Moonstone chamber.

He'd forgotten how high the roof soared above the floor and how beautiful the Moonstone was. It glittered with the light of countless stars.

"Go on, touch your nose against it." Brambleberry nudged him forward.

Fear gripped his heart. "But who will be waiting for me?"

She blinked at him. "I don't know," she admitted quietly. She ducked away, leaving him alone in the cave.

Padding slowly forward, Crookedjaw closed his eyes. He crouched down and leaned forward till the tip of his muzzle touched the stone. He waited for light to flood through him, to be swept into the stars in a dazzling dream. *Please!*

He blinked open his eyes. He was standing in a huge, empty hollow. Shadows pressed at the edge of his vision. His heart tightened. *The Dark Forest! They've come to claim me.* His breathing quickened. He backed away, shaking his head, desperately trying to find a way out of the dream.

Silvery light began to spread from the top of the hollow, gathering speed as it spiraled down around him. It lit faces and pelts that sparkled with stars until the slopes were filled with countless cats staring down at him. Crookedjaw spun around, watching more and more faces light around him. He smelled the river and the forest and heather and pines—all Clans mingled as one, eyes blazing, pelts shimmering. Had the whole of the Dark Forest come to gloat? A gray pelt stirred from the mass and padded forward.

Hailstar!

"Welcome to StarClan." Hailstar dipped his head. He

looked young and strong, his pelt sleek, his eyes bright. "I'm proud of you, Crookedjaw," he meowed. "You saved your Clanmates from the rats."

"But not you."

"It was my time to die." The old RiverClan leader leaned toward him. "Now it's your time to live."

Crookedjaw bent his head, mouth dry. This wasn't the Dark Forest, not if Hailstar was here. But would he receive StarClan's blessing?

"With this life I give you courage," Hailstar whispered. "When you feel doubt, let your heart lead you forward, not back."

As Hailstar's muzzle touched his head, agony blazed through Crookedjaw. He tried to flinch away but his paws were rooted to the ground. Hailstar's memories flared in his mind. Battle flashed around him, claws slashed, teeth snapped, enemies screeched. Crookedjaw found himself falling, plummeting from Sunningrocks, splashing down into the river, bubbles exploding around him.

He gasped as Hailstar stepped back and the memories faded. He swayed on his paws, weak with relief. "Thank you," he croaked.

Another cat stepped from the ranks of StarClan.

Duskwater. Her name flashed in his mind, though he'd never met her; she'd died in the flood on the night he was kitted. Yet Crookedjaw knew her as though he'd been born knowing her—as though he'd been born knowing all his ancestors.

"I died in the storm that gave birth to you," Duskwater

mewed. "With this life I give you a mother's love." She stretched up to rest her nose on his head. Shock pierced Crookedjaw as love, fierce as tigers, dazzled through him, hardening his heart until he knew no fear. Was a mother's love for her kits really this ferocious?

Duskwater stepped away and Crookedjaw found himself blinking into the eyes of a long-haired tabby. "Troutclaw!" Crookedjaw greeted him with delight.

Troutclaw's pelt rippled like moonlit water. "With this life I give you justice." His mew had lost its rasping croak; he sounded young and confident. As he leaned close, Crookedjaw felt certainty flow over his heart like water over stone. He would always know what was right, though seasons changed and moons passed. *Time may smooth the stone, but time will never wear it away.*

Troutclaw moved aside and another took his place.

"I'm Mossleaf." The ancient RiverClan cat had the bright eyes of a young warrior. "With this life, I give you trust." He touched his muzzle to Crookedjaw's head and Crookedjaw felt the peace of a wide blue sky move through him.

He heard another name. *Lilyflower.* He nodded his thanks as the RiverClan queen padded forward. Her blue eyes sparkled with starlight. "With this life I give you compassion." Warmth swept him as her muzzle touched his head; love for his Clanmates, for cats who were injured or frightened or displaced, flooded him until he felt his heart would burst.

She turned away and a young tom appeared in front of Crookedjaw. "I'm Lightningpaw." He nodded to Crookedjaw.

"With this life I give you humility." As the RiverClan apprentice touched Crookedjaw with his muzzle, the world shifted around him, widening till he could only see RiverClan's territory at the edge of his vision, a tiny speck in a spreading ocean of meadows, rivers, and forest. *The world is so big! What we do matters to us, but there is always something more happening in a different place.*

As Lightningpaw pulled away, Crookedjaw stared excitedly at the cat who replaced him. *Brightsky!* He recognized her pelt with a surge of joy. Peeking behind her he saw three tiny kits, their eyes round and shining. Brightsky gazed at him with happiness glowing in her eyes. "With this life I give you hope," she whispered. "Never be afraid of the future, for it brings wonderful things." As she touched his head Crookedjaw felt himself skimming over meadows, running like the wind, hardly touching the ground, the horizon ahead of him lit by a rosy dawn.

Brightsky's kits trotted around her, ducking under her soft belly, as she took her place among the rest of StarClan.

"With this life I give you patience." Crookedjaw blinked as a tom touched his head. *Sparrowfeather.* The name flashed in Crookedjaw's mind as though he'd spoken it all his life. Peace seeped into his pelt, slowing his heart until the present existed only as a single beat.

As Sparrowfeather ducked away, the moment of perfect stillness passed and the future and the past crowded into Crookedjaw's thoughts once more. *Rainflower?* He scanned the crowd for his mother. Did she have a life to give him?

"Crookedjaw."

He looked up as he heard Shellheart's mew. Bittersweet joy touched his heart. "She is here," Shellheart murmured as if Crookedjaw had spoken out loud. "But your last life is mine to give." His eyes burned into Crookedjaw's. "Long ago, you lapped water at a poisoned spring. I'm sorry I didn't know until too late. I would have guided you better."

Crookedjaw shook his head. "You couldn't have guided me any better."

Shellheart silenced him with a look. "With this life I give you loyalty, to your Clan and to the cats who love you. Promise you'll use it wisely."

Crookedjaw shuffled his paws. *He's warning me to turn my back on Mapleshade.* "I walk alone now," he vowed.

"No, not alone." Shellheart gazed down at him. "Your ancestors walk alongside you, always. Travel well, Crookedstar. You will make a great leader."

Crookedstar closed his eyes as the cats of StarClan lifted their heads to the sky and called his new name. He *would* be a great leader. He could feel the certainty of it tingling in his paws. He couldn't wait to get back to his Clan. As StarClan spun away, Crookedstar blinked open his eyes. *Where's the Moonstone?*

"We did it!" A familiar hiss sounded in his ear.

Mapleshade!

She stood beside him, her eyes glowing. "You kept your promise and I kept mine! You've proved that nothing is more important than leading your Clan. Are you going to thank me for the sacrifices I made for you?"

Crookedstar stared at her. *Sacrifices?* Did she mean Rainflower? Hailstar? Did she really think she'd made him leader by persuading him to abandon the cats he loved?

"I promised to be loyal to RiverClan, but not at the cost of my Clanmates!" he snarled. "Leave me alone! That's the only thing you can do for me. The promise I made you means nothing!"

As he turned away, she curled back her lip, revealing sharp yellow teeth. "You can't walk away from me," she hissed. Crookedstar felt her claws snag against his pelt, even though she was several paces away. "This will never be over!"

CHAPTER 37

Crookedstar sat back on his haunches, pressing a hollow into the snow, and let Loudbelly and Piketooth pass.

"At least we know why you're called Loudbelly," Piketooth teased. "It's been rumbling since we left camp."

Loudbelly scooped up a pawful of snow and hurled it at his Clanmate. "I've had half a sparrow in two days!" he reminded him. "Of course it's rumbling!"

"We'll catch something before we go home," Crookedstar mewed hopefully as they trudged into the willows above the camp. He tried to sound cheerful, but he hated watching his Clan grow so scrawny.

"We've been out since dawn and we haven't caught anything yet," Loudbelly muttered. The sun was already sliding toward the horizon.

The river had been frozen for half a moon, the ice too thick to break. Without fish, they'd had to rely on meager pickings from the woodland. Crookedstar had forgotten what a full belly felt like.

"You must eat and stay strong for your Clan," Willowbreeze begged him every night. But Crookedstar could not take food from his Clanmates. He'd rather starve.

Loudbelly squawked as he disappeared into the snow. He struggled back to the surface, cursing. "Why do I find every dip and hollow?"

"Let me go first." Crookedstar bounded ahead, throwing up snow in his wake.

"Thanks a lot!" Piketooth ducked as his leader sprayed him. "I wasn't quite cold enough." A growl edged his mew.

Tempers were as short as the days. "Hungry bellies make angry hearts," as Birdsong liked to say.

Tanglewhisker had snapped at her the last time she'd said it. "Can't you think of something helpful to say for a change?"

For once Birdsong had no quick reply. She simply stared at her mate, her eyes dark with pain. Like the rest of her Clan, she was still mourning the death of Graypool's kits. The whole Clan moved quietly around the camp now, not knowing how to comfort the grieving queen. The two kits, Splashkit and Morningkit, had been born sickly, and had never grown strong, dying less than a moon after they'd been kitted.

Graypool had been very ill afterward. Mudfur and Brambleberry had taken turns to sit with the ailing queen and now she was finally strong enough to leave the camp from time to time, ranging out over the frozen river and yowling her heartbreak out loud.

"She's calling to them," Crookedstar had heard Shimmerpelt whisper to Piketooth. "She knows they won't be coming back but I think she believes they can hear her from StarClan."

Crookedstar had paused from his washing and pricked his

ears, his heart twisting as he heard Graypool's heartbroken cry echo eerily across the river.

He shook away the memory. "Come on!" He scrambled up the slope to a clearing ringed by rowan and willow. Piketooth struggled after him, through the churned snow.

Loudbelly tasted the air. "Squirrel!" The young warrior dropped into a crouch. A gray squirrel was scampering between the willows, its tail rippling behind it. As it skittered up a trunk, Loudbelly sprang after it, wallowing through the snow. He jumped up the tree and chased the squirrel along a slender branch, shaking clumps of snow on to Crookedstar and Piketooth.

"Watch out!" Piketooth crossly shook snow from his pelt as Loudbelly leaped from one tree to another. But the squirrel darted upward, safe in the highest branches, and bounded away, tree to tree, leaving Loudbelly hanging from a narrow branch with his hind legs churning empty air.

"Frog-dung!" Loudbelly let go and dropped into the snow. He sat up, shaking it from his ears.

Crookedstar shook his head. "Tough luck," he meowed. If only Oakheart were with them. He was fast and light enough on his paws to cross the snow without breaking the frosty crust. But Oakheart was resting. A vicious battle with Thistleclaw three moons ago had left him with a wrenched leg that still ached in the cold weather.

Crookedstar wished he had been there to protect his brother. He'd trained in the Dark Forest, too, and he'd have known a few of Thistleclaw's battle moves. Crookedstar shuddered at the memory of that dank, stinking place. Rumors from the border hinted that Tawnyspots was dying; ThunderClan would need a new deputy soon, and even though Adderfang had been carrying out Tawnyspot's duties during his illness, Thistleclaw's name was the one whispered at the Gatherings. Crookedstar closed his eyes, dreading the thought of a Dark Forest cat becoming leader of a Clan. A shower of snow splattering against his muzzle jerked him back to the present.

"Mouse!" Loudbelly squealed as Piketooth shot away, skimming the snow, fast as a fish. He slammed his paws on it as it darted toward the roots of a rowan and killed it with a bite.

"Let's get back to camp," Crookedstar meowed. It was getting colder and all the cats were shivering.

"But we've only got a mouse," Loudbelly argued.

"It'll have to do," Crookedstar told him. "We've been out all day. It's freezing. We don't want to get sick." He knew Brambleberry's supply of herbs was dangerously low.

As they padded into camp, Piketooth carried his mouse to the fresh-kill pile and dropped it next to a dead frog, which was already stiff with frost. Willowbreeze was hurrying toward the nursery, feathers trembling in her jaws.

Crookedstar crossed the clearing and stopped beside her. "Who needs feathers?"

Willowbreeze's eyes shone. She beckoned him forward with a nod. Squeezing in after his mate, Crookedstar felt his mouth fall open in astonishment. Graypool was curled in her nest with two kits squirming at her belly.

Kits?

Willowbreeze quickly tucked the feathers around the kits and sat back, purring. "It's a blessing from StarClan!"

Crookedstar closed his mouth, speechless.

"I found them." Graypool anticipated his first question as she gently nuzzled the kits, encouraging them closer.

"A tom and a she-kit," Willowbreeze announced proudly. The tom was pale gray and mewling; the dark gray she-kit stared around the den, her eyes bright with fear.

Crookedstar leaned forward and touched the she-kit's ear with his muzzle. "Don't worry, little one. You're safe here." He narrowed his eyes at Graypool. "What do you mean, you found them? Where?"

"At the border." Graypool wrapped her tail tighter around the kits. "A loner must've abandoned them. It's a blessing I discovered them before they froze." She looked up with a gleam of defiance in her yellow eyes. "I'm going to keep them and raise them as my own."

"But what if their mother comes to find them?"

Graypool flattened her ears. "A mother who abandons her kits won't come back to claim them."

Willowbreeze pressed against Crookedstar. "StarClan must have led Graypool to them."

Fallowtail squeezed through the entrance. "Can I see them?"

Lakeshine peered in, Softwing crowding behind her.

"Come on." Willowbreeze began shooing away her

Clanmates. "These kits need rest." She guided Fallowtail out of the nursery. "They're still weak from their ordeal."

Crookedstar hopped out after them, glancing back at Graypool. The gray queen was staring at the kits as if they were the only things that mattered in the world. Outside the nursery, Willowbreeze fended off questions from her Clanmates.

"They're strong and healthy, just frightened."

"I expect you'll be able to see them in the morning."

"Graypool's smitten with them, and I think they like her."

Voleclaw nudged Crookedstar. "Willowbreeze seems to have everything under control," he purred. "She'll make a good mother herself one day."

Crookedstar hardly heard him. *What if the loner comes back? Graypool's heart would break to give them up. Would a loner be prepared to fight for her kits? Would it be fair to make her fight?*

What would Hailstar have done?

Distracted, Crookedstar padded toward the willow.

"Have you seen them?" Oakheart limped through the snow and stopped beside him.

"Seen them?" Crookedstar was still lost in thought, but he noticed the limp. "Are you all right? I thought you were resting that leg."

"It'll be fine." Oakheart shrugged away his concern. "What about the kits? Aren't they great? Just what Graypool needed. It really is a blessing from StarClan."

"Then you think we should keep them?" Crookedstar

searched his brother's bright gaze.

"Don't you?" Oakheart frowned. "Are you worried the mother might come and claim them?"

Crookedstar nodded. "They're not our kits. Can we really decide their fate?"

"What else can we do?" Oakheart pointed out, with a hint of anger in his mew. "Take them back and leave them where Graypool found them? They'd die before moonrise."

Crookedstar looked up at the clear evening sky. The setting sun had stained it pink. A frost was setting in. Oakheart was right: The kits wouldn't survive long outside. "I suppose we need new kits." They had lost so many. First Brightsky's, then Softwing's, and finally Graypool's.

"Why don't I go and guard the place Graypool found them, and if a loner turns up I'll bring her back to camp?" Oakheart offered. He sounded tense, as if he was furious at the idea of these kits being claimed by the cat that had abandoned them.

Crookedstar pricked his ears. "Good idea." He glanced at Oakheart's wrenched leg. "I'll send Cedarpelt to relieve you at moonhigh," he promised.

"And if no loner comes, we can keep them?" Oakheart leaned forward. It must be cold. He was trembling.

"Yes." Crookedstar rubbed his frozen nose with a paw. "They'll never know anything but RiverClan, and Graypool deserves to raise a litter."

Was that relief flashing in his eyes? Crookedstar swallowed back a purr. Perhaps it was time Oakheart got a mate of his own.

* * *

A moon passed. The snows melted and new buds softened the stark willow. As the sun slid toward the distant forest, Crookedstar sat at the edge of the clearing, his belly full, and watched Willowbreeze tugging a bulrush along the ground for the kits to chase. Stonekit scampered after it, his fluffy tail sticking straight up. He was a stocky little kit. Crookedstar could imagine him diving for fish already. Mistykit was slender and pretty. She watched the bulrush twitch, her clear blue eyes narrowing, before she pounced, landing right on top of it.

"Hey!" Stonekit complained as his littermate sat proudly on her catch. "Graypool!" He called to the queen watching fondly from outside the nursery. "She's doing it again!"

"Now, now." Graypool padded over and nosed Mistykit gently away from the bulrush. "Let Stonekit have a turn."

Willowbreeze left the game and padded across the clearing. She sat beside Crookedstar. "They're going to make good hunters," she meowed. "They already hook their claws under the bulrush as though they're catching a trout. Anyone would think they were Clanborn."

The reed bed trembled and Oakheart climbed from the river, a fat carp in his jaws. He carried it over to the kits. Graypool's eyes lit up. "Look what Oakheart's caught for you!"

Mistykit reared up, reaching for the fish with her tiny front paws. When Oakheart dropped it, she started gnawing at it hungrily.

Stonekit wrinkled his nose. "It smells fishy."

"I know, dear." Graypool lapped between his ears. "That's because it's a fish."

Stonekit sniffed at it tentatively before taking a bite. "Can't we have mouse instead?" he asked, his mouth full.

"Another time, precious," Graypool promised.

"Fox!" Sedgecreek skidded into camp, her pelt bushed up.

Crookedstar leaped to his paws. "Where?"

"Downstream, by the hawthorns!" Sedgecreek circled Crookedstar. "I could smell it."

"But you didn't see it?" Crookedstar's hackles smoothed. "It may have passed through already."

Timberfur hurried from beneath the willow. "Should I organize a patrol?"

Crookedstar had made him deputy when he'd returned from the Moonstone. Oakheart would have been his first choice, but RiverClan owed the old warrior a reward for his long loyalty and courage. Crookedstar knew Oakheart wouldn't mind waiting his turn.

"I'll go and check," Crookedstar told him.

"Alone?" Timberfur's eyes darkened. "Is that wise?"

"If I pick up fresh scents, I'll come back for help," Crookedstar promised. Foxes rarely strayed from ThunderClan's shady forests, especially once the river ice had melted. The scent had probably drifted across the border and startled Sedgecreek.

He padded out of camp, following the grassy path for a few paces before hopping through the bushes on to the shore. The river washed the pebbles, low now that the snowmelt had gone. The wooded banks were bright with new growth.

Crookedstar breathed in the familiar scent of fresh leaves and soft earth. Fish stirred the surface of the river and there were spiky claw prints in the mud where a moorhen had walked.

Crookedstar followed the river along the border of his territory. Reaching the hawthorns, he climbed the bank and tasted the air. There was no sign of fox, just the smell of primroses on the warm evening breeze. And something else. Crookedstar froze.

Mapleshade!

He snapped his head around, scanning the riverbank, hackles high. His heart lurched as a hawthorn bush quivered and Mapleshade stepped out.

Her eyes were dark, her orange-and-white pelt sleek. "You fool!" she hissed. "Where is your loyalty to your Clan now?"

Crookedstar turned and began to walk away. He didn't want to fight her. He just wanted to get away from her. She darted in front of him, blocking his path.

He unsheathed his claws. "Leave me alone!"

"Someone has to warn you!"

"Warn me about what?" He stared at her.

"You trust what *any* cat tells you!" she spat. "Mouse-brain!"

Crookedstar growled.

She eyed him malevolently. "Those kits!"

"What about them?"

"Do you really think a loner left them in the snow? Is it just a coincidence they look like RiverClan cats? That they pounce like RiverClan cats?"

"What are you trying to say?"

"Are you stupid or blind or both?" The fur lifted along her spine. "Why do you think your brother spends all day hunting for them? Watching them as if they're his next meal? He's more attentive than most fathers—but then he is raising them without their true mother."

Anger pulsed beneath Crookedstar's pelt. "I'm not going to listen to any more of your lies! Oakheart has no kits! He's never even had a mate!"

Mapleshade's eyes glinted. "Not in RiverClan." She jerked her head toward the far bank. "Look across the river, you fool!"

Crookedstar stared at the trees lined along ThunderClan's bank. He suddenly felt cold. "What are you saying?" He snapped his gaze back to Mapleshade but the Dark Forest warrior had gone.

Crookedstar whirled around and raced back along the shore. *Don't be dumb!* He leaped on to the grassy path. *It's just more of her lies! There's no way these kits have anything to do with Oakheart!* He skidded into the clearing out of breath, scanning the camp. "Oakheart!"

"What's going on?" Oakheart darted, bristling, away from the nursery.

Crookedstar lowered his voice, suddenly aware that he was frightening the kits. "Come with me," he ordered quietly.

Oakheart followed him through the reeds to the shore below the camp. "What is it?" He climbed onto a smooth rock and sat down, wrapping his thick, tawny tail over his paws. "Something's wrong." Worry sharpened his amber gaze.

Crookedstar was aware of the river sliding past and the

birds chattering in the trees behind them. A kingfisher was sitting in the branch of an overhanging willow, studying the water for the tiniest flicker of a fish tail. Crookedstar took a deep breath. "Are they your kits?"

Oakheart stared at him. There was no twitch of his whiskers. No flick of his ear. His pelt was as smooth as fish scales. "Yes."

"And Bluefur's?" *Who else can it be?*

"Yes." Pain flashed in Oakheart's eyes. "She gave them up to become ThunderClan's deputy." His voice dropped to a pained whisper. "She couldn't let Thistleclaw take over." He shrugged. "She didn't say why, just that her Clan needed her. She was so certain that she was doing the right thing, Crookedstar! What else could I do?"

Should I have told Sunstar what I knew about Thistleclaw? Crookedstar scraped his claws through the pebbles. *It would have helped Bluefur. She might have kept her kits. Instead I left her to stop Thistleclaw by herself.*

The secrets he'd been carrying suddenly felt like stones in his belly. If he dived in the river now, they'd drag him to the bottom.

Oakheart leaned forward. "What are you going to do?" A challenge edged his mew, the challenge of a father willing to do anything to protect his kits.

"Nothing."

Oakheart blinked.

"We're going to raise them as RiverClan," Crookedstar went on. "They are our kin, after all." He looked down at his paws. "But I wish you had confided in me. You know you can trust me with anything."

Oakheart sighed. "I guess we all have our secrets."

Crookedstar lifted his gaze and stared into his brother's clear amber eyes. *If only you knew.*

CHAPTER 38

Crookedstar tossed another trout to Timberfur lying by the reed bed. A good day's hunting had given the Clan all it needed for the feast. The past four seasons had treated them kindly and they were well fed and sleek. The sun was finally slipping toward the river and a cool greenleaf breeze wafted over the camp.

Stonefur rolled on to his back. "I'm stuffed." He lapped awkwardly at his bloated belly. For a young warrior, he was as solid as his senior Clanmates and longer-legged.

Mallowtail poked him with a paw. "You deserve it," she purred. "I've never seen anyone chase off a Twoleg before."

Graypool's ears twitched. "I wish you wouldn't take so many chances, Stonefur," she chided. "It wasn't long ago you were an apprentice."

"It wasn't just me," Stonefur reminded her. "It was the whole patrol."

Mistyfoot gently nudged Graypool. "You worry about us too much."

Graypool snorted. "Well, someone has to."

Timberfur swished his tail. "You did get a bit close, Stonefur."

"It shouldn't have come so near the camp," Stonefur argued.

"Attacking Twolegs can only lead to trouble," Echomist fretted.

"He didn't attack it," Mistyfoot defended her brother. "He just hissed at it."

"And now it's gone off yowling to its Clanmates about you." Echomist shook her head. "They'll be invading the camp, just you wait and see."

Rippleclaw yawned. "Twolegs are too dumb to organize an attack."

Crookedstar sat up and stretched. "We'll send out extra patrols just in case." He glanced at the fresh-kill pile, wondering whether to offer another carp to Willowbreeze. She was always hungry these days.

Fallowtail got to her paws and stretched. "I'm sleepy." She nodded to Birdsong. "Are you ready for your nest?" Fallowtail had moved to the elders' den last leaf-bare, after Tanglewhisker had died. She'd been feeling her age for moons, and keeping Birdsong company had been a good reason to give up her den to Mallowtail and Dawnbright.

Birdsong shook her head. "I had a long sleep this afternoon," she rasped. "I'll just lie here a little longer and listen to the warriors boast."

"We don't boast!" Dawnbright puffed as Fallowtail headed up the slope.

Loudbelly purred. "Doesn't telling us you caught three fish in three dives count as boasting?"

"It was *true!*" Dawnbright sniffed.

Crookedstar licked a paw. "I suppose you never boast, Loudbelly." He wiped his muzzle clean.

Frogleap's whiskers twitched. "He collects a reed for every warrior he's fought and weaves it into his nest!"

"I have to keep count," Loudbelly meowed. "We've won so many battles these past moons, it's hard to remember them all."

Crookedstar began to wash his ears. He loved to listen as his Clan shared tongues, proud of his strong, loyal warriors. No other Clan had dared threaten their borders since newleaf. And they'd taken back Sunningrocks. Sunstar's mission to the RiverClan camp had only given ThunderClan the rocks for a few moons.

"Crookedstar?" Willowbreeze called softly to him. She was on her paws, beckoning him away from the clearing.

"What is it?" He followed her toward the entrance.

"I thought you might want to go for a walk." Her amber eyes glowed in the fading light. "There's something I need to tell you, away from prying ears."

Crookedstar tipped his head on one side. His mate was definitely acting a little strange. "Are you all right?"

"Of course." She flicked his ear with the tip of her tail as she ducked out of camp. The stones on the shore were still warm from the sun as they wandered downriver.

"So?" Crookedstar glanced at her expectantly. "What is it that can't be said in camp?"

"I'm going to have kits."

Crookedstar halted, his heart pounding with delight. "Really?"

Willowbreeze purred. "Really."

"When?"

"About three moons."

"How many?"

She snorted with amusement. "I don't *know!*"

"You should move to the nursery at once." Crookedstar wasn't taking any chances. Too many RiverClan queens had lost their kits.

"Don't be silly," Willowbreeze argued. "I can carry on with patrols for ages yet."

"Then don't catch anything heavier than a minnow."

She looked at him, the tip of her tail twitching impatiently.

"Okay!" Crookedstar realized he was fussing over fish-brained details. Willowbreeze was having his kits! He pressed his muzzle against hers. Happiness sparkled beneath his pelt. "I have to tell Oakheart!" he meowed. "I have to tell everyone." He charged away, skidding to a stop as he hit the grassy path. "It's okay, isn't it?" he asked, looking back. "If I tell everyone?"

Willowbreeze nodded.

Crookedstar raced into camp. "Willowbreeze is expecting kits!"

"Congratulations!" Owlfur was on his paws at once.

Oakheart stopped washing. "At last!" He trotted across the clearing and weaved around Crookedstar.

Softwing nodded. "It's about time."

"Did someone say kits?" Fallowtail ducked out of the elders' den, ear pricked.

Birdsong's whiskers twitched. "Willowbreeze is expecting."

Fallowtail hurried stiffly down the slope. "I hope she'll be moving to the nursery," she mewed, sounding fretful. "Where is she?" She scanned the camp as Willowbreeze padded through the entrance. "Come and rest, dear." Fallowtail hurried over to her and guided her beneath the willow.

Shimmerpelt sniffed. "Stop fussing. She'll be fine."

Crookedstar nodded to Timberfur. "I want her taken off border patrols."

Willowbreeze bristled. "You'll do no such thing," she told Timberfur. She looked at Brambleberry. "I don't have to lie around like a helpless kit, do I?"

Brambleberry shook her head. "Of course not." She glanced at Crookedstar. "But let him fuss a little. It's not every day a warrior hears that he's going to be a father."

"I'm not fussing!" Crookedstar puffed out his chest. Above him, the sky was darkening. It was getting late. "Perhaps you should be resting though, Willowbreeze. I'll see you to your nest."

Willowbreeze purred as he nudged her toward their den in the roots of the willow. "Aren't you going to sleep, too?" she meowed as he began to nose his way out through the moss.

"Later," he replied. "I'm too excited to sleep." He padded into the clearing.

His Clanmates were heading for their dens. Cedarpelt nodded to him as he passed. "Congratulations, Crookedstar."

"Thanks." The moon was rising and stars were beginning to prick the sky. The camp suddenly felt small and stuffy. Crookedstar headed out through the reeds and followed the trail toward the willows. The sky was as dark as moleskin as he wove between the slender trunks. Wildflowers scented the air. His paws were wet from the dewy grass.

Thank you, StarClan. Please protect her.

Memories stirred behind his eyes, crowding into his vision even though he tried to force them back. He could see Rainflower lying on the shore, her eyes clouded. He felt the weight of Hailstar's body on his back.

"Willowbreeze is mine, Mapleshade!" he yowled into the trees. "Do you hear? She isn't part of my promise, whatever you think! Don't you dare hurt one hair on her pelt!"

He stared around the clearing, alert for any paw step, tasting the air for the familiar bitter scent. But only the willows answered, with the rustling of their leaves.

Crookedstar sniffed the air. The flowery scents of greenleaf had deepened into a musty richness; leaf-fall was closing in. Timberfur, Sunfish, and Stonefur streamed past him into camp. They'd patrolled the Sunningrocks border, re-marking the scent line. Crookedstar padded through the reeds and stopped in the clearing. He checked the fresh-kill pile. It was well stocked with fish.

"Willowbreeze!" He gasped when he saw her, vast-bellied and tottering as she tried to drag a bundle of reeds from the shore. "What in the name of StarClan are you doing?" She was far too close to kitting to be doing such heavy work. Crookedstar darted over and pulled the reeds away from her.

Willowbreeze bristled. "What's the matter?"

"Can't someone else do this for you?"

"I can make my own nest, thank you!" She glared at him, a challenge in her eyes.

Crookedstar swallowed his frustration. "Then at least let me help you," he meowed. He picked up the bundle before she could argue and carried it to the nursery. Hauling the reeds inside, he dropped them beside her nest.

Sunfish looked up from the edge of the den. She was expecting Beetlenose's kits and would be kitting soon after Willowbreeze. "I told her she should ask for help."

Willowbreeze squeezed, puffing, into the nursery. "I don't need any help," she muttered through gritted teeth.

"Who needs help?" Brambleberry slid in after her.

Crookedstar flicked his tail. "Willowbreeze thinks she should be dragging reeds around camp!"

Brambleberry shrugged. "Of course she wants to fix her nest before she kits. It's perfectly natural." She glanced at the bundle Willowbreeze had collected. "I'll ask Shimmerpelt to give you a paw weaving those in."

"Thanks." Willowbreeze was still glowering at Crookedstar.

Crookedstar glowered back. "I still think you shouldn't be—" He stopped as Willowbreeze started coughing. A chill rippled along his spine.

Brambleberry narrowed her eyes. "When did you start coughing?" She padded to Willowbreeze and pressed an ear against the queen's flank.

"This morning," Willowbreeze spluttered. "It's just a tickle. I must have swallowed a feather in my sleep."

"It's probably nothing," Brambleberry meowed breezily. "But I'll get you some catmint and marigold anyway."

Crookedstar watched the medicine cat carefully. He knew how well she could guard her true feelings. He'd visit her later in her den to make sure that Willowbreeze wasn't in any danger. Just to be sure.

"Ow!" Willowbreeze gasped and dropped into a crouch.

Crookedstar froze. Willowbreeze was scowling with pain.

Brambleberry touched Willowbreeze's belly with a paw. She looked a little surprised. "Well! The kits are coming."

Crookedstar stared at her in shock. "Now?"

Brambleberry nodded. "Fetch Mudfur and Fallowtail." She glanced at Sunfish. "It'll be your turn soon enough. Do you want to watch?"

Sunfish's eyes glittered. "Yes, please," she mewed nervously.

Brambleberry whisked her tail toward Crookedstar. "Hurry up!"

Crookedstar squeezed out of the nursery and raced across the clearing. He poked his head through the medicine den entrance. "Willowbreeze is kitting!" he called to Mudfur.

The medicine cat's apprentice was sorting through herbs. He looked up, ears pricking. "Okay, I'm coming." He grabbed a pawful of leaves.

Crookedstar ducked out and headed for the elders' den. "Fallowtail?"

The old queen looked up from her nest. "Has she started?"

"How did you guess?"

"You look as scared as a kit dropped in the river for the

first time." Fallowtail got stiffly to her paws and headed for the entrance.

Crookedstar followed her down the slope and watched as she disappeared into the nursery. Mudfur trotted across the clearing with a bundle of herbs between his teeth and followed her inside. Crookedstar's pelt pricked with frustration. He paced the clearing, trying to block out memories of Brightsky's kitting.

Oakheart padded into camp, a fish in his jaws. One glance at Crookedstar and he dropped the fish and raced across the clearing. "Willowbreeze?"

"She's just started kitting." Crookedstar kept pacing. "Brambleberry's with her."

"She'll be fine." Oakheart fell in beside him, gently slowing the pace. "She's a strong warrior. I've seen her beat a ThunderClan tom with a single swipe. A kit or two won't be any bother."

Crookedstar's heart was racing.

"And what a hunter! She can hold her breath underwater even longer than Rippleclaw," Oakheart went on. "And everyone knows Rippleclaw's half-cat, half-fish."

Ottersplash padded out of her den. "What's going on?" The old warrior squinted across the clearing. Timberfur had been trying to persuade her to move to the elders' den for moons, but she insisted she could carry on with her warrior duties for as long as he did. They'd been mates for moons and the whole Clan knew she'd be lonely away from the graying Clan deputy.

Oakheart padded to her side and guided her to the edge of

the clearing. "Willowbreeze is kitting."

"I thought I smelled fear." Ottersplash sat down. "Yours, not hers. Don't worry, Crookedstar. She'll be fine."

Timberfur trotted over and sat beside her. "I think he's forgotten that it's Willowbreeze doing all the work."

It was sunhigh by the time Mudfur slid out of the nursery. "Three kits!" he yowled triumphantly.

Crookedstar blinked. "How's Willowbreeze?"

"Doing fine." Mudfur beckoned him toward the entrance. "Come and meet your daughters. They're all she-kits!"

Crookedstar squeezed inside, excitement fizzing in his paws. Willowbreeze was lying in her nest, her eyes dark. Fallowtail crouched beside her. Sunfish was sitting up in her nest, straining to see the new kits.

Brambleberry nudged Crookedstar forward. "She's very tired," she warned.

Willowbreeze coughed.

"She'll feel better after a long sleep," Fallowtail murmured. "Why don't you welcome your kits to the Clan, Crookedstar?"

Crookedstar dragged his gaze from Willowbreeze to the three tiny, damp bundles lying at her belly. They looked perfect. He leaned into the nest and sniffed them one at a time. The biggest was dark gray, the middle-sized one almost black, and the smallest a silver-gray tabby just like her mother.

Crookedstar's heart ached with love for them. He pressed his muzzle against Willowbreeze's cheek. It felt warm.

"They're beautiful," he whispered.

"I know," she rasped.

Pride swelled in him, blossoming like a flower.

Brambleberry leaned closer and whispered in his ear. "You should let her rest." Gently she ushered him toward the entrance. Crookedstar felt a wave of gratitude toward the medicine cat. She had delivered the most beautiful kits in all the Clans. *And thank you, StarClan, for forgiving me.* Nothing could compare with the blessing of Willowbreeze and their daughters.

Crookedstar woke early. The sun had just broken the horizon as he padded out of his den and crossed the clearing, yawning. Quiet as a fish, he slid into the nursery and peeked into Willowbreeze's nest. She was asleep with the three kits curled peacefully beside her. Crookedstar guessed she'd be hungry when she woke. He slipped into the clearing and headed out of camp. He'd caught a fat carp by the time the rest of the Clan was stirring.

"Is that for Willowbreeze?" Oakheart called from his den as Crookedstar pushed through the reeds with the carp dangling from his jaws. Crookedstar nodded, slowing as he saw Mudfur standing outside the nursery. He dropped the fish at the medicine cat apprentice's paws. "Is everything okay?" he asked. There was something about Mudfur's expression that made the pelt rise along his spine.

"You can't go in," Mudfur told him softly.

Crookedstar bristled. "What do you mean I can't go in?" He heard Willowbreeze coughing inside. The kits were mewling.

"They're hungry!" Crookedstar protested. "And Willow-breeze will be starving. I'm taking this fish in." As he leaned down to pick it up, Mudfur moved in front of the entrance.

Crookedstar glared at him, fear rising in his belly. He spat out the fish. "Let me in!"

Mudfur met Crookedstar's gaze steadily. "Brambleberry says she mustn't be disturbed." He glanced over his shoulder. "By *anyone*."

"Is Brambleberry in there?" Crookedstar's heart was racing. "What's wrong? Why can't I see Willowbreeze?"

"She's a little sick," Mudfur explained. "But the kits are fine, and I'm keeping a close eye on them."

Crookedstar growled. "Let me in!" He tried to push past Mudfur, but Mudfur pushed back. He'd lost none of his warrior strength.

Brambleberry slid out of the den. "I thought I heard you," she meowed cheerfully. "Nothing to worry about. Willowbreeze just has a little cough and I don't want the infection spreading. You'll have to stay outside till I tell you it's okay to go in."

Crookedstar couldn't believe his ears. He was the leader of these cats, for StarClan's sake! "How come *you're* allowed in? And Mudfur! It's not fair!" He was arguing like a scared kit. "Even Sunfish is in there."

"Sunfish has moved to the elders' den." Brambleberry tipped her head on one side. "And if we were going to catch it, we'd have caught it by now."

"But I was in there yesterday and I didn't catch it!" Crookedstar argued.

"You were only there a few moments." Brambleberry held his gaze. "It's really better if you stay outside. You're our leader. We can't risk you getting sick, too."

Crookedstar opened his mouth. There was nothing to say. The Clan needed him. But Willowbreeze needed him, too!

"Get better quickly!" he called through the wall of the nursery. "I love you! And our daughters!"

CHAPTER 39

❧

Crookedstar jumped to his paws as Brambleberry slid out of the nursery. "Should I fetch more honey?" he offered.

"No." Brambleberry's eyes were dull and the end of her tail trailed on the ground.

A soft drizzle soaked the camp. In the days since her kitting, Willowbreeze's cough had grown steadily worse. Two of the kits had begun coughing, too. Brambleberry had kept Crookedstar out of the nursery but he stayed close, pacing the clearing, one moment praying to StarClan, cursing them the next. All the hope, courage, trust, and patience bestowed on him by his ancestors meant nothing to him now. Where was their loyalty to him? How could they let him suffer like this? *Make them well! Please make them well!*

"Crookedstar." Brambleberry's mew jerked him back to the present. "She has greencough."

"Then I'll fetch some catmint!" Crookedstar headed for the reeds.

"I've given her catmint already." Brambleberry called him back. "It's not working."

The nursery shook as Willowbreeze burst into another

hacking fit. Tiny coughs spluttered alongside hers. Crookedstar flattened his ears. "What can I do?"

"You can go in and see her." Brambleberry stepped aside. "She wants to name the kits."

Why now? Crookedstar stared into the shadowy den, his paws suddenly rooted to the ground.

"Go on," Brambleberry prompted.

Crookedstar steadied his breath and climbed inside. The nursery was dark, the air sour and stuffy. He blinked, letting his eyes adjust to the half-light.

"Willowbreeze?"

She was curled in her nest, their three kits huddled against her belly. She lifted her head as Crookedstar called her name. "You came."

He crouched beside the nest, brushing her cheek with his muzzle. "Brambleberry wouldn't let me in before now. But I've been outside all the time."

"Has it been long?" Willowbreeze's eyes were streaming. Her muzzle was damp. She coughed weakly, making her whole body shudder.

"No," Crookedstar whispered. "Not long."

Willowbreeze gazed into his eyes. "I'm sorry."

He tipped his head on one side. "Why?"

"For leaving you to raise our daughters."

"You're not going anywhere!" Crookedstar pressed his cheek hard against hers. "I won't let you leave me."

"You'll be a wonderful father." A purr rumbled in her throat, making her cough again. This time she struggled to get her breath. "I'm so happy Hailstar brought me back from WindClan. I've loved being with you and with RiverClan."

"Don't talk like that!" Crookedstar fought to keep the panic from his mew. The kits were lifting their heads, turning their muzzles toward him, straining to open their eyes. "You can't leave the kits. They need you." *I need you.*

"Oh, my precious love." Willowbreeze brushed her muzzle along his twisted jaw. "Be brave for me, please."

"You're going to be fine!"

"Help me name our daughters."

Numbness crept beneath Crookedstar's pelt, deadening his heart, slowing his thoughts. Willowbreeze was right. Their daughters needed names. He reached a paw into the nest and touched the darkest gray kit. "Minnowkit," he murmured. He already knew what it would be. He'd planned their names days ago as he paced the clearing.

"Minnowkit," Willowbreeze echoed with a wheeze.

"And Willowkit." Crookedstar stroked the smoky black kit. "I want her to have your name."

Willowkit mewled and caught hold of his paw, churning her hind legs against his pad. Purring, he shook her off gently and touched the palest of the three.

"And this is Silverkit."

"Silverkit." Willowbreeze relaxed against him, her cheek resting on his. "They are lovely names." Her breathing eased. Curling herself around her kits, she rested her nose on her paws and closed her eyes.

Crookedstar buried his muzzle in her pelt. "You rest now,

my lovely." He slid into the nest and wrapped himself around her. "I'll keep you warm." He closed his eyes and breathed in her soft scent.

"Crookedstar?" The den rustled as Brambleberry crept in. She leaned into the nest and touched his pelt. "I heard the names you gave your kits. They're beautiful."

He lifted his head. *How long have I been here?*

Brambleberry's mew was no more than a breath. "I'm so sorry. Willowbreeze has gone."

"No!" Crookedstar sat up with a jolt, realizing that Willowbreeze's pelt was cold to the touch. "No!" He scrambled from the nest and burst from the den. "No!" His yowl ripped through the camp. "I never promised you this!" Shocked gazes flashed from his Clanmates. He raced out of the camp, pounding the wet grass as he pelted into the willows. "Mapleshade!" he roared. "Where are you? Is this another of your *sacrifices*? Is this so I can be the greatest warrior ever? I don't *want* to be the greatest warrior! I take it back! I take back my promise! If this is what I must suffer, I don't want it!"

"Crookedstar!" Oakheart's yowl rang through the trees.

Crookedstar collapsed, panting.

His brother's pelt brushed his. "What are you talking about?" Oakheart pressed against him. "What did you promise?"

Crookedstar shook him away. "I can't tell you!" Guilt raged through him. "I can't say!"

Oakheart smoothed his pelt with his tail. "Come back to

the camp, Crookedstar. Our Clanmates are worried."

Crookedstar pushed himself to his paws. He padded blindly after Oakheart, back to the camp, into the clearing. Sunfish was squeezing out of the nursery, Silverkit dangling in her jaws.

Crookedstar ran toward her. "Where are you taking her?"

Sunfish flinched away, her eyes wide. Brambleberry darted between them. "She's taking Silverkit to the elders' den where she'll be safe from infection. She'll nurse her and keep her warm."

"What about Willowkit and Minnowkit?" Crookedstar demanded.

"They're asleep in the nursery."

"And . . . and Willowbreeze?" Her name stuck in his throat, choking him. Brambleberry's gaze flicked past him. Crookedstar turned and saw Willowbreeze's body already laid out in the clearing, rain drenching her pelt. With an agonized moan, he barged into the nursery. "I'm going to stay with my kits," he growled.

He curled into the nest with Minnowkit and Willowkit. They were trembling with fever and coughing as he tucked himself around them and held them tight. "Hush, little ones. I'll take care of you."

Anxious mews erupted outside.

"It's all right." Brambleberry soothed her Clanmates. "He's grieving."

Crookedstar flattened his ears and held on to his kits. They coughed, jerking against him, fragile as prey, mewling and squirming as the nursery grew darker. Night fell and Crookedstar heard paws scuff the clearing and soft whispers stir the air as his Clanmates sat vigil for Willowbreeze. Crookedstar lapped gently at his daughters' pelts until they grew quiet. Relieved, Crookedstar closed his eyes.

"Crookedstar."

He woke up, blinking against the dawn light filtering through the roof. Mudfur's dark pelt moved beside the nest. Crookedstar sat up. Minnowkit and Willowkit tumbled away from him. Crookedstar stretched out a paw to nudge them back into the nest.

Mudfur touched Crookedstar lightly with his muzzle. "They're dead, Crookedstar." He stared down at the tiny bodies. "They're with Willowbreeze now."

Crookedstar hardly heard what he was saying. He pushed past him, out of the nest, out of the nursery. He stumbled blindly across the camp, ignoring the grief-stricken mews of his Clanmates, seeing nothing but a blurred sea of pelts as he staggered toward his den.

"I'm so sorry!" Fallowtail's cry trailed after him.

"Not the kits, too!"

Crookedstar blocked out Graypool's desperate wail as he burst into his den. Collapsing in his nest, he buried his nose in the moss. It smelled faintly of Willowbreeze. Swallowing back a yowl, he screwed his eyes shut. Whatever he did, he couldn't escape his promise! He couldn't take it back. *I'm destined to lose every cat I care about!* Memories swirled—tragedy after tragedy: Willowbreeze; his kits; Rainflower; Hailstar; Oakheart's betrayal; Bluefur's sacrifice. *Mistyfoot and Stonefur don't even know their real mother!* His promise was a stone flung into the river, sending never-ending ripples not just through his life but through his Clan's, through everything! All because of Mapleshade!

Mapleshade! A growl rumbled deep in his throat. *I'm coming for you, Mapleshade.* He dived into sleep, willing it, wanting it, and woke in the Dark Forest.

Mapleshade was watching him. "Crookedstar." Her mew oozed with satisfaction.

Rage scorched through him. With a roar, he leaped at her. Silverhawk's death bite was seared in his memory. Swiping the old she-cat sideways with a hefty blow, Crookedstar lunged for her throat.

She ducked away, growling. Pleasure lit her eyes. "You think you're stronger than me?" she hissed. She darted forward and reared up at him, slamming her forepaws against his cheek.

He staggered, lifted by the force of her blow, and stumbled to the ground. He spun away in time to knock aside another strike. Claws outstretched, he hooked Mapleshade's pelt and flung her backward. She scrabbled at the dark earth with her hind legs, recovering her balance in a heartbeat and throwing herself at him, forepaws stretched out, claws glinting like pike teeth. Crookedstar ducked and slid underneath her, swiping her hind legs away. Then he turned and leaped, twisting in the air, kicking out his hind legs, swiping with his fore, landing on her back as she struggled to find her paws. Mapleshade groaned beneath him but he held her hard and snapped his teeth around her spine.

She pushed up with a force that shocked him. Crookedstar lost his grip. Flying backward, he turned, reaching for the ground. It hit him before he found it, knocking the breath from him. He grunted as he felt her weight on his back. Her claws pierced his pelt as she pinned him to the earth.

"Go on then, kill me!" Crookedstar hissed. "I've got nothing left to live for."

"Oh, no." Mapleshade's honeyed mew dripped in his ear. "Letting you live is far better revenge."

"Revenge?" Crookedstar twitched. "What did I ever do to you?"

Mapleshade jerked him backward and stared into his eyes. Her gaze flamed with hate. "You were always destined to become leader of RiverClan. It was never anything to do with me. Your path was marked out by the stars countless moons ago." She thrust her muzzle closer. "But who cares about destiny except fools? *I* should have been ThunderClan's leader! But ThunderClan cast me out when I took a RiverClan mate." Her lip curled. "Familiar, eh? Oakheart isn't the only traitor you know." She gave Crookedstar a vicious shake, her claws hooking deeper into his flesh. "Our kits were perfect!" Her eyes blazed harder. "But they *drowned*. After ThunderClan cast me out, I tried to carry them across the river to their father's Clan. But the water snatched them from my grasp and carried them away."

Crookedstar tried to wriggle free.

"Oh, no!" Mapleshade yanked him back to face her. "You

must listen to the whole story." Her rank breath bathed his muzzle. "Their father blamed *me*! And RiverClan cast me out, too. Can you imagine what that feels like? To be rejected twice? To be a loner when all you tried to do was to love? But don't worry, I made them pay. I looked for revenge wherever I could! Why do you think I'm here?" Her gaze flicked around the clearing. "I *earned* my place in the Dark Forest. But what made it worse was that the father of my drowned kits took a RiverClan mate! He promised he would only love *me*! They had a daughter, and she had a son, and do you know who that son was?"

Crookedstar shook his head, trying to keep up.

"Shellheart," Mapleshade snarled. "Your father." Her paws were trembling. "Do you see now? Do you understand?"

"Understand what?"

"You mouse-brain! *My* kin should have been the leader of RiverClan, not his! If ThunderClan hadn't driven me across the river, my kits would never have died. If RiverClan hadn't rejected me, *I'd* be their father's mate, not some fish-hearted RiverClan queen." Her breath was coming in gasps now. "I've endured so much betrayal! So many cats have hurt me beyond measure. And then *you* came, destined for so much greatness, when you should never have been born!" She shoved him away from her. "I wanted to test your loyalty," she hissed. "I wanted to see if you were as weak and disloyal as your kin. I wanted to see if you'd betray me like *they* did." She circled him, her lip peeled back. "Do you remember what I said? Do you remember my exact words? *I can give you everything you ever dreamed of, power over all your Clanmates, if you promise to be loyal to your Clan above all other things. Do you make that promise?* And you did! You *promised!* You chose to sacrifice every cat you ever loved. Your mother, your brother, your mate, and now your own kits: From that one promise, I could take them all!"

"You're crazy!" Crookedstar whispered.

Mapleshade thrust her muzzle close. "But I'm also dead." Her gaze glittered wildly. "Which means you can't hurt me!" She barged past him and Crookedstar woke in his nest with blood welling on his pelt.

CHAPTER 40

Crookedstar nosed his way through the moss draping his den. Dawn was flooding the sky. Timberfur was already beside the reed bed organizing the patrols. Frogleap, Echomist, Owlfur, and Lakeshine clustered around him. Reedtail and Skyheart hurried from their den, closely followed by Blackclaw and Loudbelly. Crookedstar watched them listen to Timberfur's orders. All of RiverClan's warriors, keen and ready for duty, loyal to their Clan and expecting nothing but the same from their leader.

"Echomist, you take Skyheart and Reedtail fishing," Timberfur meowed. "Head upstream. We've been over-fishing beside the stepping-stones. Owlfur, you take—" He glanced up as Crookedstar walked into the clearing. His expression was somber, clouded, as he studied his leader. Crookedstar tried not to flinch as, one by one, the warriors snatched a look at him before turning away, pelts pricking with unease. Suddenly Crookedstar felt like a kit again, leaving the medicine den for the first time after he'd broken his jaw. But this was worse.

"They don't know how to comfort you." Brambleberry's

mew snapped him back to the present. She stopped beside him, smelling of herbs and dew, and dropped a bundle of fresh leaves on the ground.

"There's nothing they can do," Crookedstar rasped. It was his first dawn without Willowbreeze. He could hardly believe the sun had risen. "How's Silverkit?" he asked quietly.

"She's fine. I'll tell her you asked after her." Brambleberry glanced at her herb-stained paws. "I've been collecting marigold for her, just to be safe. She doesn't have any symptoms but I don't think we can be too careful."

Crookedstar cut her off. "I have to talk to you." His ears twitched. "Alone." He led her out of camp and down to the shore, padding on to a wide, flat stone that jutted at the water's edge. The willows were starting to brown. Crookedstar watched a leaf flutter on to the river. The water swirled it and carried it gently away.

"Well?" Brambleberry prompted.

"I didn't tell you everything." Crookedstar searched the medicine cat's gaze, frightened of what he'd find. She might never trust him again.

She blinked. "Go on."

"I wasn't just trained by a cat from the Dark Forest." Crookedstar felt hot. "I made a promise to her. She told me she'd give me everything I ever dreamed of. She told me I'd be leader, but I had to promise to be loyal to my Clan above all other things." He waited for Brambleberry to comment but she just watched him. "It seemed like such a small promise," he went on. "*Of course* I'd be loyal to my Clan. I'd always be loyal to my Clan. But she wanted me to promise loyalty above *all other things*." The words felt sour on his tongue.

"What did she mean by that?"

"I didn't ask. I just assumed it would be easy." His shoulders sagged. "I didn't realize she meant I had to sacrifice every cat I ever loved."

"You mean Willowbreeze?" Brambleberry asked.

"And Rainflower and Hailstar."

"But you didn't sacrifice them." Brambleberry stared at him in dismay. "It was their time to die. It had nothing to do with you."

"But it *did*!" Crookedstar lashed his tail. "They'd still be alive if I hadn't made my promise. And Oakheart would never . . ." He stopped himself. Brambleberry didn't have to know Oakheart had betrayed his Clan with a ThunderClan cat. He swung his head miserably. "Things would have been different if I hadn't been so determined to become leader. Mapleshade would have left the Clan alone."

I'll have to stop being leader. Now that Brambleberry knew it was his fault that RiverClan had lost so much, she'd make StarClan take back his lives. Crookedstar hung his head and stared at the flat gray stone beneath his paws. He deserved it.

Brambleberry narrowed her eyes. "Why are you so certain that things would have been different? Does this Dark Forest cat really have the power to change a Clan's destiny?" There was a challenge in her gaze. "Do *you*? Are you really so powerful that you can hold the lives of cats in your claws? Even when StarClan can't?"

Crookedstar shifted his paws, his fur crawling with confusion.

"Oh, Crookedstar." Brambleberry's eyes glistened. "You've had to walk a dark and terrible path alone." She climbed onto the stone beside him and leaned against his flank. "None of these deaths are your fault. I doubt if they're Mapleshade's fault, either. Sometimes bad things happen for no reason, or for reasons we can't begin to understand." She stepped back and held his gaze. "Please never feel like you need to suffer alone again. I will always be on your side. I'm your medicine cat. You can trust me with anything."

"Really?" Crookedstar swallowed the emotions that bubbled in his throat.

"Really." Brambleberry licked him on the cheek. "And hopefully Mapleshade has had her revenge and will leave you in peace."

For the first time since he was a kit, Crookedstar felt free. He'd shared his secret. Completely. He felt light, relief washing his pelt. "Let's get back to camp." He hopped off the stone. "Timberfur may need help with the patrols." He'd faced the Clan after he'd broken his jaw. He could face them now. They were his Clanmates; he was their leader. They needed him as much as he needed them.

"What about Silverkit?" Brambleberry's question took him by surprise.

"Sunfish is looking after her, isn't she?"

"I'm sure she'd like to see her father."

"Later." Crookedstar leaped up the bank. "I have patrols to organize."

Beetlenose swam through the reeds and hopped onto the shore. Water streamed from his crow-black pelt. A minnow dangled from his jaws.

"Is that for Sunfish?" Shimmerpelt called. "Should I take it to her?"

Beetlenose shook his head and headed for the nursery. Crookedstar watched from the shade of the willow. He guessed Beetlenose wanted to see Vixenkit and Grasskit. The black tom had been padding proudly around the camp ever since his kits had been born, making excuses to visit the nursery every chance he could.

Shimmerpelt crossed the clearing and sat beside Crookedstar. "Why don't you go visit Silverkit?" she prompted.

"It'll be too crowded." Crookedstar watched Beetlenose disappear into the den.

A quarter moon had passed since Willowbreeze had died. The Clan still trod quietly around him, careful of his grief. But he was determined to prove that Hailstar had made the right choice, and that he could lead the Clan whatever happened. He was happy Sunfish had kitted, providing littermates for his motherless daughter. Silverkit had a family of her own now. She didn't need him. And with leaf-bare just around the next bend, there was so much to do. He was far too busy to visit the nursery. He signaled to Petaldust and Frogleap with his tail. They were weaving reeds into the elders' den to strengthen it for the coming cold moons.

"What is it?" Frogleap hurried down the slope and crossed the clearing. Petaldust finished tucking in the end of a stray reed before trotting after him.

"The fresh-kill pile's looking a bit bare," Crookedstar meowed to Frogleap. "Take Reedtail, Leopardfur, and Blackclaw hunting." He turned to Petaldust. "I'd like you to take Cedarpelt, Softwing, and Rippleclaw to check the Sunningrocks boundary."

Petaldust shifted her paws. "Timberfur checked it this morning."

"Then check it again!" Crookedstar snapped.

Shimmerpelt got to her paws and headed toward the elders' den. "I'd better finish weaving those reeds," she meowed. There was a trace of disapproval in her tone but Crookedstar ignored it. Warriors shouldn't question his orders.

He crossed the clearing, kicking through the willow leaves littering the ground. He slowed as he passed the nursery.

Beetlenose hopped out. "Silverkit is quite a pawful, but so cute!" Purring, he dived into the reeds at the edge of the clearing.

Crookedstar pricked his ears, leaning closer to the nursery wall. He could hear tiny paws scrabbling across the reed nest.

"I'm the biggest! I get to go first!"

That must be Silverkit. He wondered how much she'd grown. Were her markings like Willowbreeze's?

"Sunfish! She won't let me into the nest."

"Hush, Vixenkit," Sunfish soothed. "She'll let you in if you ask nicely."

Silverkit piped up again. "I'm just trying to make you grow," she squeaked. "Oh, hurry up and get bigger! I want to go out and explore the camp!"

Crookedstar heard paws scuff on the ground behind him. He turned, surprised to see Oakheart.

"Why don't you go in and see her?" Oakheart meowed.

"I've got other things to worry about."

"Really?" Oakheart's ear twitched. "You can't avoid her forever, you know. She's going to be racing around camp playing hunt the frog before you know it." He narrowed his eyes. "Don't you want her to know who her father is?"

Crookedstar scowled. "What? Like your kits knew who their father was?"

Oakheart flinched. "That was different. I was always there for them, hunting for them, playing with them. Silverkit hardly knows you exist."

"Leave me alone." Crookedstar turned away. "It's none of your business."

Oakheart ducked in front of him. "Actually it *is* my business." He thrust his muzzle closer. "You're my littermate! Silverkit is my kin, too! You're being a fish-brain and every cat knows it. I'm just the only cat brave enough to tell you."

"Brave? You?" Crookedstar snorted. "You couldn't even tell me that Bluefur was expecting your kits. If she hadn't dumped them on you so she could be deputy, it'd still be a secret."

"Really?"

"Really!" Crookedstar flexed his claws. "Don't pretend you understand how I feel, because you don't!"

"No, I don't!" Oakheart spat back. "But I do understand there's a kit in there whose father doesn't want anything to do with her." His pelt bristled. "How can you lead a Clan when you won't even take responsibility for your own kit?"

"Like you did?"

"Like I've *done*!" Oakheart glared at him. "I don't know how you can let her grow up thinking you don't love her." He turned away, shaking his head. "You, more than anyone, should know how terrible that feels. But you're doing it to your own kit."

Fury exploded inside Crookedstar. "How dare you accuse me of that?" Hissing, he lunged at Oakheart and flung him to the ground. Oakheart yowled in rage and swiped at Crookedstar's muzzle.

Crookedstar gasped as Oakheart's claws raked his cheek. "You snake-heart!" Rearing up on his haunches, he slammed his front paws down on to Oakheart's chest. Oakheart grunted and rolled away, springing to his paws. He crouched down, facing Crookedstar with his tail swishing, eyes like slits.

"Stop them!" Shimmerpelt raced across the clearing.

Timberfur shot out from the warriors' den and circled them, bristling.

"Let them fight!" Mudfur called his Clanmates away. "Sometimes it's the only way."

Crookedstar glared at his brother and growled, "I'm

nothing like Rainflower. I'm doing what's best for Silverkit!"

"I bet Rainflower thought she was doing the right thing, too!" Oakheart hissed. "I bet she made excuses just like you."

"That's not true!" Crookedstar sprang, kicking out his hind legs, slashing with his forepaws in a move he had seen being practiced over and over, in a forest where the trees were gray and slimy and starlight never broke through the leaves.

What am I doing?

Horror seized him as he realized he was about to use Thistleclaw's killing move on his brother. He writhed in the air, twisting just in time, and thumped clumsily on to the ground.

Oakheart stood over him. "Finished?" he snarled.

Crookedstar looked up at him. Grief tightened his throat. "How can I love her when every cat I love dies?"

Oakheart's eyes clouded. "*I'm* still here."

Crookedstar got slowly to his paws. "You're here for now."

Oakheart stared at him. "It's a risk *every* cat has to take. Would you rather have no feelings at all? Do you wish you'd never loved Willowbreeze?" His mew trembled. "Where's your courage, Crookedstar?"

A squeak sounded from the nursery. "Sunfish! Sunfish!" Silverkit was staring from the entrance, her eyes stretched wide. "The big warriors are fighting!"

Oakheart nudged Crookedstar. "Go on," he whispered.

Taking a deep breath, Crookedstar forced himself to walk toward the nursery. *When you feel doubt, let your heart lead you forward, not back.* Hailstar's words echoed in his ears. StarClan had trusted him to give him nine lives; Crookedstar had to prove that he was worth it. He leaned forward and touched Silverkit's ear with his muzzle. "It's okay. Nobody's hurt."

The little cat flinched away, trembling.

"Don't be frightened," Crookedstar soothed. "We're not really fighting." *She smells like Willowbreeze!* Her fur was just as soft and the markings on her head matched her mother's exactly. "We're training, that's all. Everything's fine."

Silverkit took a step forward and peered past him at Oakheart, who was standing on the far side of the clearing, watching them. Then she stared up at Crookedstar, her bright blue eyes shimmering. She was so like her mother—and like him, too, in the shape of her ears and the length of her tail. Crookedstar gazed down at her, feeling a lifetime of hope open up in front of him. For the first time that day he felt the warmth of the sun. *Watch over us, Willowbreeze. We still need you.*

"You're really just training?" Silverkit mewed. "Do you promise?"

"I promise." Crookedstar ached with joy. "I'm your father, Silverkit, and that means I will always keep my promises."

TURN THE PAGE TO SEE WHAT HAPPENS NEXT IN AN EXCLUSIVE MANGA ADVENTURE. . . .

CREATED BY
ERIN HUNTER

WRITTEN BY
DAN JOLLEY

ART BY
JAMES L. BARRY

RIVERCLAN HAS BEEN DOING WELL. I WISH OAKHEART COULD SEE IT. I MISS HIM.

I ALSO WISH THE SHADOW HANGING OVER ME WOULD LEAVE... BUT I KNOW IT WON'T. NOT EVER.

BECAUSE, YEARS AGO, I MADE A PROMISE.

MUDFUR--HAVE YOU NOTICED ANYTHING...OFF ABOUT SILVERSTREAM LATELY?

I DON'T THINK SO. SHE SEEMED FINE WHEN SHE CAME BACK TO CAMP, AND THEN SHE WENT RIGHT BACK OUT ON PATROL.

IT'S NOT LIKE HER TO BE SO SECRETIVE, OR TO DISOBEY ME. SOMETHING'S UP.

THERE SHE IS! AND SHE'S WITH SOMEONE...IT'S...

...I SMELL THUNDERCLAN! SHE...

SEVERAL MOONS HAVE PASSED SINCE I SAW MAPLESHADE FOR THE LAST TIME AND...HAD TO SAY GOOD-BYE TO SILVERSTREAM.

MY DAUGHTER LIVES ON IN HER KITS, FEATHERPAW AND STORMPAW.

SHE'D BE SO PROUD OF THEM. AND IT WOULD HAVE ASTONISHED HER WHEN GRAYSTRIPE DECIDED TO JOIN RIVERCLAN.

IT HASN'T BEEN EASY FOR HIM. NOT ALL OF US ACCEPT HIM, DESPITE HOW HARD HE TRIES.

BUT HE'S HERE, DOING THIS FOR THE SAKE OF HIS SON AND DAUGHTER. SILVERSTREAM WAS RIGHT...HE IS A GREAT AND WORTHY WARRIOR.

I HAVE TO TRUST THAT SILVERSTREAM WILL FORGIVE ME IF I STILL WISH SHE HAD CHOSEN A RIVERCLAN MATE.

IT MIGHT NOT HAVE CHANGED HER FATE... BUT IT WOULD HAVE MADE THINGS SIMPLER.

  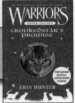

Delve Deeper into the Clans

Warrior Cats Come to Life in Manga!

Visit www.warriorcats.com for the free Warriors app, games, Clan lore, and much more!